EMMA'S WATERLOO

TOM TISCH

outskirts
press

This work is dedicated to victims of violence and injustice.

Waterloo, noun, geographical name, often capitalized
waw·ter·loo | wô′tər-loo̅

1. Waterloo: a town in central Belgium near Brussels. Napoleon met his final defeat in the Battle of Waterloo (June 18, 1815).

2. Waterloo: a village located in Waterloo Township, Jackson County, Michigan, twenty-five miles west of Ann Arbor; founded in 1830.

Waterloo, proper noun, often capitalized

Waterloo: a final crushing defeat; an unsuccessful ending to a struggle or contest. To encounter one's ultimate obstacle and to be defeated by it: *She met her Waterloo.*

Shall the trumpet sound in a city and the people not be afraid?
Shall there be evil in a city, which the Lord hath not done?

The Holy Bible
Book of Amos, Chapter 3, Verse 6

CONTENTS

INTRODUCTION

O n Sunday, May 31, 1896, an event of horrific magnitude took place in the small village of Waterloo, Jackson County, Michigan. The lives of three young individuals from three prominent families, whose lineages went back generations to neighboring hamlets in southwest Germany, were destined to collide in the parlor of a local farmhouse.

Not a Coincidence

The events leading to that day started seventy-one years earlier, in 1825, when news spread that plentiful inexpensive land in America's Great Lakes region had become reachable by the opening of the Erie Canal in New York State. Opportunistic Germans and others who left their countries for a variety of reasons began streaming into various eastern coastal ports, including New York City. Those arriving in New York mainly boarded available boats on the Hudson River. They then traveled north to Albany, where the new canal began, eventually disembarking in the city of Buffalo on Lake Erie. The canal allowed the lands surrounding it to become easily accessible, and many cities were established along its path. Those whose goal it was to reach what was then known as the American Northwest traveled by lake boat from Buffalo, following Lake Erie's southern shore to ports westward bordering the states of New York, Pennsylvania, and Ohio, and to the Territory of Michigan where Lake Erie meets the Detroit River. It was an arduous journey that often took up to a month to complete.

Prior to that year little had been known about the area that was to become Jackson County, located in southeast Michigan, about thirty miles west of the early settlement of Ann Arbor. This region was mostly unexplored, except by the few who, in the service of the government as land surveyors or protectors of the settlements around Detroit, were sometimes obliged to travel there. Those who did followed established Native American Indian trails. Along the way they would have encountered packs of gray wolves, black bears, Mississauga rattlesnakes, and swarms of mosquitoes as they charted the land. Early surveys had concluded that most of the land was too marshy for cultivation, so little attention was paid to it until fur trappers reported otherwise. They correctly surmised that much of the land had valuable agricultural potential.

With that news, government officials met with the region's naive indigenous people and made treaties in preparation of making the land available for settlement. On July 6, 1818, the sale of new lands outside Detroit was opened.

In the winter of 1829, the Michigan Territorial Council in Detroit passed an act establishing several new counties in the forested wilderness to the west, including Jackson County. A new road was commissioned to access the land, and was built over a well traveled Potawatomi Indian trail several miles north of the established Detroit-Chicago Road, which had been constructed by the federal government in 1825 over an ancient Sauk Indian Trail, which began at the banks of the Detroit River and terminated at Fort Dearborn, an army installation located at the mouth of the Chicago River on the southern shore of Lake Michigan in Illinois. This new road, aptly named Territorial Road, served as a pathway for settlers into the newly opened land. The first recorded settler to what would become Jackson County, Horace Blackman, from Tioga County, New York, arrived in July 1829. Others arrived that year, and soon the first hamlet in Jackson County was founded and named Jacksonburgh, later called Jacksonopolis and, ultimately, Jackson. Word was sent to their families and friends that, with hard work, there was abundant opportunity—and to come before it was gone.

As the news made its way east to New England and across the

Atlantic, more pioneers began making the journey. Many stopped at the Detroit land office, located at the corner of Jefferson and Randolph streets, to purchase land from the federal government. One hundred dollars in cash would purchase an eighty-acre plot. Title to the land had one caveat: the buyer was required to build and occupy a structure on the property. Before leaving for the rough country, pioneers acquired vital provisions for their journey, along with wagons and work animals.

Rugged Pioneers

Pioneers typically constructed a rudimentary wooden lean-to for temporary shelter as they prepared materials to build a permanent log cabin. Building materials came from harvesting the plentiful virgin hardwoods that included trees of oak, hickory, and chestnut. Once felled, the logs were trimmed, measured, sized, and notched to fit a rectangular foundation approximately twenty by thirty feet. The roofs were often gabled to allow sleeping lofts. Gaps between the logs were commonly chinked with stones and strips of wood, followed by ropes of oakum or moss, then finished with a daubing of clay mixed with lime that was wet-troughed to seal it. The same process was used for the interior. A stone fireplace, used for both cooking and warmth, was usually positioned near the center wall. The fireplace was vital for survival, as the winters in Jackson County would often bring freezing temperatures. The floors were constructed of slabs of roughly hewn timber; the roof was built the same and covered by wood shingles or thick bark. As additional space was required, these cabins could be expanded using the same process. Construction of wood cabins required minimal tools, including a broad axe and hand saws. Using the same tools, skilled settlers could construct bed frames, tables, and chairs from the same local resources. As they labored, these industrious pioneers dreamed of a future when their humble log cabins would be replaced by stately homes as they prospered from their cultivated fields.

Once their cabins were completed, settlers were faced with clearing the forest of trees and underbrush. This was a grueling task.

Many trees were cut and trimmed for use as lumber for outbuildings. Others were felled and split to burn in the fireplace. Then tree roots had to be cut and the stumps pulled up. Other trees may have been girdled—the bark was cut away from around the base of the tree to kill it before felling. Ditches were dug to drain swampy areas. It would take many months of grueling labor to prepare their acreage for cultivation. While working the land, farmers grew plots of corn, beans, squash, and grain for their own consumption. Abundant game, including deer, fowl, and fish from the numerous local lakes and streams, along with wild fruits and berries provided sustenance. Established settlers often offered their skills to assist newcomers to the area, helping clear the land and build cabins.

A sawmill, grist mill, and general store were quickly established in Jackson County. The new residents formed militias to protect their communities from perceived threats from Native American tribes living in the area and from unknown transients searching for unscrupulous opportunities. At the same time they established governance in accordance with the laws of the land.

Settlers to the Michigan Territory shared the same drive as those who had emigrated from Europe two centuries earlier to colonize the Atlantic coast. They were men and women eager for opportunities and freedoms that were either denied them or were beyond reach in their homelands. Those who ventured to the Territory of Michigan were not afraid of the hardships of frontier life. Early settlers were typically young and rugged frontiersmen and women. Most had been reared on farms and possessed the knowledge necessary to tame the land and survive off it. Their skills were versatile enough to make ends meet with little dependence on the outside world. These pioneers were driven by dreams of what the future could bring as they took full advantage of the unique opportunity.

In January 1833, the Potawatomi Indian nation ceded to the United States Federal Government all title and interest to what they had claimed as their land in the states of Illinois, Indiana, and, in the Territory of Michigan, the area south of the Grand River, Michigan's longest river. The Grand River's headwaters originate just south of

Jackson County and flow north through the county's marshes before twisting and turning for over 270 river miles to the west and into Lake Michigan at Grand Haven. During these demanding years, pioneers shared the land with the few remaining Potawatomi, most having been relocated west of the Mississippi River and to areas near Green Bay, Wisconsin—and with an occasional black bear and gray wolf, as they, too, were rapidly losing their habitat to open, cultivated fields.

In 1836 the widening of the Erie Canal system created an enhanced gateway to the Michigan Territory. With the knowledge that abundant, cultivatable land was still available and that the native inhabitants were mostly gone, an influx of people from New England and immigrants primarily from the British Isles and Germany began arriving at a steady rate.

During the two decades between 1840 and 1860, steamships rapidly replaced sailing ships from Europe to America's East Coast, reducing transit time from an average of six weeks to about two. At the same time, railroad track was being laid between cities on these lands, eventually reducing travel time by rail to Michigan from cities such as New York, Boston, and Philadelphia to less than a week.

Jackson County settlers continued sending word to their families and friends that the land was indeed good and plentiful, and the population rapidly grew. Immigrants generally traveled in groups from their local villages and settled in the New World together. Many shared common heritages dating back several generations from where they came, and began establishing churches that served their religious traditions.

During the mid 1800s a large number of Germans arrived in Jackson County and settled in what became the township of Waterloo. They formed "The Lutheran Evangelical Fellowship Society of St. Jacob Evangelical Lutheran Church," commonly referred to as the German Lutheran Church, or simply St. Jacob. The church was quickly constructed with the land, material, and labor provided by the congregants. Elder Friederich Schmidt, from Ann Arbor, conducted the inaugural service in the spring of 1841. The building quickly outgrew its congregation, so in 1853 the German congregants built a larger church a short distance down the road on land donated by parishioner Jacob Harr. By the time the new church was built, the Potawatomi, after centuries of inhabiting the area, having ceded their native lands twenty years earlier, were gone, as were the thick virgin forests, as no fewer than five commercial saw-mills were operating in the county. The indigenous Americans' former hunting grounds had become farming fields.

It was important to the local Germans to protect their heritage. The German language was frequently spoken exclusively at home and church, and German families worked and traded together. They also insisted that marriages stay within their Lutheran faith. Upholding these traditions resulted in an enclave where every one's business *was* everyone's business.

As Jackson County rapidly developed, so did its politics. Some immigrants from across the Atlantic had left their countries in search of freedom from political oppression. Many jumped at the chance to participate in nation building as they started new lives in their new world.

———— ⚬⚭⚬ ————

The legal institution of slavery and its expansion to America's new states and territories was greatly debated in Michigan. The people of Jackson County, along with a majority of those living in surrounding areas, fervently opposed slavery on both moral and religious grounds. In January of 1854, the United States federal government passed the Kansas-Nebraska Act, which allowed conditional slavery in those two U.S. territories. Opposition to the Kansas-Nebraska Act in Michigan and bordering Wisconsin was so great that it led to the creation of the Republican Party, which conducted its first official meeting at a tree-shaded park known as "Under the Oaks" in Jackson, Michigan, on July 6, 1854. It rallied great numbers of antislavery proponents and was successful in having its first candidate for the presidency of the United States, Abraham Lincoln, elected in 1860. Lincoln's Emancipation Proclamation on January 1, 1863, was the beginning of the end to slavery during the Civil War.

While this was occurring, abundant milled lumber made it far less difficult to build dwellings, allowing newer landowners to prepare their fields for cultivation and start farming almost right away. Milled lumber allowed more than houses to be quickly constructed. Farmers required barns, stables, and other buildings to be productive. These structures—outbuildings—included much more than the necessary privy, or outhouse. Outbuildings were structures designed for specific functions away from the main house. Farms that maintained livestock required structures to house the animals, such as barns and stables; granaries and cribs were necessary for storing feed. Other outbuildings included smokehouses and chicken coops. In Jackson County, barns served multiple uses, including a place to store blocks of ice cut from local lakes during the winter. The ice blocks were coated in sawdust for insulation and stored for future use during the warm months ahead. Another outbuilding would have been built over an excavation several feet deep that was used to keep dairy products and root vegetables at moderate temperatures year-round. Cisterns near or attached to the main house held rainwater funneled from the roof to be used for bathing and laundry. Pump wells provided fresh water for drinking, cooking, and for livestock.

Rapid Development

By 1895 the land in Jackson County had been mostly cleared of forest and drained. Roads traversed and connected farms, and railroads were servicing several towns within the county. Most farms averaged over one hundred acres. Many of the settlers' log cabins had been either demolished for their lumber or repurposed as outbuildings. For many settlers, dreams of stately homes made of brick and frame had become reality.

The rail routes and roads allowed transport to growing urban areas. Many farmers had become prosperous as rising populations readily purchased their grain, fruit, dairy, meat, and wool.

Education

Proper education was required, and several publicly funded one-room schoolhouses were constructed throughout the county, typically served by a single teacher—usually a "schoolmarm," who taught grades one through twelve. Younger schoolmarms were sometimes about the same age as their twelfth-grade male students, which may have led to the term *teacher's pet*. Schoolmarms typically boarded at nearby residences. The children were schooled in the English language from the beginning, allowing for the essential three R's—*Reading, wRiting, and aRithmetic*—to be taught *only* in English. American history was also a required subject. Because the teacher had to deal with multiple levels of subject matter and students' ages ranged from about eight to eighteen, strict discipline was enforced. Socializing was not allowed, except for recess when students burned energy by playing running games such as pom-pom-pullaway. Older students sometimes used the time to either engage in conversation or, perhaps, prepare for their lessons.

In Waterloo Township, German Lutheran parents often removed their children from the public schools at about age twelve to thirteen for one year to attend the school at St. Jacob and prepare for the rite of Confirmation, during which older children approaching adulthood officially proclaimed their Lutheran faith.

After completing their education at the local public schools, students could undergo additional schooling for trades such as carpentry and masonry, provided by St. Jacob tradesmen.

Literacy and population growth created enterprise opportunities for newspaper publishers, some local to the smaller communities within Jackson County. The two most widely circulated were variations of the *Jackson Citizen* and the *Jackson Patriot*. There was also a German language weekly, *The Michigan Volksfreund.*

Rural Relationships, Lasting Relationships

The German settlers who found their way to Waterloo Township worked together in transforming the rugged wilderness to the productive lands from which they profited. Their children also reaped the fruits of their families' pioneering spirit and unfaltering determination to build quality lives in their Michigan home. It was a united effort that spanned decades, from hamlets in Germany to their growing enclave in Waterloo Township. They were linked by community and lived and moved as a singular entity.

PROLOGUE

May 31, 1896

Sunday, May 31, 1896, started out like every other Sunday in Waterloo. It was a welcome day of devotion, fellowship, and relaxation. St. Jacob Lutheran Church served the local German community as its place of worship. It also served as an essential meeting place that allowed men the opportunity to talk business and politics, and women a venue in which to discuss families, social happenings, and neighborhood chatter. For children and young adults, it was a time to make friends and build relationships.

For some, a friendship would blossom into a romantic relationship, as it did for Lewis Heydlauff and Emma Moeckel.

Their families' houses were a short distance apart, separated only by the church, where both were parishioners. As children, they had attended the same one-room schoolhouse nearby. As the years progressed, they grew ever closer to each other. On Emma's sixteenth birthday, March 11, 1891, she and twenty-year-old Lewis made a secret pledge to someday marry. By 1895, the two were commonly known to be going together exclusively.

From the time he was a child, Lewis Heydlauff carried himself with self-assurance. As a young man, he kept his face clean-shaven. His deep-set brown eyes, almost dark as night, at times peered outward as if he was in profound thought—although it was sometimes difficult to determine if he wasn't simply daydreaming, a peculiar trait that some, including Emma, found amusing. Lewis kept his chestnut hair cut short and combed to the side—he was told by his friends that it looked distinguished. Lewis also had a curious tendency of smugly pursing his lips during conversations, which made him appear self-righteous.

Lewis's attire for farm work consisted of dark denim bib overalls, a cotton shirt, leather boots, and sometimes a wide-brim straw bowler hat. On Sundays and socially he dressed fashionably for the day in well-tailored suits, wing-collared cotton shirts with silk neckties, coordinated vests, leather shoes, and always, a charcoal-colored derby hat.

Lewis came from a prominent, respected family and had always been known by the community as hard-working, quiet, and polite.

Emma was gracefully tall and slim as an adolescent. Her figure began maturing when she was about thirteen years old, and by eighteen, her once girlish frame had become elegantly curved. Her oval face, pleasantly high forehead, well-defined cheek bones, small nose, and rounded chin were in perfect balance. Emma's fair, rosy skin had the texture of smooth porcelain. Tiny freckles dusted her nose. Emma's almond-shaped eyes, the color being similar to that of a precious green emerald with a subtle bluish cast, were accentuated by long, dark lashes. Her thick, curly, copper-red hair flared out like a fan over her shoulders and down her back. At times, she wore it braided, tying it at the end with a bright ribbon. Emma's lips were sensuously full, her upper delicately arched. Emma's girlfriends often teased her, saying they could capture any man they desired if her lips could be borrowed for just one kiss. When Emma smiled, her mouth opened in a way that formed long, cheerful dimples. Her voice was melodic and soothing.

During the day, Emma was frequently seen wearing full length cotton or flannel dresses, sometimes with a laced bodice, other times simply gathered at the waist with a colorful sash tied at the side. Her workday frocks were simple, but she wore them stylishly. On her feet, Emma wore top-of-the-ankle, black leather, laced shoes. On special occasions, she would wear one of her stylish gowns over a sateen petticoat. Some of her fashionable gowns were made with colorful satin, trimmed with velvet. For a grand event, such as a wedding, Emma enhanced her figure by wearing a corset. When wearing a gown, she often wore matching cotton gloves that covered her long, delicate fingers. On certain occasions, she would wear a small bonnet trimmed with feathers, ribbons, and lace. When Emma walked she held her head high; her gait was steady and straight. Emma was frequently surrounded by several friends. She was known to be righteous, trustworthy, and faithful.

George Tisch, twenty-seven years of age, was a good-natured acquaintance of both Emma and Lewis. His family lived about four miles north of the village of Waterloo, in Munith. George socialized at times with Emma and Lewis at local events. He attended St. Jacob with his family, where they frequently visited with the Heydlauff and Moeckel families before and after church services.

Unknown to these three young people, their lives were destined to collide in an unimaginable way.

* * *

Those who had attended church services at St. Jacob that Sunday morning were already aware of the shocking event that had occurred a half mile up the road. Word had spread of a tragedy in the village of Waterloo, near the wooden church, but the greater community learned of the calamity after 4:00 p.m., when local Sunday afternoon newspapers came rolling off their printing presses. The telegraph service was used to transmit early information from the Munith Grand Trunk railway station, four miles from Waterloo, but served primarily in bringing news reporters from around the county who scurried to the scene to interview those who lingered where the crime had occurred. The persons involved in the dreadful event were well known in the area, so there was considerable information to be had. By the time the reporters filed their stories, friends, neighbors, physicians, lawmen, and county officials had readily offered intimate details about the crime and few questions remained as to what happened and why—or so they thought.

One of the first newspapers to circulate that day was the *Stockbridge Sun*, published nine miles to the north of where the horrible event took place. Readers who had not heard what happened near the Lutheran church were shocked by the headline news—they would have known the families involved.

Nothing like it had ever happened in Waterloo.

CHAPTER ONE

---❖---

SUNDAY, MAY 31, 1896

The Stockbridge Sun

KILLED HIS SWEETHEART

THE DOUBLE CRIME OF A WORTHLESS LOVER

WATERLOO, Michigan, Special Telegram, May 31—Love, liquor, and jealousy combined were responsible for a double tragedy, which occurred four miles south of the village of Munith, at 9:15 o'clock this morning. Lewis Heydlauff, 25 years old, shot and instantly killed his affianced bride, Miss Emma Moeckel, about 20 years of age, then, turning the weapon upon himself, sent two balls into his body from which he will probably die.

The Heydlauffs and Moeckels live but a short distance apart, both being prosperous farmers. Between their farms is located the German Lutheran Church, of which Miss Moeckel was the organist. Both young Heydlauff and Miss Moeckel were highly thought of in the neighborhood. As children they had played together, cementing a friendship which, with their growth, ripened into love and culminated in an engagement.

For four years they had been almost incessantly together. Lately however, it was noted that young Heydlauff developed an attachment for the bottle, which eventually caused a rupture between the young lovers. The breach widened until it terminated in the terrible crime committed today.

This morning Miss Moeckel attended church as usual, taking her accustomed place at the organ. Among the congregation was a young man named George Tisch. He had been showing considerable attention to Miss Moeckel, and Heydlauff was insanely jealous of him.

Heydlauff called at the Moeckel residence before service was finished and awaited the return of his former fiancée. Though gloomy and morose, he gave no evidence of the tempest of passion raging within him.

Tisch accompanied Miss Moeckel to her home. This seemed to madden her former lover. As she entered the house Heydlauff followed her into the parlor.

Without a word of warning, and in a deliberate, cool manner, he drew his revolver and shot her three times. As she fell he turned on his heel and put two bullets into his own body.

Staggering into the backyard, he tried to reload his revolver to finish his job when the horrified father of the murdered girl sprang forward and, seizing the weapon, wrenched it from the murderer's grasp. Heydlauff then grabbed a stone and endeavored to batter his brains with it, but was overcome and held until the arrival of his parents. He was taken to his home, only a quarter of a mile distant, where he now lies probably dying and guarded by a deputy sheriff.

Justice Orville was sent for. Impaneling a jury he held an inquest immediately, the jury finding a verdict in accordance with the facts.

The parents of young Heydlauff are brokenhearted at the terrible crime committed by their son, while the relatives of Miss Moeckel are prostrated at the calamity which visited their peaceful household, turning the day of rest into one of gloom and sadness.

The murder and probable suicide created a tremendous excitement in the formerly quiet neighborhood. The sympathetic and curious lingered around the scene of the tragedy all day, recounting again and again in hushed whispers the details of the tragedy.

Heydlauff is still alive, but the physicians attending him say there is very little probability of his recovery.

CHAPTER TWO

———❦———

BACK IN TIME

Summer 1895

Lewis Heydlauff lived at home with his parents, John and Christina, in a large, ornate house with several specialized outbuildings. John and Christina's youngest son, August, along with his wife Carrie and their infant daughter Hannah, also shared the house.

Lewis and August worked for their father, who also employed an additional workman, Henry Gates, who slept in a small bedroom the size of a closet near the house's rear door.

John Heydlauff's property spanned over three hundred prime acres in Waterloo on which he grew crops and raised cattle for market. He was respected as a resourceful farmer, rancher, builder, and clever businessman. John Heydlauff was presumed to be quite wealthy.

Some Heydlauff fields were used to grow fodder for hay, which consisted of winter wheat, alfalfa, and orchard grass. Other fields were used for cultivating corn, oats, and barley. A portion of pasture was left for cattle to roam.

Lewis and August tended to the livestock and managed the fields. Henry Gates was responsible for maintaining the farm's equipment and outbuildings.

During midsummer of that year, the hay crops were such that

John Heydlauff hired a team of threshers from Wilhelm Tisch in Munith. Wilhelm's youngest son, George, managed the field operations for his father. Using three McCormick iron reapers and twine binders, each pulled by two heavy draft horses, six seasonal laborers and George harvested and baled a bumper yield for John Heydlauff.

----•⌒⌒•----

Emma had multiple chores around her house, which included housekeeping and cooking with her mother. She was occasionally hired by neighbors to do the same, sometimes to help with their children, especially when newborns came into a family.

When Emma was at home and her chores were completed, the Moeckel house was often filled with music. At a very young age, Emma was taught by her mother how to read sheet music and play the family's Estey harmonium parlor organ, which she quickly learned and loved. By the time she reached sixteen-years of age she had also mastered playing the pipe organ at St. Jacob, and was known to be skilled at extracting the maximum sounds from the instrument. At eighteen, Emma had become its primary organist.

The church's pastor, the Reverend Emil Wenk, chose the music to accompany the liturgical readings at church services. He collaborated with Emma on Wednesdays at 9:30 a.m. before the choir members arrived thirty minutes later. She enjoyed her two-hour rehearsals with the choir as they prepared for Sunday services. She considered playing the church's pipe organ a privilege.

----•⌒⌒•----

Days for Emma and Lewis were filled with everyday responsibilities and obligations, so when their work was completed, they strove to spend time together. When weather permitted, they would often ride out to one of the area's lakes or ponds to share a basket meal at water's edge, and sometimes to explore the ancient Potawatomi paths connecting them. They would frequently challenge each other as they attempted to navigate local Waterloo roads and paths with their bicycles. Sometimes they took short trips to shop or visit with family and friends. On occasion, they rode the Grand Trunk Railroad from Munith to experience the bustling streets of Jackson. Special dates and events were boldly marked on their calendars.

Emma and Lewis also socialized separately.

Emma had several girlfriends and enjoyed visiting with them. They frequently traveled together by buggy to Chelsea or Stockbridge, sometimes by train to Jackson, to shop or simply walk fashionably about the towns.

Lewis often joined his friends and cousins, who he referred to as his "Waterloo boys," to do much of the same, with one exception—they sometimes visited saloons.

During the peak of summer when days were hot and steamy, local lakes and ponds were refreshingly cool. Emma and her friends, along with Lewis and his "boys," sometimes gathered for late afternoon swims at the Trist millpond. Emma's uncle, Henry Moeckel, owned property bordering the east side of the pond—a secluded grassy area—where he allowed Emma and her friends to gather. The millpond had a steady slope to the center, and was trusted for its predictable bottom—less than five feet deep—as few of the boys or girls could actually swim.

The young ladies provided baskets of food to lie out on checkered tablecloths; the boys enthusiastically ate whatever was prepared. At times, a bottle of whiskey was secretly shared by some of the older boys.

Before entering the water the girls discreetly changed into loose-fitting smocks made from dark flannel, a fabric that protected their modesty when wet. While in the water, they instinctively huddled together with their feet and toes wallowing in the thick moss covering the gravelly bottom.

Guys typically stripped to their not-so-modest cotton union suits. Aware that they could stand upright at any point, they often pretended to swim, but mostly splashed water at each other. One of Lewis's close friends, Fred Artz Jr., was skittish of water, so he preferred staying on shore, near the food, where he would entertain with his Hohner pocket harmonica.

After sunset and away from the girls, some of the young men sometimes discarded their union suits. Giggles would be heard from the ladies, some whom dared doing the same, as both groups strained to see what was exposed below the evening sky, and above the surface of dark, refreshing water.

------------⚬------------

The late summer of 1895 was rapidly leading to final harvests and dawn-to-dusk work in the fields. Knowing that the season would limit her time to be with Lewis, Emma decided to plan a birthday party for him. On Monday, September 2, Emma surprised Lewis on his twenty-fourth birthday by hosting an evening party at her parents' home. She had worked for two days decorating the house with colorful ribbons; she baked pies and other pastries, and prepared fresh lemonade. When Lewis called on Emma at about 7:00 p.m., she led him to the parlor where their friends were assembled. After she opened the door for him, he immediately heard, "Surprise, Happy Birthday, Lewie!" from the jolly group inside.

For the next two hours Lewis seemed delighted as he celebrated with his and Emma's friends. During that time, unnoticed by Emma, Lewis had occasionally stepped outside for brief periods of time. Toward the end of the party he was appearing belligerent with some of his friends, yet quickly smiled when his eyes met Emma's.

After the guests had left and Emma's family had retired for the night, Lewis sat on a bench in the foyer and rested his head against the wall. Seeing this, Emma came to him, took his hand, and led him to the parlor. They sat together on the sofa and quietly reminisced about the evening. She was troubled when Lewis began stumbling over his words, and asked, "Lewis, you're mumbling. Are you feeling all right?"

Lewis hesitated, and then said, "I'm very tired; I should leave for home." He stood, yawned, and exhaled as he stammered, "Emma, thank you fo . . . for the party. You are ver—" Lewis belched, grinned, and mumbled, "very thoughtful." Lewis flushed as he awkwardly swallowed a hiccup, and then continued to say, "The fixins' were delicious. Maybe I . . . I ate too much? Thank you a . . . again for all you did for me. I gotta g . . . go home now."

Emma was surprised by Lewis's sloppy demeanor. She stood up from the sofa, smiled, and put her head against his chest. Softly, she said, "Lewie, you work so hard; you deserved the party. I'm happy you enjoyed it; we'll have many more together, just like tonight." Ignoring that his breath had developed a pungent odor, Emma gave Lewis a kiss on his cheek and led him to the front door. She looked into his eyes and, noticing they were quite bloodshot, said, "Lewie, you do look very tired. Please be careful on your way home, and get a good night's rest."

"Yep, I'm tired as an old dog. Goodnight Emma."

"Goodnight to you, Lewie."

Emma watched as he stepped from the porch and began walking to the road. Then she closed the door and put her back against it. She sighed deeply, looked down the hall to the empty parlor, and wondered *Why was Lewie tripping over his words? What soured his breath? Why had he been belligerent with his friends? Why did Lewie seem so weary toward the end of the party?* Emma closed her eyes and thought about how happy he seemed, and then dismissed her concerns by deciding that he was simply exhausted from a very long day. She was worn-out as well, so she extinguished the lighting and readied for bed.

After covering herself with a blanket, Emma's thoughts of Lewis's odd demeanor resurfaced and disturbed her. There was something reminiscent about his breath. As Emma tossed and turned, she remembered: two years earlier, she, along with Lewis's Uncle Gottlieb, brought him to a dentist in Chelsea because of a painfully throbbing toothache. Before seeing the dentist, his uncle brought Lewis into a saloon to drink some whisky, saying it would help ease the pain, especially if the tooth was to be pulled. When Lewis came out, Emma was embarrassed by his strange, boorish behavior and repulsed by his foul breath. Had she smelled it again?

The summer's accommodating weather resulted in abundant crop yields throughout the county. Several successive dry October days were followed by clear, moonlit skies, permitting fieldwork well past dusk. Friederich Moeckel mostly grew feed for his flock of Black Top sheep. He also had a bountiful yield, and hired George Tisch and his thresher team to harvest his fields. Friederich, and his young sons Albert and Florenz, spent time away from the fields shearing the sheep before cold weather arrived. Emma worked alongside, bundling wool.

By late October the arduous work was completed. The Moeckel fields were harvested, winter wheat sown, and the wool had been sent to market.

Emma had time on her hands, so she sent word to relatives and friends that she was available for work outside her house.

At John Heydlauff's farm the bulk of work was finished as well. His cattle herd had increased significantly through calving during the summer. A few bull calves were sold at auction and several cows were culled and driven to a slaughterhouse in Jackson.

Carrie had delivered a daughter, Hannah, at home on March 15, 1895. Hannah was the center of attention as doting mother and grandmother spent considerable time with the baby girl. August, Carrie, and baby Hannah occupied an upstairs bedroom next to Lewis's.

When August brought Carrie into the house as his wife, at the invitation of his parents, Lewis was welcoming at first. Soon afterward Carrie got pregnant and Hannah was born. As with all newborns, Hannah cried from the start. After several nights of being awakened every few hours by the baby's bawling, Lewis became short-tempered with Carrie, and demanded that she keep her child quiet. Lewis became increasingly annoyed by having his once-tranquil home life disrupted and displayed it with rudeness toward Carrie. This did not go unnoticed by August and his parents.

By June, Hannah was slumbering through most of the night, but that did not stop an occasional squeal. It continued to frustrate Lewis and his spiteful remarks to Carrie continued.

Later that month while tending to the livestock, August approached Lewis and told him to stop treating his wife with disrespect. Lewis denied anything of the sort. August countered by saying, "Just this morning, Carrie told me that you said to 'cork that spoiled child's mouth.' "

"Carrie has thin skin, Auggie. I was only joking," Lewis scoffed.

August was not sympathetic. He brought up another time when Carrie told of Lewis grumbling in his bedroom loud enough for her to hear, "Carrie changed everything when she moved in. Auggie and his precious wife and baby should find their own place to live; they don't belong here."

From that day forward, conversation between Lewis and August—and Carrie—came only from necessity. Friction in the house was so heavy that the family rarely spoke when Lewis was present.

Lewis told of what was happening at home to one of his Waterloo boys. His friend suggested that a quick gulp of whiskey—or more—during the day would ease his feelings; make him feel better. Lewis's friend told him how to acquire some cheap locally made white whiskey—*liquid lightning, moonshine*—but to keep it quiet because its maker did not have a government permit to produce it; it was illegal booze. Lewis asked him if it was the same whiskey he brought to the Trist millpond. His friend said that it was, and that it was the same booze he shared with Lewis at Emma's house during his birthday party.

Lewis wasted no time acquiring his first two bottles. He also purchased a metal flask from the general store in Munith—a flask that he could easily conceal in his pants pocket.

In the beginning, two or three drinks during the day relaxed him. Lewis was able to better tolerate the tension at home. But in little time, it led to Lewis being short-tempered as its effects wore off, so he started drinking more.

Then he made a second trip to the clandestine moonshiner, not far down the road.

Lewis began noticing that his father was spending considerable time explaining the financial workings of the farm to August. Lewis had always believed that he and his younger brother would manage the farm together when their father got old and gray. Each time Lewis saw his father with August reviewing work ledgers and other journals, he felt ignored—unwelcomed—and would walk away sulking, fearing that he was about to be pushed out to fend for himself. Lewis was ignoring the fact that he was an elder brother, and that his father accepted his lineage's tradition of passing landholdings to the youngest son. Lewis could not conceive the idea that, someday, he could be working for August.

CHAPTER THREE

TIME TO LEAVE

On a misty, late-October afternoon, Lewis and August were work-ing together with their father in the main barn. Their father told August to go join his wife and daughter in the house, and that he and Lewis would finish the job. Lewis's father grabbed a pine stool and sat. He called to Lewis, "Come, join me. I want to have a word with you." Lewis pushed a small bench to his father and sat.

"Son, it's time we've had a talk. Winter is comin' and there won't be much for you to do here. You've always given me a fair day's work for what I pay you, but I can't pay enough for you to live on your own."

Lewis's head dropped. His ears had been scorched by the words, "I can't pay enough for you to live on your own." He immediately felt sick, as if he had been kicked in the gut. He was afraid to hear what may be said next, but looked up as his father continued.

"Lewis, you were eighteen when I agreed to put you on my pay-roll. That was six years ago. How much money have you saved?"

Lewis replied boastfully, "I've put over eight hundred dollars in the bank."

His father looked pleased. "Eight hundred dollars is a good amount of money. What do you plan to do with it?"

Lewis looked down to his feet and quietly replied, "Father, you know that Emma and I have been together for over four years.

Someday, I want to make her my wife. I've been saving most of my wages to help give us a good start."

Looking dubiously at his son, he asked, "Lewis, where do you intend to live when you decide to take on a wife?"

Lewis paused. He thought of August and Carrie sleeping in the bedroom next to his with their baby, and realized *There is no place for me and Emma in my father's house.* He then slowly answered in an uneasy tone, "I would use my savings to purchase property and build a fine house."

"Eight hundred dollars would be a good start, but you will need to borrow money from the bank. How else would you intend to pay the note and still provide for your wife and children to come?"

"I was hoping to work for you, Father."

Lewis's father sternly countered, "Son, I cannot pay what you need to make that possible. You cannot own property, build a business, and feed your wife and family working for me. It's time for you to be more than just a farmhand working for me. You must learn to live on your own, build a business, control your own day, and make the money that I cannot pay you."

"Father, what is it you want me to do?"

"That is something you must determine. Your time with me has taught you about farming and raising cattle. But Lewis, I've noticed lately that you don't seem to have your heart in the work. Farming is difficult and offers few days of rest. I was raised on a farm, but I also learned carpentry and home building. Over the years I've built many houses to earn money to acquire more land and livestock, and have grown what I have to what it is today. Lewis, you must put *your* skills to work for yourself, whether it is farming, ranching, or being a tradesman, you must make that determination. To be successful, there will be little time to rest. Son, it's time for you to be on your own."

Lewis lamented, "Why now? Is it because of what Carrie told Auggie?"

"That's part of it, son. You're causing problems by your temperament around Carrie. This is now your brother's home. I'm getting older, and I intend for August to manage what I own."

"But Father, I have nowhere to go," Lewis said in a quivering voice, tears beginning to flow. "Why so soon, why not until after winter? I can find work to do here."

"Lewis, there isn't enough. You must find work elsewhere. It's time to provide for yourself—and for Emma, if you plan to wed. I've taught you several skills, now use them to build your life."

Lewis was stunned by his father's decree. He had been dismissing his father's repeated message during the past several months. The message came in variations, but the theme was always: *When I came here as a young boy with my parents. We worked together clearing the land so it could be farmed. It was hard work, a hard life in the beginning, but as time went on I was able to earn and bank enough of my wages to own land, build a house, and raise a family. When I was your age I refused the thought of being someone else's farmhand. I wanted my own business to control—earn my own money. Lewis, what is it you want?*

When asked that question Lewis would think, *I want what is yours,* but would answer, "I hope to own a house with some land."

His father would ask, "How are you going to do it—what is your plan?"

Lewis could never offer the answer his father was looking for. He would often simply reply, "I'm working on it."

Lewis was at a loss for words. After a minute of looking down at the straw-covered floor, he said, "When do you want me to leave the house?"

"Lewis, there is no profit for you here. I'll pay your back wages, but you must build your future. You will always be welcome to visit as you wish, but now it's time for you to find your way."

Lewis got the message, and acknowledged, "Father, I understand. I'll do as you wish."

His father nodded, then said, "Lewis, if you are to succeed, there is no place for whiskey in your future."

Lewis's head jerked when that was said. His father stood, looked disapprovingly at Lewis, and then left the barn, not looking back.

Lewis felt sick as he watched his father stride toward the house as the numbing reality of what was said sunk in. As his father walked further away, Lewis thought of all the chores, all the labor, all the hours of work he provided, and assumed there was more than enough for him to stay busy. Lewis questioned why his father was putting him out so abruptly. He searched for a reason. He wanted to blame Carrie for talking against him, and August for gaining his father's favor. He was further puzzled by his father saying there was no place for whiskey in his future—*Why did he say that? Sure I have a drink every so often. So what?*

Lewis desperately felt a need to see Emma and tell her what had happened. He started walking to the road. Then he stopped. His throat was parched, and he was thirsty. Lewis made his way back to the house and up to his bedroom. He closed the door and reached for his hidden flask, then silently left his room, and the house, without being noticed.

Lewis slowly shuffled his feet along the muddy road leading to Emma's. Along the way he stopped, dropped his head, and experienced a terrifying feeling of anguish and despair. He had never felt such an emotion, and began to fully realize that he had been told to leave home and, for the first time in his life, find a job on his own. He removed the flask from his pants pocket; the burn of white-lightning drizzling down his throat gave him the courage to keep walking.

When Lewis reached the Moeckels' he paused and stared vacantly at the house, not knowing how to tell Emma. He then decided to continue on the muddy road to call on his friend, Fred Artz Jr.

Lewis knocked twice on the rear door. Fred peeked through the window curtain and was surprised to see Lewis standing outside in the heavy mist.

"Come in Lew, what can I do for you?"

Lewis stepped in and asked his friend, "Do you have time to talk?"

"Sure, Lew, let's sit at the kitchen table. What's going on?"

Lewis told of the conversation with his father—of having to leave the house and find a job. He talked about his brother taking over the farm, and how his sister-in-law, Carrie, had disrupted everything. He asked Artz, "How do I tell Emma? What will she think?"

Artz suggested telling Emma that it was *his* decision to leave home; that it was time to be independent from his father, start his own trade, and by doing so, earn more money. He could then purchase a house on a few acres, and he and Emma could get married and start a family.

Lewis thanked his friend for the advice and left for home.

On the way back the mist turned to rain. When Lewis approached the Moeckel house he decided to keep walking. Minutes later he was home and entering the house soaked from the rain. The family was finishing supper. His mother asked, "Lewis, where have you been? You must be hungry."

"Oh, I went to see Fred Artz. Sorry Mother, I'm not feeling well and have no appetite. I'm going to dry off and rest on my bed awhile."

Lewis stayed his bedroom, where he was awake most of the night wondering what he did wrong to be abruptly told by his father to leave the house—and what to tell Emma. At dawn he awoke, overwhelmed by a feeling of abandonment.

CHAPTER FOUR

THE WINDMILL

Most farmers had completed harvesting their crops by the end of October. Many would use the coming winter months to build upon and repair their farms' infrastructure. For Friederich Moeckel, the winter was planned for constructing a new windmill that would be used to pump water for his livestock. Friederich selected the ten-foot model (as measured across the blades) with a thirty-five-foot wooden tower from the Perkins Wind Mill Company, located in Mishawaka, Indiana. Their products were considered amongst the most durable and versatile of modern windmills, with accessories available for grain milling, irrigation, and other applications. The unassembled windmill arrived by train in several crates during the last week of October. Realizing much of the construction was a two-man job, Friederich had decided to hire a helper to assist with assembly and installation.

When Lewis awoke the morning after being told it was time for him to work and live on his own, he carefully crafted a story to tell Emma as to why he was leaving his father's employment. He would say that he had a good sum of money in the bank and wanted to learn a trade that would free him from being dependent on his father, and that by finding work elsewhere, he would begin his path to independence. Lewis's story did not include that he was told to find a new place live.

Later that day Lewis was standing at the front door of the Moeckel house. After calling out Emma's name, she greeted him with a smile and invited him in.

"Emma, could we talk somewhere privately?" Lewis asked.

"Of course Lewie, is everything all right?"

"Yes, I have something I want to tell you."

Emma led him past the kitchen where her parents were quietly talking and into the empty parlor, where she then closed the door. They then sat together on the sofa.

"What is it, Lewie?" Emma asked.

Lewis told his story.

Emma listened with great interest, and when he finished, she replied, "Lewie, that's so exciting! What are you going to do first?"

Lewis was not prepared for that question.

"Oh, ah, well . . . I'm considering many things. I . . . I haven't decided yet," he stammered.

Emma, knowing of her father's plans to hire a helper for constructing the windmill, offered, "Lewie, you know, my pa is going to start building his new windmill soon. He's looking to hire someone to help. Maybe that would be something you could learn about."

Lewis knew about the windmill, but was unaware that Emma's father was looking for help. He seized on the opportunity, replying, "Emma, yes! Helping build a windmill is something I would very much value." Lewis then took his good fortune one step further by saying, "I know that your father starts his day very early, and we live only a short distance apart, but during the winter storms it could be difficult getting to and from your house."

"Oh Lewie, I'm sure you could stay here. That would be so much fun! Do you want me to ask?"

Lewis lowered his head and smiled slyly in a way that Emma could not see. He then looked at Emma and said, "That would be good for me. I would promise to stay out of everyone's way."

Emma laughed as she replied, "Lewie, you're practically family!

I'll talk to my pa after you leave. Come back in the morning."

As Emma was leading Lewis from the parlor, Friederich saw him from the kitchen and said, "Lewis, what brings you here today?"

"Just came by to see Emma, that's all. Good day to you and Mrs. Moeckel."

After Lewis left Emma walked into the kitchen and proudly announced Lewis's unexpected availability.

Friederich liked Lewis, but wondered why he made his plans without discussing them with Emma beforehand. Regardless, Emma persuaded her father to offer Lewis employment.

Early the next morning Lewis was back at the Moeckel house. Emma led him to the kitchen where her father was having his breakfast.

Friederich looked up and said, "Good mornin' Lewis. I've been expecting you."

With some trepidation, suspecting there was more to know about his sudden availability, Friederich asked Lewis if he was willing to help with the construction and installation of the windmill, starting as soon as possible. He offered the attic as a bedroom, plus two meals a day for the work's duration. His wage would be fifteen dollars per sixty-hour week. On Christmas and Thanksgiving there would be no work or pay. Friederich was very specific about the number of work hours, telling Lewis that he would be keeping a daily log of his time, and when the job was complete, would reconcile his final pay.

Lewis accepted without hesitation, relieved to have a place to work—and to live

A New Day

Lewis arrived at the Moeckel residence at dawn, Monday, November 4, carrying two canvas-covered grips: one containing his work clothing, the second packed with social attire. Lewis was happy and energized. Now he and his girl would be together as never before.

Lewis had been scheming how to use the arrangement to entrust and persuade Emma's father to help him finance a business. Yes, he had saved eight hundred dollars, but if he could persuade Mr. Moeckel to lend him another eight hundred, Lewis figured he could purchase about twenty acres, build a modest house, acquire a small number of sheep, and have Emma's father get him into the wool trade through his contacts. And, with that collateral, he could borrow future money from the bank to expand the business. Lewis assumed that this would provide the prerequisite to asking for Emma's hand in marriage.

Lewis was enthusiastic the first few days as he worked alongside Mr. Moeckel. Conversation between them was cordial, but rarely did Lewis speak of Emma, nor did he approach Friederich about the business idea. Lewis quickly learned that he had a demanding boss who expected a full day of flawless work. In the beginning, the workday began at dawn and ended at about 4:00 p.m., when supper was served. After the first week, Friederich expected Lewis to return after supper and work additional time to fulfill his sixty-hour weekly commitment. At home, Lewis's winter workdays started early, but normally concluded when supper was served. His father rarely expected work afterward.

Except for Sundays, Lewis was able to visit with Emma for a short time at breakfast, longer during supper, and sometimes in the parlor after her father announced the workday was over. This frustrated Lewis. It seemed that he was able to spend more time with Emma when he was living at home. Now that he was sleeping in her house he hardly saw her.

Alone Time

Lewis began showing signs of frustration after the second week at the Moeckels'. When Friederich proclaimed that the workday was over, Lewis would approach Emma—if she was home—and say he wanted to calm down with a quiet walk. Without waiting for an answer, he would leave the house, and return high-spirited a short while later ready to spend time with Emma and the family. In the evening, they frequently retired to the parlor where a card or a board game was played, or sometimes to hear Emma or her mother play the families' harmonium organ. After an hour or so, Lewis often slipped into a weary, gloomy state, apologized for being tired, and left for the attic bedroom. The Moeckels did not think much of it; they figured Lewis was tired or, maybe homesick. There was little concern at the time; Lewis was working hard and needed his rest.

When Lewis first began taking his alone time, it was only for a half hour or so. Then his time away increased. After three weeks, his absence grew to an hour. Lewis would sometimes say, "I'm going to visit my parents for a bit," or, "I want to see how my friends are doing." Emma thought it strange that he never invited her, but respected his desire to go by himself.

Lewis began returning from his longer jaunts appearing exhausted. He started being less social and did not speak with his usual lucidity. His former fashionable self was getting shoddy, his eyes glassy, and his breath increasingly pungent. Lewis had changed. Emma suspected—but wanted to deny—that Lewis was returning after drinking alcohol.

Thanksgiving

Thanksgiving Day arrived on November 28. Emma and her mother prepared a meal consisting of domestic turkey, cranberries grown in nearby marshes, potatoes, carrots, onions, and Hubbard squash—all harvested earlier from the family garden. The same garden also produced the sugar pumpkin used for Emma's dessert pie. Lewis joined the Moeckel family for dinner, his disposition polite, quiet. Emma and her mother served the scrumptious dinner at 2:00 p.m. After Friederich offered prayers of thanksgiving, the family and Lewis took their seats. Lewis mostly spoke to Emma's young brothers, Albert and Florenz, about the Perkins windmill, and to her father about raising sheep. Emma, who reluctantly sat next to Lewis, barely acknowledged him as she and her mother spoke about their friends and neighbors.

Two hours later dinner was finished. Emma and her mother cleared the table and washed dishes. Emma and Lewis then excused themselves so they could visit Lewis's family, most of who were at his sister Paulina Schumacher's house not far down the road.

Emma and Lewis walked the short distance, where they joined Paulina, her husband Christian, and their two young children, along with his other sister, Lydia Archenbraun, her husband Albert, and their six children. Lewis's brother August and wife Carrie were there with eight-month-old Hannah, along with Lewis's parents John and Christina.

Paulina had prepared a large turkey, smoked ham covered in cloves and brown sugar glaze, pork sausages, and side dishes of potatoes and other root vegetables. Dinner was finished, but the evening was just beginning.

Emma headed to the kitchen where Christina, her daughters Paulina and Lydia, and Carrie, closely holding Hannah on her left hip, talked and laughed while they washed and dried dishes and tableware. Emma offered to help and was handed a towel. Laughing children ran in and out, including little six-year-old Nora Schumacher, who had been constantly asking, "Mommy, what can I do, what can I do Mommy?" Her mother assigned her the important task of carrying used kitchen towels to the laundry room, near the backdoor, one at a time.

In the parlor, the men had just begun a game of dominoes. Lewis's brothers-in-law Christian and Albert were enjoying small glasses of amber-colored bock beer from Jacob Reithmiller's small brewery in Grass Lake, ten miles south of Waterloo. Neither August nor his father drank alcohol; they preferred freshly pressed apple cider. Before the first hand was finished, Lewis excused himself for the privy, metal flask hidden in his pocket. When he returned, Christian offered Lewis his seat for the next hand, saying, "My children are going crazy! I best keep after them. Lewis, please take my seat at the table."

Lewis joined, and while playing, drank water from a cream-colored porcelain cup. Between each hand, he excused himself for the privy.

An hour later, when work in the kitchen was finished, the women and children joined the men in the parlor. The women noticed that Christian and Albert had emptied both quart bottles of Reithmiller's brew, and that Lewis was drinking water from a cup. They played one last hand and totaled their scores. John Heydlauff easily won; Lewis scored lowest.

The children were tired and morning chores came early, so Thanksgiving festivities had to conclude. Emma gathered her cape and loosely wrapped it around her shoulders. She hugged Paulina, thanked her for being invited to the gathering, and began saying her goodbyes when Lewis, in an uncharacteristically boisterous way, stood and shouted out, "Goodnight everyone, Emma and I gotta get away from this place!" Embarrassed by Lewis's outburst, Emma took his hand and led him to the front door. As they walked out, Lewis stumbled on the steps and dropped down to his hands and knees. Lewis's father saw this, shook his head, and frowned to his wife, saying nothing.

Emma helped Lewis to his feet and asked, "Lewie, are you OK?"

"Yes, I'm fine," he barked, "I tripped on . . ." Lewis's upper body shook from a hiccup, "on that goddamned last step. It has a loose nail; Christian's gotta fix it. Damn it all."

Lewis brushed the dirt off his pants, noticing he had ripped his favorite trousers. Emma scanned the wooden step for a loose nail, seeing nothing of the sort.

"Lewie, you've been drinking. I can smell it on you," she said, also noticing how flushed he was.

"Did you see me drinking?" Lewis scoffed, saliva sputtering from his mouth, splattering Emma on parts of her face.

Emma wiped off his spit, and angrily said, "You've been drinking, Lewie, and you've had too much. I know it."

"You . . . you don . . . don't know what you're talkin' 'bout," Lewis stammered, attempting to stand still.

Emma cynically shot back, "I'm heading home now Lewie. Are you walking with me or crawling on your hands and knees?"

Lewis stared blankly at Emma, as if he was in a daze.

Paulina came to the door and asked, "Is everything all right?"

Lewis said nothing, but Emma fielded her question, "Yes, Paulina, everything's OK. Lewis stumbled on something. Thank you again. He's OK." Emma turned and grabbed Lewis's hand and tugged him along.

Paulina watched for a minute, wondering why Lewis was acting strangely, returned inside, and asked Lydia if she had noticed Lewis drinking anything besides water during the evening, to which she responded, "No, I didn't see anything, but he was leaving the house quite often, maybe for the privy."

Emma dragged Lewis for several steps, not saying a word. She then jerked her hand away and said, "I'm ashamed of you, and I know what you do on your walks at night." Emma gained ground, arrived at her house, and waited impatiently for Lewis to stagger his way back. When he finally stumbled in, Lewis went directly to his attic bedroom without looking at Emma, not uttering a sound.

Emma's family had retired for the night, leaving one lamp burning dimly on the kitchen table. Emma lit a candle in a walking holder, and then extinguished the lamp on the table. She walked to her room feeling sick from anger, humiliation, and frustration. As she changed into her bedclothes she wondered why Lewis was drinking. Emma let down her hair, cleaned her face and neck at her washstand using a scented soap ball, patted her skin with a linen towel, and climbed into bed. She blew out the candle and pulled the covers to her neck. Emma then tightly closed her eyes knowing that something was very wrong in her life. As Emma lay in bed, she could not stop thinking about leaving the Schumacher's house, when Paulina came to the door to ask if everything was all right. Lewis could barely stand or speak.

"No, everything is not all right," Emma whispered into her pillow. She had been deeply embarrassed to be with Lewis in that condition. With that thought, tears began trickling unto her pillow.

At dawn Emma confronted Lewis when he came down from the attic bedroom.

"How are you feeling, Lewie?" Emma asked mockingly. She

continued, "You don't look so good, and you smell bad."

Lewis refused to look at Emma. He stood for a moment, and then tried passing. Emma put her hands out and stopped him. "I know that you're drinking . . . you can't hide it from me anymore. What's going on, Lewie? Why are you doing it?"

Lewis looked sternly at Emma and pushed her hands away. He coldly answered, "I'm not doing anything wrong, Emma; I rarely drink alcohol, and I have *never* had too much."

"I don't believe you, Lewie," she cried. "I know that you were drinking last night; you were drunk. You embarrassed me. You're not like you used to be. You have to stop it. It's changing the way I feel about you."

"I'm not doing anything wrong, Emma. I'm going to work now," Lewis said angrily. He gave Emma a condescending glance as he turned his back to her and left for the barn.

With Lewis away from the house, Emma ran up the stairs to the attic. It did not take her long to find three pint bottles and a metal flask tucked behind a wooden rafter—two empty bottles, and one half full with a clear liquid. The flask was empty. She removed its cork, put her nose to the opening, sniffed, and immediately recognized Lewis's pungent body odor. Next, she uncorked the pint bottle containing the clear liquid and sniffed it. When she did, her nostrils stung so badly she sneezed to the point of going faint. The pungent alcohol odor was so strong it burned her eyes.

Before supper Emma privately confronted Lewis about his nightly walks, told him what she had discovered, and demanded that he stop drinking. Lewis said his walks were to simply relax, and denied that what she discovered in the attic was his, sarcastically implying, "Maybe they're Albert's—maybe they're Florenz's. Why don't you ask them?" He went on to say, "I only drink a smidgen once in a blue moon with my friends." He then announced that he was not hungry and was leaving to visit his parents for the night and would return in the morning—but not before saying, "Emma, stay out of my room."

Emma was furious. "Lewis, you're a liar. Those are your bottles.

Keep your liquor away from my house."

Lewis left, and along the way tried to remember exactly what he had done or said at Paulina's house that made Emma so angry. He recalled playing dominoes. He knew he drank from his flask, but was surprised it was empty in the morning. He tried to remember leaving his sister's and wondered why his favorite trousers were soiled with a rip in a knee.

Emma's trust and affection for Lewis were gone. He had driven a wedge into their once-fond relationship, a wedge formed from a toxic combination of whiskey, rudeness, and deceit. Emma was becoming repulsed by the very thought of him.

Lewis returned early the next morning looking fatigued. Emma ignored him as she went about her chores, but noticed that he was wearing the same clothes from the day before and emitted an unpleasant odor as he passed her on the way to the attic bedroom. Minutes later Emma heard him dragging his feet as he came down the stairway. From around the corner, she watched him slowly walk to the barn, his head hanging low. Later, during supper, he picked at the food on his plate. Afterward, when Friederich declared work was finished for the day, Lewis went directly to the attic for the night.

From that day forward Lewis declined breakfast, saying his stomach hurt. His personal hygiene steadily deteriorated. Lewis had always meticulously groomed himself; now his hair was greasy and messy. He had stopped shaving, and his teeth were stained and filmy.

Emma and Lewis's relationship digressed to being cantankerous. They argued in petty ways at first; then it went caustic. Lewis became increasingly profane and insulting, sometimes demeaning Emma, ending arguments with, "Damn you, girl, you have no idea what you're talking about," then storming off in a huff. Lewis would later regret what he said—although he could not always remember exactly what he said—and attempted shallow apologies. That would then lead to more quarrelling. Lewis began going about his days without seeing Emma.

It was obvious she was avoiding him.

Lewis's concealment of his drinking, his escalating peevishness, and his shoddy appearance —it all repelled Emma. Lewis was fully aware that her affection for him had waned, and would think, *What's wrong with Emma?*

Emma could not comprehend why Lewis had changed into someone she barely recognized. She prayed daily that the drinking would stop, the arguing would stop—that Lewis would return to being the friendly, polite, and charming man he seemed to be only a few weeks earlier.

The change in Lewis was not unnoticed by Emma's parents and her brothers.

Friederich and Lewis continued their work on the windmill, but Lewis's workmanship had significantly slipped. Friederich was fixing small errors and pointing them out to Lewis, who then would apologize and improve for a brief period of time, then again get sloppy. Although this exasperated Friederich, he felt an obligation to keep Lewis employed until the windmill was completed.

Christmas

During work on the Friday before Christmas, Mr. Moeckel announced to Lewis that he had decided to suspend work on the windmill starting at noon, Monday, December 23, but would pay him for the full day. He also told Lewis that he was to grant him a full day's pay for December 24, as a Christmas bonus. Lewis thanked Friederich for his unexpected generosity.

Early Monday morning, December 23, Lewis made his way down the stairs and toward the kitchen where the Moeckels were having breakfast. He could hear Emma and her brothers excitingly discussing their plans for the next couple of days. When Lewis showed his face, the room went silent.

Friederich looked up, said "Mornin' Lewis," and reminded him that it would be a short day, and to have a quick bite to eat because there was much to do before noon. Lewis nodded as he helped himself to a cup of coffee, two hard-boiled eggs, and a freshly baked bread roll. He then left for the barn, saying, "I'll see you at work, Fred."

The two men worked quietly together until Friederich instinctively checked his pocket watch and announced that it was almost noon, and that work was finished for the day. He then dismissed Lewis until the morning after Christmas.

Lewis had nothing more to do at the Moeckels', and Emma was avoiding him anyway, so he decided to leave at once to stay with his parents. He packed one of his two grips, and as he was leaving asked Emma if they could meet later at the Christmas Eve service at St. Jacob. Emma replied curtly, "If you must."

Lewis put on his overcoat and derby, foolishly considered an embrace, but wisely stepped back and said, "I'll see you at church then?" Emma did not reply. He then picked up his worn grip and simply said, "Bye," as he left the house and began walking alongside the frozen road to his parents' house, passing St. Jacob church halfway along the way.

When Lewis reached his parents' house his mother met him at the front door. She frowned at his appearance and told him to look presentable before his father saw him. Lewis prepared a tepid bath, washed, trimmed his hair, and shaved. Afterward, Lewis dressed in clean clothes, looked in a mirror, and smiled; his reflection reminded himself of the Lewis Heydlauff that had left for the Moeckels' back on November 4—seven weeks earlier.

That evening Lewis ate supper with his parents, August and Carrie, and little Hannah. Lewis enjoyed the food, quickly devouring it and asking for a second helping. They talked about Friederich Moeckel's windmill. Lewis's father commented that Fred had made a wise decision to go with the Perkins brand; it had the best accessories, including a mechanical linkage for driving a small table saw. He laughed and commented, "Fred could make a pretty penny if he wants to cut some trim."

Christina asked about Emma. Lewis responded, "Fred Moeckel has me working from dawn to dusk. I see Emma at supper, but that's about it. Sometimes after work I'll sit with her in the parlor where she's been sewing on her mom's new Singer machine. Emma's also knitting something, but won't say what it'll be. Emma doesn't say much when she's doin' those things. Other than that, she's in bed early, and so am I."

"Well, I'll be looking forward to seeing Emma tomorrow evening at St. Jacob. I adore seeing her at the organ. Christmas Eve service would not be the same without her," Christina commented.

After supper Lewis left for his upstairs bedroom and closed the door. He opened the lower drawer in his dresser and reached under a layer of clothing. Not finding what he was searching for, he walked to his closet and moved a small trunk. Not finding what he craved, he walked down the stairway to the front foyer where he had hung his overcoat. He reached into a side pocket and found his flask; it was empty. August approached Lewis on his way to bed and asked, "What are you looking for?"

"Oh, I . . . I was looking for my gloves; I must have left them at the Moeckel house," Lewis answered.

"I have an extra pair that you can use."

"Thank you, I don't need them now. It's been a long day. I'm going to bed. Goodnight Auggie." As Lewis walked back to the stairs he called out, "Goodnight, Mother and Father."

Lewis had kept two bottles of moonshine secretly hidden in his room. He could not ask his mother, father, or August—or Carrie—if they had searched his room and removed them.

Several days earlier when Lewis came to spend the night, he had been approached by his mother before bed. She told of finding an empty whiskey bottle under his bed after he left for the Moeckels' and scolded him, saying she would not have a drunkard living in her house. She told Lewis that if she ever found another, his father would hear about it, and there would be consequences—liquor was not permitted in the house. Lewis wondered if she had found the others.

Lewis thirsted for a drink, but there was no way he could leave the house after saying "Goodnight," so he climbed into bed where he lie awake for hours wondering if he had actually hidden the two bottles. Lewis figured he could keep them concealed, but where were they? Perhaps he needed to do a better job of it next time.

And where did the empty bottle that his mother found come from? He could not remember. Shortly before dawn he descended into an uneasy sleep.

———— ⤙ ————

Tuesday, December 24, arrived bitterly cold and blustery. An overnight winter storm had blanketed Waterloo with several inches of snow. Dead, sepia-colored grasses and fuzzy, brown-tipped cattails surrounding the fields and frozen marshes poked through the vast whiteness and swayed wildly in the frigid wind. Sheets of snow migrated from field to field, sculpting wavy drifts around trees and fence posts. Fragile remnants of dried leaves skipped along the surface before being jettisoned upward, twirling wildly as they mysteriously disappeared. Wispy clouds swirled above as blinding sunlight occasionally peaked through the pewter sky.

Many of the Germans in Waterloo Township worked a short day so they could attend the 4:00 p.m. Christmas Eve service at St. Jacob. For some, the journey would take an hour or more as they precariously navigated deeply rutted, icy, snow-covered dirt roads.

At 2:30 p.m. a large, welcoming bonfire was lit in the St. Jacob's courtyard. Soon afterward, parishioners began arriving, thankful to see the hot, towering flames. After securing their horses in a stable west of the church, warmly dressed attendees assembled by the large, crackling fire, greeting each other with "*Fröhliche Weihnachten*," while many younger people called out in English, "Merry Christmas." The church's choir was caroling, with many of the congregants singing along. The merriment was contagious—it looked as if casual acquaintances were now the best of friends.

John and Christina Heydlauff, along with fellow parishioners George Hannewald and his wife, Louise, were conversing cordially as they warmed themselves near the fire. Lewis, who came with his parents, stood with them as he watched the bonfire, fixated on the undulating flames.

The Moeckel family arrived and made their way to the raging

fire. Through the flames, Lewis saw the Moeckels and called out, *"Fröhliche Weihnachen!"* Albert and Florenz both ignored him. Lewis then walked to Emma—she was surprised to see him neatly groomed.

"Hello, Emma, you look nice," Lewis said sheepishly.

"So do you," Emma replied uneasily.

Wilhelm Tisch and his wife, Katherine, along with their son, George, arrived and made their way to the gathering crowd.

"Hello Emma, hello Lewis," George said as he nodded to both. Rubbing his gloved hands together, he continued, "It's nice by the fire; feels real good."

Emma was relieved that George had interrupted. She was uncomfortable near Lewis. She smiled and exclaimed, "Merry Christmas, George. Yes, the warmth from the fire feels very good!"

George offered Lewis a handshake, saying, "Nice to see you Lewis."

Lewis reached out and acknowledged, "Likewise."

They spoke briefly about the uplifting scene and their Christmas plans. Emma then excused herself to take her seat at the organ in preparation for the many Christmas hymns she would be leading. Lewis and George made small talk for a few minutes. Lewis then went to be with his parents. George joined his, who were visiting with the Hannewalds, including their attractive, seventeen-year-old daughter, Charlotte.

At 3:50 p.m. the church bell began ringing, alerting the congregation that it was time to take their seats. As they left the fire, which had become a glowing mass of hissing red embers, the choir stood at the church entrance singing *"Stille Nacht, Heilige Nacht* (Silent Night, Holy Night)." Congregants slowly passed and took their seats; the choir followed and made its way to the chancel.

Inside, the temperature was comfortably warm. The building was heated by a coal-burning, brick and iron furnace situated in the dirt cellar, its two heating vents leading to the floor above. From the ceiling, four kerosene lamps provided a pleasant yellow light. Candles burned in brass candelabras on each of the church's eight windowsills, with two additional ones at the front altar. Next to the pulpit stood a fresh, seven-foot-tall balsam tree, decorated with strands of golden beads, colorful ribbons, and several thin beeswax candles flickering in counterbalanced tin holders. The church was filled with a fragrant balsam scent, with a hint of outside smoke from the now smoldering fire.

Every pew was filled as Emma led the choir with *"Fröhliche Soll Mein Herze Springen* (All My Heart with Joy Is Singing)," with the entire congregation joining in song. Pastor Wenk then began the Christmas Eve service with a prayer celebrating the birth of Jesus Christ, the *Christkind*. The space within St. Jacob warmed with every hymn. When Pastor Wenk concluded the service by saying, "May the Lord bless you and keep you," the entire congregation sang, *"Von Himmel Hoch* (From Heaven Above to Earth I Come)."

At about 5:00 p.m., parishioners began leaving for their homes. Lewis waited near the back row of pews for Emma as she continued playing the organ. He was delighted to see Emma smiling as she played her final piece, a slow tempo version of *"In Dulci Jubilo* (In Sweet Rejoicing). "* She finished her music for the evening in cheerful spirits. Seeing Lewis, she was surprised to feel a sudden, unexpected affection for him, and thought to herself, *Why am I having this feeling—maybe because it's Christmas? It is a time of celebration— a time to be happy. Is that the reason?* Emma decided not to fight the feeling, and guardedly approached Lewis. "Did you enjoy the service, Lewie?" she asked.

"Yes, Emma, I did. Your music was magnificent."

Emma was perplexed by her sudden emotion. "Thank you, Lewie. You know, we both have parents waiting for us outside in the cold. We should go now."

"I agree, let's not keep them waiting." Lewis's expression suddenly went sullen, "But first Emma, I want to apologize for the way I've been acting. I don't know what got into me, but I'm sorry. Will you please forgive me?"

Tears came to Emma as she looked into Lewis's eyes. Not saying a word for several seconds, she then slowly responded, "Lewie,

I want you to be like you used to be; for us to be like we used to be. You must stop drinking. Can you do that?"

"Yes, I'll do anything that you want." Lewis smiled, and continued, "Emma, I have a Christmas gift for you. Can I bring it to you tomorrow?"

Emma had almost stopped praying for a return to her happy life with Lewis. Now, with a new glimmer of hope, Emma took a deep breath, returned Lewis's smile, and replied, "Yes, Lewie, that'll be OK. Is twelve noon all right?"

"Yes, Emma, I'll be at your house at noon."

"Lewie," Emma said softly, "I have something for you, too. Now let's not keep our parents waiting any longer."

Families were boarding their rigs and leaving the church for their homes, most in hungry anticipation of a traditional Yuletide evening supper. Upon arrival, the dining room table would quickly be topped with plates loaded with sausages, smoked meat, pickled cabbage, and boiled potatoes mixed with bacon and onion. Carrots, turnips and other root vegetables shared the same plate, and fruit-filled Christstollen was served to finish the meal. Following the feast, small fir trees would be decorated in parlors as families sang Christmas carols and read about the Nativity. Afterward, gifts were exchanged around their beautifully decorated trees. Tired families would then retire for the night in anticipation of more celebration on Christmas Day.

Christmas morning in Waterloo was colder than the day before. The deep-blue sky was cloudless. The sun's blinding rays reflected off the pure-white snow covering the ground. Just before noon, from a frosty parlor window, Emma saw Lewis walking up the lane to her house in the bitter cold. She had spent more than two hours getting dressed for the day, starting with her mother tightening a new woolen corset above her petticoat. She was wearing her Christmas gift from her parents—a long, dark-green satin gown, draped in front, flared and pleated in the back, accentuated by a matching bodice secured by sixteen small brass buttons. Emma's ankle-high, black, laced boots had stylish heels, which elegantly enhanced her tallish stature. Her curly, copper-red hair flowed over her shoulders and down her back.

As Lewis walked up the steps to the house Emma opened the door, squinted, and greeted Lewis with, "Merry Christmas, Lewie," as her hair glistened in the radiant sunshine.

Amiable as the evening before and smelling of rosemary scented soap, Lewis was nicely dressed, his face cleanly shaven and his chestnut-colored hair neatly combed. He smiled and nervously echoed, "And a happy Christmas to you, Emma." Stepping back, he looked at Emma from top to bottom and commented, "You are absolutely gorgeous."

Emma smiled, "You look nice too," she said as she took Lewis's overcoat and derby, placing both on a bench in the foyer.

Lewis did look good. He was dressed in his favorite special attire: a dark-gray, double-breasted wool suit over a white, rounded-collared shirt. He wore a wide, red necktie and had a corresponding pocket square stuffed in his coat pocket; on his feet were polished black leather boots.

Lewis offered Christmas greetings to Emma's brothers as they came into the foyer, but neither responded. He and Emma then walked together into the kitchen. Lewis greeted her parents with, "Hello, Mr. and Mrs. Moeckel, happy Christmas!" Both replied in German, "Fröhliche Weihnachten." After exchanging pleasantries, Emma led Lewis into the parlor where he took a seat on an upholstered chair facing the sofa where Emma sat.

Emma felt guardedly comfortable with Lewis. For the first time in weeks they conversed cordially. They spoke of the evening before, what they each had for their Yuletide suppers, and of singing carols as they decorated their Christmas trees.

As Emma listened to Lewis she was still haunted by his recent behavior. But it was the Christmas season and she wanted to be happy. Since feeling the unexpected surge of emotion the night before, Emma believed she could carefully put her guard down for the day and be cordial with Lewis. As they talked, she wondered if her prayers for Lewis's return to being the person she remembered, the person she had admired, the person she once had a growing affection for—maybe loved— were being answered. For today, at least, Emma was willing to put the past behind her. Emma thought, *Today I'm going to try and remember the way I once felt for Lewie.*

Emma reached kindly for Lewis's right hand, held it in hers for the first time in many weeks, looked into his eyes, and asked, "Lewie, would you like to exchange gifts?"

Lewis cheerfully answered, "Yes, let's do it! After all Emma, it is Christmas!"

Lewis smiled and handed Emma a small package wrapped in heavy, yellow paper, and tied with a bright green ribbon. As he intently watched, Emma untied the ribbon, and laughed as she said, "Lewis, I can use this for my hair!" Emma then carefully removed the wrapping, revealing a purple, velvet-covered jewelry box, and exclaimed, "Oh my, Lewie, what could this be?" Emma slowly opened the box, revealing a delicate, sterling silver heart locket and necklace.

"Oh, Lewie, you shouldn't have. This is beautiful. Thank you, thank you so much." Emma held it in her hand as she admired the engraved flowery pattern on the locket. She then opened the locket and saw that it was empty. "Lewie, what shall I put into this?"

Lewis replied, "A photo of us would be nice."

Emma smiled and announced, "I'm going to try it on." She walked to the mirrored sideboard and placed the necklace around her neck, attached the clasp, and allowed the locket to slide and position itself just above the contour of her bosom. Emma looked at it in the mirror, then pivoted to face Lewis and thanked him by saying, "Lewie, I love it!"

Lewis smiled as Emma reached under the sideboard for a package. It was wrapped in brown paper and tied with a red, braided cord. "This is for you, Lewie," Emma said as she handed it to him.

He squeezed it while saying, "This is soft . . . I wonder what it could be?" He then pulled the red cord and removed the paper, revealing a tightly knitted wool scarf. Lewis began unfolding it, bringing his hand up higher and higher, until the twelve-inch wide, ivory colored scarf dropped to its full length, over five feet long. Lewis beamed as he coiled the scarf around his neck and said, "This is the best! It'll keep my neck warm when it's cold . . . like it is today! Thank you, Emma."

"You're welcome, Lewie. It's made from our own wool, which I spun myself. It was fun. I want you to know that it took a long time to knit it!"

Lewis closed his eyes for several seconds, and then asked, "Is this what you were knitting last autumn in the parlor?"

"Yes! How did you know?"

"I didn't know. Remember, you wouldn't tell me. But I know now!"

Emma and Lewis laughed together as he gently stroked the scarf. He looked affectionately at Emma and said, "Emma, thank you again. I'll think of you each time I wear it."

Emma began experiencing a feeling that the distance, which had grown so severely between them, was in some miraculous way being bridged. She felt as if Lewis, the man she once fondly cherished—her best friend for so long—had somehow returned. Maybe, she thought, the last several weeks had merely been a bad patch for Lewis. On the other hand, she thought, maybe it was from the Christmas excitement, and to not trust her emotions. For certain, it was a feeling she dearly missed.

"Lewie, don't move, I have something else for you." Emma skipped from the parlor and ran up the stairs to her bedroom. She opened her wooden keepsake chest and removed a small cedar box holding photographs. She chose one, and then hurried back to the parlor. "Lewie, this is for you!"

Emma handed Lewis a photo of herself in an elegant dress, similar to what she was wearing.

Lewis looked at the photograph, smiled, and said, "Emma, this is a splendid photo of you. I'm going to have this with me no matter where I am. Thank you."

For the first time in weeks Lewis felt comfortable around Emma. Since they exchanged pleasantries the night before, and now, with a personal gift and a smile from his girl, all seemed as it was back in October. Lewis felt relieved—the same feeling he had experienced the November morning he arrived at the Moeckels' to work with her father.

Emma and Lewis then sat together on the sofa and talked for over an hour, during which Lewis told Emma that he had ordered the locket and chain late last summer from a catalog at the DePay department store in Stockbridge, and that it took weeks for it to arrive. He laughed when he explained how worried he was that it wouldn't show up by Christmas, and how excited he was when the store finally notified him, by mail, that it was at the store. Emma assured Lewis that it took nearly as much time for her to spin the wool, bleach it, and knit the scarf. While they were admiring their gifts to each other, Lewis glanced at his pocket watch and saw that it was almost 2:00 p.m. He commented that he was expected home for the family supper. Lewis rose from the sofa and offered his hand to Emma, which she accepted, and gently helped her up. They then walked together to the kitchen, where Katharina was finishing preparation for their annual Christmas open house, and said, "It was nice seeing you, Mrs. Moeckel. I need to leave for our family get-together. I hope to see you again tomorrow."

Katharina agreed cheerfully, "Thank you, Lewis, me too. Tell me, Lewis, are your parents having a houseful this afternoon?"

"Yes. I know my sisters, Lydia and Paulina, and their families are coming. Auggie will be there with Carrie and Hannah. I believe my sister, Sarah, and her husband, Charles, are coming all the way from Ann Arbor. I'm not sure about my brother Immanuel and his wife Edith. I have so much family around here that if they all stop for a visit, I'm certain the walls will be busting out!"

"Well, that's the way it should be, Lewis. Please give my warmest regards to all your family."

"I will, Mrs. Moeckel," Lewis promised as he began walking with Emma toward the dining room, where Friederich and his sons were taking turns looking at *Wonders of the World* photographic stereocards through the boys' Christmas gift, a new Holmes stereoscope viewer. Lewis asked, "Fred, when do you want me back to work on the windmill?"

"At eight o'clock tomorrow morning."

"I'll see you before eight, ready for work," Lewis agreed with a smile.

Emma then escorted Lewis to the front door and helped him with his overcoat. Lewis wrapped his new scarf around his neck and said, "This feels good—actually better than good, because I know you made it for me."

Emma faced Lewis, tightened the scarf she had knitted— without much affection at the time—and told Lewis, "Now, you keep this around your neck so you don't catch your death of cold," and for the first time in weeks, lowered her shoulders and embraced him, pressing her head to his neck. She allowed her body to relax, and thanked him again for the silver locket and necklace.

Lewis posed for a kiss, but Emma pulled back, thinking, I should know better . . . not yet, definitely not yet.

Lewis looked disappointed, then smiled, flipped on his derby, and left for his house, saying, "I have your photograph right here," as he tapped his right pocket. "See you tomorrow, Emma."

When Lewis left, Emma watched him walk down the road wondering if her sudden change of heart was only a Christmas truce, or if their lives together could return to the way things used to be. Emma whispered under her breath, "Oh Lewie, we were so happy together before you started drinking so much. Have you finally realized what you have been doing to us?"

Lewis's face strained in the bitterly cold air as he began his walk. He stopped, glanced back to the Moeckel house where Emma was still watching from the front steps, waved, then turned and formed an oddly shaped grin. Under his breath he mumbled, "It's about time Emma's come to her senses," repeating it again and again as he continued along the frozen road. With his parents' house in sight, he made a diversion. Lewis had decided earlier to stop along the way where some liquid lightning was waiting in a friend's shed.

The Moeckel family was exhausted after a full day of receiving family and friends. After the last visitors left, Friederich checked on the livestock as Katharina and her three children finished straightening up the house. After the chores were completed, the boys left for their bedroom, yawning deeply along the way.

Emma's mother commented to Emma, "Oh my, what a busy day," and left to prepare for bed.

Her father returned and said to Emma, "Lewis seemed in better spirits today."

Emma agreed with a tired smile and nodded, "Yes, he did."

At 9:00 p.m. Emma was in her bedroom. She washed, changed into her nightgown, and climbed into bed holding the locket from Lewis. She wanted to forget the awful way he had been behaving and treating her. When Emma closed her eyes for sleep she thought back to the time when all she had wanted was to be with Lewis. She reminisced about holding his hand for the first time when she was fifteen years old and the innocent embrace shortly afterward. Emma smiled as she recalled their first kiss on her sixteenth birthday. She was then pleasantly carried into a dream.

Emma sees herself standing next to a devoted husband and feeling the sensation of his warm hand holding hers. She admires golden wedding bands sparkling on their fingers. She looks outward from the threshold of a fine house, her and her husband's warm home, and sees three little girls dressed in colorful clothes joyfully chasing a brown and white puppy, its ears flopping and tail wagging wildly as the small ones laugh and play in the yard. The air is fragrant and the sun is shining brilliantly; the gardens are plush and vibrant in the blazing light. She is euphoric as her earth touches heaven and floats weightlessly with her husband and their giggling children and cute puppy. From high above the verdant fields, lush meadows, crystal clear lakes, and shimmering marshes surrounded by swaying rushes and reeds, she is liberated and free of all fear. Aching for her husband with a burning desire to hold him tightly, she reaches out and puts her hands to his face—but there is none. She strains to look again, and as she does, an empty space begins contorting into an un-recognizable frightful form, crying out her name in a fading prolonged wail, "Emma . . . Emmaaa . . ."

The light in her dream is eclipsed by an undulating hideous shape as a growing shadow brings total darkness. Her husband, her children, the puppy, the house, the eupho-ria—all are replaced by a malevolent force. She gasps for a breath of air and feels a hand covering her mouth. She's unable to breathe . . . she's suffocating and panics as she is being pulled down into a spiraling fall . . . falling . . . spin-ning . . . falling . . . spinning . . . falling to the dark-ness . . . can't breathe . . . can't breathe . . . can't breathe . . .

Emma screamed!

She snapped from her dream soaked in sweat, her chest feeling paralyzed as she struggled to catch her breath. The unlit room seemed as if its walls and ceiling were collapsing on her. Emma leaped from her bed with a feeling of absolute emptiness and reached for a lamp on the nearby dresser. Her hand trembled as she put a match to its wick. She then looked for her locket, finding it on the floor—far away from her bed.

Emma stayed awake for fear of returning to her terrifying night-mare. Light from the lamp made flickering shapes on the walls that frightened her, but it was better than what she experienced in her horrible dream. Emma sat at the side of her bed and thought about Lewis—and her future.

As dawn's purple glow began flooding the room, Emma extin-guished the lamp and got dressed for the day.

Lewis returned Thursday shortly after dawn to resume work with Mr. Moeckel. Emma, still haunted by her nightmare, saw Lewis from her bedroom window and rushed down the stairway to open the front door for him. Wearing her new silver locket, she quietly said, "Morning, Lewie," offering and wanting as never before an assuring embrace, but quickly pulling back when she was overcome by the all-too-familiar stench permeating from his body and breath. Emma at once burst into tears as she looked into Lewis's bloodshot eyes and cried, "Lewis, how could you?"

Lewis looked coldly at Emma as he lowered and straightened his arms. He formed tight fists and callously said, "Girl, what I do is not your business. Where is Fred?"

Emma, frightened by Lewis's increasingly unpredictable demeanor, answered despairingly, "In the barn."

Lewis pushed past Emma and into the house, dropped his grip in the foyer, and hurried through the kitchen, not saying a word to Emma's mother.

Emma followed Lewis as he stormed out the backdoor to the barn, leaving her speechless. All she could think was, I'm finished with him. It's all over with him. Never again . . . never ever again will I open my heart to that scoundrel.

The span of emotions Emma had been experiencing collided and she began to cry. Her mother saw what had happened and took Emma into her arms. She tightly held her shattered daughter and whispered, "Shhh . . . I know, Emma, something has happened to Lewis. Give it time and you'll be all right."

Emma wept, accepting that the amorous flame that flickered briefly in her heart was fully extinguished by a stark reality that Lewis was no longer a person she wanted in her life.

After being comforted by her mother, Emma went to her bedroom and opened a dresser drawer. She reached for a small wooden sewing tread box containing some unused and broken jewelry items. She removed the silver locket and necklace and coldheartedly dropped them into the box—not caring to see either ever again.

From that day forward, Lewis, except for his personal appearence, acted as nothing had occurred between he and Emma. He went through the day with little emotion, not interacting with the Moeckels unless it related to work with Friederich. Lewis's morning breakfasts were brief; he often skipped them and headed directly to the barn for the windmill work. During supper Lewis would sit quietly as he ate. The family, particularly Emma, ignored Lewis as they shared the events of the day with each other. A heaviness surrounded them all; the Moeckels had witnessed the change in Lewis, and would have preferred to not have him at the family table, but the patriarch had told them that he intended to use Lewis until the windmill was completed; he had given his word, not just to Lewis, but privately to John Heydaluff.

Lewis continued working with Friederich but never spoke of Emma, nor discussed much of anything other than the work required to complete the project. Lewis's chronic sloppiness annoyed Friederich, but he intended to keep his word, and allow him—barring his inability—to finish the job.

Lewis spent his time away from work either alone in the attic or taking walks, saying he was going to visit his friends or family.

Emma began spending more time away from home, much of it at St. Jacob mastering new musical selections on the pipe organ, afterward meeting girlfriends, often staying overnight in their homes. This did not trouble her parents; they knew the reason why.

When circumstances forced Emma and Lewis together with her family in the house, there was little communication between them, except for what was absolutcly necessary. If they suddenly found themselve alone together, Lewis's demeanor would abruptly shift from ambivalent to combative, and Emma would promply leave.

When New Year's Day, 1896, arrived, any remnant of fondness Emma once had for Lewis was gone. The short-lived affection she felt on Christmas was an aberration; Lewis had undeniably changed. His once-steady behavior had become erratic. His once-dapper appearance was now disheveled—sometimes just plain ragged—and he almost always smelled bad. Emma felt that Lewis considered her an object, his possession. His kindness had been displaced by rudeness, his sobriety lost to an ever-growing thirst. Those close to Lewis saw this, but could do nothing to prevent him from sinking down the sewer of self-destruction.

During an unusually frigid January and February, Emma and Lewis had few conversations. They had none as the raw, earthy smells of March began wafting in and around Waterloo as winter melted into spring.

Emma's Birthday

Emma's twentieth birthday arrived on Wednesday, March 11, 1896. A few days earlier Lewis rode to Stockbridge and purchased a card with an ornate cover depicting two curly-haired, angelic winged children embracing above the caption, "Happy Birthday, my Dear One," and on the backside, "Best Wishes on Your Birthday." Under that he signed, "Fondly, Lewis." Rather than personally giving it to Emma, he posted it from Stockbridge.

During supper that evening, Emma's mother recounted her first pregnancy and how it seemed like forever as she labored for hours waiting for her baby girl to be born. She laughed when she spoke of how the sunny day had turned to dusk about the time a young doctor and his wife arrived from nearby Lima to assist with the delivery in her bedroom. Emma's father told how he was a nervous wreck as he anxiously paced in the parlor. He told Emma, "You were the firstborn; I had no idea what was happening. I can still recall your mother's cries coming from the bedroom. I guess you were pretty rough on her!"

Albert and Florenz joked to each other about their sister. Albert laughed as he said, "Emma, I heard that a really ugly stork dropped you down the chimney, and that you were covered in soot!" The two boys each asked about their own births, but were told if they really wanted to know the details, they had to wait until their birthdays.

Emma's family laughed and wished her a happy birthday as they ignored Lewis, who sat quietly with his head lowered and shoulders hunched inward, slowly picking at his food.

Following supper, Christina and her two sons cleared the table. Emma's father left for the barn to work on the windmill, not asking Lewis to follow.

Lewis looked to Emma and asked quietly, "Emma, did you receive my card in the mail?"

"Yes," Emma coldly replied.

Lewis waited for her to say more, but there was none. He then tried engaging Emma in conversation. Without looking directly at her, he said apprehensively, "The circuses will be coming to Munith and Jackson in May. I sure hope the weather will be good."

"Yes," Emma numbly acknowledged as she rose from her seat, leaving Lewis sitting alone at the table, and left for the parlor. Emma called to the kitchen, "Albert, Florenz, come to the parlor; let's play a game." Her brothers quickly joined her.

Lewis, abandoned at the table, knew he was not wanted in the parlor or anywhere else where Emma was. He got up and walked dejectedly down the hall toward the stairs leading to the attic. When he reached the partially closed parlor door he stopped and looked in. He stood for a minute hoping to be noticed and hear Emma say, "Lewie, come join us for some fun!" That did not happen, and he walked the rest of the way to the stairway. Halfway up, Lewis stopped and listened to Emma as she laughed with her brothers. When he entered his room, Lewis lowered his head and stared at the floor. He hated the way he felt. Lewis sat in a chair at the corner of the attic, hung his head, and moped, "Why has Emma changed? Why is she ignoring me? I haven't done anything wrong. What's wrong? What's wrong with Emma?"

After Lewis stopped sulking he quietly left the house.

For the next several days Emma and Lewis rarely spoke. Emma kept her distance, avoiding him whenever and wherever she could. Lewis frequently missed supper and stayed in the attic. He and Friederich were nearing the end of the windmill construction and both were ready for the work to conclude. Friederich was disappointed with Lewis's increasing lack of motivation. He knew that alcohol was involved, but not to the extent that he would later learn. Lewis was no longer earning his keep, but Friederich Moeckel tolerated him in respect to John Heydlauff.

Lewis Leaves the Moeckel House

On Wednesday, April 1, Lewis's brothers-in-law, Christian Schumacher and Albert Archenbronn, assisted in positioning the windmill's base over eight massive iron bolts, which were previously cemented into four concrete footings that Friederich had set during the fall. In the center, a well had been drilled previously for the windmill to draw its water from. After several hours, Friederich, Lewis, and his two brothers-in-law successfully anchored the windmill's base. Over the next two days they assembled the remaining sections to complete the work, and by sunset Friday the windmill became functional.

"Great job, fellows!" Friederich announced as water began flowing from the discharge pipe into a large, round, in-ground steel water trough. Friederich invited Lewis's two brothers-in-law to his house to settle payment for their work. Lewis followed.

———•—❧•———

Early Saturday morning Friederich waited for Lewis at the foot of the attic's stairway. When Lewis came down, Friederich met him, saying, "Lewis, please join me in the parlor. I want to talk to you." Lewis complied without saying a word, suspecting what was to come.

In the parlor Lewis stood and stared curiously at Friederich.

"Lewis, please sit down," said Friederich.

Lewis sat at the end of the sofa.

Sitting at a small desk in the corner of the room, Friederich continued, "Lewis, we've finished the windmill."

Lewis acknowledged with a nod.

Friederich opened a worn, hardcover ledger and said, "Lewis, you came to work for me last fall on Monday, November 4, and as of today, your job here is finished. I'm now using what's recorded in this ledger to settle your final pay."

Friederich's finger traced a page as he said, "Lewis, you've worked for me for twenty-two weeks, and I've paid you in full for that time. When you agreed to the wage of fifteen dollars per week, you were required to provide me sixty-hours each week. Before you came to work for me, I told you that I'd be logging your time. Lewis, I've been forgiving at times with your lack of skillfulness, but I'm not forgiving for missing work time. My ledger entries show that during the past twenty-two weeks, you've been absent a total of seventy-eight hours. At twenty-five cents per hour, that totals nineteen dollars and fifty cents. Lewis, I'm subtracting that amount from your final pay, which nets you ten dollars and fifty cents."

Hearing this Lewis seemed embarrassed, and then angered. He knew there were times he had arrived late, times when he disappeared for short periods, but did not believe that Fred was keeping such close tabs on him—and that it had amounted to that much money. He thought Fred miserly, but did not dispute his record keeping.

"Fred, I'm glad to see the windmill in your field. It was a big job, and I thank you for the work. It's nice to see it finished," said Lewis, looking uncomfortable as he spoke.

Lewis accepted his final payment without comment. He was then unceremoniously told by Friederich to gather his belongings and be on his way.

Lewis quickly packed his two grips. He looked for Emma, but she was away from the house. He found Katharina in the kitchen and thanked her for her cooking. Albert and Florenz were at the windmill with their father.

Lewis left the Moeckels' not noticing that the windmill was humming a pleasant song as its blades whirled smoothly in the wind.

When Emma returned home she had not realized Lewis was gone until her brother, Albert, told her, "Lewis is gone; said he was moving back to his parents' house and will maybe see you at church in the mornin'."

Emma was thankful and relieved to finally have Lewis out of her house. The Lewis that Emma once knew, maybe even loved, was gone as well. She wondered if he would ever change back to the way he was when they were together, but Emma knew for certain she would never take him back. The damage to their relationship was irreversible.

———————

Easter Sunday morning arrived clear and mild on April 5. Emma was scheduled as the organist for both morning church services. The Moeckel family had a light breakfast and was dressed and ready to leave for St. Jacob Church one hour before the 8:00 a.m. service. Friederich asked his family if they would prefer walking to church rather than using their carriage because it was such a delightful morning. Before allowing anyone to answer, Katharina stepped out to the lane to make sure it was dry, felt the warm southerly breeze, and looked to the bright glowing sun working its way above the horizon. She returned to the house and declared, "Hallelujah! God has given us a beautiful morning and strong legs, so let's use them!" The family agreed and left their home for the short walk to St. Jacob, arriving fifteen minutes later.

Every pew was filled at St. Jacob for the early morning service, and would be again at the second service. Regardless of how infrequently Pastor Wenk saw some parishioners, he was guaranteed to see all of them on Easter Sunday. When the Moeckels arrived they were joyfully greeted by others in German with, "*Fröhliche Ostern!*" with the younger people and children shouting out, "Happy Easter!"

Emma made her way to the organ, near the chancel, where the choir was assembling. Emma and the choir had practiced the Easter hymns on both Tuesday and Wednesday during the preceding week and looked forward to their performance. Shortly afterward the pews began to fill. They were completely filled at 7:55 a.m., when the church bell began ringing in rapid cadence. Emma began to play, "*Christ lag in Tobesbanden* (Christ Lay in Death's Bonds)." The choir and congregation followed along, singing in reverent voices. Pastor Wenk followed his acolytes to the front of the church. After moving to their positions, Pastor Wenk waited for the hymn to conclude, opened his arms wide to the congregation, and shouted out, *"Christ ist erstanden!"* Emma played one line of notes to the hymn of the same name and the choir began singing in German, *"Christ ist Erstanden* (Christ is Risen)." More hymns were sung between Biblical readings. Pastor Wenk delivered his sermon, in which he assured the congregation, that through Christ's sacrifice, they too will be resurrected on the *Last Day*. Easter service concluded a few minutes before 9:00 a.m. with Emma playing and the choir singing, *"Auf, auf! Mein Herz, Mit Freuden* (Awake, My Heart, With Gladness)."

Emma left her seat at the organ to join her parents, who were talking with John and Christina Heydlauff. Emma was greeted by Christina, who offered a hug, which Emma was hesitant to accept, feeling strangely guilty about it.

"Where's Lewis?" Emma asked.

"Lewis wasn't feeling well this morning. He said he was sick and didn't think he should come to church today," Christina answered.

Emma and her mother looked at each other, their facial expressions acknowledging what they both assumed. It was about 9:30 a.m. when Emma politely excused herself and rejoined the choir in preparation for the next service.

⟶ ⟝ ⟞ ⟵

During the following week the temperatures warmed daily. The ground was fully thawed and emitted the earthy scents that notify farmers that it is time to prepare their fields for planting.

Lewis stayed at his parents' home for two weeks hoping his father would put him back on the payroll. After not getting his wish, his sister Lydia, at the request of her father, persuaded her husband, Albert, to hire Lewis as a farmhand and provide him meals and a bedroom. Her husband unenthusiastically complied.

The Archenbraun house was near to where one of Lewis's Waterloo boys lived, and where an outbuilding was used for hiding liquid lightning.

With Lewis out of her house and seemingly out of her life, Emma felt as if a heavy, smothering blanket had been lifted. Her eyes had been opened to see Lewis for what he was, or, had become. Emma's affection for Lewis was gone, but her liberation from him was not. She had a lingering fear that he would suddenly appear at her door, begging her to take him back. Emma also worried that her childhood pledge to Lewis had not been renounced, and that he was clinging to it.

Traditional Roles

In this late-nineteenth-century rural German enclave, traditional roles were generally observed, as in much of the American patriarchy. Men were heads of the household, and made virtually all decisions. Women were expected to be acquiescent to their men, and generally be responsible for domestic chores and looking after children.

Civil laws favored men, offering few legal rights to women. Women had limited divorce rights, child custody rights, and estate rights; they had no jury rights, voting rights, and so forth. Laws were passed by men for men. And by custom, once married, or even engaged to be married, women were essentially considered to belong to their men.

For Lewis, Emma was still his girl, his sweetheart. After he left the Moeckel house, Emma did not attempt to contact him—she wanted nothing to do with him. That did not change Lewis's sense of entitlement. He understood that Emma had, for some foolish reason, gone cold on him, but that was her doing, not his. Yes, he carried a flask—men drink whiskey—and yes, he spoke rudely at times, but Emma had to know her place. Lewis simply assumed Emma should awaken one morning realizing how stupid she was and beg for his forgiveness. Emma was his girl. Some in the community saw it that way as well.

Emma not only had an aversion to her former companion, but was deeply troubled by his unpredictability. She wanted desperately to tell him—to make him understand—that she was no longer his girl, not his betrothed, and for him to accept it without any repercussions.

Emma frequently recalled how, years earlier as a young child, she, along with other children, was confined to St Jacob's balcony during services. After Confirmation, at about the age of fourteen, they were allowed to sit on the main floor below. As her older church friends left the balcony, she could get a good look at them from above. From there, she was able to watch with infatuation her friend, Lewie Heydlauff, sitting with his family. She lamented on how those days of wonder were gone.

Nightly, as Emma lay in bed, her thoughts wandered from feeling liberated to being fearful that Lewis would suddenly break into her house and claim her as his . . . until her weary eyes finally closed, only to abruptly awaken from her recurring nightmare of being trapped in a dreadful future.

Emma's time at church, practicing with the choir and performing at the organ on Sundays, brought the little joy she had in her life since Lewis had destroyed most of the rest. When church services ended, so would her cheerfulness, knowing that when she returned home Lewis would be loitering about.

Emma thanked God for answering her prayers when Lewis finally departed. Yet, since that day, she had been haunted by her continuing nightmare of being imprisoned in a dark existence.

Emma asks for Advice

Emma was well acquainted with the church's pastor, Emil Wenk, and his wife Sophie, who was only a few years her senior.

Less than one week after Lewis had finally left her house, Emma quietly asked Sophie during Wednesday's choir practice if she could confide with her afterward. Emma said it was about a delicate situation, to which the pastor's wife agreed. Sophie invited Emma to the parsonage so they could talk in private.

Emma went into detail about how she had known Lewis Heydlauff for most of her life, and that he was the only boy she had ever wanted to be with. She talked of Lewis's sudden change in behavior, his excessive drinking, and how she was now repulsed by him. She explained how the fondness she once had for him had been replaced by fear and loathing. She described her frightening nightmares and her prayers for a future with an attentive and loving husband and her hope for having children—but not with Lewis. She had to put him out—put him out of her future— forever.

Sophie asked, "Emma, are you engaged to Lewis Heydlauff?"

"No, never have been. On my sixteenth birthday we kissed for the first time, and Lewie asked that I promise to always be true, so I pledged myself to him. Later on, Lewie talked about being married someday, but no, we were not engaged," Emma explained.

"Emma, how old was Lewis when you turned sixteen?"

Emma shrugged her shoulders, blushed, and answered, "Lewie was twenty-one."

Sophie rolled her eyes and said, "Emma, you were only sixteen!"

Emma lowered her head and replied, "I know, but he told me to be a good girl and swear that I belonged to him, and to him only."

Sophie closed her eyes and shook her head. She then looked compassionately at Emma and said, "Emma, if this is how you truly feel you must distance yourself from Lewis Heydlauff in any way possible. But first, remember, you were only sixteen years old when you pledged yourself to him—you need to understand that you were just a girl. At the time you may have believed otherwise . . . but you were only sixteen."

Emma nodded in agreement. "I realize that, Mrs. Wenk, but I had been with him for so long—I'm not sure how to make him understand. Besides, even though I'm no longer with Lewie, his friends seem to believe I'm still his girl."

Sophie then advised: "Emma, if you want the new beginning that you are praying for, one that doesn't involve Lewis, you must tell him; you must make him fully know your feelings. That may be difficult after having known him for so long but, Emma, if you're unhappy, and if you truly believe all is finished with him, you must completely put him out before you can move forward with your life."

"Yes, Mrs. Wenk, I know that's what I must do, but I'm also afraid of how Lewis may react. The way he was acting when he left my house frightened me. He even said that if I ever put him out, he would no longer want to live."

"Emma, that's no reason to feel trapped in a relationship. If you're fearful of what Lewis may do to himself—or to you—end it with him and make company with a different man. He'll have to accept that it's over with you."

"How do I find another man, a man I could love and raise a family with? Lewis is the only beau I have ever had. I wouldn't know what to say or do with someone else."

The pastor's wife told Emma, "You are a beautiful, personable young woman. I think you'll know how to get any man's attention if you so wish. But first, you must make clear that it's over between you and Lewis Heydlauff. If not, a man you're attracted to may not want to interfere if he thinks you're still involved."

"Mrs. Wenk, I understand all that you're saying." Emma then queried, "Mrs. Wenk, how do I find a good man?"

Sophie Wenk smiled and suggested, "May I propose someone that you already know?"

Emma asked shyly, "Who might that be, Mrs. Wenk?"

"May I suggest a faithful man, a trustworthy man, a man I believe you would be proud to be seen with, a man who would surely make you smile, a man from a good family and, Emma, a man I know would protect you?"

"Yes, please do, tell me who."

"George Tisch," Sophie replied with confidence.

Emma smiled demurely at the suggestion. She had known George from an early age; their families had attended church together. Emma was surprised by how quickly she opened her mind to Mrs. Wenk's suggestion. As Emma further thought of George, she acknowledged, "George is very handsome."

Sophie agreed, and told Emma that if she wanted to attract a man like George Tisch, she had to seize an opportunity to be alluring in a friendly way; a man like him would certainly get the idea and respond accordingly.

Emma stepped close to Mrs. Wenk and reached for her hands. Holding them warmly, she thanked her saying, "Oh, Mrs. Wenk, you have helped me so much. I pray that God will guide me."

"Emma, time heals all wounds. With Lewis out of your life, and with a good man in it, your nightmares will become peaceful dreams.

Emma replied softly, "Mrs. Wenk, love and peace is all I want. Oh, Mrs. Wenk, thank you for talking to me."

The pastor's wife squeezed Emma's hands and said, "Emma, please call me Sophie."

With that, Emma left for home wondering just how to get George Tisch's attention.

George Tisch, twenty-six years of age, was more than six feet tall with broad shoulders, a chiseled face, a high forehead, and slightly freckled skin. George's eyes were an intense, bluish gray. In the bright sun they looked transparent. He kept his wavy, reddish hair cut short and combed to the left. His thick mustache was neatly trimmed to the top of his upper lip. George's prominent chin was rounded with a small cleft. George's low and rhythmic voice was almost hypnotic when he spoke. He had not gone unnoticed by the young ladies at church and other girls in the township.

George, always well dressed, enjoyed a solid reputation as being trustworthy, firm to his convictions, socially proper, attentive, and good-humored.

What the pastor's wife did not share with Emma was that she had been privately asked by Emma's father to interpose her influence to get Emma away from Lewis Heydlauff and sway her toward George Tisch.

Separately, George's mother suggested to her son that he should get to know Emma Moeckel better; she had heard that Lewis Heydlauff was out of her life, and that Emma had expressed interest in George.

In this German enclave, prominent families were always positioning behind the scenes.

———

Soon after her private conversation with Sophie Wenk, word was sent to Emma from Reicka Tisch, George's brother Henry's wife, offering a position as housekeeper, and for help watching her three young children as Reicka was about to give birth to her fourth. The position would pay ten dollars and fifty cents per week, including room and board, and would begin on Monday, April 20. Emma could have Wednesday mornings free so she could lead choir practice at St. Jacob, and her Sundays could be spent at home with her family. Reicka also explained to Emma that she would be flexible if necessary.

The Henry Tisch house was near the village of Munith, about four miles distant from Emma's home. George's parents' house, where he lived and worked for his father, was only a quarter mile from Henry and Reicka's, each facing Territorial Road. Emma's heart jumped when she received the offer, knowing how near she would be to George. Without hesitation, Emma approached her mother and asked if she could accept, to which Katharina, already aware of the offer, agreed by saying, "Yes, my dear, they are fine people; they'll treat you well."

Prior to Emma's change of heart with Lewis, she had never thought of a relationship with any other man. But that had changed, and now she was feeling an attraction to another. Emma felt a trifle uneasy as she began hoping for George to approach her.

Emma prayed for guidance on how to keep Lewis away.

CHAPTER FIVE

CONFLICT

Emma had her hands full at Henry and Reicka's. They had four children, the eldest being five years of age. The youngest, Martha, had been born on Friday, April 24, four days after Emma arrived. Reicka tended to her newborn while Emma, with help from Reicka's mother, Mary Maute, looked after the older children, helped prepare the meals, and kept house.

Late Saturday afternoon, the day after Martha was born, Emma was delighted when George was heard calling at the front door.

Seeing George through a window caused Emma's heart to begin thumping as her freckled cheeks flushed. She formed a bright smile and her throat went dry. Emma opened the front door.

"Greetings, Emma, good to see you here. How's our little Martha doing?"

Emma swallowed hard, and then answered in a soft, silky voice, "Hello, George, so nice to see you."

Before she could say another word, Henry, who was sitting at the kitchen table with a cup of coffee after a full day in the fields, heard George's voice and called out, "Brother George, get in here and meet our Martha!"

Emma held the door open for George as she thought to herself, *Thank you, God, thank you!* George walked in. After Emma closed the door behind him, she put her hands together and, without being noticed, danced on her tiptoes. She then followed George to the kitchen, where his brother greeted him with a big smile and a strong handshake.

Emma whispered, "I think Reicka may be napping with the baby. I'll check on them and see." She walked down the hallway and quietly tapped on the bedroom door. There being no answer, Emma cracked it open and peeked in. Seeing that both mother and child were fast asleep, she came back to the kitchen and softly reported, "They're both sleeping. Let's play quietly with the little ones in the parlor."

Henry told his brother that he had to wait until Reicka awakened to see the baby, which seemed all right with George. He and Emma joined the children's grandmother, Oma Mary, who had the three older children with her in the parlor.

Henry then excused himself, saying he was going to take a short nap himself.

⁕⸻⟨∞⟩⸻⁕

During the next few days, George was a frequent visitor to his brother's house. He enjoyed time with his niece and nephews. Sarah was five years old, Herman, four, and Walter, who required considerable attention, fifteen months. Emma welcomed his help, and she loved being with him.

Emma and George started being noticed together around the neighborhood, sometimes shopping at the stores in Munith, and at times riding together in George's buckboard.

George had known Emma for several years. He became increasingly interested in her when he saw that she had grown into a charming, strikingly beautiful young woman.

George and Emma had always exchanged pleasantries when they encountered each other around town or at church, but because he respected that she was with Lewis Heydlauff, he never approached her as a potential suitor. The past three weeks had changed everything. Emma had ended her relationship with Lewis, George believed, and was now free to do as she wished. George thought of no reason not to pursue Emma.

George was becoming increasingly smitten with Emma Moeckel. He constantly thought of how to convey his romantic interest without being too bold. Had George known that Emma was hoping to be amorously approach by him, he would never have struggled with his dilemma.

───⌘───

Word found its way to Lewis that Emma was living at the Henry Tisch house, and that George was spending considerable time with her. He confided with some of his Waterloo boys that Emma had distanced herself from him after working with Friederich Moeckel on his windmill, and that he could not bear the thought of his girl leaving him, especially for someone like George Tisch—he was not a Waterloo boy.

When Lewis's friends asked him why Emma had put him out, he claimed not to know. He said he was nice to her, even bought her an expensive silver locket and necklace for Christmas. He mentioned how much Emma's parents liked him, and could not understand why she was avoiding him; he did nothing wrong.

Not admitting that his future with Emma was lost, Lewis constantly reminded himself, Emma is pledged to me—she belongs to me. Emma is my girl, and yes, she will come to her senses.

Lewis did not visit Emma where she now worked and lived, and Emma prayed he wouldn't. At times Lewis started riding in the direction, but as he neared, his fear of not being welcomed forced him to turn around—and return to his flask. Regrettably for Lewis, rather than the solace he sought through its contents, jealousy and anger flooded his mind as he visualized Emma with George.

Emma pondered if she had ever truly known Lewis. She wondered if his transformation from good to bad was the revelation of a dark side she had never noticed until he worked and lived at her home. She reflected on her years with him, asking herself if she had ever actually loved him, or if she simply felt comfortable with him because they had known each other for so long. She asked herself,

What did I know about love? I was only sixteen when I pledged myself to Lewis. I was little more than a child. I'm now a woman of twenty, and now I do know what love is.

Emma's mounting attraction to George caused a sensation that she had never experienced—a desire—a hunger to be with him. Emma felt wonderful when she was near George; he made her happy. At night, Emma went to bed hugging her pillow, thinking only of George and imagining her life with him. When Emma closed her eyes, she longed for his embrace and a passionate kiss. She yearned to see him the next day.

During the second week and after three consecutive evenings of stopping by Henry and Reicka's to see baby Martha—and Emma— George stayed until the children were in bed and the parents had retired for the night. It was getting late. Emma and George found themselves alone together in the quiet and dimly lit kitchen. George, noting the hour, looked at Emma and started to say, "Emma, it's late, I should be heading home—"

Emma put her finger to his mouth and quietly whispered, "Shhh . . . you'll wake the family." Without saying another word, Emma lifted the mantle light from the kitchen table with one hand and took George's with her other and led him into the parlor where she had him sit on the sofa. Emma placed the lamp down and sat next to George, sinking into the cushion as her hip and shoulder pushed against his. As the mantle light made delicate, flickering patterns on the walls and ceiling, Emma looked to George and their eyes met.

George slowly put his arm around Emma's shoulders and breathed, "Emma, may I kiss you?" Without answering, Emma surrendered herself to George and their lips met for the passionate kiss they both desired.

When word got back to Sophie Wenk that Emma and George were frequently being seen together, she was delighted to know that her clever intervention was succeeding.

CHAPTER SIX

·•·•———— ⟨ᢒᢁᢒ⟩ ————•·•·

LETTERS

It was apparent to the Waterloo community that a breakup was oc-curring between Lewis Heydlauff and Emma Moeckel, and that Emma was frequently being seen with George Tisch.

Lewis dejectedly realized that Emma was avoiding him. After going to work at Henry and Reicka's house, Emma made no attempt to contact him. Lewis refused to accept the truth as to why he was being jilted by his girl. He blamed George Tisch, suspecting he was trying to steal his girl. When his friends asked Lewis about Emma, Lewis told them that she was acting foolishly—she wasn't thinking right—probably because she was having female problems. He said that if she didn't snap out of it, he would rather die than go crazy without her. His friends laughed when Lewis said things like that, but from Lewis's unusual facial contortions, they were concerned that he may have meant it.

At the Archenbraun house, Lewis awakened at first light no matter how he felt. After getting dressed for the day he joined the family for breakfast. Afterward, Lewis would work at whatever his brother-in-law, Albert, had planned for the day.

During breakfast on Saturday, May 1, 1896, Albert told Lewis, "Lewis, I want you to drag the twenty-acre field today. Think you can do it?"

"Yes, but only if the weather holds," Lewis countered.

Lewis walked with Albert to where two large draft horses were stabled. Lewis looked upward to the threatening sky as he and Albert attached the two animals to the tiller and led them to the field to be dragged. Once in position, Lewis climbed to his seat, snapped the reins, and called, "Getup," and the horse team lunged forward. As Lewis steered, he once again started repeating to himself, "Emma, Emma, Emma . . . what have I done, Emma, Emma, Emma . . . what have I done?" Lewis continued having the same thought throughout the day.

The weather held—only a few sprinkles fell before noon.

After cleaning the heavy black soil off his boots and washing his hands and face, Lewis joined the family for supper. His sister, Lydia, noticed that Lewis ate only a small amount after such an arduous day. When she began to clear the table, Lewis politely excused himself for a walk outside.

While walking the footpath that led to Emma's house, Lewis again repeated, "Emma, Emma, Emma . . . what have I done, Emma, Emma, Emma . . . what have I done?" Lewis was unnerved. He reached for his flask, brought it to his mouth, and emptied the last of his liquid lightning. Lewis refused to recognize that his relationship with Emma was over. He had confided to several friends that he was so upset with Emma that he was having thoughts of suicide; he told them that if his girl jilted him for another man it would be too much to bear. He had become intensely jealous when he heard Emma was being seen with George Tisch.

After a long winter, traveling circuses provided opportunities for people to break from their routines to be entertained by some of the grandest attractions on the face of the earth. Two were coming to Jackson County during May, 1896. The first, the Barnum Circus, was scheduled in Munith for the weekend of May 17. The second, the infamous Forepaugh & Sells Brothers Circus, one of the country's most exciting entertainment venues, was coming to the Jackson County Fairgrounds two weeks later during Decoration Day weekend. Both events provided a setting for folks to share time together. These events also provided an ideal setting for couples to be together, and to be seen together. Emma and Lewis had circled the dates on their calendars the summer before and planned on attending both together.

That had dramatically changed. Emma and Lewis, once almost incessantly together, were no longer. Emma was now being seen in the company of another man, and Lewis was nowhere in sight.

Less than two weeks before the Barnum would arrive in Munith, Lewis came to the Sunday morning service at St. Jacob. It was the first time he had attended church in weeks. Lewis sat alone, positioning himself where he could easily see Emma at the organ. During the service Lewis kept his head lowered, but frequently turned for short glances of Emma. Emma first noticed him as she glimpsed out to the congregation while playing her first hymn, causing her hands to shake, and accidently hit two keys together. During Communion, she fumbled notes while playing, "*Ich komm zu deinem Abendmahl* (Oh come, O Savior, to Thy Table)", when Lewis passed by her. Emma was unnerved by the eerie way he was staring at her.

After Emma played the final hymn she waited at the organ until the nave had cleared; she wanted to be certain Lewis was gone. Rather than exiting through the main doors and risking confronting Lewis, she used a small door near the rear of the church. When she opened it, Lewis was waiting.

Emma was startled to see Lewis standing in front of her. He grinned and awkwardly said, "Um, hello, Emma, how have you been?"

Emma's heart pounded from an anxiety she had not felt since Lewis left her house in early April. Without a smile, she nervously replied, "I'm all right, Lewis, how are you?"

Emma made her way down the steps. Lewis moved in front of her and continued, "I've been working for Albert Archenbraun. It's been good work. I hear you're at Henry Tisch's."

Emma tried moving forward, but Lewis blocked her. She then

said in an impassive, monotone voice, "Yes, they have a newborn girl. Her name is Martha. I've been helping out. Lewis, please step aside."

Lewis stayed put, and in an odd, high-pitched voice, rapidly said, "Emma, the circuses are coming soon. Remember last summer when we talked about going? The Barnum circus will be in Munith in a couple weeks. Will you come with me?"

Emma was annoyed. She looked at Lewis and thought, *What is he thinking? We're finished*, and responded, "No, Lewis, I'm not interested."

"What about the Forepaugh Circus, in Jackson, on Decoration Day?"

"No, Lewis, I don't care to go. You can go with your friends. Go on your own if you want," Emma told him.

Lewis lowered his head, put his hands into his coat pockets, and shuffled his feet. His frustration surfaced when he blurted, "Emma, we agreed to go last summer! Why won't you come with me?"

"Lewis, I'll be busy. I'm working at the Tisch's."

Lewis's lips pressed tightly together as he wickedly narrowed his eyes. He then angrily asked, "Emma, are you putting me out?"

Emma wanted to scream, yes, you fool; yes I did—weeks ago, but stayed calm and said, "Lewie, we aren't meant for each other. I'll be your friend if you'd like, but not like before. Now I need to be alone, and not with you."

Lewis raised his voice and responded indignantly, "Emma, explain to me exactly what I have done wrong?"

Emma, not wanting to spark an altercation by dredging up the many reasons that destroyed her feelings, replied, "Lewis, during the past few months what was between us has changed."

Lewis's eyes bulged. He pulled his hands out from his pockets, dropped them to his side and formed tight fists. He declared in an almost frantic voice, "Emma, you're my girl; you can't put me out. I've done nothing wrong. If you do, I'll binge on a drunken bum and never come back."

Emma replied bluntly, "Lewis, if that is what you wish to do, it's your decision. I don't care. Do as you want. It's your life, not mine."

Lewis stepped closer to Emma. He indignantly pushed his face close to Emma's and shouted, "Emma, my friends say they've seen you with George Tisch—tell me why?"

Lewis's breath and spittle suddenly made Emma nauseous. She stepped back as she pushed against Lewis. Emma tried repressing her voice, but couldn't as she cried, "Lewis, it's not your business who I'm seen with or why." Emma shoved Lewis aside and ran toward her parents' house without looking back, praying he wouldn't follow.

Emma's harsh rebuff left Lewis not just dejected, but resentful and mad—mad to the point of feeling hate for her. He watched as Emma ran from him, and then walked in the opposite direction as he cursed her name.

⏤⏤⏤⏤⏤⏤

The morning of Saturday, May 17, Lewis left for the Barnum Circus in Munith with his friend, Fred Artz Jr., and later joined with other Waterloo boys before the main event to roam the sideshows. Later, during the main event in the circus tent, Lewis was being loud and obnoxious, annoying several people sitting near him. From a distance, George Tisch saw this, and stayed away.

After the show was over, Lewis and his group were walking toward where George was chatting with some local acquaintances, including his young neighbor, Charlotte Hannewald.

When George saw Lewis and Artz approaching with their friends, he called, "Hello gentlemen!"

Artz heard George and returned his greeting while laughing, "Gentlemen? What gentlemen?" Artz nudged Lewis and said, "Lew, do you see any gentlemen here?" Lewis frowned at George and mumbled unintelligible profanities as he and his boys kept walking, making their way to the Hurst Saloon.

Charlotte asked George "Was that Lewis Heydlauff? He looked different. Is there something wrong with him?"

George acknowledged, "Yes, that was Lewis. I haven't seen him lately, but he did seem a little off." George looked at his watch and mentioned to the group that he had chores to attend to before night-fall, and that it was time for him to leave.

"It was nice to see you, George," said Charlotte as she offered a warm smile.

George tipped his hat and replied, "Always good to see you as well, Charlotte." George then said to the group, "Goodbye my friends, enjoy the rest of the evening," and departed for home.

Lewis and his boys would finish their reveling in Munith at Frank Bosson's tavern, attached to the Breitmayer Hotel, across the street from the Hurst Saloon.

The next morning, George was surprised to see Lewis in church. Emma, who was at the organ, also saw Lewis, who was blankly star-ing at her from a nearby pew. Not wanting to confront Lewis, she hoped to somehow avoid him at the end of the service.

When Emma finished her last piece of music and as the congre-gants filed out, she watched George approach Lewis.

George caught Lewis's attention, "Lewis, what did you think of the Barnum yesterday?"

"I don't recall seeing you there, George." Their conversation was brief, with no mention of Emma. George, curious that Lewis did not remember seeing him, walked away. Lewis looked frantically over to where Emma had been sitting, only to see an empty bench. While Lewis had been distracted by George, she had darted to the side door and ran to the parsonage to take sanctuary with Sophie, the pastor's wife.

Lewis did not see Emma leave. He looked for her everywhere in the church. He then sarcastically called out into the empty space, "Emma, Emma, where are you?" He then walked through the court-yard, the stable, and even knocked on the privy door before fling-ing it open. Lewis then noticed that the drapes were drawn in the parsonage. He sneered, and left to join his boys in Munith for the second day of the Barnum circus.

Letter to Emma

During the following week Lewis became increasingly distraught knowing that Emma had deliberately avoided him after church. He knew Emma saw him sitting nearby as he tried to get her attention during the entire service; why didn't she acknowledge him? The more he thought about his girl hiding from him, the more he thought of what must be done do to bring Emma to her senses. He decided to make his case in a letter. He figured once Emma received it, by mail, she would open it, read it, think about her foolishness, and then their relationship would resurrect. *It would return to where it was supposed to be*, he thought, *me and Emma forever together, just like it was always meant to be.*

Each day that week, Lewis worked the Archenbraun fields, constantly thinking about what to say to Emma in his letter. He barely touched his nightly supper, leaving before the family was finished to take refuge in his bedroom where he sat on the floor, paper and pen in hand, scribbling incoherent sentences. After an hour or more he would surrender to his metal flask, tear the paper and toss it across the room. Finally, during his sixth attempt, he wrote: "My Dearest Emma."

Lewis was able to continue writing. He rambled on, asking why she had put him out, what had he done wrong, and what he must do for her to take him back. He asked why she refused to join him for the Barnum circus, why had she avoided him at church, why would she not go with him to the Forepaugh circus in Jackson. He told her that they were pledged, that she was his girl, his sweetheart, and that he could not bear to be without her. If he was not to have her, he would surely go on a drunken bum and would not be seen for a long time. He concluded by writing, "Without you I care not live," and signed it: "Your friend, Lewie."

Early the next morning Lewis addressed the letter using the Moeckel address in Waterloo. He sealed, stamped, and mailed it from the Munith post office. It was postmarked on Sunday, May 24, 1896.

After mailing it, Lewis began his return trip to the Archenbraun house, convinced that after Emma read it she would come back to him. She had to—Emma was his girl; she had pledged herself to him.

Along the way, Lewis imagined Emma running to him and throwing her arms around his neck saying, "Lewie, I'm sorry for the way I've been treating you. I'm so very, very sorry. I don't know what was wrong with me. Please take me back. I love you."

As Lewis pulled his buggy alongside the Archenbraun house he was feeling a wave of euphoria as he imagined Emma reading his letter and coming to her senses. He laughed about the time Emma hid from him after church—a child's antics. Lewis thought of their first kiss and that there would be many, many more.

Lewis pulled his horse to a stop and stepped off his rig. When his feet reached the ground, the elation abruptly stopped as a dreadful thought surfaced: *Has my girl actually put me out?* The thought of Emma with the other man—George Tisch—made him queasy. Lewis put his hands to his knees, wanting to vomit. He swallowed hard, and then started rapidly breathing. Unaware that jealousy had blinded his ability to see things as they were, and that the contents of his flask were destroying his ability to understand why, he whispered to himself, "Emma's mine; she knows that. She'll come running to me after she reads my letter."

The envelope containing Lewis's letter to Emma arrived at the Moeckel residence on Wednesday morning, May 27, while she was at Henry and Reicka's house. Her brother, Albert, had been asked earlier that morning by his father to ride to Crane's General Store in Stockbridge to purchase some hardware for the windmill. Knowing that he would be passing by the Henry Tisch house along the way, he took the envelope and delivered it to Emma. She thanked him for dropping it off, and asked how everyone was doing at home.

"Doin' just fine, Emma. Me and Florenz been busy with Pa. Ma's been doin' lotta cookin'. Looks like we're gonna have a big supper later. How are you doin', Emma?"

Emma laughed as she said, "It has been very busy around here. The children have lots of energy, but it's been fun."

"Heard you and George Tisch been ridin' around together."

Emma smiled and replied, "George and I have become good friends."

"Emma, I miss you not being at home."

"Miss you too, Albert."

With that, Albert left for Stockbridge, and Emma, seeing the envelope was from Lewis, walked to the parlor, sat down, and opened it. She pulled out a folded sheet of paper and began to read. It began with, "My Dearest Emma."

After Emma finished reading the letter, she put her head back and closed her eyes. She then read it a second time.

George walked in the back door without knocking and called, "Hello, hello, George here! How's my cute baby niece doing?" Reicka and her mother were sitting at the kitchen table where Oma Mary was holding baby Martha against her chest.

"Afternoon, George. Emma's in the parlor," said Reicka with a smile.

Entering the parlor, George beamed when he saw Emma. "Hello, Emma. How are you this morning?"

Emma placed the letter on a table next to where she was sitting and stood. With melancholy eyes she faced George and responded solemnly, "Mornin', George, I'm all right."

"Emma, you look sad, has something gone wrong?"

Emma paused, wondering if she should tell George of the letter.

George stepped closer to Emma and asked, "Is there something I can help you with?"

Emma looked anxiously at George and said, "Oh, George, I received a letter from Lewie today." She reached for Lewis's letter and, holding it in her hands, told of its contents.

Emma returned the letter to the table.

George stood looking perplexed, astonished that Lewis still thought of Emma as his girl.

"George, please take a seat on the sofa." Emma sat next to him. "George, you need to know what has happened to Lewis, and why I put him out."

Emma began by telling of the adolescent pledge she had made years earlier when Lewis asked her to do so. She assured George that at no time were they engaged, but that Lewis considered her exclusively his girl. Emma explained that it felt fine in the beginning—that that was the way it was supposed to be—but as time went forward she began feeling uncomfortable by his possessiveness.

She went on to tell how Lewis started to change soon after taking residence in her house to work for her father. She told of his drinking, his behavior, and that they were no longer together. Emma assured George that she no longer had any affection for Lewis, and that he had to know that she was no longer his girl. It was over between them, and had been for months.

George thanked Emma for explaining what had happened. He never questioned why she had left Lewis. George only knew that she was free to be courted and that she accepted his romantic advances.

George suggested to Emma that Lewis's letter may offer her the opportunity to again tell Lewis, in writing, that she had put him out and, perhaps, say that she is now with another man. Emma thought about it, and decided to say exactly that. She then asked George if he could tend to the children in the parlor for a little while so she could write a reply, to which he agreed.

Letter to Lewis

Emma sat at the kitchen table contemplating on how to start her letter, and decided upon: "Friend Lewie." She wrote an answer to each of Lewis's questions and told him that all was over between them and that she was now spending time with a different man, expecting that statement would surely send the message their relationship was, indeed, over.

After she finished writing, Emma folder her letter and sealed it in an envelope addressed to Lewis at his parents' house in Waterloo. She then called, "George, I'm finished. Will you please mail this for me if you can?"

"Yes, Emma. I'm about to head over to Stockbridge. I'll take it to the post office there."

Emma thanked him for looking after the children and kissed him on the cheek as he departed. Watching him leave, Emma held Lewis's letter one last time, ripped it to shreds, and deposited it in the wasted bin.

Emma's letter to Lewis was posted from Stockbridge on Wednesday, May 27, 1896.

Lewis rode home from the Archenbrauns' after work the next two days to see if Emma had sent him a reply. On Friday, May 29, Lewis received the envelope he was anticipating. As he held it, his heart pounded, his palms went sweaty, and his hands shook. He hoped with all his heart that Emma would say in her reply that she had come to her senses, that she felt bad about the needless pain she had inflicted on him and tell him everything was going to be OK. Or, he feared, maybe she would not say that at all.

Lewis wanted to open the envelope and read the contents privately, so he left the house and walked to a large pile of granite boulders at the far end of his father's main field.

With his heart rapidly pounding against his chest, he kissed the envelope, opened it, and removed two pages. He began to read the first page. It started with, "Friend Lewie." That was a relief—she wrote, "Friend." As he read further, she acknowledged receiving his letter. It went on to say that he could go to a circus without asking her. Reading on, she wrote that if he wanted to go and binge on a drunken bum, she cared not. As he continued reading, his jaw dropped when she wrote that the pastor's wife even said she should put him behind her. Lewis turned to the second page, and near the top he saw the name "George Tisch," and in an abrupt rage Lewis shrieked and ripped it out, shredded the remnant and threw into a gust of wind. When he further read the torn page, it went on to say "I can now go with a man I need not be ashamed of and so this letter ends all between us." The letter was signed, "Emma."

Lewis's knees buckled. Despondent, he collapsed against the granite stones, his heart shattered by Emma's words: "ends all between us." He sat against the stone pile for several minutes and wept. He then rose to his feet, tucked the torn remainder of Emma's letter into his right hip pocket, and started walking across the field to the road that led to the Moeckel residence.

As Lewis approached the Moeckel property, their house within sight, he saw Emma's father working his south field. Lewis walked to him and called out, "Fred . . . hey, Fred, do you have some time to talk?"

Friederich was using a long steel spade to push large soil clumps away from the tiller furrows in preparation for planting beans when he heard Lewis call. Turning to look at Lewis as he approached, he wiped the sweat beading on his forehead with the back of his glove and loudly returned, "Lewis, what is it?"

Lewis shouted back, "Fred, it's about Emma; she's gone back on me and I'm afraid she has abandoned me forever."

Those were the words Friederich Moeckel was hoping to hear from Lewis. Lewis had become strangely different. Friederich was more than aware that his daughter no longer wanted Lewis in her future. But he was concerned by how Emma could leave Lewis without casting a dark shadow on his reputation by letting the truth be known. Besides, the Heydlauffs had been good neighbors for a long time, and Friederich wanted to keep the peace.

Friederich was irritated by Lewis interrupting his work, but called back, "Emma is old enough to look after herself. Lewis, I will not interfere between you and my daughter. If she wishes not to see you, that is her decision, not yours." Friederich went further to say, "Lewis, you have never asked me if you could go with Emma and now she must do as she likes."

Lewis jumped over the shallow ditch between the road and the Moeckel field and approached Friederich, pleading, "But, Fred, Emma's my girl."

Aggravated by what Lewis claimed, Friederich told him, "Emma will decide whose girl she is, and Lewis, if she has put you out, it is no longer you."

Lewis could think of nothing more to say. He gazed directly into Friederich's eyes with an eerie glare. Friederich stared back curiously, then broke the look by saying, "Lewis, it's time for you to go."

Lewis nodded, turned, and began walking away toward the Archenbraun fields. Then he stopped and called back, "Hey, Fred, you still owe me the nineteen dollars and fifty cents you didn't pay me."

Lewis smirked, then walked away thinking about the next day and the Forepaugh circus in Jackson without his girl—and of George Tisch—whom he now loathed.

After Lewis shouted out that he was owed money, Friederich reminded himself that he had vastly overpaid Lewis for his shoddy work on the windmill, and how little respect he now had for the boy. Friederich continued to watch Lewis and took notice of how he was shuffling his feet along the wagon ruts with his hands deep in his pockets. Watching this, he thought of the weeks when Lewis was living at his house. He had tolerated Lewis's disturbing behavior, believing they had made a deal, and he felt obliged to honor it. He remembered struggling to ignore Lewis when he arrived at work disheveled and smelling acrid from what he had correctly assumed was cheap whiskey. He recalled being so appalled at his poor workmanship that he wanted to send him away, but felt obliged to tolerate it because he was John Heydlauff's son. And he was still suspicious of Lewis's motives when he talked about needing some money to get a business going. He had become especially angered by Lewis's disrespect for Emma.

Friederich leaned on his spade and shook his head thinking, I don't know what happened to Lewis—but I don't ever want him around my Emma again.

That same day while Emma was tending to Reicka's children, Reicka mentioned to her that George's mother had sent word asking if she could borrow her on Saturday morning to help hang drapes, and if she could, to please come early. Reicka then winked when she said, "Oh, I think George will be home."

Emma blushed and asked, "Is that OK with you?"

"Emma, I have already sent word that you should be expected at their front door bright and early. Oh, by the way, wear something nice. You may have to go into town."

Emma's usual workweek ended on Saturdays at 6:00 p.m. She would then leave for home and spend the night and all day Sunday with her family, returning early the following Monday. She had arranged for her brother, Albert, to pick her up on Saturday after her workday.

"Reicka, my brother, Albert, will be coming here tomorrow afternoon to bring me home. He'll be here at about six o'clock. Will you please ask him to wait for me if I'm not back in time?"

"Emma, don't you worry. If you're not back before Albert arrives, I'll let him know that you'll be next door at George's house, and I'll send him to you. By the way, I think you should bring your satchel along just in case you're not back," suggested Reicka.

"Thank you Reicka, I'll do that."

After helping put the children to bed, Emma went through her clothes. She had packed extra for the week hoping to have an opportunity to wear them. She laid out the favorites she had with her, wanting to dress nicely for going to town, and especially for George.

CHAPTER SEVEN

———⟨∾⟩———

JACKSON CIRCUS

Saturday morning, May 30, arrived sunny with a warming breeze flowing from the south. Newly leafed trees and tall prairie grasses bordering Territorial Road swayed rhythmically in the gentle wind.

Emma said goodbye to Reicka and the children as she left for the Wilhelm and Katherine Tisch house, about a twenty-minute walk down Territorial Road. Emma was wearing a cream-colored wool shawl over a long-sleeve cotton day dress trimmed with black zig-zag stitching around its buttoned collar, low hem, and above the wrist cuffs. Emma had gathered the dress tightly above her waist with a thin dark belt. She wore her comfortable ankle-high leather laced shoes and toted her satchel on her shoulder. Her thick copper-red hair was gathered and tied at the end with a black silk ribbon.

Walking peacefully along the way, Emma smiled thinking only of George, hopeful that he would greet her at the door when she arrived. She began quietly singing one of her favorite J.P. Skelly songs, "Tell Me I'm Not Dreamin'": "Speak again those words so sweet that to my heart bring such a thrill, while love's moments fly so fleet, again my soul with rapture fill! Oh 'tis like a dream this joyous feeling so divine. Let your eyes upon me beam, and say again that you are mine!"

Emma threw her head back and belted out: "Let us by the gate delay, although 'tis late, a longer while, lighted by the moon's soft ray, and the rich radiance of your smile—"

Emma stopped singing when, in the distance, she saw George standing on the front porch dressed attractively in tan-colored trousers, a pinstripe shirt, and a gray vest with matching bowtie.

George spotted Emma coming up the road and immediately leaped off the porch. He started jogging to her and called out, "Greetings, Emma. Greetings! Sure is nice to see you this morning!"

Emma called back, "And you too, George!" her smile wide and dimpled, her green eyes sparkling in the morning light.

George beamed, "Emma, you look charming in that splendid dress!"

"Thank you George! You look rather dapper," she answered, curious as to why he was so nicely attired.

"Emma, let me take that for you," George insisted as he motioned to her bag. Emma handed him her satchel, and they continued cheerfully to the house, her long hair bobbing in rhythm with each happy step.

George's mother, Katherine, was standing outside the door leading into the kitchen. "Guten Morgen!" she called out to Emma.

"Guten Morgen, Frau Tisch!" Emma returned.

Katherine waved her hands toward the door saying, "*Kommst in die Haus.*"

"*Mutter*, please, use English!" George called out jokingly.

With a heavy accent, Katherine gleefully countered, "*Mutter* or Mother . . . vhat's the difference?"

George's mother welcomed Emma into her home and thanked her for coming. Katherine then promptly confessed, "I vas'nt sure if the drapes vould be here, and they're not. Emma, I'm sorry, but there's not much else to do around the house."

After apologizing, Katherine smiled at Emma, then looked at George, and said, "It' such a nice day, and you know, the big circus opens in Jackson today. George, vhy don't you ask Emma if she vould like to go vith you and then the two of you go there for the day. Emma, I vill still pay you a full day's pay."

George let out a burst of laughter as he looked at Emma, whose expression was a mixture of surprise and joy, and said, "My mother will pay you a *full day's wage*! Now, doesn't the circus sound a whole lot better than hangin' drapes? What do you think, Emma?"

"That would be wonderful, George. Are you sure, Frau, I mean, Mrs. Tisch?"

Katherine answered, smiling, "You two vill have loads of fun. Emma, I'll put your satchel in our guest bedroom. But before you leave, come have some breakfast."

———✦———

May 30 was the date America set aside as Decoration Day, some calling it Memorial Day, a solemn day to commemorate the hundreds of thousands who died while serving in the military during the Civil War. This particular Saturday was also the opening day of the Forepaugh & Sells Brothers Circus extravaganza in Jackson.

There was excitement everywhere that morning in Jackson County. In Waterloo Township, some locals had already begun their way to the circus by horse and carriage, but most would journey by rail from Munith.

A steady stream of people traveling on foot, bicycle, and horse dotted the roads leading to the Munith Grand Trunk railway station. Upon arrival, horses were left at nearby liveries. Bicycles were secured to racks alongside the station's platform.

The Grand Trunk would then carry the circus goers to Jackson's Central Station, from where passengers would ride electric streetcars powered by nearby dynamo generators to the county fairgrounds where the spectacle was being staged.

At Munith, Lewis and some of his boys were among the growing crowd waiting for the Grand Trunk to arrive. Unnoticed by them were Emma Moeckel and George Tisch. What everyone noticed was the dark billowing smoke surrounding a rumbling locomotive pulling its coal tender and four olive-green passenger cars toward the Munith station. When the train's engine driver applied its metal-on-metal brakes, an ear-piercing screech drowned the din surrounding the awaiting passengers. It ceased as the train slowly inched forward to the station's platform, and persons of all ages began lining up for the doors to open. A few passengers exited; then the conductors called out, "All aboard!"

Emma and George boarded the first car behind the coal tender along with some familiar faces, but none of the Waterloo boys. The final passengers were loaded within a couple of minutes and the doors closed. The locomotive then chugged, and a billow of white steam puffed from the engine's chimney and the train jerked noisily forward. It then began moving slowly away from the station as the chuffing increased with its speed. Emma reached for George's hands and held them in hers. Along the way they looked out the window, marveling at the explosion of spring colors as an electrifying charge flowed from their intertwined fingers into their pounding hearts.

Upon the train's arrival at 1:00 p.m. passengers quickly boarded waiting streetcars for the ride to the fairgrounds. Once there, Emma and George walked with the swarm of excited circus attendees toward queues forming at the ticket booth. As they neared, Emma noticed her neighbor friends, Karrie and Laura Hoffman. Emma pulled George by the hand and led him to the Hoffman sisters.

"Hello girls!" Emma called as she and George approached. The sisters turned and saw it was Emma calling. Karrie was stunned to see Emma with George Tisch. A minute later, Emma and George, holding hands, stepped in front of them and joined the queue.

Karrie was acquainted with George and his family through membership at St. Jacob Church. Several years earlier, Karrie, about ten years older than Emma, was rumored to have had an impassioned spat with George's elder brother, Charles, shortly before his marriage to Caroline Malcho. Afterward, Karrie was not friendly to Charles, and George reminded her of him.

"Where's Lewis?" Karrie asked disapprovingly, a chill in her voice.

"Oh, I don't know," Emma replied nonchalantly.

Hearing Emma's reply, Karrie's younger sister, Laura, raised her eyebrows and gave George an inquiring look. George smiled in return. He was then at the ticket window, where he purchased two passes: one for himself, one for Emma.

Emma then took George by the arm and sang, "Enjoy the circus, girls!" Karrie frowned and Laura smiled as they watched Emma and George, arm in arm, leisurely walk toward the main entrance.

Meanwhile, Lewis and his friends mixed with the horde as they pushed their way to the show's main entrance.

Along the way Lewis thought he saw Emma a short distance ahead. He mumbled to himself, "Can't be Emma, she's working today." Taking a second look, he was shocked to see that it was, indeed, Emma. Lewis was stunned when he realized Emma was strolling on the street with her arm wrapped around that of another man. He became outraged when he realized she was with George Tisch. Without hesitation Lewis ran quickly to them shouting, "Emma, Emma, why aren't you at work?"

Emma looked back and saw that it was Lewis.

Lewis got closer and called between huffs, "Emma, Emma, I thought you weren't going to come today?" Before she could reply, he yelled, "What are you doing with him?" as he extended his arm and pointed his finger directly at George.

Lewis finally reached Emma and George, who kept their arms locked together. Lewis, his face flushed and beading sweat, rudely positioned himself directly in front of Emma. She looked at Lewis without emotion and simply said, "Hello," while George tipped his hat without saying a word. Emma and George then moved around Lewis and strolled on, leaving him standing dumbfounded with his hands in his pockets as he watched them walk together into the show smiling, arm in arm.

Lewis's friends caught up with him, and in a jovial way, made remarks about Emma being with George, wanting to know why Lewis had not brought his girl to the circus, but received no answer. As the group headed for the entrance they talked about the circus—but Lewis said nothing.

During the show, Lewis paid no attention to the acts. His friends figured he was thinking about Emma with George. At times they noticed Lewis staring at the audience across the way, not realizing that he was watching Emma and George throughout the entire show. Lewis's anger increased with each passing minute, climaxing when Emma buried her head into George's chest during a daring trapeze act. In that instant Lewis became paralyzed by vitriolic rage.

After the show Lewis was seething with jealously. He left his friends when he spotted Emma and George holding hands as they walked and began following them. He stalked them from the fairgrounds to the streetcar depot, where he boarded the same car. Emma and George both nervously tried to ignore Lewis, aware that he was staring at them during the entire ride.

When the streetcar unloaded at Jackson's busy Central Station, Lewis finally walked away, his head throbbing in agony from seeing his girl with George. Lewis then stepped behind a large iron column, reached into his pants pocket and pulled out his flask. He looked around, and then drained the contents into his mouth before returning it to his pocket. Quietly he uttered to himself, "That'll hold me for the time being." Lewis then rudely pushed others on the platform sputtering profanities as he made his way to a different passenger car.

"Hey, Lew, there you are," Lewis's friend, Fred Artz Jr., called when he saw Lewis approaching. "I thought I might've seen you at the circus. What'd ya think?"

Lewis was frowning when he reached Artz, indifferently addressing him, saying, "Oh, hello Fred—sorry, I didn't see you—I wasn't paying much attention to the show today."

"Why was that, Lew?" Artz asked, concerned by his friend's lowly demeanor.

They boarded the train and sat together. Lewis began rapidly blinking tears as he told Artz about Emma being at the show with George Tisch when she was supposed to be at work. As the train pulled from Central Station, Lewis stopped talking and looked out the window, not seeing the lights illuminating the tracks, but remembering his girl's head buried in Tisch's chest at the show. His twisted rage returned.

After several minutes, Lewis looked at Artz and said, "Emma told me she couldn't come to the circus with me because of work. Why was she with Tisch? Fred, she's my girl. What am I to do?"

"Lew, maybe Emma was dismissed for the day. Maybe George asked her at the last minute. Don't worry about it. Lew, calm yourself. Talk to Emma; she'll make it right with you."

Artz had not seen Lewis for over a week and was not aware of the letters between him and Emma. Lewis had talked to him about Emma weeks earlier, telling that he and Emma were on the outs and, that he had heard about Emma and Tisch being seen together in town.

Artz continued, "Lew, Emma will be at church tomorrow morning. Wait for her afterward and talk to her. She'll come back to you."

"She'd better," replied Lewis, "I can't live without her. Fred, she's my girl, not George Tisch's or anybody else's for that matter. Fred, if Emma doesn't take me back, I'll kill myself. I can't live without her."

"Come on, Lew, don't say that," Artz said, alarmed that maybe his friend meant what he was saying.

When the train arrived in Munith Lewis's throat was parched. A fierce headache was causing intense throbbing in his temples. Knowing he could drink the remedy once he refilled his flask, he accepted the pain.

After the train unloaded, Fred suggested they have a quick whiskey at Hurst's saloon, to which Lewis countered, "No, best not, Fred. I have an Archenbraun field to drag before nightfall, and it's gonna take me a while to get back. My sister's husband wants it ready by tomorrow mornin' so he can do some planting."

"So be it, Lew. The Archenbraun house is on my way home; I'll walk with you."

Along the way Lewis told of the letters and of his thoughts of taking his own life after reading Emma's words "I can now go with a man I need not be ashamed of and so this letter ends all between us," and that the man was George Tisch.

Artz became increasingly alarmed when Lewis told him these things. He had noticed that Lewis had been acting differently of late and now began to understand why. Artz thought that maybe . . . maybe that explained why Lewis had been drinking so much over the past few months. When the two reached the Archenbraun house, they stopped in the road and Artz told Lewis, "Talk to her, Lew, just talk to her. It hasn't been that long; Emma will take you back."

"Best she does, Fred," Lewis said in an unnerving tone. "One thing is for certain: George Tisch will never take Emma to any more shows."

As Artz walked away he could be heard making sweet sounds with his harmonica; then the music stopped. Fred thought about what Lewis had said, and called back, "Talk to her, Lew; talk to her."

CHAPTER EIGHT

STORM CLOUDS

Emma and George returned to Munith on the same train as Lewis. They were relieved that he had boarded a different passenger car after having been deliberately followed from the streetcar depot to Jackson's Central Station. It unnerved them both.

It was almost 5:00 p.m. After a delightful morning the day had become very hot and humid. Billowing clouds were forming, and the sky to the southwest was darkening. Seeing this, the couple walked briskly up Territorial Road on the way to George's house.

Along the way, Emma told George that she had arranged for her brother, Albert, to collect her at Reicka's house to bring her home. Emma told George that Reicka would send him to his house if she had not returned by that time. As they walked, Emma scanned the threatening sky, and asked George if she could stop and wait for her brother at his house, mentioning that her satchel was already there.

"Yes, Emma, and my parents would enjoy seeing you. If we're lucky, my mom may have some warm supper on the stove."

Suddenly an erratic wind started swirling and, along with it, the rumble of approaching thunder. Emma reached for George's hand and said, "It's gonna rain; let's hurry," which they did, holding hands as they dashed to George's house, laughing loudly along the way.

"Hello, we're home," George panted as he and Emma entered the house through the side door and into the kitchen.

George's mother answered with her heavy accent, "I bet you two are hungry. I have something for you to eat. Vash your hands and have a seat at the table."

Knowing Emma and George would be famished upon arrival, she quickly served the hungry twosome hot bowls of lamb stew and warm bread. Both, voraciously—but politely—attacked their food. George's parents sat with them as they dined and joyfully shared some of their favorite experiences at the circus.

Soon after Emma and George finished their meals the sky suddenly turned dark gray. Rapid lightning flashes began sparking within the clouds. Rumbling thunder increased in volume until a deafening crack shook the house.

George's mother looked at Emma, and said, "Emma, you are velcome to spend the night here."

She smiled and softly responded, "Maybe . . ."

Emma's brother, Albert, arrived just before 7:00 p.m. He apologized for being late because along the way he saw Lewis, who wanted to talk. Emma said that was all right.

Suddenly, the sky went from gray to almost black as ominous, turbulent clouds boiled overhead. Strong, swirling gusts caused the trees to sway wildly. Tall grasses along the edges of the fields were being pushed flat to the ground by the howling wind. George told Albert he'd better tie his horse in the stable behind the house and take shelter on the porch with them because a strong storm was coming. Albert agreed and quickly unhitched his buggy and secured his horse.

Just after Albert returned to the porch a powerful lightning strike produced an ear-piercing crack of thunder. Within seconds, heavy rain began pelting the ground. Tempestuous winds and a quick succession of lightning bolts produced strobes of intense brightness and deafening thunder cracks. The sharp smell of ozone permeated the moist air. Sheets of rain mixed with pea-sized hail hammered the house's clapboard siding. Emma, George, and Albert stayed dry on its covered porch.

While they watched the storm, Emma asked her brother, "Albert, where did you see Lewie?"

"He was workin' the Archenbrauns' west field. When he saw me, he called me to stop and came out to the road—Lewis even left the horses standing there by themselves. He was angered. He asked me where you were and I told 'em you were at Henry Tisch's house and I was comin' to get you."

George asked Albert, "Did Lewis say why he was so mad?"

"Said he was angered at Emma 'cause she had put him out—was fuming because she was at the show with you, George—said that if she didn't come back to him he was gonna kill himself."

Emma questioned her brother, "Are you sure he said he'd kill himself?"

"Yes," said Albert. "Lewie also said that if he had hold of you right then and there he'd choke your neck till you couldn't breathe no more."

"Are you certain that Lewis said he would hurt Emma?" George asked.

"Yep, and he even said if Emma married you, she'd have a damned hard life before she died."

When Albert said this Emma's mouth gaped as she looked worriedly at George.

Another bolt of lightning cracked overhead, producing a brilliant flash of pure light on the house and trees. The sharp sound spooked the horses in the stable.

Albert asked, "George, should we check on the horses?"

"They should settle; let's wait for a minute or two. Did Lewis say anything else?"

"Yes, he did. Lewis said that I oughta be damned sure to bring Emma back home with me," Albert tensely replied.

After about ten minutes the storm quickly subsided and moved to the northeast. The temperature dropped several degrees and the sky began brightening as the sun reappeared low in the sky. A fine mist sparkling like tiny diamonds filtered the reemerging sunlight.

"Look, George!" Emma pointed to the east as a rainbow

appeared, its dazzling bands forming a perfect arch, its ends seemingly anchored to the dark fields. "Oh George, it's so beautiful."

Emma and George gazed at the spectacle.

Albert broke the spell when he said, "Emma, looks like the rains' stopped. I'm gonna get my horse and rig 'em to the buggy, then we can get goin'."

Emma looked out and watched the fine mist floating in the air. She asked, "George, are you sure it's all right to spend the night?"

"Yes! My mother already invited you. I'll bring you back first thing tomorrow morning."

"Albert, I really don't care to get soaked on the way home. I've been invited to spend the night, and I have clothes for the morning with me, so I have decided to stay here."

"But Emma, the rain has stopped. Look, the sun is out," Albert insisted as he pointed to the clearing sky. "I'll pull up the canvas top on the buggy."

Emma smiled. "My dear brother, it's still misting and it feels like more rain is coming, so be sure to pull up the top. I've decided to spend the night here and stay dry. George can bring me directly to St. Jacob in the morning where I'll be playing the organ at the eight o'clock service. Tell Momma and Papa that I love them and that I'll be home afterward, at around nine-thirty."

George helped Albert rig his horse to the wet buggy. Albert then stepped up, brushed the rainwater from its seat, flipped a leather cushion, sat, whistled once, and then called out, "Gehen! Let's go home," and commenced his muddy ride.

George returned to the porch and joined Emma, who had been silently watching him work with Albert. Emma took George's hands into hers and, raising them to her chest, looked warmly into his eyes and said, "Thank you, George, for helping Albert; you are very kind."

Emma and George each cleaned their hands and faces at a small washstand by the backdoor. They then moved to the warm comfort of the parlor, which was heated by a coal-fired iron stove. George stoked the glowing embers. He then walked to the center of the room and lowered a large kerosene lamp hanging from the ceiling, struck a match and lit it below its floral glass shade, then raised it midway to cast ample illumination for the room. He and Emma sat closely together on the sofa under its pleasant glow, taking turns looking at photographic card sets through George's stereoscope, which included the 1893 World's Columbian Exposition in Chicago and a new series of images from the P.T. Barnum Museum in New York City.

George's parents joined them a short time later. Katherine sat at her harmonium organ, as she did almost every evening, and began playing familiar songs which they all enjoyed. Wilhelm sat back in his rocker and paged through a new 1896 copy of the *Sears Roebuck and Company* catalog, referencing pages describing items he would later consider ordering from the *Cheapest Supply House on Earth.* While Emma was focusing on a stereo image of a mummy contained in an open Egyptian sarcophagus from the Barnum set, George was reading a recent edition of the *Jackson Patriot.* He suddenly exclaimed with a cackle, "That is one holy cow!"

Emma put down the stereoscope, raised her brow, looked at George who was now laughing as he held the paper, and asked "What's with the holy cow?"

George laughed as he said, "Yes, holy cow! Listen to this, I'll read it to you: 'Baker McNeil, of Imlay City, owns a cow of which he is proud. The animal is part Jersey, and gives such a quantity of the lacteal liquid that she has to be milked three times a day. She averages about forty-five quarts of milk a day.' Now that is one holy cow!"

Wilhelm chuckled, "Son, find me that cow and nine like her and we'll make a go of it in the dairy business!"

"I'd rather be a thresher; less to shovel!" George snorted.

When George snorted, Emma laughed so hard that she could barely catch her breath. George's parents smiled to each other as they approved of Emma and George sitting comfortably together on the sofa.

George put down the newspaper, looked up to the ceiling while stretching out his arms, and said, "What an eventful day. It seems as if today has lasted an eternity."

Emma yawned deeply. As she groggily exhaled she announced, "Oh my, I'm tired." She looked over to the wall clock hanging next to the parlor's archway and continued, "It's almost nine o'clock and I'm the organist in the morning. George, we must be on the road early in the morning. I need to be at church by seven-thirty. If I don't close my eyes soon I may not awaken in time."

"Don't you worry, Emma, my mother will be sure you're awake early. I'll have you at St. Jacob with plenty of time to spare," George assured her.

Emma stood and thanked Katherine for allowing her to spend the night. She then said goodnight in a tired, mellow voice, "Danke, und gute Nacht," to George and his parents and retired to the guest bedroom down the hallway.

Emma closed the door and pulled back the bed's covers. She removed the clothes she had worn during the day, then, at the washstand in the room wiped her face, neck, and arms with a damp cloth and cleaned her teeth.

After slipping into her cotton nightgown she thought of what Lewis had told Albert and decided to shrug it off. After all, she had ended it with Lewis—it was finally over. Emma extinguished a lamp on the dresser and climbed into bed. She pulled the blankets to her chin and thought of George upstairs in the bedroom above. Emma then rolled to her side, hugged a pillow tightly to her chest, and fell into a deep and peaceful sleep.

After Albert left his sister with George, he quickened the pace to arrive home by dark. As he was passing the Archenbraun farm he saw that Lewis was just leaving the field he had been dragging.

Lewis heard the sounds of an approaching horse and buggy, turned, and saw that it was Albert—alone. He jumped from his rig and ran to him shouting, "Stop Albert, stop! Where the hell is Emma?"

Albert slowed and called back, "Emma's staying the night at the Tisch House."

"What, she's workin' at Henry Tisch's tomorrow?" Lewis yelled in reply.

Lewis was out of breath when he reached the edge of the road where Albert had stopped. He put his hands to his hips and inhaled deeply, then snapped, "Why is Emma staying at Henry's house?"

"Emma's not staying there; she's with George Tisch at his house," Albert replied.

Lewis became enraged and stammered, "Emma is . . . is stay . . . staying the night with . . . George Tisch?"

Albert smiled and replied, "Yes, Lewis, with his family. George is bringin' Emma home in the mornin'. She'll be back after nine."

Lewis became more incensed and grumbled, "You oughta brought Emma with you."

Albert did not reply. Unnerved by Lewis Heydlauff's hostile demeanor, he looked away and continued his ride home.

───── ⁙ ─────

Lewis was miserable as he stabled the two horses used to drag the Archenbraun field. He was wet, cold, and overtaken by jealousy and resentment. After drawing water from a wooden barrel to wash mud from his arms and face, he walked to the house, and seeing his brother-in-law Albert sitting at the kitchen table, called through an open window, "The field is ready."

Lewis then walked to his sister Paulina's house where he mystified the Schumacher family by wandering in and out of their kitchen and around their barn before returning to the Archenbrauns'.

Lewis removed his soiled boots at the backdoor and walked into the kitchen where his sister Lydia and her husband Albert were sitting at the table. When Lewis entered, Albert said, "Lewis, it was raining; you could have finished in the morning."

Lewis countered, "No, I had to finish the job. I have something to attend to in the morning."

Lydia looked over to her husband and then to Lewis and asked, "What do you need to do in the morning?"

"I want to see Mother and Father. I haven't visited with them for a few days. I may stop by the Moeckels' on the way."

Lydia and her husband both noticed how haggard Lewis looked. Lydia asked, "Lewis, you must be hungry. Let me serve you something to eat."

Lewis wearily responded, "Thank you, Lydia, I'm too exhausted to eat. I'm heading up to get some rest."

Lydia looked at her brother's strained, pale face and said, "Lewis, you haven't been eating much. Are you feeling well?"

Lewis quietly replied, "I'm just very tired is all. Goodnight," and left the kitchen for his upstairs bedroom. After he walked into the bedroom he closed and locked its door, then lit a table lamp. Lewis wiggled out of his rain-soaked clothes and tossed them against the door. He then opened the bottom drawer to his dresser, from which he removed and slipped into a dry union suit. Then he reached under a second layer of clothing and put his hand on a full bottle of liquid lightning. He immediately moved it to his mouth and guzzled, wiping his chin after gasping for a breath. Lewis refilled the metal flask that he had emptied during the day and finished what remained by sucking out the last drop. He then returned the empty bottle to the dresser drawer.

Lewis sat on the floor and rested his back to the bed as he savored the rush he craved. He closed his eyes as the alcohol burned his gut and numbed his head, bitterly thinking of Emma and George together at the circus, and his girl now staying the night in the Tisch house.

Lewis reached under the bed and slid out one of his two grips, the other being stored in the closet. From the grip, he removed a wooden case. Lewis opened it—inside was a Smith & Wesson .32-caliber five-shot double action revolver with a three-inch barrel and a paper carton containing fifty cartridges. He took the gun from the case and pressed its cylinder to the side. He placed it on his lap and opened the carton of cartridges. Lewis removed one bullet and gazed at it as he rolled it between his thumb and fingers, and then dropped it into one of the cylinder's five chambers. He slowly filled the other four and snapped the cylinder into firing position. He leaned further against the bed, holding the gun in his right hand. With his finger on the trigger, he pointed its barrel to the middle of his forehead and whispered "Pop!" Lewis scoffed, then moved the barrel to the right side of his head and held it to his temple, squeezing the trigger ever so slightly—then released it. Again he scoffed, and put the gun's three-inch barrel into his mouth, shrieking as the sharp metallic taste of nickel-plated steel stung his tongue. He jiggled the barrel up, down, and around as his front teeth clinked against the barrel. Lewis callously giggled after pulling it slowly from his mouth.

Lewis then looked around the room and, for the first time, noticed a small glass-framed image hanging on the wall: a charcoal drawn side silhouette of a woman's head with long flowing hair. For several minutes he fixated on the gray silhouette and began to see it as Emma's. Lewis blinked, and the silhouette appeared to move. He froze, paralyzed by fear, and forced his eyes shut, and then opened them wide—the silhouette *had* turned. The silhouette had eyes— large black eyes—and they were staring blankly at his. Terrified, Lewis stammered, "Em . . . Emma," and strained to stretch out his trembling arm and aim the gun at the image. Lewis curled his lips and sounded, "Pop, pop . . . pop," and the silhouette was back to the way it was before. Lewis then held the barrel to his gut and uttered, "Bang bang."

He bowed his head and lowered the gun to his lap.

Rather than returning the loaded revolver and cartridges back to their case, he placed them in the closet on top of his Sunday pants, whispering under his breath, "Not here, not now, not like this—I have more to do."

Lewis sat on the edge of his bed. His head was throbbing. He put his hands to his temples and pressed. The agonizing pounding intensified; he began to dry heave. Lewis remembered having laudanum, a medicinal tonic, in the same grip as his gun. He reached for a small brown glass bottle. He removed its cork and swallowed the contents. Its ingredients consisted of alcohol, sugar, and opium. A soothing surge quickly flowed through his veins and numbed his brain. He returned the empty bottle and revolver case to his grip and slid it under the bed, on which he then collapsed and stared blankly at the shadowy ceiling. Lewis had made his decision—he knew for certain how to end the misery.

During the night the sky had cleared and the temperature dropped. A mostly full moon and sparkling stars radiated a soft, bluish light over Waterloo. The quiet of the night was broken sporadically by owl screeches and haunting howls from distant coyotes. When dawn's early purple glow appeared in the eastern sky and the creamy moon hovered low on the western horizon, throaty, rolling-rattle calls from hundreds of sandhill cranes foraging the area's shallow marshes began mixing with trills from birds of many types.

Sunday Morning

Sunday morning, May 31, 1896, arrived clear, cool, and crisp following the purifying rain of the evening before.

At the Wilhelm Tisch residence, George and his father were tending to the livestock. By sunrise, they had finished and washed. Katherine, who awoke with her husband, started her chores by stoking coal in the kitchen's iron stove, adding a few small lumps to raise the heat for cooking.

Emma opened her eyes drowsily when the glow of early dawn painted the room's windows with soft hues of rose and violet. While cozy in bed, she thought of all the wonderful times she had been enjoying with George, then dozed back to sleep. Her eyes opened a second time when the brilliant red glow from the rising sun sent rays of light through the bedroom's two east-facing windows, its beams scattering through delicate lace curtains, producing flickering shapes on the walls and furniture. Emma imagined the shapes as petite angels playfully twirling as they celebrated the beginning of the new day. She arose and removed her nightwear. Stretching her arms upward, she giggled at the angles dancing whimsically across her gentle curves. Emma moved her hands over her body and to her satchel, where she removed fresh undergarments and a white gown. As Emma dressed for the day she was entranced by the magical scene around her.

While Emma and the Tisch folk continued getting ready for Sunday's activities, the early morning's sunlight became vividly orange. The sky overhead lightened to turquoise, and wispy, coral clouds gathered above the risen sun. By the time everyone finished getting dressed, an intense, yellow light was bursting through the windows. Blossoms on the apple trees behind the house opened in full bloom with the warming sun, their sweet fragrance filling every room.

Katherine walked to the guest bedroom to check on Emma, who had left the door slightly ajar after getting dressed and using the privy. She looked in and saw that Emma was wearing a beautiful white gown and shaking out her long hair. Katherine announced herself by saying, "*Guten Morgen, Emma! Hast Du gut geschlafen?* Oh, I'm sorry, English—did you sleep vell?"

"*Ja, und einen guten Morgen zu Ihnen, Frau Tisch*—whoops, English! Good morning to you, Mrs. Tisch! Yes, I slept like a baby. What a glorious morning!"

Katherine moved close to Emma and placed her hands to the sides of Emma's head and ran her fingers through her curly hair, saying, "Emma, let me help you vith your hair. Come vith me to the parlor and take a seat."

Emma smiled and said, "Why thank you, Mrs. Tisch, that would be grand," and followed Katherine to the parlor and sat on the sofa that she and George had contentedly shared the night before.

"Emma, vould you like a pretty Deutsche braid for the day?"

Emma checked the time on the tabletop clock, and seeing that it was not quite 5:30 a.m., answered, "Oh, yes. That would be divine, Frau—I mean, Mrs. Tisch."

Katherine reached for a small porcelain carafe on the sideboard, and from it sprinkled several drops of rose-scented oil into her hands. She then began massaging Emma's scalp with her fingertips. After about two minutes, she held Emma's long, thick hair with her left hand, and with her right, gently pulled a boar-bristle brush through it from top to bottom in slow, steady strokes. After repeating it a few times, Emma's hair began glistening in the morning light. Katherine then separated Emma's hair into three strands and began braiding. As her hair was being fussed and pulled, her eyes got heavy, flickered, and closed. Emma found herself in a dream . . . hazy at first . . . then

Emma is running barefoot through a verdant glen in early morning dew. She's dressed in a brilliant white gown flowing behind as she effortlessly dashes to the top a lush hill, a hill blanketed by a chorus of yellow, red, and blue flowers cascading down to a magnificent house framed by a dazzling tangerine sun beaming its brilliant rays in all directions. There's a long, winding stone pathway bordered by rose bushes blooming with radiant white blossoms leading to its front door. Suddenly she's walking gracefully on the path toward the stately house. Its front door opens wide, and a tall, handsome man dressed for a wedding stands at the door. It's George, waving for her to come to him. His voice warmly calls, "Emma, come, come to me Emma, come to me." She feels weightless and effortlessly drifts toward George, his eyes blazing with passion. His arms open wide as she floats over the threshold and falls gently into his waiting embrace. She lowers her shoulders and raises her head to his. Their lips touch. She pushes her body close to George and feels his heart beating strongly against hers and is overwhelmed by a sensation of immense desire. She is engulfed by rapture and pulls herself closer.

Emma's body twitched and her chest swelled, longing in her dream for all of George's touch. Emma moaned . . . and then released a long, prolonged sigh.

Katherine, who had been at it for only a few minutes, smiled as she watched Emma, curious as to what she was dreaming, then finished the braid. Katherine walked quietly to the sideboard and opened a drawer containing colorful ribbons. She selected a long, scarlet strip of silk that matched the red embroidery around the neckline and at the ends of the sleeves and hem of Emma's white gown. Katherine returned to Emma, who was now taking rapid, shallow breaths, and tied the bright ribbon into a butterfly bow at the end of her thick braid.

Katherine left Emma to check on breakfast. After a few minutes she returned. Emma's freckled face was flushed. Katherine smiled when she saw this, and being time to eat, she bent down to Emma's ear and quietly whispered, *"Es ist Zeit zum Essen,"* which caused Emma's chest to heave as she audibly moaned, "Ohhh . . ." and was drawn from her enchanting, passionate dream.

Feeling somewhat awkward when her eyes popped open, Emma simply said, "Oh, I'm afraid I was asleep." She then said in German, *"Danke, ich bin hungrig,"* and with a wide smile thanked Mrs. Tisch for braiding her hair as her stomach rumbled at the smell of fresh bread and the sound of sizzling ham coming from the kitchen.

When she stood, Emma knew she had been changed by her dream. She had never experienced such a feeling of exhilaration, euphoria, and absolute jubilation. And the intense passion, it was a sensation she could not explain but only feel. Emma wondered, "Is this what love feels like?" Emma could hardly wait to see George as she walked to the dining room.

Emma entered beaming and fresh as a wild rose. George and his father also walked in from having harnessed and rigged their draft horse, Bob, to a small buggy for Emma and George's ride to church. George was wearing his church clothes: dark wool pants, white shirt with a low, rounded collar, and gray vest with his pocket watch tucked into a small pocket, its gold watch-chain draped and attached to a buttonhole.

George smiled at Emma, dressed radiantly in white, and cheerfully said, "Good morning, Emma! You look very, very nice."

Emma sighed, and then replied quietly, "Thank you, George, so do you. Your mother braided my hair this morning."

"Your hair is absolutely beautiful," George complimented as his face blushed.

Emma's face blushed as well when she replied, "George, thank you again."

Katherine placed platters of boiled eggs, fried ham slices, warm bread lathered with rich pork schmaltz, a large bowl of applesauce, and full pot of hot coffee on the table. George looked to his mother and nodded in appreciation.

His mother smiled back.

Before sitting down to eat, the four stood before the table in preparation of grace; Emma and George stood side by side, their shoulders' touching. Emma discreetly took hold of George's hand. With their heads bowed, Wilhelm offered a short prayer to bless the food, closing with, "*Im Namen unseres Herrn Jesu Christi*. Amen."

At the table, there was pleasant conversation as they spoke of the morning's gorgeous sunrise, fragrant apple blossoms, the beauty of vibrant spring growth, and of the absolutely delicious food being consumed at the table.

After breakfast, George excused himself to bring his horse, Bob, and his buggy from near the barn to the house for the four-mile, forty-five-minute ride to church. George's parents were not sure they could attend the later service. Wilhelm had been suffering with an aching lower back during the prior week and was concerned that the ride may be too painful to endure; they would decide later.

Sunday morning music at St. Jacob had brought some of the only joy to Emma during Lewis's rapid descent into his flask. This bright Sunday morning, a new joy filled her heart. At 6:00 a.m., Emma thanked Mr. and Mrs. Tisch for the hospitality, saying, "*Danke für alles*," wrapped her shoulders with her shawl, gathered her satchel of neatly packed belongings, and walked through the house to the backdoor. George met Emma, politely took her bag, and placed it in his buggy. He helped Emma to her seat and then sat to her right. He reached for a thick wool blanket and placed it across her lap. She pulled it to her shoulders and said, "Thank you, George, this feels good."

Lovely Emma, dressed in white, her long, curly, red hair braided and tied with a gleaming, crimson-colored silk ribbon, along with her attentive, well-dressed man, departed Munith to begin their early morning journey to Waterloo. It was clear to both of them that an extraordinary force had pulled them closer together.

Soon after leaving, George, seeing they were alone on the road, pulled his buggy to a halt, removed his brown fedora and looked into Emma's sparkling emerald eyes.

"Emma, I'm so happy that we've been able to spend so much time together. I've always enjoyed seeing you at church and around town and now, getting to know you so much better, it means a great deal to me." George took a deep swallow and said in his low, smooth voice, "Emma, I'm very fond of you; you mean so much to me. I have never felt like this before; I love our time together."

George reached into his coat pocket and produced a small silver ring. "Emma, this isn't much, but I'd like for you to have it," George said as he pressed the ring into the palm of her open right hand.

Emma smiled and warmly replied, "Oh, George, this ring is beautiful!" as she tried it on each of the fingers on her left hand, sliding it onto her ring finger. "George, look, it fits perfectly, and it belongs there!" said Emma as she held her hand up to show him.

Emma turned to face George, looked into his bluish-gray eyes, and smiled demurely as her heart pounded like in her dream. She put her hands around his head and neck and kissed him, the warmth of his lips sending an electric current throughout her entire body. George closed his eyes as he savored the soft tenderness of her lips against his and realized his heart was racing in sync with Emma's. Her kiss felt as if it would never end, and then she tightly hugged him and breathed into his ear saying, "Thank you, George. I'll treasure this for as long as I live."

George, having tasted Emma's warm breath and inhaling the fragrance of her neck, was nearly overcome. He became transfixed by her eyes and without hesitation proclaimed, "Emma, I'm falling in love with you."

Emma inhaled deeply, and as she exhaled tenderly confessed, "George, I already love you." She put her hands on George's face and said, "I'm so glad we are together now. My dear George, I'm so incredibly happy when I am with you."

An exhilarating sensation surged between Emma and George as they embraced a second time. After another rush of passion, they smiled adoringly at each other. George had become lost in Emma's green eyes only to have his trance broken when she beamed, "George, I wish we could pull off the road and vanish together in the glen, but we need to get to church on time!"

George laughed and checked the time on his watch, "I'll have you at church with plenty of time to spare; maybe we have time for one more kiss?"

Emma pecked him on the cheek and giggled as she said, "George, you're going to have to wait! Let's get going!"

George snickered, tightened his horse's reins, and whistled. Bob snorted and once again began the saunter on the muddy road to St. Jacob.

Emma looked at George and slowly moved her hand from under the wool blanket, reached for his arm, and gently pressed it against her chest. Emma then rested her head against George's shoulder and released a long, pleasant sigh. George looked at Emma and smiled; Emma's eyes looked up to George as she bashfully grinned, and the two continued reminiscing their Saturday at the circus, and the stunning rainbow following the violent storm. They spoke of the morning's tangerine sunrise and turquoise sky, all the while thinking of their next kiss, their next embrace, and a future of torrid intimacy. Along the way, they pointed out the reflection of the calm, blue sky shimmering on the water-filled ditches along both sides of the road. At times they spotted an occasional deer prancing across a field. Emma and George looked out to the splendid plethora of spring grasses swaying in the gentle wind. Some of the fields were lime green with winter wheat, contrasting the dark fields that had been freshly dragged for planting. The sides of the ditches were lined

with wildflowers blooming in many colors. The chirping and singing of numerous birds created a glorious symphony that blended
with the rhythmic sounds of Bob pulling the carriage.

Emma spotted yellow finches and bluebirds with rust-colored
breasts. George pointed to a brilliant orange and black oriole. Birds
of many types were singing their unique calls to attract mates. Near
the marshes, tall, gray and ochre sandhill cranes squawked out their
rolling "Awk . . . awk" calls as they foraged in the shallows. George
pointed to the cranes and commented how their red crowns made
them all look the same, and remarked, "Emma, sandhill cranes mate
for life. I've always wondered how they find each other when they
join huge flocks during migration—they all look alike!"

Emma smiled. "George, my dear, I think they see something in
each other that no other crane sees."

"I'm beginning to understand," George agreed.

As Bob pulled the buggy with a steady cadence of clip-clop,
clip-clop, clip-clop from its hooves, George thought only of Emma's
warm kisses, the intoxicating taste of her breath, the sweet smell of
her neck, her arousing touch. George had fallen in love—in love
with all of her, inside and out.

Emma continued admiring the delicate silver ring gracing her
left hand as her heart fluttered and parts of her body ached in a pleasant way. Hypnotized by the cadence of the horse's trot, Emma's eyes
closed and she returned to her early morning dream and was again
overwhelmed by a sensation of an immense desire for George's
touch.

George had purchased the silver ring during a lonely time in his
life with the hope of someday giving it to a special girl. He had kept
it in a small leather valet box along with other treasured items—until that morning. Finally, it was that special day.

At the Archenbraun house Lewis had not extinguished the table
lamp nor slept the entire night. He had gotten in and out of bed

thinking relentlessly about his miserable, hopeless life, at times pacing on the room's squeaky wood floor with increasing resentment toward Emma. He decided to end his wretched life that morning, as death would release his tortured soul. But he could not bear the thought of leaving Emma behind and letting George Tisch have his girl. Lewis assured himself that two important things would be accomplished when he pulled the trigger on his Smith and Wesson: Emma would be horrified, and Tisch would feel guilty. He'd be blamed for everything.

At daybreak, Lewis did his chores without talking to anyone. Afterward, he changed into his church clothes—his best wool pants, finest white shirt, and favorite silk vest—and wandered in and out of the house without saying a word.

Lewis then temporarily sat in the kitchen with the bewildered Archenbraun family as he ignored his breakfast. At 7:30 a.m. he left for his bedroom and locked its door. He went to the closet, collected his loaded revolver, and carefully positioned it into the front right pocket of his pants. He then took the carton of cartridges and dumped the bullets into his hand, then dropped them into the other front pocket, and hid the empty carton under a pile of clothes. He put on his Sunday coat, slipped his full flask into its inside pocket, and then wrapped the scarf Emma had knitted for him around his neck. He put his derby atop his head, walked down the stairs and, before leaving the house, stared forsakenly at his sister, her husband, and their daughter for a while, forced a smile, and departed saying, "I have something to attend to," and trudged across the field toward his parents' house. Lydia thought it strange that Lewis was wearing a winter scarf on such a pleasant morning.

Lewis thought along the way, *Maybe I should just go to that damned boulder pile where I read Emma's letter and get this over with.*

The Moeckel house was along the way. Lewis had to see Emma one last time.

Bob pranced with style as he pulled Emma and George closer to St. Jacob. They began encountering buggies and carriages along the way to the same destination. Men tipped their hats and women smiled, many saying, "*Guten Morgen*," as young people and children waved joyfully to each other calling out, "Good morning!"

Emma and George sat closely together, backs straight, heads held high, as they neared St. Jacob Church.

For the first time that morning, Emma thought of Lewis, praying that he would not be at church. She looked to George and voiced her concern, "George, what if Lewie is here this morning?"

"I've thought of that as well. Emma, whether he's here or not, Lewis Heydlauff is no longer your concern or mine. You've made it clear that you are not his girl. If Lewis is here and tries to make trouble, I'll look after you."

Emma squeezed George's arm, saying, "Thank you, George. I know that you will protect me."

The night before, at George's house, Emma had asked him if they could leave for her house immediately after service had concluded, to which he naturally agreed. With that being the plan, George pulled his buggy into the courtyard and stopped at a rail nearest the church, leaped to the ground, and tied his horse. George then offered Emma his hand and asked, "May I?"

Emma gladly accepted and stepped down from the buggy, saying, "Thank you, my dear. George, should I meet you here after church?"

"We'll be waiting for you right here," George answered as he patted his horse on its mane.

Emma locked arms with her man. Her smile was infectious and her step graceful as she and George proudly strolled toward the entrance, warmly greeting other couples along the way, some of whom whispered to each other afterward.

When the happy couple reached the open front door, they were greeted by Pastor Wenk.

"Good morning and may God's blessings be upon the two of you. Emma, the choir is assembling."

Emma smiled as George answered, "Thank you, and God bless you, Pastor Wenk," and they entered the church.

Emma discreetly squeezed George's hand and said, "I'll come to you at the end of service."

"I'll be waiting for you outside. But first Emma, I look forward to hearing you play, and it will be more than the music I'll enjoy."

"Why thank you, George," Emma chimed, and walked up to the choir chancel, next to the organ.

George sat and positioned himself so he could easily see Emma. She took her seat at the organ and turned to see where George was sitting, caught his eye, and flipped her braided hair over her right shoulder. Emma then grinned and winked.

Emma normally played the organ at both Sunday services. She had asked Pastor Wenk one week earlier if it would be all right to use the alternate organist for the second service on this Sunday. Pastor Wenk did not query Emma as to why. He trusted that whatever the reason, she would make certain everything would be properly arranged—and it was.

Emma's reason for her request was that she had been longing for more time at home, even if it was only an extra hour or two. On this particular Sunday, she now hoped to invite George into her house and use that extra hour or two to be alone with him.

The church bell began ringing and Emma played the first notes to, *Wir Glauben All An Einen Gott* (We All Believe In One True God)." The congregation rose to their feet as Pastor Wenk followed three acolytes, one carrying a brass cross with a long wooden handle, the other two holding lit torches. As they processed up the aisle to the altar, the choir and congregation sang the hymn in German.

When the hymn ended, Pastor Wenk offered opening prayer. It being Trinity Sunday, he read from the Gospel of Saint Matthew, the story of Jesus commanding his disciples to "Make disciples of all nations, baptizing them in the name of the Father, the Son, and of the Holy Ghost."

After reading the Gospel, Pastor Wenk explained the Holy Trinity as one God united in three divine persons; Father, Son and

Holy Ghost. He preached on the power of prayer and that all things are made possible through the Holy Trinity. Emma listened intently, and agreed with her pastor that, with prayer, all things are indeed possible. After having been made miserable by Lewis, she believed her prayers for a good man, a man she could truly love—a man who equally loved her—had been answered. She dreamed of being blessed with children, and how they would leap for joy as they were born into her loving, nourishing family.

Following his sermon, Pastor Wenk consecrated bread and wine at the altar. He then offered and served Holy Communion to the congregation.

After prayers concluded, Emma played "*Te Deum Laudamus* (We Praise You, O God)," with the choir singing its melodious verses. Throughout the service Emma's exceptional organ performance had filled the space with booming sounds that resonated throughout, helping many of the faithful as they prayed for renewed religious piety. Following the hymn's final verse, attendees began departing for the courtyard, many spiritually reinvigorated, where they would commensurate with fellow parishioners.

As Emma lifted herself off her seat at the organ she turned to admire the round, stained glass window high above the altar. The bright morning sun amplified the vivid colors in its many cut-glass pieces. She marveled at how the glass was leaded together to depict Martin Luther's Seal, a black cross set in the middle of a red heart surrounded by a fully bloomed white rose and blue sky; a golden ring encircling the entire image. Emma was suddenly drawn to the black cross. She thought of Jesus, that he came to the people of the world to preach love—only to be crucified. She fixated on the window and her vision blurred.

Emma closed her eyes, and when she opened them, she saw a fuzzy image of a little boy imposed upon the black cross. She became frightened and squinted hard, then strained to open them, and panicked when she saw it *was* a little boy—a boy with warm, compassionate eyes dressed in a scarlet robe, his small arms reaching out to her. Emma rubbed her eyes, and the cross behind the boy seemed to sail away.

Emma was terrified. She looked away from the window and then down to the altar, again squeezing her eyes and praying for the vision to disappear.

She opened them, and the image was gone. Emma was in shock as she gazed at the altar. Her eyes began to flutter and her eyesight dimmed. She rubbed her eyes, then forced them open, and another vision suddenly formed: a ghostly image of a young woman dressed in a radiant wedding gown standing on a plush bed of pure-white rose petals, alone at the altar with a black veil draped over her face— *her* face. From above, a blinding column of light began emanating through the round window. The column made Emma squint as a deafening buzzing sound filled her head and she felt the presence of an immense power. She began shaking in terror and again shut her eyes. Terrified that she might see herself engulfed by the blazing column of light, she was too scared to look, but knew she had to. Emma opened her eyes wide as she could, and the vision rapidly vanished; the buzzing stopped abruptly.

Trembling, Emma looked up to the window. Everything was exactly the same as before—stained glass depicting Martin Luther's Seal. Emma was mystified by what had just occurred. Why was I alone at the altar? Why was I dressed in a wedding dress? Why was the veil black? What was the bright light, the sound—what did it mean? Emma was overwhelmed. She pushed her moist palms together and began wondering, Was it a just figment of my imagination—a wild daydream? Emma snapped from her bewilderment when, from behind, she heard, "Emma, you played beautifully this morning."

Emma took a deep breath, turned, and saw that it was her friend, Sophie, the pastor's wife. She reached out and took Sophie's hands in hers and said, "Thank you, Sophie. Oh my, George Tisch is waiting for me outside; I need to go. Sophie, I'm grateful for all you've done for me. Goodbye for now."

Sophie smiled and remarked, "Emma, I'm very happy for you."

————◦◦————

Emma walked briskly down the aisle to meet George. She stopped at the front door, still awestruck by what see had seen—or, what she thought she had. Emma looked back at the window, and thought, *Nonsense—I saw nothing, it was only my imagination, a crazy daydream.* Again however, she wondered why she imagined her ghostly image was alone at the altar. Then a flood of bad memories began cluttering her mind: Her anxiety as she hid from Lewis that Sunday after church; her resentment of what Lewis said in his letter; Lewis stalking her at the circus; Lewis telling her brother he wanted to choke her. There had been so much to worry about during the past few weeks. Emma wanted Lewis out of her mind forever to fully make room for her fast-growing love for George.

Emma inhaled deeply and determined it was stress that caused whatever it was she imagined—yes, imagined. It was just a strange daydream, an aberration—nothing more. Emma determined that a long nap after getting home was what she needed, then time with the family, and early to bed.

Emma took one more deep breath, then stepped from the church and saw George standing next to his horse. She ran to him saying, "Thank you for waiting, George. It took me longer than I expected."

"That's all right, Emma."

George had left church immediately after the service ended and walked quickly to his horse and buggy where he had waited eagerly for Emma—George would have waited until nightfall.

Before George could offer an assisting hand to Emma, she sprang onto the buggy, beating him to the seat.

"In a hurry, girl?" he chuckled.

George got on and sat close to Emma, their hips and shoulders touching. He whistled to his horse, which neighed in reply, and the buggy lunged forward. They began the short ride to the Moeckel house.

Emma, so proud to be seen with George Tisch, was elated. She was now riding next to a man she was delighted to be with—in love with—and her letter to Lewis earlier in the week had finally made certain he knew that she was no longer his girl—had not been for months—and would never be again. As they continued up the road to her house she felt very good; the sunny morning could not be any finer.

Emma touched the silver ring on her delicate finger and reflected on her passionate morning dream and the way her body felt when she embraced George. Emma had fallen deeply in love and had a growing desire, a burning desire, to embrace all of him.

George turned to Emma and was overwhelmed by the beauty of her radiant face, her stunning emerald eyes, her gorgeous copper-red hair, and by how complete she made him feel. He thought of how he longed to be with her every minute of every day—and every night.

Their eyes met. George pulled his horse to a stop and proclaimed "Emma, I love you."

Emma's dimpled smile graced her face as she tenderly replied, "George, you know that I love you too."

Emma and George warmly embraced, kissed, looked into each other's eyes and kissed again, then continued on their way.

Following services at the St. Jacob Church, some parishioners lingered awhile. Men often talked farming and business, women about their children and of social happenings in the area. Children played like children, often running together in no particular direction. Young adults gathered in groups, some flirting, some ignoring; others whispered rumors of what they knew or may have heard within their communities. This morning when church service concluded, it was noticed by many that George Tisch and Emma Moeckel had arrived together and left together, and that Lewis Heydlauff was nowhere in sight.

CHAPTER NINE

AMBUSH

Lewis Heydlauff trudged along a footpath leading to his parents' house, the Moeckel residence being along the way. He knew from Emma's brother the night before that she would be home. Lewis was tired; he had been unable to sleep during the past several nights, and was dragging his feet. Lewis stopped—he thought he heard indistinguishable whispering, and looked in all directions. He saw nobody, lumbered forward and began hearing voices, loud voices, chanting *Emma . . . Emma . . . Emma . . . Emma.* He stopped again, looked to the sky, put his hands to his ears, and screamed, "Shut up you bastards, shut the hell up!" The voices stopped and he moved on, his forehead beading sweat.

Lewis then began thinking about what Emma said in her letter, "ends all between us," and of seeing his girl with Tisch in Jackson the day before, intensifying his misery and, absurdly, justifying his plan. As he continued plodding along Lewis was unable to imagine any reason to live without his girl. Emma told him that he was out of her life. He questioned why—he had done nothing wrong. Lewis blamed only one person—George Tisch. He ruined everything. With each painful step Lewis repeatedly grunted, "Emma is *my* girl, Emma is *my* girl, Emma is *my* girl."

With no one in sight, Lewis called out, "If I can't have Emma neither will George Tisch!"

Lewis reached into his coat pocket, grabbed his flask, and drank much of its contents.

Lewis had considered killing himself the night before with one shot to his head—his suicide would be swift. Lewis only needed one bullet to die, but decided that there was more to do. The revolver in his pocket was loaded with five cartridges, and in the other, forty-five additional rounds. Lewis was prepared for however he chose to die and had enough bullets to make certain he finished the job.

A short distance before the Moeckel house stood a small stand of mature bur oaks, the trees' delicate new-growth green canopy reaching nearly sixty feet to the clear, blue sky. As Lewis neared the trees, a large number of black crows perched in the upper, veinlike branches began calling in loud, grating caws. Lewis stopped on the path as the crows continued their sharp rattling, clicking and cawing. The harsh sound from high in the stately trees broke Lewis from the continuous echoing in his head of *Emma is my girl . . . Emma is my girl*. He looked up to the sinister looking birds and listened to the maddening noise. Lewis recalled a time, as a boy, when he was frightened by a large horde of deafening crows peppering a huge shagbark hickory tree next to his parents' house. His father referred to the birds as a *mord an krähen*—a murder of crows—and when they gathered like that, it was to hold court to judge one of their own.

"Don't judge me," Lewis bellowed as the deafening sound flooded his ears, each caw a piercing nail being driven deeply into his temples. He was suddenly overcome by nausea, fell to his knees, and began vomiting. After several empty, violent heaves, he got up, wiped his mouth with the sleeve of his coat, cursed the repulsive crows, and moved on.

Lewis reached the road leading to the Moeckel residence. At 8:45 a.m., he was standing in the lane, fixated on their house—the house where he had been so many times. His mind flooded with fragments of memories: Emma laughing as they chased after each other in the winter snow . . . Emma looking at him with her beautiful green eyes while walking alongside the quiet marshes in early spring . . . Emma looking over to him in joyful excitement as they raced their horses together across open fields . . . feeling Emma's hand holding his as they socialized with friends . . . hearing the splashing sounds while swimming together at Trist millpond . . . her promise of a future together . . . and kissing Emma for the first time on her sixteenth birthday.

Lewis snapped back to the reality that Emma had put him out, but longed to feel her soft lips on his one last time. He thought about George Tisch's name in Emma's letter of rejection, and then of seeing his girl with him at the circus. He continued staring at the house, wondering what he had done that brought him to this point. He blamed Tisch—George had used his charm to steal Emma. Then Lewis started hearing voices again . . . *Emma . . . Emma . . . Emma.*

Lewis reached for his flask the second time.

Lewis thought of his conversation with Fred Artz after the circus. "Talk to her," Artz told Lewis—more than once.

As much as Lewis was determined to end it all this Sunday morning, he heard two conflicting voices, one demanding, *"Wait for Emma, see Emma and just do it,"* the other pleading: *"Talk to Emma first; you haven't done anything wrong. Emma knows that; she'll come to her senses, and then everything will be like it used to be."*

Pulsating pain was hammering Lewis's head. He pulled out his flask and took his third swig of liquid lightning—his liquid courage—and nearly emptied his flask. He then took one step toward the house, and another, and another, and deliberately paced his way to the Moeckels' front door. When he reached it the Moeckels' guard dog approached, bared his teeth, and growled.

"Shut up, dog," Lewis hissed before knocking three times and calling, "Lewie here."

Friederich Moeckel was dismayed to see Lewis standing at his door. He responded indifferently saying, "Mornin', Lewis."

"Fred, I'm here to see Emma."

"Emma's at church. I expect her home in about half an hour or so."

Lewis knew Emma was probably not at home, but at church. He grinned and asked, "Fred, I have something I need to tell Emma. It'll just take a minute. I'd like to wait for her. May I come in?"

Friederich hesitated. Then he thought, *Just because Emma and Lewis have grown apart did not make him entirely unwelcomed.* Yes, Lewis had changed, but that was of little concern now; Emma had put him out. The two would move on in different directions. Besides, Lewis and his family had been good neighbors and fellow church congregants. Friederich did not want that to change. He saw no harm in allowing Lewis to wait inside for his daughter.

"You may come in and wait. Take a seat with me in the parlor."

Lewis stepped over the threshold into the Moeckel house. He quickly removed the scarf Emma had given him and discarded it on the coat bench near the front door. He looked down at it, rolled his eyes without being noticed, and followed Friederich into the parlor.

Friederich sat with Lewis making small, insignificant talk about the windmill, crop rotation, and sheep shearing, but not a word about Emma. While they were talking, Lewis was thinking about Mr. Moeckel telling him earlier during the week that he would not interfere with Emma's decision to go with whom she wished—but Lewis thought, *I haven't asked Mrs. Moeckel to talk with Emma. She'll get Emma to come to her senses and take me back. I'll talk to Mrs. Moeckel—she likes me.*

Lewis asked to be excused, saying he would like to say hello to Mrs. Moeckel.

"In just a minute; my wife is getting ready for church. She's been between the bedroom and kitchen. Wait here until she's back in the kitchen," Friederich told Lewis.

Emma's brother, Albert, walked into the parlor, and was disappointed to see Lewis sitting with his father. Albert reluctantly said, "Good Morning," and left.

After a few more minutes of random conversation, Lewis heard Katharina Moeckel in the kitchen. Lewis got out of his chair and left the parlor. "Mornin' Mrs. Moeckel," Lewis announced quietly as he entered. Friederich thought nothing of it and remained in the parlor.

"Hello, Lewis. You look nice. Are you on your way to church?" Katharina asked with a smile.

"No, well, maybe . . . yes . . . maybe yes. I'm actually on my way to see my parents first," said Lewis, unsure how to answer.

"I haven't seen you for a while, Lewis. How have you been?"

Lewis looked down to the floor and responded, "Not so well, Mrs. Moeckel"

"Lewis, what's wrong?" Katharina asked with concern.

Lewis's eyes went glassy as he answered forlornly, "Oh, Mrs. Moeckel, Emma has put me out. We haven't been seeing each other at all lately and yesterday she went to the Jackson circus with George Tisch."

Katharina, already knowing that her daughter had distanced herself from Lewis, asked, "Why didn't you ask Emma?"

"I did, Mrs. Moeckel, I did. Emma said she didn't care to go, and that if I wanted, then go by myself. So I did, with some friends. Then I saw her there with George Tisch; she was supposed to be at work, Mrs. Moeckel."

Katharina had always been fond of Lewis and felt for him after what occurred with Emma. But she had seen Lewis change as well and was in agreement with her husband that Emma's future was not to include Lewis Heydlauff.

She asked Lewis, "Have you talked to Emma about what happened?"

"No, but I wrote her a letter asking what I did wrong and she wrote back saying that it was over between us. She put me out, Mrs. Moeckel."

Not quite sure how to finish the conversation, Katharina said, "Lewis, when Emma comes home . . ."

Lewis's head was pounding in excruciating pain. While she was talking he thought to himself, *Mrs. Moeckel won't make a difference. I'll wait for Emma. If she doesn't take me back, I'll pull the trigger and my pain will be over,* he then continued to hear her say,

"I can have a talk with Emma, but Lewis, Emma's decisions are hers and hers alone. But first, I need to tend to a few details before church. Lewis, please wait for Emma in the parlor."

The morning sun shined brightly behind George and Emma, Emma glowing in her long, white dress, George handsome in his church clothes. George pulled his rig to a stop on the lane in front of Emma's house. Before George could tend to his horse, Emma enthusiastically grabbed her satchel from the buggy and hopped off without his help. She looked up to George and said, "George, take care of Bob and join me in my house!" She then merrily skipped toward the house as her braided hair swung in rhythm. Halfway, the Moeckels' dog came running to Emma, barking loudly with his tail wildly wagging, and hunched down in front of her wanting to play. Emma set her satchel to the ground, leaned, and reached to the big dog and cheerfully said, "Hello Rolfie, I've missed you!" Emma petted Rolf behind his ears and around his head and neck with her hands and exclaimed, "Good Rolf, good boy, good dog! We'll play later, Rolfie."

Faithful Rolf followed Emma as they raced to the front door, where she was delighted to hear Albert announcing, "Emma's comin', Emma's comin', Emma's home!"

From the parlor, Lewis heard Albert's happy proclamation, "Emma's home," got up and stood in the room's doorway. He quickly emptied his flask and thought of what Artz had repeatedly told him: "Talk to her Lewis, talk to her."

"I'm home!" Emma cheerfully announced as she entered the house.

Emma's parents warmly greeted her. Katharina gave her daughter a tight hug; her father offered Emma a broad smile. Emma's brothers, Albert and Florenz, each gleamed with delight as they welcomed their sister home. The family stayed in the foyer talking about what they all had done during the week, having entirely forgotten that Lewis was waiting for Emma in the parlor. While they were talking, Friederich saw George outside grooming his horse and said, "Emma, I'm going to ask George to come in."

"I already have, Papa," Emma announced.

"That's good Emma, I'm going to go out and formally invite him in!" Friederich replied with a chuckle.

"George, please tie your horse to our rail and come in. I want you to say hello to Emma's mother and our boys."

"Are you sure, Mr. Moeckel? It's after nine o'clock, almost church time for you. I don't want to get in your way"

"Yes, plus Emma has already invited you in! We have time. It will be a while before the church bell rings," assured Friederich.

In the foyer Emma mentioned that she had to use the outside privy. She dropped her satchel by the front door and walked out. After she left, her mother and brothers made their way to the kitchen.

George saw Emma heading to the privy, waved to her, and then followed her father into the house and to the kitchen.

George was greeted by Katharina with a cheerful, "Good morning, George."

With a big smile, George reciprocated, "Good morning to you, Mrs. Moeckel, and to you Albert, Florenz. How are you all doing this magnificent Sunday morning?"

"George, I'm feeling very good, thank you for asking. What a beautiful day God has given us!"

Her sons nodded in agreement.

Katharina smiled warmly and asked George, "Would you like some hot coffee?"

"Thank you for asking, Mrs. Moeckel. Yes, that sounds very good, but only if you have time before church."

George sat with Albert, Florenz, and their father at the kitchen table.

Emma returned from the privy, collected her satchel, and walked from the foyer and rounded the corner to the hallway leading to the parlor—and was shocked to see Lewis standing at its door.

"What . . . oh . . . I didn't expect to see you here," Emma snapped, furious that Lewis was in her house.

Lewis stepped in front of Emma and pompously said, "Mornin'

Emma, I'd like a word with you."

"Good morning, now leave," Emma frigidly replied,

From the kitchen window Friederich saw his friend, George Hannewald, pulling his carriage to a halt in front of his house and went to greet him. Hannewald stepped off the coachman's seat and tied his two-horse team to the sturdy rail next to George Tisch's rig, while his wife, Louise, and their daughters, Charlotte and Rose, stayed inside the coach.

"Good morning to you all. What brings you here this morning?"

"Good morning, Friederich, do you have a little time to talk? It won't take but a minute. I'd like your input on a church matter before worship."

"Yes, what is it?" Friederich asked.

"Friederich, it's about something you should know about one of our fellow parishioner's sons."

Deeply annoyed that Lewis was in her house, Emma said, "Lewis, I have nothing to say to you, please step out of my way and leave my house."

Lewis replied arrogantly, "Excuse me if I'm in your way, Emma," and abruptly stepped aside to allow *his* girl to pass with her satchel. Without hesitation he turned and followed Emma into the parlor, where once inside with her, he closed the door.

Emma stopped, turned and asked indignantly, "Lewis, what are you doing here? Why are you following me? What do you want?"

Now alone with Emma, Lewis began pleading with her to take back everything she had written in her letter, to come to her senses, to be his sweetheart like she always had been.

"Emma, you're my girl, I need you, take me back. I didn't do anything wrong; I'll do whatever you want."

As Emma listened to Lewis she recognized his all too familiar cloudy, red eyes and the repulsive stench of his breath, and said, "Lewie, you're drunk. Please leave."

Lewis's eyes squeezed to narrow slits as he sarcastically snarled,

"You know, Emma, this could be the last time you need to look into my eyes or smell my breath." He then taunted her by saying, "Just be my girl again and all this will stop."

Emma was startled by what Lewis was saying and cried out, "I will not, Lewis, and I am not your girl. It's over between us. It's over. Get out of here."

Raising his voice, Lewis demanded, "Emma, if you don't take me back I'm going to kill myself. You'll be sorry—it'll be your fault!" He then noticed a silver ring on Emma's left hand and, in a brutally jealous voice, asked, "Where did you get the ring, Emma?"

"It's not your business," Emma angrily replied.

Lewis did not ask again—he knew where it came from.

Emma began to panic and shouted, "Leave my house, Lewis! I don't want you here, leave me alone. I don't ever want to see you again. Get out or I'll call for help!"

Lewis looked into Emma's frightened, tearful eyes, and said sardonically, "OK, Emma, I'll go, but first, one last kiss."

"No!" Emma screamed as Lewis forcibly put his left arm around her neck, jerked her close, and forced her face to his. Emma dropped her satchel and tried shoving Lewis away, crying out, "No, Lewis, no. Let me go, let me go, let me go!"

Refusing to release Emma as she pleaded, Lewis forced his lips onto hers, muffling her cries as she tried in vain to push him off. In one motion, Lewis reached into his pants pocket with his right hand, removed his loaded revolver, pushed the barrel to Emma's left side, and pulled the trigger as he stared into her eyes, watching curiously as her pupils instantly dilated and her mouth gaped, unable to voice a sound. Keeping her from falling, he quickly fired a second shot downward at her chest, and released her. Emma's limp body melted to the floor and rolled to its side. Lewis stood over Emma as she began convulsing, and perversely watched her vanishing expression as her eyes slowly fluttered. He then fired a third time, striking the back of Emma's neck, pulverizing her spine, and snuffing out a once brilliant light by a darkness that was not to be overcome. Having seen what he had done, Lewis closed his eyes and turned the revolver to himself, sent two bullets into his abdomen, and reeled away from Emma's lifeless body as he fell onto his back.

While Friederich and George Hannewald were outside talking they heard five loud pops in quick succession. Hannewald asked Friederich, "Do you have firecrackers going off somewhere?" to which Friederich yelled at the top of his voice, "No . . . oh my God—Lewis!" and sprinted into the house and to the closed parlor door. He grabbed the knob and pushed the door open. The room was filled with hazy white smoke and smelled of sulfur—and he discovered his beloved daughter lying motionless on the floor, her neck bent unnaturally. A sickening gurgling sound came from her mouth as it oozed a bubbling, red froth. Emma's white dress was soaked in blood, with more pooling around her contorted body. Lewis was sprawled next to her lying on his back holding a revolver near his hip, his arms and legs sporadically twitching as he looked wideeyed at Friederich.

Shocked by what he was seeing, Friederich immediately put his hands to Emma's bloody neck and felt no pulse, saw no sign of life. Her face rapidly turned ashen; her eyes were open and motionless. Friederich cried out, "My dear God! What has happened here?" He grimaced at Lewis and shouted, "You killed Emma! Why did you kill my daughter? Why did you do this?"

Hearing her husband's desperate calls, Katharina, her sons, and George Tisch rushed to the parlor where they were mortified to see Emma's lifeless body, blood everywhere, with Lewis lying nearby and bleeding below his chest.

Lewis, conscious and wondering why he was alive, oddly spoke in a weak and quivering voice, "Fred, for God's sake, help me up, I'm dying."

Friederich, in his panic, had not noticed Lewis's revolver. He frantically shouted, "Lewis, just stay put," then looked at George and told him to get help at once.

George ran from the house to Hannewald and told what happened. Hannewald followed George back into the house and saw Emma dead on the floor with Lewis squirming near her. Both

Hannewald and George then immediately left the house and ran into the road, calling out in all directions for a doctor.

Friederich once again put his fingers to Emma's neck and felt no pulse. He then dashed from the house shouting, "Emma's been shot! Emma's been shot! Oh, no, no, no, I think she's dead. Get help at once!"

Katharina and her sons were frozen in fear by what they saw. Suddenly, Lewis moved and slowly got up without looking at them. Startled and scared, they moved aside without saying a word as he passed them holding his gun and slowly careened down the hall to the front door.

From the middle of the dirt road, George saw Lewis flounder into the yard holding his gun. Fearing he might be shot next, George bolted to where his horse was tied and positioned himself behind his buggy. Lewis's hands were weakly trembling as he slipped a new cartridge into the revolver's cylinder. He then dropped to his knees before loading another.

Friederich then came running from the house yelling, "My daughter's been shot! Get help at once, please get help!" He then saw that Lewis was out of the house with his revolver and what he was doing. He hurried to him and took the gun from his grasp and kept it.

Lewis then strangely uttered, "Fred, I'm going home now."

"No you're not!" Friederich yelled as he grabbed Lewis by his coat collar and dragged him back into the house to the foyer.

"Don't you move," Friederich shouted.

Lewis leaned against the wall and quietly mumbled, "Hey Fred. Fred, take . . . the . . . take the money you owe me . . . use it for your girl's coffin."

Friederich stood in shock, looking at his daughter's killer, unable to comprehend or understand what had just happened.

So bewildered were Emma's father and mother that they hardly knew what else to do as they fully realized their daughter was dead. Friederich repeatedly ran in and out of the house as he kept his eyes on Lewis. In the parlor, Emma's mother was on her knees deeply wailing as she held her daughter's head in her hands. Emma's brothers were frozen in shock, unable to move or speak.

George had watched Friederich take the gun from Lewis and drag him back into the house. Not knowing what to do, George ran back into the house, stopping in front of Lewis.

"Lewis, what have you done?" George cried out between rapid breaths.

Lewis looked up to George, curled his upper lip and sneered, saying nothing.

George raised his fists, wanting to beat Lewis to a pulp as he watched the shooter slowly close his eyes. Leaving him for dead, George returned to the frantic scene in the parlor. The shock of again seeing Emma, whom he had warmly embraced such a short time ago, sprawled grotesquely on the bloody floor with her mother embracing her breathless head, overpowered him. George collapsed onto a chair and howled, "My good Lord, why has this happened?"

After a few moments, and not knowing what to do next, George left the horror of the parlor and quickly walked through the house to the foyer. Staying mindful of Lewis, dead or not, he passed him, moving through the door and out to where his horse was tied. He stood cautiously near his buggy as onlookers began appearing in the distance.

Without being noticed, Lewis slowly rose to his feet and staggered to the front door. George was startled when he saw Emma's killer standing, and watched in dread as he stumbled down the steps. Lewis then tried running in the direction of his parents' house, but fell next to a stack of building bricks in the yard. He reached for one, rolled onto his back and began bashing his forehead as he attempted to beat his brains out. Seeing this, Friederich moved quickly to him, easily wrestled the brick from Lewis's hands, and again pulled him back toward the house, leaving him near the front doorsteps. As Lewis lay motionless on the ground, Friederich returned to his dead daughter and weeping wife, who still had Emma's head cradled in her lap.

George Hannewald, not finding anyone who could help, had driven his carriage to get Lewis's parents and tell of what happened and for them to come with him at once.

Lewis, almost forgotten in the frenzy, regained consciousness and crawled on his hands and knees back to the bricks, grabbed another, and again attempted to bash his head, but was so weak he crumbled facedown to the ground.

Rolf, who was running haphazardly in the yard and barking wildly during the frenzy, began snarling at the motionless body. Tisch left the shield of his buggy and walked to Lewis, assuming he was dead, and stood.

John and Christina Heydlauff arrived a moment later with Hannewald. Shocked at the sight of their son, presumably dead, they both leaped from their seats and ran to him, Christina hysterically screaming, "No, no, no . . ."

When they reached Lewis, John dropped to his knees and rolled his son onto his back. Lewis's eyes opened weakly. "Dad, Dad, help me," he moaned.

"He's alive, my son is alive! We need to get him to a doctor at once!" John shouted out.

Christina added hysterically, "My dear, what have you done?"

Lewis's eyes fluttered and closed, but his shallow breathing continued. She then looked to George, and not having fully comprehended what Hannewald had told them, asked, "How is Emma . . . is Emma OK?"

George looked sadly at Christiana, paused, and then replied dismally, "Mrs. Heydlauff, Emma is dead."

Christina's body went limp as she began to faint. George steadied her, and she wept as he held her close to him.

"Mrs. Heydlauff, Mrs. Heydlauff. It's time to bring Lewis home," and he stepped aside as she regained her stature.

Christina watched as her husband and Hannewald lifted Lewis from the ground. Lewis regained consciousness as he was being placed in Hannewald's carriage. Hannewald looked at Lewis, whose blood was slowly oozing through his vest, and asked him why he did the shooting, to which Lewis faintly uttered, "I can't live without Emma. I just wanted to die and take her with me."

Lewis then lost consciousness as Hannewald brought him and his shocked parents home while medical assistance was being summoned from Munith.

Word was also sent to Dr. C. Brogan in Stockbridge to come at once to the Moeckel house, who upon arrival at 10:30 a.m. confirmed the girl dead from gunshot wounds.

Thirty minutes later, Dr. John E. Conlan arrived from Munith to find Lewis Heydlauff at his home in grave condition with two gunshot wounds, one a flesh wound below his chest, the other near the center of his abdomen, and moderate to severe bruising to his head.

Lewis again regained consciousness and weakly told the doctor not to probe for the bullets as he had to die. Dr. Conlan, having been told of what occurred, asked Lewis why he did it. Lewis told the doctor that he had intended to kill himself and Emma, as he could not die and leave his girl behind, but had made a bad job of it. Knowing Emma was dead, Lewis pleaded with the doctor to administer poison so he could die as intended and be with his girl, to which Dr. Conlan refused.

Later that day an inquest was called by local justice of the peace, Orville Gorton, and was conducted at the Moeckel house. Justice Gorton had impaneled a coroner's jury consisting of six local farmers: Henry Lehman, John H. Hubbard, Andrew Rumiman, Emanuel Harr, Friederich D. Artz, Sr., and Charles Crane. After the physicians and Justice Gorton had examined the scene of the shooting and collected evidence, and after hearing the details from five witnesses consisting of Katharina and Friederich Moeckel, George Tisch, George Hannewald, and Dr. John E. Conlan, the Coroner's Court rendered a verdict: Emma Moeckel had come to her death by means of gunshot wounds the morning of Sunday, May 31, 1896, at approximately 10:30 a.m., caused by Lewis H. Heydlauff.

After the inquest concluded, Emma's distraught parents tried as best they could to gather strength to bathe and dress Emma's cold body and lay her in bed as if she were sleeping—a task no mother, no father, should ever endure.

George Tisch stayed with the grieving family throughout the

day, helping with whatever he could at the scene of the tragedy. At dusk, he left for his home in Munith.

When George arrived, he was met by his mother and collapsed into her arms. Katherine held her brokenhearted son with deep compassion. George looked at his mother and burst out in tears, "Emma's dead. Lewis Heydlauff killed her. I was there and I couldn't save her."

"I know, son. Charlotte Hannewald came to us and told what happened. I'm so sorry, George."

George had tried to be strong while at the Moeckels' but now, in his mother's warm embrace, he cried, "Oh, Mother, I should have stayed with Emma; I didn't known Lewis was waiting for her. It's my fault Emma is dead."

"No, George, it's not your fault; do not blame yourself. The Heydlauff boy is to blame. He shot and killed Emma."

George moved to the parlor and wept.

Two of George's brothers, Charles and Henry, came into the house to console George, assuring him that he had nothing to do with Lewis Heydlauff killing Emma.

"Lewis is crazy, George, he's a crazy drunkard," Henry told him. "There was nothing you could have done."

George was sitting on the sofa that he had shared with Emma just the night before. He lowered his head and wept, "Emma was my friend, and I loved her."

Katherine sat next to George and held his hands. Charles and Henry stood behind their brother with their hands on his shoulders. Wilhelm stood in the background wondering what form of evil led the Heydlauff boy to commit such a wicked deed.

At the Heydlauff home, Lewis, who began his morning determined to carry out his plan, lay dying at home—his parents almost dead with grief. Dr. Conlan had taken leave at nightfall with little hope for Lewis's survival, saying he would return early the next morning. Deputy Sheriff David Croman had been put in charge of Lewis following the inquest and sat silently on a wooden chair in the corner of the room to keep watch on the killer.

At the Moeckel house, Emma, who had felt an exhilarating rush of a new life when she had kissed George only hours earlier, lay life-less in her bed, following the kiss of death from Lewis.

Later that night, the grieving Moeckel family sent word to George asking him to please come to be with the family. George came back at once and joined the family and some of their dearest friends, all of whom mourned and prayed for beloved Emma until dawn.

CHAPTER TEN

Morning After

Early Monday morning, Pastor Wenk came to the Moeckel home to console the grief-stricken family. As he prayed with them for the repose of Emma's soul, he assured them that she was now with the Almighty in paradise.

Emma's brother, Albert, was unable to look at the pastor during prayer—all he could think of was hearing the shots, seeing his sister dead and covered in blood, and seeing his mother and father in deepest anguish as they knelt by Emma's body. He was further distraught about having talked to Lewis on the way to get her when Lewis told him, "Emma would have a damned hard life before she died, and that he oughta be damned sure to bring her back home with him." Albert believed that if only he had told his father what Lewis had threatened, he would not have let Lewis into the house, and Emma would still be alive.

Following his visit with the Moeckels, Pastor Wenk rode his carriage the short distance to the Heydlauff house to offer support, prayer, and something more.

John Heydlauff led Pastor Wenk to the bedroom where Lewis lay semiconscious with Katharina at his bedside. Deputy Sheriff Croman sat in the corner by a window. The pastor asked the officer if he and Lewis's parents could be alone with the boy for a few minutes. The deputy agreed, but said he would be on the other side of the door.

Pastor Wenk prayed with the inconsolable parents as Lewis awoke and drowsily looked at the pastor and his parents. His eyes then fluttered and closed. After Pastor Wenk finished, he asked to be alone with Lewis for a private prayer, to which they agreed.

Pastor Wenk, in the hope of keeping Lewis's soul from descending at death to the fiery chasm of hell for his transgression, whispered to Lewis if he wished to receive Holy Absolution by confessing to God all his sins and beg for forgiveness. Lewis slowly opened his eyes and weakly sighed, "Yes."

Pastor Wenk responded, "Lewis, there are no secrets between you and the Lord, so hold nothing back."

Whatever sins Lewis privately confessed to Pastor Wenk would stay between both to the grave.

Shortly after Pastor Wenk departed, Dr. Conlon returned from the night before to assess his patient.

As Dr. Conlon started examining Lewis, he gradually became conscious, allowing the doctor to ask, "Lewis, I'm here to help you. Can you tell me how you are feeling?"

Lewis replied tiredly, "I'm sick doctor; my head hurts so bad . . . all of me hurts. I wanna die. Please let me die."

Lewis became fully alert when Dr. Conlon told him he was going to look at his bullet wounds, and he attempted to sit up.

"Doctor, I'm very thirsty; may I have some something to drink first?"

Dr. Conlon placed a pillow behind Lewis's head and offered him water. But as he tried to hold the glass, Lewis began trembling so badly that he was unable to keep it at his mouth.

Lewis then surprised the doctor by asking, "Dr. Conlon, do you have some whiskey I can drink?"

Dr. Conlon then recognized the pungent odor emanating from Lewis's body was likely from alcohol and that his trembling might be a symptom of withdrawal from abuse. The doctor told him, "I don't believe that would be good for you. Tell me, do you drink much liquor?"

Beads of sweat were forming on Lewis's forehead. The doctor put his hand to it—it was damp and cool to the touch. Lewis then responded, "No doctor, not much. I once had too much to drink, but that's it. I only have some once in a while."

Dr. Conlon found Lewis's answer difficult to believe, but needed to examine his wounds, so he took the pillow from behind his head and told him to lie still, and then removed the bloodstained bandages. While the doctor was probing the oozing bullet holes, Lewis began convulsing. Dr. Conlon quickly rolled Lewis to his side and kept watch on him until it stopped, almost two minutes later. Afterward, Lewis was profoundly confused by his surroundings and his heart was racing so rapidly that Dr. Conlon was certain he was about to lose his patient. But Lewis gradually regained lucidity and told again of his desire to die.

Dr. Conlan was deeply concerned by what he had observed, and prepared and administered a mixture of powdered opium and a bromide serum to suppress the pain and reduce the chance of another convulsion. Numbed by the remedy, Lewis promptly lost consciousness.

At the end of that day, Dr. Conlan informed Lewis's parents the chances of their son's survival were at best equally divided.

As word of the tragedy spread across Waterloo and beyond, the peaceful residents were taken aback by the crime. No one could comprehend how such a respected boy from the Heydlauff family could commit such a depraved crime against his sweetheart. Many talked of George Tisch, curious to how he was involved. There was an ongoing question of Emma Moeckel's role in the shooting, asking what she may have done to warrant being murdered by her lover. Gossip was callous and cruel—and traveled fast.

CHAPTER ELEVEN

DAY OF THE FUNERAL

At dawn, Tuesday, June 2, it was warm and misty with gray clouds rolling overhead. At around 7:00 a.m., light rain was falling as a black, glass-windowed funeral hearse, drawn by two Clydesdale horses the color of a raven, pulled up to the Moeckel residence. Two somber-looking men, dressed in coal-black tailcoats and stovepipe hats, stepped off the hearse. One of the two walked to the house and was met at the door by Friederich. They had a word, and the man returned and joined the other at the rear of the hearse, where they unlatched the two doors and pulled out a brown, wooden coffin. They then carried it to the open door and into the house. Friederich led them into the bedroom where the body of Emma lay in bed, as if asleep. Sitting next to the bed was Katharina and her two young sons. On the other side of the bed sat Pastor Emil Wenk. The two men placed the coffin at the foot of the bed, removed their hats, and stepped off to the side.

Friederich nodded to Pastor Wenk, who at once stood and said, "Allow me to pray."

Katharina knelt at the side of the bed in deepest grief, her head pressed against her daughter's cold body. Albert and Florenz sobbed through the entire prayer. Friederich stooped behind his wife and placed his hands on her shoulders. Pastor Wenk concluded his prayer, and said, "Together, let us pray the Lord's Prayer." The tearful pastor struggled as he began, "Our Father, who art in heaven, hallowed be thy . . ."

The Moeckel family joined, "Hallowed be thy name. Thy kingdom come, Thy will be done . . ."

The two carriage drivers standing to the side were shedding tears as they whispered along with the anguished family, "Thy will be done, on earth as it is in heaven. Give us this day our daily bread. And forgive us our debts, as we forgive our debtors. And lead us not into temptation, but deliver us from evil."

The prayer was finished, and all that could be heard in the room was the gentle pattering of light rain against the bedroom's windows. Pastor Wenk then stated Emma's body would return to dust, from whence it came, but assured the family that Emma's soul now lived forever with the Creator in heaven.

Pastor Wenk turned to the Moeckel family and offered a consoling smile. He then left for St. Jacob to prepare for Emma's funeral. Starting with Friederich, followed by Albert, then Florenz, and finally Katharina, all dressed in mourning black, each walked to Emma, leaned over and kissed her forehead, then stepped aside.

Friederich looked to the two men standing to the side and nodded, as if to say, "It's time."

The two men from the hearse approached the coffin and removed the top. Katharina gently gathered Emma's favorite quilted blanket, which was draped over her daughter's corpse, and lined the coffin with it. Friederich nodded again to the two men, who then slowly approached the bed and slid their arms under Emma's body. Friederich gently placed his hands under his daughter's head, her red hair still braided and tied with the scarlet ribbon. One of the two from the hearse softly said "Now," and all three lifted Emma's body and gently placed it into the open coffin. Friederich tenderly moved his daughter's braided hair over her shoulder. Katharina moved next to her husband, knelt, and lovingly smoothed and straightened the beautiful gown they had chosen for Emma—their Christmas gift to her—to wear until the end of time. Katharina wept profusely as she leaned and kissed her daughter one last time and whispered, "Sweet dreams, my love."

Friederich then asked his sons to wait in the dining room. The mournful parents watched in tears as the two men placed the cover over the coffin. The sorrowful mother and father left the bedroom holding hands, Friederich closing the door behind them. Moments later they heard the wretched twisting of eight brass coffin screws being turned to secure the top to the coffin. After the agonizing screeching sound stopped, one of the two men opened the door and indicated that it was time to carry the coffin to the hearse. Friederich led them through the house, passing the parlor along the way. He opened the front door, and Emma's coffin was taken to the waiting hearse, where it was carefully placed inside. As this was happening, several carriages had arrived and positioned behind the black hearse, waiting for the cortege to make its way to St. Jacob Lutheran Church.

The Moeckels, boys first, then Friederich and Katharina holding hands, walked out through the same front door that Emma had entered so joyfully just two days earlier. The family was met by a third attendant, who led them to an enclosed funeral carriage behind the hearse. The driver then positioned himself in the coachman's seat, put his arm up, and waved to alert the hearse in front to start the solemn journey to St. Jacob. The carriages that had been queuing behind the funeral carriage had grown to 228, all of which followed in the long cortege.

As the two Clydesdale horses pulled the glass-windowed hearse into the church courtyard, those awaiting its arrival were able to see the coffin inside, causing women and men alike to bemoan the reality of the young girl's tragic death. Pastor Wenk met the hearse and instructed the drivers to remove the coffin and follow him into the church.

The Moeckel family exited their carriage and followed the men carrying Emma's coffin into St. Jacob's. It was then placed on a long table at the front of the altar. The coffin was then draped by a black, silk pall.

The Moeckels sat together in the first pew.

The funeral of Emma Maria Moeckel began at 10:00 a.m. on that gloomy Tuesday morning. The church was overflowing with grieving relatives and friends, including John and Christina Heydlauff, who mourned for Emma—and for their son, Lewis.

Wilhelm and Katherine Tisch attended with their son, George, who was devastated by Emma's murder and had withdrawn to the point where he was barely able to speak without breaking into uncontrollable tears.

The love for Emma and esteem in which she was held were evidenced by the great number present and the many floral arrangements throughout the church.

After the tearful funeral service concluded, Pastor Wenk led the pallbearers carrying the black-draped coffin with Friederich, Katharina, and their sons alongside to the churchyard cemetery. John and Christina Heydlauff followed close behind, along with the other funeral attendees, to where the coffin was placed on a low, rectangular-shaped taupe-colored tarpaulin next to a freshly dug grave, its black dirt piled to the side. The mourners bowed their heads and Pastor Wenk began reading Psalm Twenty-Three from his Bible:

The Lord is my Shepherd; I shall not want.

He maketh me to lie down in green pastures: He leadeth me beside the still waters.

He restoreth my soul: He leadeth me in the paths of righteousness for his name's sake.

Yea, though I walk through the valley of the shadow of death, I will fear no evil: For thou art with me; Thy rod and thy staff they comfort me.

Thou preparest a table before me in the presence of mine enemies: Thou anointest my head with oil; my cup runneth over.

Surely goodness and mercy shall follow me all the days of my life: And I will dwell in the house of the Lord forever.

After a long pause, he dismissed the attendees. The Moeckel family and the Heydlauffs stayed at the grave with Pastor Wenk, along with two of the hearse drivers.

John Heydlauff was suddenly stricken with immense grief and begged to have one last look at Emma. Friederich and Katharina looked to each other for a fleeting moment, and then tearfully nodded in agreement. Friederich motioned to the two drivers. They approached the coffin, unscrewed each of the eight coffin screws, lifted the top and placed it along its side. Friederich held his umbrella over his daughter's body, shielding it from the mist. Friederich and Katharina held hands with their sons as they looked, one last time, at Emma. John and Christina, the distraught parents of the murderer, looked at Emma's ashen face. Christina began wobbling and, as she began to faint, her husband grabbed hold before she slid into the open grave. Pastor Wenk waited for Christina to regain her composure, and then led them with the Lord's Prayer, followed by saying, "Emma's short life with us was a gift to be cherished. We can take comfort in knowing that she is now with our Creator in heaven."

Friederich nodded to the hearse drivers. They approached and closed the coffin's top, quickly resecuring it with the eight long thumb screws, their tops each stamped with a dove. They lifted the coffin, and with the use of two ropes, slowly lowered it down to its final resting place. Friederich gathered a handful of dirt and sprinkled it over the coffin, as did Katharina, Albert then Florenz, and the tearful Heydlauffs. Lastly, Pastor Emil Wenk did the same, as his final act of committal.

From a distance, the pastor's wife had tearfully watched her friend being lowered into the grave, fighting a feeling of guilt as she pondered having intervened in Emma's affairs.

The remaining dirt was then shoveled into the pit by the hearse drivers, ending Emma's via dolorosa to the grave.

During the funeral, Lewis was attended to at home by Dr. Conlan. When he heard the bell tolling for Emma at nearby St. Jacob, Lewis thought of what he had done and began hysterically howling so severely that the doctor thought he would surely die. Lewis cried to Dr. Conlon to leave and just let him be so he could close his eyes and never awaken.

Also during the funeral, Waterloo's Deputy Sheriff David Croman, who was keeping watch on Lewis, was called to Jackson to meet with Jackson County Assistant Prosecuting Attorney Henry E. Edwards and Jackson County Deputy Sheriff Kniffin. Afterward, Edwards directed Kniffin to lodge a complaint against Lewis Heydlauff, charging him with murder. The deputy sheriff made the complaint in Justice D. Gibbs Palmer's court in Jackson, and a warrant for Heydlauff's arrest was issued. Kniffin was told to proceed at once to the Heydlauff house to serve the paper. Justice Palmer, having heard of Lewis Heydlauff's precarious condition from his wounds, instructed Kniffin that, if Heydlauff's condition was such that he could not be moved, to stay with the accused until fit for travel.

At the end of the day, intimate friends of the Moeckel family came to console them at home, not wanting them to grieve alone.

CHAPTER TWELVE

STILL ALIVE

WEDNESDAY, JUNE 3, 1896

JACKSON DAILY CITIZEN

HEYDLAUFF STILL LIVES

BUT IS FAILING FAST—HE WISHES TO DIE

On Tuesday afternoon, June 2, a resident of Munith stated he visited Lewis Heydlauff, the young man who shot and killed his sweetheart, Emma Moeckel and attempted suicide Sunday. He found the young man alive, but failing rapidly. Lewis Heydlauff was perfectly conscious and told his visitor he regretted his deed, but as it was done, he wished to die also.

Sherriff Peek received a message Wednesday morning from Dr. Conlan, of Munith, who is attending Lewis Heydlauff, stating the would-be suicide had improved a little and that chances for recovery or death were about evenly divided.

CHAPTER THIRTEEN

NEWSPAPERS

Reports published by the local newspapers telling in great detail of the Moeckel murder triggered immense interest. Three prominent and respected families were involved and a great number of persons who read or heard of the killing and attempted suicide were personally acquainted with them. The tragedy also generated considerable interest throughout neighboring counties. The first published accounts were so dreadful that the public was hungry for details. Readers wanted more—more about the dead girl, more about the boy who murdered his sweetheart, more about the other boy's involvement.

The Waterloo community knew Emma Moeckel for her uncommon beauty, her welcoming nature, and by her relationship to the popular Heydlauff boy. To the greater community the Moeckel girl and Heydlauff boy appeared to have been the perfect couple and some wondered what she may have done to be so brutally killed by her lover. Hearsay about George Tisch's involvement with Emma Moeckel was that he was being seen with Miss Moeckel just before her death; rumors were circulating that he had something to do with what made Lewis Heydlauff kill the girl he loved and attempt suicide.

The owners, editors, and reporters of the two primary Jackson newspapers, the *Citizen* and the *Patriot*, knew the crime would develop into a sensational court case. They also knew the public was starving for more information. This was the ideal story to sell papers, so the publications' top reporters were assigned to chronicle what was to follow.

Reporters from each newspaper had networks of sources, named and unnamed, who would tell of what they knew or may have overheard. Information was also generated by the reporters' personal observations and investigations, and by facts obtained from trusted sources. A reporter's journalistic duty was to gather, sort, and verify facts—but there would be times when some details wouldn't quite fit, but appeared to be circumstantially factual. Some reporters rolled the dice to meet press deadlines. Whatever the case, reporters would collect, verify as best they could, write the story, and allow the editors to approve or not.

It was recalled that the Emma Moeckel murder had been the first in the vicinity since 1852, when James Hitchcock stabbed a man named Stevenson near Stockbridge during a drunken row. Hitchcock, who was said to have been twenty years old when convicted, served over thirty-five years at Jackson State Prison before being pardoned.

The Waterloo community was hungry for salacious details relating to the Moeckel murder, the most sensational crime ever to occur in Waterloo, and waited impatiently for each new edition.

CHAPTER FOURTEEN

JACKSON COUNTY JAIL

Mr. John Heydlauff owned and successfully operated one of Jackson County's most productive farms. He raised cattle and feed crops for the animals; any surplus feed was sold locally to other farmers. He was also involved in building several stately homes throughout the community. With his profits, he invested in a slaughterhouse in Ann Arbor, a brick company in Britton, and in shares of other businesses. His investments were producing handsome profits and, as a result, he had the financial means to hire whomever he wanted to medically treat or legally defend his son.

Mr. Heydlauff wanted two things for Lewis: full medical recovery, and avoidance of prison.

Lewis was already under the care of his doctor of choice, Dr. John E. Conlan of Munith.

The day after Emma Moeckel's funeral, Mr. Heydlauff traveled to Jackson and met with John W. Miner, a thirty-one year-old defense lawyer who had gained a reputation as the county's preeminent defense attorney. After reviewing Miner's impressive history of winning acquittals, and listening to his persuasive presentation, Heydlauff accepted Miner's terms and hired him to represent his son.

As Lewis lay in bed wanting to die, there was little in the way of advice that John Miner could offer to the dying boy's father—but he was already thinking of possible defense scenarios. Miner considered tactics for minimizing prison time, and long-shot strategies for full acquittal.

The early evidence was condemning. The defendant admitted that he killed the victim. There was motive. The victim, his former girlfriend, rejected him for another man, so he deliberately went to her house with a revolver, demanded she be his girl again, and when she refused, shot and killed her. The killer's motive, admissions, and evidence of the crime were overwhelming.

John Miner's first action as Lewis's lawyer was to contact the sheriff and arrange to have Lewis confined at home under the watch of his father, not by the county's deputy sheriff.

Lewis surprised Dr. Conlan when he unexpectedly regained strength later that week. He stunned everyone by dressing for the first time on Sunday, June 7, only one week after the shooting.

Early the next morning Lewis was visited by Deputy Sheriff Kriffin, who deemed him fit for transport, and sent word by telegraph to the county sheriff in Jackson. Later that day, four sheriff deputies from Jackson arrived by carriage, and Lewis's father and brother turned Lewis over. Lewis was handcuffed and transported in the carriage to the Munith Grand Trunk rail station; John Heydlauff and his son, August, following closely behind.

A small crowd of gawkers had already gathered at the station when word spread of what was occurring. When the sheriff-carriage arrived, the people watched intently as the deputies led Lewis to the platform and boarded the train to Jackson. Lewis's father and brother boarded as well. Lewis sat at the aisle with a deputy at his side, the other directly across. John Heydlauff and August were allowed to sit behind Lewis.

Along the way, Lewis said nothing, hanging his head in lingering pain and shame. When the train arrived at Jackson's Central Station, a waiting sheriff's jail wagon transported the accused at once to the county jail. Lewis was processed and brought to the jail's guarded medical apartment, where he was held to allow physicians to attend him—he was still experiencing considerable pain in the vicinity of his self-inflicted wounds—and would remain until well enough for transfer to a standard cell. Lewis was to not be arraigned for the charge against him—murder—until he gained more strength. This arrangement had been negotiated by his defense attorney, John Miner.

During his first week in county jail, Lewis was treated by two physicians, Dr. Conlan, from Munith, and the county jail doctor, Charles DeWitt Colby. Lewis's parents and his brother, August, came to see him daily. His sisters Lydia, Paulina, Sarah, and eldest brother, Emanuel, each came once. The pastor from St. Jacob Lutheran Church also made a visit.

Although Lewis said he did not care to live, he was recuperating. At the end of the first week, his physicians concluded that Lewis Heydlauff would probably live.

Lewis's parents continued to see him each day during his second week. They were thankful for their son's improving health, but were equally troubled by his fixation with death. They tried to be sympathetic to what had occurred, but Lewis had little interest in conversation, mostly repeating that he wished he had died. At one point, however, Lewis told his mother that he wanted to see Mrs. Moeckel, and to ask her to come.

CHAPTER FIFTEEN

* · — ❧~❧ — · *

Reality

THURSDAY, JUNE 11, 1896

The Stockbridge Sun

Lewis Heydlauff Taken to Jail in Jackson

TO BE ARRAIGNED FOR THE MURDER OF EMMA MOECKEL

Waterloo, Michigan—Lewis Heydlauff, the young man who murdered Emma Moeckel in Waterloo, May 31, and then shot himself, but not fatally, has so far recovered as to be able to be taken to Jackson, where he will be arraigned for murder. His father and brother took him up and turned him over into the custody of the sheriff, just as they promised that they would do. The young man is respectably connected, and the family have the sympathy of everybody; but the stern requirements of law and the sacredness of human life demand that young Heydlauff shall be punished for his criminal conduct just the same as though he were not so well connected.

CHAPTER SIXTEEN

DEFENSE STRATEGY

Upon hearing from the physicians that Lewis was expected to live, attorney John Miner called on John Heydlauff at his Waterloo home to discuss the devastating evidence against his son, and how best to build a defense strategy.

As they sat in the Heydlauff home library, Miner explained that they had to decide on the most promising approach to defend Lewis against the murder arraignment that was certain to come. Miner explained that there were two options with four possible outcomes.

"What are they?" John Heydlauff asked.

Miner began, "Nobody saw your son shoot Emma Moeckel that Sunday morning, but Lewis admitted doing it soon afterward to Friederich Moeckel, George Hannewald, and to Dr. John Conlan. There is no doubt that Lewis will be arraigned for murder, and it's not possible for your son to prove he didn't shoot Miss Moeckel.

"The first option is to avoid trial by offering a plea. We could approach the prosecution and offer to have Lewis plead guilty to the lesser charge of voluntary manslaughter and negotiate reduced prison time."

"What exactly is voluntary manslaughter?" Heydlauff asked.

Miner answered, "It varies by the conditions under which the crime was committed, but in this case, it would mean that Lewis didn't have a motive, and that he shot the girl in a rage of emotional passion. We would have to convince the prosecutor that that was Lewis's state of mind at the time of the shooting."

John Heydlauff nervously asked, "If they accepted that, how much time would Lewis spend in prison?"

Miner paused and started tapping a pencil against his notepad, then answered, "Considering this case, I estimate the sentence to be somewhere between fourteen and sixteen years. Oftentimes, prisoners are released early for good behavior, so possibly ten to twelve years."

John Heydlauff looked dismayed as he inquired, "What if my son is convicted by jury—how many years?"

"The jury will likely be given two charges to consider. If convicted of murder, life in prison—if voluntary manslaughter, likely twenty years, with possible reduced prison time for good behavior."

John Heydlauff closed his eyes and groaned, "Oh my God."

Miner paused and again started tapping his pencil, then continued, "The second option is to plead *not guilty by reason of general insanity*."

John Heydlauff snapped his head and indignantly responded, "My son is not insane."

"I'm not saying he is, Mr. Heydlauff, but it's the only possible defense your son has for an acquittal. The newspapers have been reporting that according to his friends your son had been threatening suicide because he couldn't live without his sweetheart. The news stories have implied that your son was insane by asking *why else would he have killed the girl*. We will interview your son's friends, family members, and anyone else who Lewis had contact with to gather information that he may have been acting irrationally before the shooting."

John Heydlauff scratched his forehead and asked, "With that defense, what are the possible outcomes?"

"Before I answer that, there are reports that your son was drinking a considerable amount of alcohol during the weeks leading to the shooting. Are you aware of this?" Miner asked.

"I know Lewis had been drinking now and then, but my son is

not a drunk. Those reports are false," Heydlauff insisted.

"That's very important, Mr. Heydlauff. If it was established during the trial that he decided to kill the girl during a drunken binge, he would likely be found guilty of voluntary manslaughter—if not, then the murder charge. We will need to convince the jury that those reports are false—that he is not an imbiber—and we will require witnesses who will testify to it. Without that, it will be nearly impossible to use insanity as a defense." Miner narrowed his eyes and said, "Now, back to your question. If the jury finds that your son was not insane, he'll be found guilty of either murder or manslaughter. If the jury determines that your son was insane when he killed Miss Moeckel—not guilty."

"Not guilty? But if the jury determines that Lewis was insane, wouldn't he be sent to the asylum?"

"Unlikely. I've talked with your son and he certainly seems despondent about what happened. But, if we make the case that Lewis was insane at the time of the shooting, but not necessarily now, we will use temporary insanity as the defense. That's for medical experts to determine and explain. My job is to carefully weave it into the defense."

John Heydlauff immediately asked, "What will it take?"

Miner clarified, "I'm going to need some help. I've already spoken to a colleague about this case, Richard Price, who has considerable experience in using emotional insanity as a defense and has gained a wealth of knowledge regarding a form of insanity known as melancholia. I will need him on my team."

"What is melancholia?" Heydlauff asked.

"It's a medical term for emotional insanity. It's a form of mental illness that can be triggered by a shocking event. While suffering from the disease, memory is disrupted," Miner explained.

"But my son admitted that he shot the girl," Heydlauff argued.

"Yes he did, but that does not mean he remembers having done it.

John Heydlauff raised his voice and stated, "Friederich Moeckel, George Hannewald, and Dr. Conlon all said my son admitted doing the shooting."

"Yes, that's what they said at the inquest, but in each instance, they asked your son why he killed Emma, so Lewis *assumed* he had done it, but your son may have no memory of it because he was insane when he pulled the trigger. That would be temporary insanity caused by melancholia."

John Heydlauff sat silently for a time, and then announced, "I want to save my son, so please inform Mr. Price that he should be on your team."

Miner continued, "Mr. Heydlauff, I want you to fully understand that there will be considerable cost if we follow this route. We will hire medical experts—physicians who are knowledgeable of brain diseases—to evaluate your son and testify at the trial, and they will charge for their services. Are you agreeable to this condition?"

"Yes, I don't want my son in a prison or an asylum. I'll do whatever is necessary for my son to be free—no matter the odds, no matter the cost," Heydlauff firmly stated.

"Thank you, Mr. Heydlauff, it's a good decision you make."

CHAPTER SEVENTEEN

PRAYERFUL EXONERATION

Katharina Moeckel agreed to call on her daughter's killer on Friday of that week. It had been about three weeks since Emma's funeral and her grief was great.

Katharina gathered some belongings as she prepared for her trip to visit Lewis at the county jail. At the last moment she remembered the silver locket Lewis had given Emma for Christmas. She entered Emma's bedroom and opened a dresser drawer. Reaching in, she removed a small, round sewing box containing Emma's broken and discarded jewelry items, the locket amongst them. Katharina took the locket and dropped it into her bag.

Albert drove his mother to the Munith station. Along the way, Katharina thought of the last time she had seen Emma alive, and a great resentment for Lewis surfaced—a feeling she had been fighting. Katharina accepted that Lewis had broken the commandment, *Thou Shalt Not Kill*, but reminded herself that Pastor Wenk often preached about the need to forgive—he frequently referenced Jesus' Sermon on the Mount, where it was said: "For if you forgive other people when they sin against you, your heavenly Father will also forgive you. But if you do not forgive others their sins, your Father will not forgive your sins."

Katharina was having great difficulty with this command.

Wearing her black mourning dress, black hat, and dark veil,

Katharina boarded the Grand Trunk at Munith with her Bible, prayer book, and the locket.

Along the way, Katharina opened her prayer book. In the center was a folded piece of paper. She had forgotten that after her daughter's funeral a close friend of Emma's gave it to her saying it may provide some comfort in times of need. Katharina unfolded the paper. It was a prayer, handwritten in English. The top of the page was neatly titled "The Catholic Prayer of Saint Francis of Assisi." Katharina began reading:

Lord, make me an instrument of your peace. Where there is hatred, let me sow love. Where there is injury, pardon. Where there is doubt, faith. Where there is despair, hope. Where there is darkness, light, and where there is sadness, joy. O Divine Master, grant that I may not so much seek to be consoled, as to console; to be understood, as to understand; to be loved, as to love; for it is in giving that we receive—it is in pardoning that we are pardoned; and in dying that we are born to eternal life.

Katharina began pondering what she had read and her eyes got heavy. Several minutes later the train was pulling into the Jackson's Central Station.

After coming to a full stop, Katharina stepped off the train and walked the platform as she hailed a horse-drawn taxi, taking it to the county jail.

Upon arrival she approached the front desk, identified herself as Katharina Moeckel, and asked to see Lewis Heydlauff. After a few minutes, she was led to the jail's medical apartment where her daughter's killer was confined. She introduced herself to the officer guarding the apartment, who then inserted a key into its door's lock. Watching this, Katharina recalled the day following Emma's funeral, when she felt compelled to visit Lewis on his deathbed after hearing that he was not expected to survive. Lewis only groaned during her visit, but she prayed for him at his bedside. Now, at the county jail, she began questioning why she was there. Her stomach tightened when the guard opened the door.

Katharina stood still and looked at the broken, pathetic boy, not knowing what to say.

Lewis turned his head and saw that it was Emma's mother and burst into tears. He then whimpered, "Mrs. Moeckel, Mrs. Moeckel, thank you for coming . . . I loved Emma so much."

Katharina had great difficulty looking at the man she had once admired as her daughter's best friend—now the monstrous man who took away her beloved Emma—but forced a smile and replied "Hello Lewis, I'm glad to see that your health is improving."

Lewis moved his legs as if he wanted to leave his bed, but was sharply commanded by the guard standing at the door, "Stay put."

Hearing this, Lewis lay back down and propped a pillow behind his head, then whined, "Thank . . . thank you for coming, Mrs. Moeckel. I . . . I wanted to see you . . . to tell you that I miss Emma . . . and to tell you . . . to tell you how much that I . . . that I loved her."

"Now, now, Lewis," Katharina said calmly as she moved to him, and took his right hand into hers—not thinking it was the same hand that ruthlessly fired the revolver that destroyed her daughter's precious life.

"My girl is dead, Mrs. Moeckel. I wanna die. I just wanna die," Lewis cried.

"Lewis, don't you say that. You are now in God's hands, and when He decides to take you, it will be on His time. Lewis, I regret all that has happened, but it cannot be undone. What now can be done is for you to trust in God and ask for His forgiveness."

Katharina thought of what she had read on the train, "It is in pardoning that we are pardoned," and of the Lord's Prayer, "forgive those who trespass against us," and about Pastor Wenk preaching of the need to forgive, regardless of how grievous the sin.

Lewis burst into tears while Katharina was holding his hand. She squeezed it tighter, and a rush of memories flooded her mind: Emma's birth when she first held her infant daughter close to her breast, and their eyes met for the first time. She recalled the morning when John and Christina Heydlauff first visited with their three youngest children, Sarah, Lewis, and August, Lewis being only five years old, to deliver a welcoming meal, and that Lewis could not take his eyes off little Emma. She thought of Emma and Lewis playing in the garden when Emma was only four years old, and Lewis picking a white daisy and handing it to her. Katharina reflected on how quickly her young daughter grew from a lanky child to joining the ranks of womanhood when her body developed soft curves, and Emma's questions shifted from how chickens make eggs, to how girls made babies.

Katharina was lost in memories when she heard Lewis weakly call out, "Mrs. Moeckel."

Katharina snapped back to a cold reality as she suddenly envisioned Emma in her casket, and realized she had been staring vacantly at his face, at the face of the murderer who took her daughter away in a most horrible way. She released Lewis's hand and stepped back, thinking it best to wish Lewis well and leave. Then she felt guilt—guilt that she had not done what she came to do. She looked down at Lewis, who looked back in puzzlement. Katharina came to forgive . . . but wondered *why* as she closed her eyes and pictured Emma's broken, violated body lying dead on the bloodstained floor. She wanted to turn her back on Lewis and leave, but felt obligated, by faith, to stay and forgive.

Fighting the urge to simply walk away and let him deal with God's forgiveness, she made her decision and said, "Lewis, let's pray the Lord's Prayer together."

Lewis nodded in agreement, and Katharina began,

"Our Father, who art in *Heaven*. . ."

Lewis feebly joined with, "Hallowed be thy name."

When Katharina got to, "And forgive us our trespasses as we forgive those who trespass against us," she felt bound, in some implausible way, to tell Lewis that she forgave him for murdering her daughter.

When they finished saying, "Amen," Katharina looked down at

the deplorable creature who, she had to reminded herself, was Lewis Heydlauff, the killer. She forced herself to say, "Lewis, I will never understand why you murdered my daughter, but I forgive you."

Katharina had made that most excruciating of all absolutions. She closed her eyes and experienced a feeling of liberation, but when she opened them and looked at Lewis, she was overwhelmed with a desire to see that justice be served on earth.

Lewis cried out in a high pitch, "Why did I kill Emma, oh, why did I do it . . . why, why?"

When the guard heard this, he told Mrs. Moeckel that her time was up, and to finish with her visit.

Katharina had one last thing to do before leaving Lewis; she reached into her bag for the silver locket. She took Lewis's right hand and placed the locket into his palm and pressed it closed. She whispered, "I want you to have this," then impulsively kissed him on his forehead, immediately feeling repulsed by her spontaneous act of kindness.

Lewis opened his hand and seeing what it was, groaned and began sobbing. He then cried out, "Oh Emma, why did it have to happen . . . why Emma, why?"

The guard looked on disapprovingly.

Lewis then whined, "Thank you, Mrs. Moeckel," and released a long sigh. He then tightly closed the hand clutching the locket and moved it to his chest. He then groaned, "I'm tired," and rolled to his side and curled into a fetal position.

The guard announced, "Time's up," and Katharina left the room. The guard then closed and locked the door.

On the return trip to Munith, Katharina was saddened by seeing what had become of Lewis, but calmed by her bold act of forgiveness, and imagined Lewis faithfully reading the Holy Bible—in prison.

The next morning, Saturday, June 20, Lewis Heydlauff was transferred to a standard cell within the Jackson County Jail. His living quarter was now a brick cell measuring six by eight feet with a hard concrete floor. Lewis was provided a thin mattress to be placed atop a steel platform, a wool blanket, pillow, one towel, a comb, one tin spoon, one tin cup, a small basin and water pitcher, a round steel stool, a square wooden box with a drawer, and a metal chamber pot that required emptying each morning. The cell was secured by a locked steel door with a small, narrow opening near the top, and a hinged opening near the bottom used for meals. Lighting came through the opening at the top of the door, and during the day, additional light from an iron grated window high on the cell's east-facing wall.

CHAPTER EIGHTEEN

MELANCHOLIA

After arriving at the county jail, Lewis Heydlauff had been treat-ed by two physicians: his personal doctor, John E. Conlan of Munith, and by the county jail doctor, Charles DeWitt Colby, who cared for him daily the first few days, then every other day until Lewis was transferred to the confines of a standard cell.

One week before Lewis was moved, defense attorney John Miner had asked Dr. Colby about Lewis Heydlauff's overall condition. The doctor told him that the patient was recovering, but that he was still experiencing substantial pain in the area where he had shot himself. Dr. Colby told the lawyer that he wanted to probe for the bullet still imbedded in his abdomen for fear of an infection, but that Heydlauff refused to allow him to do so. When Miner asked the doctor why the patient refused, Dr. Colby said that Heydlauff told him he did not care if he got an infection—the patient had no desire to live.

Upon hearing this, John Miner asked, "Do you think the boy will live?"

Dr. Colby responded, "The boy has made a remarkable recovery. Most men inflicted with similar injuries wouldn't live. I believe the patient has beaten the odds and will survive."

"Even with a bullet lodged in his abdomen?" Miner inquired.

"The body will often grow a mass around a foreign object to isolate it; I believe that is what's happening."

John Miner then asked Dr. Colby, "Why do you think he hopes to die?"

"I've thought about it. I believe it's because he doesn't want to live with the guilt over what he did. Out of despair he committed a dreadful crime against the girl—and to himself. She died; he wanted to—and he didn't."

Miner contemplated the doctor's opinion before asking, "Do you think the boy may have been led to insanity because the girl rejected him?"

"I've thought about that as well. I don't know. It was probably a crime of passion; he was jealous and got rejected. What man wouldn't be emotionally unstable if the girl he loved jilted him for another man?"

"Most men wouldn't kill the girl they loved, and then attempt suicide," Miner remarked.

"Most men are not driven by jealousy or rejection to be crazy enough to commit such an act," Dr. Colby quickly replied.

Miner seized on the opportunity when the doctor said *crazy*. "Dr. Colby, when you say, 'Most men wouldn't kill the girl they loved,' do you think the boy could be suffering from a disease of the brain?"

The doctor put his hands behind his head, leaned back, looked pensively at John Miner and commented, "That's an interesting question. The patient definitely committed a terrible crime, whether it was from emotional distress or a form of brain disease, well, that's a difficult diagnosis to make."

Miner then asked, "Do you think it possible that the Heydlauff boy could be suffering from a form of brain disease known as melancholia?"

"Um . . . melancholia? Well, the boy does say he doesn't want to live, and that is a symptom of melancholia. My understanding of the disease is that there are many symptoms: depression, loss of appetite, insomnia, morose and broody behavior, loss of memory—and in severe cases, violent and suicidal thoughts. I have not observed many of these symptoms with the Heydlauff boy, but that is an interesting theory."

"Doctor, if the boy was suffering from melancholia when he shot the girl, do you think he would remember what he did?"

"Ah . . . another excellent question, Mr. Miner. There could be a loss of memory. That would be determined by how the patient would answer questions asked by a medical expert."

"Dr. Colby, may I ask that you conduct such an interview with Lewis Heydlauff, and offer to me your expert opinion?"

"Certainly, Mr. Miner, but I will require adequate notice."

"Would one week be sufficient?"

"Yes, that should do."

Having delivered his intended message to the jailhouse physician, John Miner's next step was to talk with Lewis about Dr. Charles DeWitt Colby's upcoming interview, and what questions to expect.

First Day in Common Cell

The next afternoon, Sunday, June 21, John Miner came to visit Lewis at his new accommodations in the county jail.

Standing next to a guard outside Lewis's cell, Miner called to his client through the small opening on the cell's steel door, "Good day Lewis, how are you feeling in there?"

Lewis stood and griped, "I'm OK, I guess. Mr. Miner, ya know what . . . Mrs. Moeckel came to see me on Friday."

"Lewis, may I come in for a visit?"

Lewis answered, "Sure, if you want."

The guard unlocked the cell door and allowed the lawyer to enter, then closed and locked him in with the prisoner.

"Lewis, may I sit on this stool?"

"Sure, Mr. Miner, I'll sit on my bed."

Surprised to learn that Katharina Moeckel had visited Lewis, Miner asked how he felt about seeing Emma's mother. Lewis told of her visit and that she forgave him for what he had done.

"Mrs. Moeckel said she forgave you?"

"Yes, Mr. Miner. She said that's what we're supposed to do—forgive anyone who hurts us when they break God's law. She forgave me for what I did to Emma."

Astonished to hear this, Miner asked, "How did that make you feel, Lewis?"

"Better. And she even gave me Emma's silver locket, the one I gave her for Christmas. Mr. Miner, my girl loved it."

With that new information, Miner was given the opening he could only have dreamed for. If Lewis felt *forgiven*, perhaps he would be inclined to live—rather than die—and get involved with his defense.

"That was very thoughtful of Mrs. Moeckel."

Lewis smirked and agreed, "I know; Mrs. Moeckel likes me. She even kissed me before she left."

"She kissed you? That was also very thoughtful of her."

Miner was taken aback with Lewis's expression—it was the first time since meeting with his client that he had formed anything resembling a smile, but this was not a smile. Miner was also mystified by what Katharina Moeckel had done. She forgave Lewis for killing her daughter and then kissed him—was she the crazy one?

Miner moved on with his reason for visiting.

"Lewis, I had a talk with Dr. Colby yesterday. We talked about your health, which thankfully is improving, and of what may have caused you to do what you did."

Lewis's eyes opened wide.

"Dr. Colby has a theory as to what caused you to shoot Emma and yourself. He believes it possible that you may have been suffering from a brain condition on that morning, you know, the morning that you surely want to forget."

Lewis cocked his head and continued listening.

"Dr. Colby believes it possible that the awful emotions you were experiencing were because of what happened between you and Emma. You must have felt terrible when you saw Emma at the circus with another man. Who wouldn't be heartbroken—no, more like devastated—to see his girl betraying him? Lewis, those horrible emotions may have taken control of your mind and triggered a brain condition called melancholia. People who have melancholia forget things. Lewis, if you had melancholia when you shot Emma and yourself, you may not actually remember doing it. Lewis, think very carefully: do you actually remember shooting Emma?"

Lewis folded his arms and looked up to the small window in his cell. For several moments John Miner waited—he was in no hurry to have his answer. Lewis finally lowered his eyes and began stuttering as he mumbled, "Um, uh . . . I don't know."

"Lewis, what was the first thing you remember after the shooting?"

Lewis buried his head into his hands and started stomping his feet on the concrete floor and grumbled, "Mr. Miner, I don't want to talk about it."

Miner stopped his questioning and waited for his client to end his strange outburst.

Lewis stopped and took a deep breath, raised his head and, avoiding eye contact, looked at his lawyer and meekly stuttered, "No . . . I don't think . . . no, I don . . . I think . . . no Mr. Miner, I don't."

Miner looked compassionately at his client. "Lewis, I didn't think so. I believe you were suffering from brain disease when it happened. It started when you heard that Emma, your sweetheart, was being seen with another man. When you pleaded with her to stop and she didn't, your emotions, your painful emotions, sickened your brain with melancholia. Lewis, you were sick, that's why you can't remember much of that morning," Miner ascertained.

Lewis began coughing.

"Lewis, do you want some water?"

"Yes, thank you Mr. Miner."

Miner filled the tin cup and handed it to him. Lewis attempted a sip, but his throat was so parched that he had difficulty swallowing; water dribbled down his chin as he gulped.

Miner waited to allow Lewis to quench his thirst. Then, already knowing the answer, he asked, "Lewis, that other man, the one who tried to steal Emma for himself, who was he?"

Lewis grimaced, looked to the floor, and grumbled, "George Tisch."

"Lewis, I know that you loved Emma. I bet that made you very angry."

Lewis began tearing and replied, "Yes, I felt bad. I even wrote Emma a letter reminding her that she was my girl and that I needed her. I said in my letter that if she didn't come back I didn't wanna live no more. She wrote back and said she didn't care—she was now with Tisch."

"Lewis, you must have been angry when you read her letter."

"Yes, I was. I wanted my girl back. Emma was my sweetheart."

John Miner studied his client's expressions. Lewis looked tired but was listening alertly. Miner asked another leading question, "Lewis, another symptom of melancholia is depression. Did you feel depressed while this was happening?"

"Ah . . . yes, Mr. Miner. Yes, I was definitely feeling very low."

"Lewis, someone who suffers from melancholia is called a melancholic. A melancholic will often have a stooped posture and hang their head low, sometimes not even being aware of where they are—it's called a hangdog look."

"Hangdog, I never heard of a hangdog." Lewis mumbled and coughed again.

"Lewis, when I spoke with Dr. Colby about you, he showed me how a melancholic sometimes walks. I'll show you," and with that being said, John Miner pulled his stool to the wooden box and walked away to the cell wall. He then dropped his head and walked very slowly across the cement floor to the wooden box, where he stopped, and remained with his head drooped. He then sat on the stool and dropped his elbow to the box, leaned his head on his hand, and looked down to the floor without saying a word. After waiting silently for a minute, Miner stood, looked inquisitively at his client and asked, "Lewis, have you ever found yourself walking or sitting like that?"

Lewis fidgeted and answered apprehensively, "I . . . I . . . don't think . . . no, maybe, maybe I remember, but . . . no . . . I don't quite re . . . remember . . . but yes . . . yes, maybe I do."

"Lewis, if Dr. Colby determines that melancholia was responsible for your actions, we will use it in your defense. The doctor can see you later this week. Is that OK with you?"

"Yes, that's OK. Mr. Miner, I'm tired; I need to rest. Can we talk later?"

"Lewis, yes, please get some rest; we can continue our talk later."

Lewis rolled over onto his mattress and lowered his head to his pillow.

John Miner called for the guard, who then came and unlocked the steel door and released him.

After Miner left, Lewis began thinking about what was ahead of him, his thoughts foreshadowed by the dread of living the remainder of his life in a stark, dank cell with a cold cement floor, and he wanted to learn more about melancholia.

After leaving Jackson County Jail, John Miner was satisfied that Lewis received his intended message.

Miner walked quickly to his office where he immediately sent word to Richard Price that he wanted to meet with him soon as possible. Price marked his calendar for Tuesday, June 23, at 9:00 a.m.

CHAPTER NINETEEN

·•·———⟨ৎ⟩✺⟨ৎ⟩———·•·

PRELIMINARY ARRAIGNMENT

On Monday, June 22, 1896, twenty-three days after the murder of Emma Moeckel, Lewis Heydlauff was deemed strong enough to be arraigned in Justice D. Gibbs Palmer's court. He was represented by defense attorney, John W. Miner, and for the people, Jackson County Prosecuting Attorney Charles A. Blair. The accused entered the court with Miner, who immediately demanded an examination of the case—a formality to make certain the prosecution had convinced the judge that it had ample evidence and probable cause to move the case forward—which was granted and scheduled for Monday, July 6, at 1:00 p.m. Lewis was returned to his cell where he would wait two weeks until his next court date.

There were very few people besides the Heydlauff family in the courtroom, it not being generally known that Lewis was to appear in court that day. In fact, the arraignment time had not been decided until the day before.

John Miner met with Richard Price the next morning to update him on the next court date. More importantly, Miner detailed his two conversations: the meeting with jailhouse physician, Dr. Charles DeWitt Colby, and his talk with their client, Lewis Heydlauff.

"Well done, John, excellent! This is the opening we needed to get the ball rolling. I've already talked with some medical experts about the case. Two of them are Dr. John Main, and his son Fred, who practice medicine together here in Jackson. Doctors Main and Main are well experienced in treating patients suspected of suffering from episodes of emotional insanity. As I expected, they prefer to use the classification of melancholia, especially the elder Dr. Main. He's been in practice for almost forty years, and I'm certain his son will agree with his father's conclusions. As we have agreed, John, melancholia is the mental term we will use in our client's defense."

"Dr. John Main—didn't he testify in the Pelky versus Palmer case?" Miner asked.

"Yes, he did. Dr. John Main testified in the Pelky malpractice case before the Michigan Supreme Court last June in Lansing. He succinctly explained to the Court that having only one medical doctor in town doesn't protect him from malpractice; a bad doctor is still a bad doctor. The circuit court had ruled for the doctor, but Dr. Main convinced the Supreme Court otherwise, who then reversed the ruling in favor of the plaintiff.

"John Main also testified in the Latimer murder trial a few years back. In that case he testified as an expert on the subject of blood.

"More recently, Dr. Main has become recognized as an expert on brain disease, and has been frequently called to evaluate patients as to whether or not they should be sent to an asylum. The doctor is exceptionally scholarly and carries himself with powerful authority. Furthermore, Dr. Main possesses an extensive and convincing medical vocabulary—if he says someone is insane, trust me, you will assume that person is insane. On the witness stand, our venerable doctor will be extremely difficult to discredit. His son, Fred, is considerably younger but almost equally effective."

From the time Miner brought him into the Heydlauff case, Richard Price had been interviewing various medical experts who were available to interview Lewis Heydlauff—for a fee—to determine his medical condition and testify as to their diagnosis.

Price continued, "John, I've also spoken to another medical expert, Dr. John DeMay. He also gave excellent testimony in the Pelky case. I believe we need more than a father-and-son practice to convince the jury that Heydlauff has a brain disease. Dr. DeMay will testify from a different perspective. Rather than using the term *temporary insanity*, he prefers to call it *acute insanity*. Nevertheless, he will arrive at the same conclusion as I suspect from the two Dr. Mains. Dr. DeMay has more than enough experience with crazy people."

Miner nodded with approval when Price promised that the three physicians were willing to testify as experts.

Price added, "John, from what you say, Dr. Colby, the jail's physician, may very well come to the same conclusion, especially after being associated with our experts in the arena of insanity, who's combined opinion will be that Lewis Heydlauff is nuts."

John Miner smiled as he assured, "We will overwhelm the prosecution with our medical experts."

Price then explained to John Miner that the defense for Lewis Heydlauff would officially be *general insanity*, and be used as the basis for determining melancholia as the brain disease that would lead to their client's infliction with emotional insanity.

Miner smiled ear to ear and said, "Clever. By the way, Richard, you are now officially on my team, so make sure to enter your billing hours in your ledger, including what you have already done."

CHAPTER TWENTY

THE OTHER VICTIM

Emma Moeckel's murder had become a major topic of conversation throughout the area. In Waterloo, local folk were wondering how John and Christina Heydlauff must feel having raised a murderer, and how Friederich and Katharina Moeckel must be suffering after losing their daughter in such an awful way. The question always came around to, "Why did the Heydlauff boy do it?"

There was talk of Lewis being a drunkard. There was hearsay of Lewis treating Emma poorly. There were rumors of Emma being seen frequently with another man. But there was general agreement that Lewis Heydlauff must be crazy—why else would he murder the girl he loved? There was speculation by some that Emma had left Lewis for George Tisch, and that Tisch should never have put himself between Emma and Lewis.

What the community did not know was that George Tisch was devastated.

During the month of May, Emma and George had become best of friends and were falling in love. The community was unaware that George had helped Emma through a great crisis in her life. They had no knowledge that George consoled her during her darkest days—that George had become Emma's confidant. Except for George's family—and perhaps the Moeckels'—the community had no knowledge that George was crushed by Emma's violent death.

George hid his feelings as he went about his daily business. However, insensitive glances from some in the community began almost immediately. He often rode to town. Along the way acquaintances frequently ignored him. In town, persons he had known for years were hesitant to engage in conversation. At church, some parishioners would ask how he was doing, and then briskly leave him standing. Too many rumors and not enough answers were poisoning George's reputation in the community.

George felt awful about it all. When his workdays were finished, he frequently retired to his bedroom and silently wept for Emma. He tried to remember their first kiss, but his memory was lost when he thought of Emma dead on the floor. He longed for the feeling he had experienced when he was with her, but that evaded him. He tried closing his eyes, hoping to see Emma's beautiful face, her enchanting green eyes—but the only vision he could conjure was Emma lying motionless in a pool of blood. George knew he had loved Emma, but could no longer feel it.

As weeks passed, George tried his best to create a facade to the community that he was no different than before that fateful day. But distorted gossip led to absurdities that followed him almost everywhere he went.

George's family knew the truth and was aware of George's suffering. They consoled him, but were unable to ease his anguish for Emma.

The family tried to assure George that he had nothing to do with Emma's death. They knew that George was tortured by an unwarranted guilt: guilt that he should have known that Lewis was in Emma's house, guilt for wanting to run from the tragedy, guilt for getting involved with Emma at all, guilt for loving her. The family did what they could to help make George feel good about himself.

It was to be a long journey.

CHAPTER TWENTY-ONE

EXAMINATION BEFORE THE COURT

On Monday, July 6, 1896, Lewis Heydlauff was brought from the county jail to the Jackson County Courthouse on Main Street. He was led into Justice Palmer's court by two guards, where he was met by his parents and defense attorney, John Miner.

Standing at the judge's bench were Jackson County Prosecuting Attorney Charles Blair and Friederich and Katharina Moeckel, who looked on as the contingent arrived.

The small courtroom was mostly filled with family and friends of the Moeckels and Heydlauffs. Newspaper reporters and some Jackson residents who were following the case sat or stood near the rear.

Following a brief consultation between the attorneys and Justice Palmer, court was called to session.

At 2:00 p.m., Charles Blair called his first witness, Friederich Moeckel. With difficulty, Mr. Moeckel retained his composure during his testimony as he recalled the horrifying event at his residence on Sunday morning, May 31, 1896. While telling of the event, his wife, Katharina, who sat in the first row of seats behind the prosecutor's table, could not repress her tears. Lewis Heydlauff sat motionless with his head hanging low, handkerchief in hand.

At 3:00 p.m., Katharina Moeckel was next called. She, in essence, repeated her husband's testimony as she wept.

Further evidence was given by George Tisch, George Hannewald, and Dr. John E. Conlan, all of whom retold what they had seen and heard the morning of the shooting.

Waterloo's justice of the peace, Orville Gorton, who held the inquest the day of the murder, was last called, and confirmed the conclusion of the coroner's court.

Witness testimony was recorded as evidence by circuit court stenographer, Thomas I. Daniel.

The time was getting late, so Judge Palmer adjourned court until Monday, July 20. Lewis Heydlauff was returned to county jail where he would stay imprisoned until appearing at his next court date in two weeks.

CHAPTER TWENTY-TWO

PRIVATE SERVICE

FRIDAY, JULY 17, 1896

Jackson County News

Waterloo – On Friday, July 17, at 10 o'clock this morning a private service was held at the grave of Emma Moeckel, who was so wickedly and wantonly shot by Lewis Heydlauff, as it was marked by an inscribed granite monument at the German Lutheran cemetery. Service was conducted by Rev. Emil Wenk, pastor of St. Jacob Lutheran Church.

CHAPTER TWENTY-THREE

EXAMINATION, CONTINUED

Monday, July 20, arrived and the examination of the Lewis Heydlauff case from two weeks earlier was resumed in Justice Palmer's court.

The murdered girl's brother, Albert Moeckel, gave evidence of what he saw the morning his sister was killed.

It was getting late, so Justice Palmer adjourned court until the next morning at 9:00 a.m.

Next Day

Court was continued on Tuesday, July 21, during which additional evidence was given, all consistent with the prior accounts.

Justice Palmer asked Prosecuting Attorney Charles Blair if there were any additional witnesses to be called, to which he answered, "No, Your Honor."

Justice Palmer then asked the defendant's attorney, John Miner, what he intended to use for his client's defense, to which Miner stated, "General insanity."

Heydlauff was returned to his jail cell where he would await arraignment for his crime.

CHAPTER TWENTY-FOUR

BUILDING THE DEFENSE

John Miner agreed to take the Heydlauff case before reading the testimonies given at the inquest in Waterloo. After Miner analyzed the initial evidence, he was uncertain how best to defend his client, initially considering a voluntary manslaughter plea as the safest approach. But after realizing the sum of money that could be available from John Heydlauff to defend his son, Miner discussed the case with his colleague, Richard Price, who explained how to work the emotional insanity defense, who was then asked to join the team.

Price had been meeting once a week with Miner since joining the Heydlauff case. The two lawyers had been discussing how to deal with the damning evidence against their client. Options ranged from offering the pretrial guilty plea for voluntary manslaughter to arranging for Heydlauff to be deemed unfit for trial because he was hopelessly insane.

Their client's father had previously frowned on a plea, even though it could reduce his son's prison time, and had all but rejected the option of having Lewis declared insane and sent to the asylum for the criminally insane, even though he would eventually be deemed sane and released.

Price insisted on structuring a case for acquittal. He assumed that Prosecuting Attorney Charles Blair considered the case solid for a murder conviction, and might possibly be unprepared for an onslaught of testimony from physicians called as expert witnesses. Price agreed that manslaughter was the likely outcome, but told Miner, "Let's go for broke. After all, John Heydlauff is paying for it."

Miner told Price, "I think you're the one who should be sent to the madhouse—or maybe we should both be committed!"

Price shrugged and quipped, "John, it's a long shot, but if we choose the jury members very carefully and play our cards close to our vests, we might catch Blair off guard—then everything is possible."

Miner wanted to share Price's optimism, but reminded himself that juries were sometimes unpredictable, and could render verdicts that seemed to make no sense whatsoever.

Trident

Lewis's arraignment for murder was expected to occur within the next few weeks, so following the July 21 examination in Judge Palmer's court, Miner and Price settled upon a blueprint for their emotional insanity defense: melancholia-induced temporary insanity.

The two lawyers settled on a plan they named "Trident." Trident consisted of three elements: defend, deny, attack.

First: defend. The lawyers will demonstrate to the jury, through multiple witness testimonies, that Lewis Heydlauff has always been known to be a righteous person, a good and sober person, a peaceful person held in high esteem by the community, and a person who has never shown malice to anyone.

Second: deny. The defense will demonstrate how deeply their client loved his girl, a love so profound that only a circumstance out of his control could have led to the tragedy. The defense will prove that Lewis's devotion to Emma Moeckel was so great that it was impossible for him to have any motive to harm her, least of all, to kill her.

Third: attack. The defense will deflect attention away from Heydlauff by vilifying the other man, painting him as a covetous rival who caused their client's plunge into the darkness of emotional insanity—*temporary* insanity. The lawyers decided to use expert witness testimonies from various physicians to sway the jury into believing their client was unknowingly sick—sick with a dormant, underlying brain disease known as melancholia. The lawyers will illustrate how the emotional shock of Lewis's Heydlauff's sweetheart leaving him after being swooned by another left him so fragile it allowed his melancholia to trigger a response—a response so severe that his insanity surfaced just moments before Emma Moeckel was shot, and his memory of the event was forever lost.

Therefore, Lewis Heydlauff had no motive and no memory—because he was temporarily insane—and was not responsible for the girl's death.

Considering the crushing evidence against their client, Miner and Price thought their plan was a long shot.

John Miner then met with John Heydlauff to explain Trident, to which he approved.

Miner had already seeded the plan with Lewis.

———— ⟨∽⟩ ————

Miner and a law apprentice began interviewing Lewis Heydlauff's relatives, friends, and prominent folks, including public officials that John Heydlauff recommended.

The scripted questions included: How do you know Lewis? How long have you known Lewis? What do you think of him? These questions included a subset: Have you ever known Lewis to be violent? Have you ever seen Lewis drink whiskey? Are you willing to testify as to what you have said?

Miner catalogued his potential witnesses as yes, maybe, and no.

Richard Price had targeted and interviewed physicians who could be called as expert witnesses. He chose three who were recognized for their knowledge of brain diseases. He decided upon the well-respected Dr. John Main, his son Dr. Fred Main, and Dr. John DeMay. The Jackson County Jail physician, Dr. Charles DeWitt

Colby, was chosen because he had treated Heydlauff at the county jail, and after being flattered by John Miner when asked to interview Heydlauff to determine his sanity, realized that he could offer an opinion of insanity just as well as the experts in the case. With the exception of Dr. Colby, the doctors agreed to compensation for their time to interview and analyze Lewis, and then testify in court.

Dr. Colby would later be offered an unsolicited stipend for his time.

Medical experts who testify in court have an effective technique of asking leading questions of their subjects to attain the results they want.

Lewis Heydlauff was identified as a suitable and willing subject.

Miner and Price spent considerable time determining the order of calling their witnesses to the stand. They agreed that Lewis Heydlauff was to appear first, expecting that his anticipated behavior would support the medical experts' conclusions.

The lawyers decided to intersperse the physicians' testimonies with character witnesses, and with some who would testify that Lewis was acting strangely leading to the shooting.

CHAPTER TWENTY-FIVE

ARRAIGNMENT

On Monday, September 14, a number of men whose cases appeared on the criminal docket were arraigned in circuit court. Among the group was twenty-five-year-old Lewis H. Heydlauff, charged with the murder of Miss Emma M. Moeckel.

Heydlauff appeared before the Honorable Erastus Peck of the Michigan Fourth Judicial Circuit in his county jail uniform: dark gray slacks secured by drawstring, and a matching collarless shirt. He looked gaunt, his face ashen and unshaven.

With his shoulders drooped and head lowered, Heydlauff stood in front of Judge Peck as Jackson County Prosecuting Attorney Charles A. Blair read the murder charge and related information to the court.

Judge Peck, in a monotone voice, asked Heydlauff, "To this information what do you plead?"

Heydlauff stood motionless and neglected to respond.

Judge Peck asked again, "What do you plead?"

Representing his client, John Miner stepped forward and spoke for Heydlauff, entering a plea of, "Not guilty."

Miner then asked that bail be set for his client, which was denied.

Heydlauff was returned to his jail cell to await trial, which was placed on the court's docket for December 14, 1896.

As the courtroom emptied, John Miner approached Charles Blair and asked, "Charles, may I have a word with you?"

"What can I do for you, John?" Blair cordially replied.

"Charles, the defendant's father, John Heydlauff, is willing to spend a great amount of money in defense of his son. I explained to him that an option may be a guilty plea for voluntary manslaughter in exchange for reduced prison time. Are you agreeable to consider a plea?"

Blair smiled and said, "John, considering the evidence against your client, the chance for an acquittal is zero—a murder conviction is all but certain. It's unlikely that the jury would convict on the lesser charge of manslaughter, but if they did, your client will receive the full sentence for his crime. John, he murdered an innocent girl in cold blood. No, I will not agree to a plea."

John Miner had received the answer he expected, and would share it with John Heydlauff—should he ask.

CHAPTER TWENTY-SIX

<figure>⁕⸱—◦◦◦◦—⸱⁕</figure>

PROSECUTION STRATEGY

The Jackson County prosecuting attorney is an elected position, but Charles A. Blair had not been elected—he was actually appointed to serve the final fifteen months of his brother's term. Charles' brother, George H. Blair, was the duly elected Jackson county prosecutor, but had unexpectedly resigned at the end of August, 1895. Charles had decided not to run for the following term, beginning January 1, 1897, because he had formed a new law firm with two colleagues that would open its doors that same day in January.

Charles Blair was pleased that the Heydlauff murder case was receiving considerable interest. Nothing better than a conviction to leave office with; it would help build the firm. It was also excellent publicity for the assistant prosecuting attorney, Henry E. Edwards, who was running as Blair's successor on the Republican ballot against the Democratic Party's nominee, Elmer Kirkby, in the November 3, 1896, general election.

Blair was impressed by the immense hype the Heydlauff case had been receiving from the two Jackson newspapers, the *Patriot* and the *Daily Citizen*. The case had also drawn attention from other counties in Michigan and their regional newspapers, including Washtenaw's *Ann Arbor Argus,* Saginaw's *Saginaw Evening News,* Lenawee's *Adrian Daily Telegram*, St. Clair's *Yale Expositor*, Van Buren's *True Northerner*, Ingham's *Stockbridge Sun*, and others.

The story was full of intrigue—love, liquor, jealousy, murder, attempted suicide—and amongst three prominent families. It was the type of story that reporters sought and publishers cherished—it sold scores of papers.

Blair had assigned Jackson County's thirty-two-year-old assistant prosecuting attorney, Henry Edwards, to the Heydlauff case following the May 31 inquest in Waterloo. Other than a regular weekly briefing with Edwards, Blair's meetings with him on the case were infrequent.

Lewis Heydlauff had been formally arraigned for the murder of Emma Moeckel on September 14, and the trial was placed on the docket for Monday, December 14, 1896. Edwards had examined evidence from the scene of the murder, evaluated witness testimonies taken at the inquest and examination, interviewed the witnesses and others related to the event, and from early discovery, knew that the defense would be calling on expert witnesses to support the insanity defense for their client.

Blair scheduled a meeting with Edwards for Monday afternoon, September 21, at 1:00 p.m. He had Edwards send his file on the Heydlauff case beforehand.

Charles Blair was at his desk on September 21 looking through the Heydlauff file when Edwards arrived at precisely 1:00 p.m. Before any pleasantries were exchanged, Blair stated, "Henry, the information in this file clearly indicates that Lewis Heydlauff had a motive. There's an abundance of incriminating evidence from the scene of the murder, and testimony from several people that Heydlauff admitted to shooting the poor girl. Do you agree?"

Still standing, Edwards replied, "Yes, Charles, everything I've researched—the witness testimonies, the physical evidence, the circumstantial evidence, Heydlauff's own admissions—it all leads to a conviction for murder. Three witnesses have already testified that Heydlauff admitted to the shooting on the day of the murder.

Edwards finally sat and continued, "Waterloo's Justice Gordon met with Heydlauff a couple days after the murder and will testify that the defendant admitted to him that he shot the girl. And, as you may have already seen in my notes, I've interviewed some of the defendant's family. Heydlauff has a cousin who also claims the defendant admitted to shooting the girl."

Blair smiled and asked, "Henry, what are your thoughts on John Miner using emotional insanity for the defense?"

"Miner's client has admitted that he killed the girl to at least five people. What else do they have?"

Both attorneys paused and pondered the question. Blair then asked, "It looks like they're talking to some of our local physicians. What do you know of that?"

Edwards answered, "That's their plan. Miner has teamed with Richard Price, who will work the insanity angle. It's certain he will contact Dr. John Main. Dr. Main has become quite respected in the study of insanity and welcomes being called as an expert in court cases. His son, Fred, is also a physician, and he's building a reputation for diagnosing diseases of the brain. I suspect Price will use him as well."

"Yes, I'm sure Dr. John Main will spend fifteen minutes with Lewis Heydlauff and declare him crazy for a fee," Blair jokingly replied.

Edwards cautioned, "Dr. Main can be an effective witness."

"I know, Henry, but this case will be a straightforward conviction."

Edwards responded, "Charles, no doubt, but the defendant's father, John Heydlauff, is quite wealthy and will surely spend a small fortune to defend his son from going to prison. He's engaged John Miner—Miner is quite good at working the jury. Miner is using Heydlauff money to hire Richard Price, and will use more for physicians that will testify that his son was mad as a cuckoo when he killed the poor girl."

Blair warned, "The defense will spin an untruthful tale. Our job is to not veer from the facts. We must keep the jury from being deceived. Any competent juror will see that the facts are irrefutable, that whatever the defense throws out is fabricated. The fact is that Lewis Heydlauff killed Emma Moeckel because she left him for another man. That's motive with malice, it's as simple as it gets. Henry, keep this in mind: our responsibility is to present only the facts. The defense can make up any story they want. We're bound by the truth—they are not. The defense will call witnesses to support an intriguing story that the facts will discredit.

"We'll see their witness list soon enough," Edwards promised.

"Henry, that doesn't matter. We only require witnesses who matter. We need those who will support the motive, those who were there when it happened, and those who the defendant admitted the shooting to. Our witnesses—along with the physical evidence, which is substantial—will dispel any doubts whatsoever."

"We have it all," Edwards assured Blair.

Blair smiled and joked, "Henry, if we can't convince the jury that Heydlauff is guilty of murder, everybody is crazy!"

They had a good laugh.

Edwards then mentioned that there was information that Lewis Heydlauff was a boozer.

"Yes, Henry, the newspapers have indicated he was drinking a lot before the killing. Bringing alcohol into the prosecution could potentially lead the jury to reduce their verdict to manslaughter. The jurors might figure that if Heydlauff was drunk at the time he shot the girl, he did it in an emotional rage. Henry, we want to establish that Heydlauff was sane when he planned the killing, and sober when he carried out his plan. He's guilty of murder, nothing less."

Blair told Edwards to continue being in contact with their witnesses and to learn what he could of the defense's activities. Both agreed to meet frequently leading to the trial.

CHAPTER TWENTY-SEVEN

ONE WEEK BEFORE THE TRIAL

For many, the six months between Emma's death and the final week leading to Lewis Heydlauff's December 14 trial seemed like an eternity of endless dread.

For the Moeckels, each court procedure and every meeting with the prosecution attorneys invoked memories of Emma's murder. Time and time again, either Blair or Edwards were probing for more information about what they knew of Lewis and his relationship with their daughter. He asked them to write down any memories of Lewis's behavior as it changed leading up to Emma's death. He implored them to ask other family members, friends, and acquaintances if they had ever heard Lewis talk discouragingly about Emma, and if they had witnessed or heard of Lewis ever threatening her. Friederich and Katharina did their best to assist, but it was excruciatingly difficult—they believed there was already more than enough evidence to convict Lewis.

Worse than being forced to endure the ugly memories during the legal proceedings, they were becoming unnerved by the judicial system itself. The Moeckels lived by honesty and integrity. During the preliminary proceedings, the chicanery that Lewis's lawyers used to alter the truth—*emotional insanity?*—was to them a great lie. The Moeckels knew the truth: Lewis Heydlauff was resentful that Emma had put him out; Lewis would not allow her to be with another man;

Lewis carried a loaded revolver into their peaceful home and cleverly made conversation with the family; Lewis waited for Emma to come home, followed her until he was alone with her, then shot and killed her. Lewis admitted to it—how could anyone claim anything but cold-blooded murder?

The instant Emma was killed events were put in motion that forever changed the peaceful existence for each member of the Moeckel family. The emotional shock to Emma's parents and her two brothers implicitly changed their lives. Emma's brother, Albert, developed a nervous condition. He was often very restless, which caused him to have difficulty concentrating and remembering to do little things he was asked to do. Emma's youngest brother, Florenz, became unusually quiet. His frequent smiles and laughter were mostly absent. There were times when Florenz went to his bedroom and stared at a photograph of Emma that she had given him only days before she died.

Emma's parents were forced to do things no loving parent would ever think of: washing blood from their daughter's cold, lifeless body; dressing her rigid corpse into her favorite gown; enduring the heartrending funeral; watching the coffin containing their beloved daughter lowered into a dark grave; and later returning to relive it all when a granite gravestone was placed to mark where Emma would forever rest.

There was not a day that Emma's parents did not mourn their loss. Some days were more painful than others, such as birthdays and holidays. Sundays at church were sadly emotional as they pictured their daughter joyfully playing the organ.

Katharina kept a table setting where Emma once sat, and before sitting for supper, Friederich would offer a prayer of grace as he placed his hands on her empty chair, followed by a second prayer for the repose of her soul. Cheerfulness had evaded the Moeckel home since Lewis's act of ultimate wickedness.

During the final weeks leading to the December 14 trial date, Friederich's painful memories were being replaced by profound anger. He was embittered by the thought of facing Lewis in court and having to again testify to the same event, although he was anxious for the trial. Lewis would be served what justice demanded—to be imprisoned for the remainder of his life. Nothing would bring his Emma back, but at least the monster who took her away would languish in a bleak and dismal place until death.

Katharina acknowledged that the trial would result in Lewis's earthly penalty, but she was more concerned with God's ultimate punishment, and prayed for Lewis to surrender to his Creator and plead for forgiveness. Katharina's faith commanded that she forgive all those who did her wrong—including Lewis for what he did to Emma. There was no other option.

As the trial drew near she began questioning the sincerity of her forgiveness and began having misgivings that challenged her faith. Her worries so troubled her that she confided in Pastor Wenk, who advised her not to get in-between Lewis's horrible act and God's judgment, but rather to pray that her faith be strengthened.

After talking with the pastor in his parsonage, Katharina crossed the courtyard and entered the church, where she walked to the front and knelt before the altar. She lowered her head and began praying devoutly for a sign that yes, she was sincere when she gathered the courage to tell Lewis she forgave him, and to stop regretting having done so. As Katharina became engrossed in piety, her prayers carried her to loving thoughts of Emma, and her eyes began moving up to the round, stained glass window above the altar. Katharina was suddenly captured by the image of the delicate white rose blossom. While immersed in a flow of distant memories, she became enchanted by the rose as it began rapidly pulsating until it burst, sending its delicate white petals in all directions. Katharina squeezed her eyes. When she looked again, her sight was blurred. She closed them again. From total blackness, a pin of light immerged and grew, and continued growing. Katharina became overcome by joy when, through the light, she imagined Emma dressed in an elegant white gown in the midst of rose petals falling gently as fresh snowflakes. Emma turned, smiled, and lowered her palms as she lovingly reached out while being pulled away by a great power.

With her eyes still closed, the light vanished and Katharina found peace knowing that Emma was in paradise with the God. She squeezed her eyes tighter and experienced an overwhelming reaffirmation of her faith. Katharina's doubts left her when she opened her eyes.

Katharina looked again at the round window—the window she had passed hundreds of times without notice, and thanked God for the sign she was praying for. Her faith was restored—the sincerity of her forgiveness confirmed.

Katharina rushed home compelled to write a letter to Lewis, which she did. She addressed it to Lewis Heydlauff at the Jackson County Jail, and asked her son, Albert, to post it in Munith.

It was delivered two days later to her daughter's killer, who read it as he awaited the trial for murdering his girl.

Christina Heydlauff dreaded the upcoming trial. She prayed for Lewis, for the Moeckels, and for peace. She knew that her husband had met multiple times with the attorneys representing her son. Christina knew of the defense strategy but did not believe her son to be insane. There were times that Lewis came home angry from the Moeckels, and when she asked why, he often said it was because of a squabble with Emma, and that his girl would get over it. Christina knew Lewis was drinking, but not to the extent she later learned. During the weeks leading to the tragedy, she did not know that Emma had actually put him out. Christina's heart was broken by what her son had done and was unable to comprehend any reason why he did it. The trial was only a few days away—maybe it would provide an answer.

John Heydlauff was obsessed with saving his son from being locked up in prison or being caged in an asylum. Knowing the expense would be considerable, he instructed the lawyers to do whatever was necessary. There was more at stake than Lewis's freedom—he wanted to protect the family name from the shame of having a son guilty of murder or declared crazy.

The trial was days away—he would soon know if his money was well invested.

———◦✇◦———

Other than tending to livestock, George Tisch did not have much to do on the farm, which unfortunately provided more time for him to dwell on the upcoming trial—a trial for a crime he could never have imagined in his worst nightmare. The thought of being called to the witness stand and having to relive that morning—the best and the worst morning of his life—inundated most of his thoughts.

Charles Blair met with George and explained what to expect while being questioned on the witness stand. Blair advised George what to expect from the defense during cross-examination. Blair told George, as best he could predict, of what the defense attorneys may ask, and to provide only what he absolutely remembered. Blair also told George not to worry about it—he wasn't on trial. But George did worry.

———◦✇◦———

Lewis Heydlauff had fully recovered from his self-inflicted gunshot wounds. Over the past few weeks he had frequent visits from his lawyers, who at times brought a doctor along. His parents came frequently. Occasionally, a brother or sister came, especially his sister Sarah, from Ann Arbor. His good friend, Fred Artz Jr., visited twice.

At times the jail's turnkey, Deputy Sheriff William Wheat, had conversations with Lewis, usually about *his girl*. Deputy Wheat was often impressed by Lewis's depth of detail surrounding his stories, which became increasingly dramatic as Lewis's health improved—sobriety and eating regular meals will have that effect. Lewis sometimes said, "Oh . . . to have a shot of good whiskey would be such a delight." Whenever Lewis said anything like that, Deputy Wheat told him that those days were over for him, and it was best he be off booze anyway. Lewis admitted that he did feel better, and that his girl would have been proud of him.

John Miner visited Lewis each day the week before the trial to explain what to anticipate. He told Lewis the type of questions he would be asking, and how to answer them. He told him what to anticipate from the other attorneys, and how to answer those as well. He was told how to dress and how to act. Miner assured Lewis that everything was going to turn out all right—he just had to do as he said.

CHAPTER TWENTY-EIGHT

THE HEYDLAUFF TRIAL

Monday, December 14

Day One

Jury Selection

The trial of Lewis Heydlauff, charged with murder for shooting and causing the death of Miss Emma M. Moeckel, began on Monday afternoon, December 14, 1896, at 1:30 p.m. at the Jackson County Courthouse, home of the Michigan Fourth Judicial Circuit, presided by the Honorable Erastus Peck.

When court was called virtually every seat was taken. Some in the audience were residents of Waterloo, many of whom were women. Others included several newspaper reporters, some curious lawyers, and many local residents.

The defendant's parents, John and Christina Heydlauff, were sitting directly behind the defendant's table, which faced the bench to the left. The parents of the murder victim, John and Katharina Moeckel, sat in the first row opposite the Heydlauffs.

The extraordinary public interest in the Heydlauff murder trial was evidenced by the packed condition of the courtroom. Unfortunately, the inadequacy of the room was strongly shown, notwithstanding the long climb up an iron stairway to the third floor before it was reached, as fully half the room was given up to the judge's platform, the jury box, the county clerk's and stenographer's benches, and the two attorneys' tables. The room was fairly arranged for the purpose of the court, but for the spectators, about eighty persons, it was exceedingly distracting.

Defendant Heydlauff entered the courtroom in the charge of Sheriff Archibald J. Peek. Lewis stood between his two lawyers, John Miner and Richard Price. The defendant's head was hanging low, his eyes downcast.

The people of Jackson County were represented by Prosecuting Attorney Charles Blair and Assistant Prosecuting Attorney Henry Edwards, who used the prosecution table facing the bench on the right, the jury box directly to their right.

Judge Peck was announced as he entered, who then allowed the spectators to take their seats.

The panel of thirty prospective jurors were called and sworn in. Some of the men on the panel were acquainted with each other, having served previously for other court trials.

Charles Blair, for the prosecution, and for the defense, John Miner, were both prepared to interview and evaluate each prospective juror to determine their suitability. The men from the panel were questioned at length by both attorneys. Those acceptable to the prosecution were mostly rejected by defense attorney Miner for being familiar with the case, either by newspaper or hearsay, regardless of their opinions about being impartial and unbiased in the case.

For example, Eugene Straight, of Hanover, volunteered the statement that he had a relative—a second cousin—on trial at Elmira, New York, charged with the murder of his wife and sister-in-law, and that the defense in his relative's case was temporary insanity—but thought he could enter the case with unbiased mind. Mr. Straight was excused on a peremptory challenge by Charles Blair.

As the afternoon dragged on, the panel of thirty men became exhausted. Sheriff Peek was then directed to summon a group of talismen—prospective jurors from outside the original panel—to be interviewed.

The first of the talismen to be called was Ralph Snow. He was acceptable to the attorneys on both sides. Lewis I. Blashfield was next called and then excused, as were Wilson Ketchum, Edgar Rowe, and Charles Cooper.

At 5:00 p.m., jury selection for the day was exhausted. Of the thirty-five men called for the jury, eight were excused for cause. Sixteen others on peremptory challenge, ten by the defense, who clearly did not want to risk having any jurors with the slightest partiality to the events of May 31, and six by the prosecution.

Before adjournment, Judge Peck advised the eleven selected jurymen to refrain from listening to any discussion of the case and to exercise prudence. Judge Peck chose not to have the group sequestered in the charge of a court officer, but said he might issue such an order at a later time. Court adjourned until 9:00 a.m. the next day, at which time the eleven men would occupy the jury box, one short of the required twelve.

During the entire afternoon's proceedings the defendant showed no interest. He simply stayed seated, head bowed, with an indifferent, vacant expression.

The newspaper reporters were pushed back to the center of the room where they complained of not being able to hear the proceedings clearly.

Tuesday, December 15
Day Two
Jury Selection Continues

The defendant took the same position as the day before, sitting between his two lawyers with his head bowed and showing no expression. Across the aisle, the prosecution attorneys had ample space from where they commanded a clear view of the judge, jury to the right, and defendant to the left. Several local attorneys not engaged in the case were lined along the walls or moved about for a better view. Newspaper reporters were again forced to the back of the room, where it was sometimes difficult for them to hear the proceedings. The parents of the accused and the victim sat in the same seats as the day before. Family and friends of both parties occupied remaining seats.

After the opening of court, the continuation of selecting the one remaining juryman began.

As the day before, John Miner was to take no chance of allowing a potentially predisposed juror to serve. For example, Mr. Stephen Wyman of Columbia was catechized at some length, and was evidently not persona grata to the defense, for which he was peremptorily excused. Another talisman, Miles Heyser, of Jackson, was asked the usual questions by Charles Blair, who was satisfied with the answers, but the defense tossed questions at the juror unerringly, ascertained that he read the *Jackson Patriot*, and excused him. Another, William E. Thorne of Jackson was found acceptable by the prosecution, but because he had also read of the event in the *Jackson Patriot*, the defense concluded that his judgment must be tainted, so he was excused. This continued until finally, Orlando W. Pierce, of Jackson, proved to be what each side was looking for. Mr. Pierce said that he read the *Jackson Citizen* and the *Jackson Patriot*, and learned about the case from both papers' columns. Mr. Pierce convinced both lawyers that his mind was not prejudiced by what he had read, and would give the defendant a fair trial. Orlando Pierce was accepted and the jury was finally completed.

The jury names and residences were as follows: juror one, Alfred Sova of Leoni; juror two, Prentice F. Fisher of Rives; juror three, Frank Trist of Napoleon; juror four, Francis E. Olney of Henrietta; juror five, O.J. Chapel of Spring Arbor; juror six, William J. Fisher of Liberty; juror seven, Clarence W. Davis of Jackson second ward; juror eight, Chester McGraw of Jackson third ward; juror nine, Ralph Snow of Jackson third ward; juror ten, John Rockwell of Jackson; juror eleven, Hiram A. Miller of Jackson; juror twelve, Orlando W. Pierce of Jackson third ward.

At this point in the trial, Heydlauff sat with his head resting on his left hand, entirely motionless and apparently oblivious of the impressive proceedings.

John Miner asked the defendant if he was satisfied with the jury, but Lewis made no audible answer.

Judge Peck said, "All right then," and called for an intermission to allow the jury to make necessary arrangements for the duration of their civic service, and then gather in the jury room to elect a foreman and then wait to be called for what was promising to be a long trial. Juror number ten, John Rockwell, was elected foreman by his peers.

Witness Testimony to Begin

Thirty minutes later, the twelve jurymen filed into the courtroom and took their seats in the jury box.

Court stenographer, Thomas I. Daniel, was already seated. Both teams of lawyers sat at their tables, Miner and Price flanking the defendant.

All stood as Judge Peck returned and took his seat at the bench. Court was in session. Judge Peck allowed the courtroom to settle, and then proceeded to give preliminary instructions to the jury. Facing them, the judge explained that it was their sworn duty to determine the facts in the case against the defendant, Lewis Heydlauff. He declared that although the defendant was charged with the murder of Emma Moeckel, he was to be presumed innocent of that charge, and that they alone were the judges to the facts to be presented. He reviewed the process of the trial, telling them that the evidence about to be offered would consist of witness testimony, along with other items that had been received and recorded as exhibits that would be presented as evidence. He further explained what was not evidence, including statements by the attorneys. He explained objections and the meaning of "sustained" and "overruled" and that the jury was to disregard what was said in a sustained objection.

Judge Peck sternly told the jury that they were to consider only the evidence presented in the courtroom and that anything they might hear or read outside the courtroom was to be disregarded. They were not to discuss the case with anyone until they were sent to the jury room to decide on a verdict. He concluded by explaining the process the trial would take, that they were to have open minds throughout the proceedings. Judge Peck said he would give them final instructions prior to retiring to deliberate on the verdict.

Judge Erastus Peck then gave way to opening statements.

The Case for the People

Opening Statement by the Prosecution

Assistant Prosecuting Attorney Henry Edwards approached the jury and studied the face of each juryman. He thanked them for serving, then opened with a statement giving a concise history of the tragedy, detailing the location of both parties in Waterloo, the neighboring farms, and the acquaintance of Lewis Heydlauff and Emma Moeckel, which had developed into affection but was accompanied by little quarrels and jealousy on the part of the defendant. He explained that Miss Moeckel had ended the relationship and that, on at least one occasion, Lewis Heydlauff had threatened to take his life if she refused to come back to him. Edwards told them that Miss Moeckel had left her home to live at the home of Henry Tisch, where she worked, and on occasion, at the Wilhelm Tisch home, both near the village of Munith.

Edwards told that Miss Moeckel had come to Jackson to see a circus on May 30, 1896, with her friend, George Tisch. This so wrought upon the defendant that he followed them to the Jackson rail station and afterward told a brother of Miss Moeckel that if she did not come back to him, he would kill himself. The following Sunday morning the defendant went to the Moeckel house and awaited the arrival of Miss Moeckel, who came home with her friend, George Tisch, in a buggy. Miss Moeckel came into the house and, after greeting her parents, went into the parlor and was followed by the defendant.

Edwards then stated, "What occurred in the next few minutes the prosecution will not attempt to prove."

He went on to describe how Miss Moeckel's mother was preparing for church and Mr. Moeckel was outside with a neighbor. Several shots were heard. Miss Moeckel's father, followed by his family and George Tisch, ran into the parlor and found Miss Moeckel shot to death while Lewis Heydlauff was lying near her, bleeding from self-inflicted wounds. Mr. Moeckel took his gun away when the defendant was outside trying to reload, and then the defendant commenced to beat his head with a stone.

Edwards then said, "The defendant, Lewis Heydlauff, told Dr. John Conlan, of Munith, that he wanted to die; that he could not live without his girl, and could not die and leave her behind to live alone. He implored the doctor to give him drugs that would kill him quickly. The defendant told the same to other witnesses who will testify."

Edwards concluded by saying, "The prosecution has a short story to tell. It all occurred in a few minutes and the witnesses are not numerous."

First Witness for the Prosecution
Friederich Carl Moeckel

Prosecuting Attorney Charles A. Blair called Mr. Friederich Moeckel, father of the murdered girl, as his first witness.

Moeckel stood. He was wearing a black wool suit, a white shirt with a high, rounded collar, and a knotted bow tie. He walked self-assuredly as he approached the witness stand.

The courtroom went quiet as Moeckel was being sworn in by the bailiff. He took his seat on the witness stand. Only the faint sounds of clearing throats and Charles Blair's shoes shuffling on the wooden floor interrupted the hushed silence.

Blair broke the stillness. "Mr. Moeckel, I know being here is not easy for you. I'm going to ask some questions that may be difficult for you to answer, but before I do, please tell the jury about yourself."

Friederich, whose neatly trimmed auburn beard covered much of his face, stated that he was fifty-one years old and had lived in Waterloo for over seventeen years. He said he grew some crops but was primarily a sheep farmer. He described his family as consisting of his wife, Katharina, age thirty-nine, and two sons: Albert, age sixteen, and Florenz, age ten. He cleared his throat before saying that his eldest child, Emma, was twenty when she was killed in the month of May. He then mentioned having lost a son, Arthur, who died six years earlier from influenza at age eight. He stated that he was an elder at St. Jacob Lutheran Church, a quarter mile from his home in Waterloo.

Blair began, "As best you can, Mr. Moeckel, please tell the jury of the defendant's conduct before and at the time of the tragedy at your home on May 31 of this year."

"Last winter Lewis worked for me and stayed mostly at my house. Lewis was friendly to me and my family at first, but later, not so much."

"Did he appear friendly with Emma when he left your house in April?" Blair asked.

Moeckel frowned. The pronounced crow's feet that radiated outward from his hazel eyes grew deeper. He answered, "Lewis was not friendly to Emma when he was sent away."

"Did Emma continue to see Lewis after he left your house?"

"To my knowledge, not at all," Friederich responded.

"Mr. Moeckel, did the defendant approach you Friday, May 29, of this year while you were working in one of your fields?" Blair asked.

"Yes, Lewis came to the field where I was preparing to plant beans. Lewis said he wanted to talk, so I said 'All right.' He said it was about Emma, that his girl had put him out, that Emma had gone back on him and that he was afraid she had abandoned him forever. I told Lewis that he never asked me if he could go with my daughter, and that I would not interfere. I told Lewis that Emma was old enough to look out for herself and could do as she wished. Lewis then went away and I did not see him again until Sunday morning."

Moeckel's voice was fading as he spoke, and began breaking by the time he finished. Blair stopped and allowed him to take a series of deep breaths. When he regained his composure, Blair continued, "Mr. Moeckel, please tell everything you can remember of Sunday morning, May 31, 1896."

Moeckel regained his demeanor and recalled, "On Sunday morning we were dressed for church. A little before nine o'clock, Lewis came to my door and asked if he could come in and wait to see Emma. I let him in and we visited. We talked about the windmill, about farming and sheep shearing."

Blair asked, "Did the defendant speak of Emma?"

"No, only that he wanted to wait for her. Lewis never asked me about Emma. We continued talking about farming."

"Please tell the court what happened when Emma came home."

"Emma arrived from church about thirty minutes later with George Tisch. She had her satchel and said she intended to stay home. Emma was dressed for church." Moeckel's voice broke again.

"Mr. Moeckel, can you continue?" Blair asked.

Friederich Moeckel again regained his composure and continued, "Yes, yes, I can continue. I saw George Tisch in our lane and went outside to ask him to come in. George said it was about church time, but I mentioned there was time before the bell would ring, so George tied his horse and came inside the house with me."

"Where was the defendant when you and Mr. Tisch came into your house?" Blair asked.

"I did not see Lewis in the house anymore," Moeckel replied sharply.

"Did you stay with Mr. Tisch after you came in?" Blair asked.

"No, my neighbor George Hannewald stopped by, so I stepped out to talk to him. Right away we heard shots. Hannewald asked if we had firecrackers in the house and I said no and ran into the house." Moeckel struggled to continue. Very quietly and slowly he said, "I found Emma lying on the floor dead—Lewis had shot himself, too. My wife saw what had happened and was screaming." He stopped to wipe his eyes with his handkerchief, and continued," Lewis asked me to help him up because he said he was dying. I asked him why he killed Emma and Lewis didn't say anything. I told him to stay put. George Hannewald went to get help."

Katharina Moeckel, who was sitting a short distance away in the audience, audibly wept as her husband recalled considerable detail of that Sunday morning in May.

Moeckel went on to say, "I didn't know what to do. I was in shock and distracted and went in and out of the house many times while Hannewald went for Lewis's parents. After Hannewald left, Lewis came out of the house and tried to reload his revolver on the west side of my house, but I took the gun away from him and made him go inside and sit down and stay there until his folks came. Then I saw Lewis was again in the yard, pounding his head with a brick. Lewis fell down and I took the brick and threw it away from him. When I looked back he wasn't moving; I thought Lewis was dead." Moeckel paused for a long time, and then said, "I went back into the house and to the parlor. My wife was wailing over Emma's body. We didn't know what to do. I went back out to see if anyone was coming and Lewis was up again and had another brick and was pounding his head, but he was so weak he couldn't hit very hard and fell over."

Throughout his testimony, Moeckel winced in emotional pain, and frequently strained to speak clearly as he recalled the events. At times he looked at Lewis, who was hunched with his head down. Charles Blair was aware of the difficulty Moeckel was having and decided to conclude his questioning by asking, "Mr. Moeckel, what did you do when Lewis's parents arrived?"

"When Lewis's parents arrived he was loaded on Hannewald's buggy and George took him and his parents away. I had no further talk with Lewis."

Defense attorney John Miner approached Mr. Moeckel and began his cross-examination by asking, "Mr. Moeckel, did Lewis Heydlauff work for you last winter?"

"Yes, he did some work for me; he helped build a windmill."

"Did the defendant live in your house?"

"Yes, as I said earlier, he did for most of the winter," Moeckel answered, noticeably irked by the question—he had said that earlier in his testimony.

"Did you talk with the defendant about Emma during that time?" Miner asked.

"We had little talk of Emma."

"Did the defendant seem down in the dumps at times?" Miner inquired.

"Down in the dumps? What exactly do you mean by that?" Moeckel asked.

"Let me rephrase that, Mr. Moeckel. Was the defendant gloomy, did he seem depressed?"

"Yes, at times he did."

"Do you know why?" Miner asked.

"No. Maybe you can learn why from other witnesses," Moeckel indignantly countered.

Having extracted what he sought, John Miner approached the jury and said, "I wish for the jury to understand that Lewis Heydlauff had been acting queerly, not naturally, for some months leading to the act of which he is accused and that this witness, Mr. Moeckel, freely admits he thought Lewis to be gloomy and depressed when he lived and worked at his house."

Friederich Moeckel was then excused from the stand and returned to his seat incensed by how John Miner had twisted his testimony.

Second Witness for the Prosecution
Doctor John E. Conlan

Next, Charles Blair called Dr. John E. Conlan to the stand. The doctor approached the witness stand dressed in a dark suit with a lighter-colored vest. A silver pocket watch, secured by a watch chain attached to a middle button on his vest, was tucked into its left pocket. His receding hairline exposed a high forehead; his dark sideburns were trimmed on a downward slant to one inch below his ears. He was sworn in by the court to tell the truth and took his seat on the stand.

Dr. Conlan stated that he was born in Chelsea, Michigan, was forty-seven years old, and that he was a physician residing in Munith.

Blair than asked, "Dr. Conlan, please tell the jury at what time you arrived at the Heydlauff home and in what condition you found the defendant."

Conlan looked to the jury and testified, "I arrived at the Heydlauff house at eleven o'clock in the morning, Sunday, May 31. Lewis Heydlauff was lying in bed. He had two bullet wounds. One was a flesh wound far left to his upper abdomen that exited through his left side. The other was left center of his abdomen. That bullet was so far in that I did not succeed in locating it with my probe. The patient also had a bruised head but was fully conscious."

"Did you have any conversation with the defendant?" Blair asked.

"Yes, I had several conversations with the defendant as I was treating him. He was greatly excited and thought he was about to die."

"Did you ask the defendant why he shot Emma?" Blair inquired.

"Yes. Lewis told me he shot Emma because he asked her to take back what she wrote to him in a letter and to be his girl again. When she told him no, he put his arm around his girl and kissed her when he fired his revolver. Lewis said he killed her because he couldn't live without his girl and did not want to leave Emma behind when he killed himself. Lewis told me he then shot himself expecting to die but made a mess out of it. Lewis asked me to give him poison or leave it so he could take it and die. I refused, of course. He asked a second time for poison, saying he couldn't live without Emma and had to die."

Blair then asked, "When you left the Heydlauff house, did you travel to the Moeckel house?"

"Yes, I did."

"Did you examine the body of Emma Moeckel?"

"I did see the dead girl after leaving the Heydlauff house but did not examine the dead girl's wounds. Another physician had made the examination," he explained.

Dr. Conlan was then cross-examined by defense attorney John Miner.

"Dr. Conlan, when you spoke to the defendant about Miss Moeckel did he show any malice toward her?"

"No, he did not."

"You said earlier that the defendant told you during your conversations that before shooting Emma Moeckel, he put his arm around her and kissed her?" Miner asked.

"Yes, that is what the defendant told me. I already mentioned it."

Miner smiled and continued, "Would you conclude that the defendant was in a state of shock when you treated him after the shooting?"

"The patient was excited and agitated by what had occurred," Conlan explained.

"And did the defendant ask more than once for poison so he could die?"

"Yes, as I said earlier, twice and I did not comply."

"Did the defendant appear depressed by what occurred?" Miner probed.

The doctor remained silent for a few seconds and then said, "Lewis Heydlauff appeared despondent over what he had done."

John Miner turned to face the jury and emphatically stated, "The defendant showed no malice toward Emma Moeckel. He was depressed over what had occurred. Lewis Heydlauff loved Emma Moeckel. Lewis Heydlauff was irresponsible by reason of extraordinary excitement, driven to emotional insanity by the loss of his girl. He said he put his arm around his girl and kissed her!"

The courtroom erupted with tears and jeers. For the first time, there was a visible hostility between the Moeckel supporters and those who sat behind Lewis Heydlauff. "Monster," was heard from the back of the courtroom.

At once Judge Peck pounded his gavel loudly and in a bold, loud voice commanded, "Quiet! This is a court of the law and you will remain silent when in the walls of my court. If not, I will have anyone who does not respect the authority of this court removed at once."

The spectators immediately went quiet, allowing Miner to continue his cross-examination of Dr. Conlan.

"Dr. Conlan, how would you describe what makes a man insane?"

Conlan looked straight ahead and offered, "I would say that any person whose mind is not in a normal condition is somewhat insane. But my understanding of the law is that it does not necessarily mean it recognizes someone as insane until their irresponsible behavior reaches a point where they can no longer act rationally."

"Would you consider a man shooting someone he loved as rational behavior?" Miner asked.

"No, I would not," Dr. Conlan stated firmly.

John Miner faced the jury and said, "I repeat, Lewis Heydlauff was not responsible by reason of extraordinary excitement for what occurred. He loved Emma Moeckel."

Dr. Conlan glanced at Miner in disapproval as he was excused from the stand.

Third Witness for the Prosecution

Albert J. Moeckel

Sixteen-year-old Albert Moeckel, brother of the dead girl, was called next by the prosecution.

Fair-haired and tall for his age, Albert awkwardly approached the stand. The bailiff asked the boy to place his hand on the Bible and then recited, "Do you solemnly swear that you will tell the truth, the whole truth, and nothing but the truth, so help you God?"

"I do." The young witness took his seat and pulled at the cuffs on his white cotton shirt, adjusted his black string tie, and looked attentively at Charles Blair.

"Albert, please describe as best you can what you recall of the morning of May 31."

Albert seemed apprehensive to answer, but began, "After having breakfast with my family I got dressed for church and was waiting for Emma to come home. Before she arrived, Lewis stopped by to visit. I said 'Good morning Lewis,' when he and my pa were talking about farm stuff. Then I left the room to watch for Emma."

"Did George Tisch come into the house with your sister?" asked Blair.

"No, she came in by herself. My pa went outside to see George."

"Albert, where did your sister go after coming into the house?"

Albert quietly answered, "Emma went to the parlor."

Blair inquired, "Where was Lewis Heydlauff?"

Albert grimaced as he lamented, "Lewis was in our parlor."

Blair turned to the jury and saw that each of the jurors was gripped by the boy's testimony. Blair then asked, "What was Lewis doing in your parlor?"

Albert's eyes got wet as he sorrowfully exclaimed, "Lewis was waiting for Emma!"

"Albert, what happened after your sister left for the parlor?"

Albert scooted to the front of his seat and looked out to where his parents were sitting. Blair gave Albert some time before continuing. The courtroom went dead quiet until the silence was broken by Judge Peck when he said, "Mr. Blair, please ask your witness to answer the question."

Blair got the full attention from his young witnesses when he said, "Albert, you need to tell court what happened after Emma went to the parlor."

"I heard the door close and then I heard Lewis talking; it sounded like he was arguing. I could hear Emma talking loud. Then I heard bangs coming from the parlor. My pa came running in and opened the door and started yelling. My mother and George ran in. My ma screamed. When I heard this, I ran to the parlor, too."

Albert burst into tears and buried his face into his hands.

Blair looked to Judge Peck, who waved his hand as to say *Give him a minute*. Blair allowed Albert to regain his composure, and then asked, "Albert, I know this is difficult for you; are you able to continue?"

Albert wiped his cheeks and nose with his shirt sleeve, took a deep breath, and then said, "Yes, sir, I think I'll be all right."

"Albert, when you came into the parlor, tell us what you saw."

Albert took a deep breath. His voice broke when he said, "I saw Emma lying on the floor all bloody. She was not moving and my ma was screaming, 'My God, my God, my God.' "

Unrestrained wailing began filling the courtroom from the families and friends of both the dead girl and the defendant. Judge Peek reached for his gavel, but waited for the room to settle.

Albert was having increasing difficulty talking through his sniffling. He was fidgety and his voice was weakening, but Blair decided to continue.

Blair asked, "Albert, when you entered the room, where was Lewis Heydlauff?"

Albert softly, but indignantly answered, "He was on the floor next to Emma with blood on his vest."

"Albert, what did your father do?"

"My pa was asking Lewis why he shot Emma," replied Albert.

"What did Lewis say to your father?"

"Lewis was asking Pa to help him get up."

"Where was George Tisch?" Blair asked.

"George left the room, I think to get help."

Blair then asked Albert, "Are you friendly with Lewis?"

Albert harshly answered, "Not anymore."

Before continuing, Charles Blair turned to face the jury and evaluated their reactions. Some were glassy-eyed; all were leaning forward waiting for the next volley of questions and answers. Blair then turned back to face Albert and asked, "Albert, where were you Saturday afternoon, May 30, the day before your sister was killed?"

Albert had regained his composure, and answered, "I went to get Emma in Munith. Along the way I saw Lewis dragging one of the Archenbraun fields. Lewis saw me, too, and came out to the road leavin' his horse team by itself. I pulled to a stop and we talked. He was mad. He talked only of my sister, sayin' that Emma had put him out. Lewis said that if she didn't come back to him he was gonna kill himself. Lewis told me that if he had a hold of Emma he would choke her. Lewis also said that if she married George Tisch she would have a hard life before she died. Lewis asked where I was goin' and I told him that I was goin' to get Emma at Henry Tisch's house. Lewis told me to be sure to bring Emma back home."

"Did you bring Emma home?" Blair asked.

"No, sir. When I got to Henry's house, his wife, Reicka, told me that Emma was at George's house. So I drove there and it started storming. Emma would not go in the rain and said she would drive over with George in the mornin', so I left without her. On the way home I saw that Lewis was still in the field. I didn't expect to see him there because it was so wet, but there he was. Lewis came over and asked me where Emma was and I told him that she was at George's house and would drive over with him on Sunday."

"What did Lewis say?" Blair asked.

Albert eyes opened wide as he nervously recalled, "Lewis said, 'You oughta brought Emma with you.' "

"Thank you, Albert, that's all for now."

Blair looked at the jury as he returned to his table.

John Miner left his table to cross-examine the young witness. He walked very slowly to the witness stand and stopped uncomfortably close to Albert and asked, "Albert, you swore to tell the truth, is that correct?"

"Yes, sir, I did."

"Albert, do you remember being at the court examination back in July?

Albert shifted on his seat and simply replied, "Yes."

Miner leaned closer to Albert and frowned while he asked, "And did you swear to tell the truth when you were on that witness stand?"

Albert was becoming noticeably upset by the intimidating questions and looked over to Judge Peck, who told him to answer Mr. Miner.

"Yes, sir, I did. I always tell the truth," Albert affirmed.

Miner then looked scornfully at Albert and raised his voice asking, "Then why did you not mention at the July court examination that you and Lewis Heydlauff talked along the road?"

Albert answered, "No one asked me, sir."

John Miner stepped back in a huff and announced that had no further questions.

On redirect, Blair asked, "Albert, have you answered all of the questions today as best you can?"

The young witness breathed deeply and said, "Yes, sir. I've answered the questions exactly as I can remember."

Albert Moeckel was excused and court was adjourned for the noon recess.

Afternoon Session

Attendance before the opening of court had swelled to more than two hundred persons. There was no extra room. Reporters tried pressing their way toward the front so that they would not miss any of the proceedings.

At 1:30 p.m. Judge Peck entered from his chambers and called for testimony to continue.

Fourth Witness for the Prosecution
George Jacob Tisch

George J. Tisch was the next witness called by Charles Blair. Tisch stood and walked quickly from the back of the courtroom to the stand. He was dressed in a conservative double-breasted dark-gray suit, and a high-winged, white collar shirt with a black necktie. His wavy, tawny hair was cut short and combed neatly to the side; his thick mustache evenly trimmed.

Tisch was sworn in by the court and took his seat. He stated that he was born in Munith on November 28, 1869, and was his parents' youngest child, a single man, and that he worked for his father as a thresher and lived at home. Blair asked if he was a member of St. Jacob Church in Waterloo, to which George said, "Yes."

Blair faced his witness and asked, "George, please describe as accurately as possible what you saw at the Moeckel house the morning Emma Moeckel was killed."

Tisch was suddenly acting uncharacteristically nervous. He swallowed hard, looked out to the packed courtroom, and rapidly said, "I came to the Moeckel house after church to bring Emma home. Emma went in and I came in after hitching my horse. Mr. Moeckel and I were sitting in the kitchen when we heard the shots. Mr. Moeckel got up and I followed him to the parlor. I saw Emma and Lewis lying on the floor. I thought at first that they were both dead."

Charles Blair stopped and glanced at his notes. They stated that George had testified at the July examination having been with Mrs. Moeckel in the kitchen. What George had just said was not the same sequence of events. Blair decided not to question George's apparent confusion, and quickly decided to move on. Blair continued, "George, what else did you see in the parlor?"

"I was excited and didn't notice things much," George apprehensively replied, his mouth so dry his tongue felt swollen and impossible to move.

Blair knew his witness had to calm down, so he walked to his table, poured a glass of water, and offered it to George.

"Thank you," George gasped before he emptied the contents and handed the drinking glass back to Blair.

Blair sat the empty glass down and continued, "What did you do after seeing Emma and Lewis on the floor?"

George cleared his throat and answered, "I didn't know what to do."

"Did Lewis say anything?" Blair prompted.

"Yes. He opened his eyes and asked Mr. Moeckel to help him up."

"George, did you stay in the parlor?"

"No. Mr. Moeckel told me to get help. I left the room and went to the lane where my horse was tied."

"Did you see Lewis again after leaving him in the parlor?" Blair asked.

"Yes, he came out of the house. I became afraid of him; I thought he might shoot me, so I stayed behind my buggy."

"Did Lewis come after you?"

"No. Mr. Moeckel took his gun away. Then Lewis went around to the north side of the house. He didn't say anything. Then I saw

Lewis back to the house."

"George, did you follow Lewis back to the house?"

"Yes."

"Why did you not go for help as Mr. Moeckel asked?" Blair inquired.

"My cousin George Hannewald was doing that," Tisch answered.

Blair had no further questions and returned to his table.

Defense attorney John Miner got up from his seat, looked at the jury, then quickly walked the few steps to Tisch and immediately began his cross-examination.

"Mr. Tisch, where were you when you heard the gunshots?"

George replied, "In the kitchen."

"When you heard the shots, what did you do?"

"Just as I told Mr. Blair, I went to the parlor and saw Emma and Lewis on the floor."

Miner then asked, "After Lewis left the house, why didn't you run away if you were afraid of him?"

George again stared out to the courtroom, swallowed hard, and pensively said, "I don't know."

Miner walked to the attorney's table and gathered his notes, briefly studied them, glanced quickly to the jury, and then returned to George.

"Mr. Tisch, at the July examination you stated that when shots were fired, Mr. Moeckel was with George Hannewald outside. You just testified that Mr. Moeckel was in the kitchen. How could Mr. Moeckel be in two places at one time?" he cynically asked.

George was obviously uneasy when he answered, "I don't recall, sir. I don't remember much of the morning."

"Mr. Tisch, at the examination, you stated that the defendant walked out the door to the west side of the house; now you say it was the north side. Which side was it, Mr. Tisch?"

"I'm not sure. I was afraid Lewis might shoot me when he came out. It may have been the west side, or the north side. I don't recall."

Miner turned to the jury, rolled his eyes, then pivoted back to

George, looked at his notes, and started a new line of questioning.

"Mr. Tisch, did you know that Lewis was going with Emma Moeckel?"

"Yes, at one time he was. I believe Lewis had been going with Emma for a couple of years," George answered as he looked toward Emma's parents.

Suddenly, Heydlauff, who had been sitting motionless with his head resting on his left hand, snapped up and looked at George on the stand.

"Mr. Tisch, why did you take Emma to the circus in Jackson on Saturday, May 30?" Miner asked.

"Emma had the day off, so I took her to the show in Jackson, that's all."

Miner glared at the shaken witness as he fidgeted on the stand and then, raising his voice, asked, "Mr. Tisch, were you keeping company with Emma Moeckel?"

"No, I was not. I just took her to the show," George answered, noticeably upset by the question.

"What was Emma doing at your parents' house the day before she died?"

"Emma came from my brother's house where she was helping with a new baby. She came because my mother engaged her for some work. When Emma arrived, my mother said she wasn't need-ed, so we went to the circus."

The defendant looked menacingly at George, then slumped and lowered his head.

John Miner hammered George about the discrepancies between his prior statements and the testimony he had just given, but the effort was not successful, the differences being immaterial to the judge.

Miner walked to the attorneys' table and again reviewed his notes. He turned to the jury and offered them an inquisitive look, as to imply that the witness was perhaps trying to hide something. He then turned to George and resumed his questioning by asking, "Mr. Tisch, did you see Emma read a letter from the defendant a few days before she died?"

"Yes," George replied quietly.

Heydlauff raised his head and frowned at George.

"What did the letter say?" Miner demanded.

George looked resentful. "I don't know what the letter said," he indignantly answered.

Undeterred, Miner continued to probe, "Did Emma Moeckel say to you what was in the letter?"

"Objection, Your Honor! Whatever the witness may have heard is hearsay," Blair called out.

Without hesitation Judge Peck returned, "Sustained."

Miner continued, "Did you see Emma write a letter to the defendant that same day?"

"Yes I did."

Miner moved very close to George and asked "And what did that letter say, Mr. Tisch?"

Noticeably exasperated by the nature of the questions, George responded, "I don't know. Emma wrote a letter to Lewis. I didn't see what she wrote. Emma asked me to mail it and, I did, later that day from Stockbridge."

Miner quickly changed his line of questioning by asking, "Mr. Tisch, did you give Emma a ring?"

George lowered his head and replied very softly, "Yes, I did."

"Mr. Tisch, I'm not sure the jury heard what you said. Please repeat your answer," Miner asked indignantly.

As George raised his head, tears welled in his eyes. His voice broke as he repeated, "Yes. Yes, I did.

Miner raised an eyebrow and asked, "Why did you give it to Emma if you knew she was with Lewis?"

"Emma was no longer with Lewis", George replied.

Miner looked sternly at George and asked, "How could you have known that for certain, Mr. Tisch?"

George looked out to Emma's mother who was sitting with her husband behind the prosecution table and paused. George watched as tears formed in Katharina's eyes, and then he turned to John

Miner and sighed as he replied, "Because Emma told me so. I gave the ring to Emma because she was my friend."

"Mr. Tisch, I once again don't believe the jury was able to hear your answer. Please repeat what you just said."

George looked over to the judge, who instructed George to repeat his answer so the jurymen could hear.

George raised his voice with contempt and repeated, "Emma told me she was no longer with Lewis. I gave Emma the ring because she was my friend."

Without reacting to George's answer, Miner asked, "Where did you get the ring?"

Baffled by the line of questioning, George answered, "I bought it from Casper DePay at his store in Stockbridge."

"What did you pay for the ring?" Miner queried.

"I don't remember," George replied.

"Was it a small silver ring?" Miner asked.

"Yes, it was."

Miner produced a ring from his pocket and held it in front of George. "Is it similar to this one that I am now holding?"

George leaned forward to look at it, and then said, "Maybe so."

Miner walked to the jury box, held the ring between his fingers so the jury could see it, and mockingly stated, "The price of this cheap ring was fifty cents." Returning to the witness stand, he asked, "Mr. Tisch, who now has the cheap ring that you gave to Emma?"

Tears began welling in George's eyes as he quietly responded, "I do."

Further testimony from George Tisch told of his being called back Sunday evening to the Moeckel residence at the request of the family and of staying up all night with them.

It was noted by Miner that the defendant's cousin, Jacob Heydlauff and other close family friends, including the Moeckels' neighbors, Rosina Hoffman and her daughter Karrie—a close friend of Emma's—were at the Moeckels', as well.

After setting the grieving atmosphere at the dead girl's house, John Miner faced the jury and held the small ring between his fingers and sarcastically proclaimed, "Fifty cents—fifty copper pennies—just an ordinary, cheap ring."

Returning to face George, he continued, "Mr. Tisch, did Karrie Hoffman ask you to stop pursuing Emma Moeckel before she died?"

"No, Karrie never asked me that," George promptly denied.

Miner raised an eyebrow and asked, "During that night of grieving, did you talk about the ring with Karrie Hoffman?"

Perplexed, George looked at Miner and said, "No. I don't remember saying anything to Karrie about the ring."

Raising his voice, Miner asked, "When you were talking to Karrie Hoffman, did she ask why you gave Emma the ring?"

George was becoming increasingly agitated and replied sharply, "No, she did not."

John Miner looked sternly at George and brazenly asked, "That night, while poor Emma lay dead in her home, did you not ask Karrie Hoffman . . ." Miner looked to the jury and then quickly back to Tisch and bellowed, "Mr. Tisch, did you not ask Karrie Hoffman to go into Emma's room and pull the ring off the dead girl's finger, and if she couldn't do it, to break the finger off?"

The courtroom collectively gasped at the question. George's head snapped back, he cringed, his mouth gaped. Stunned by what the lawyer had just asked, George grimaced and shouted, "No, sir, I said nothing of the kind, nothing like it!"

The attorney continued his piercing attack. "Didn't Karrie Hoffman tell you she wouldn't do such a thing to that poor girl?"

"No! Karrie didn't say that. I never asked her that. None of what you're saying is true," George shouted.

In the jury box, each of the twelve men was spellbound by the exchange between the lawyer and the visibly shaken witness, undoubtedly speculating as to why Karrie Hoffman would have fabricated such a story.

Miner continued by arrogantly asking, "Then, Mr. Tisch, just how did you get the ring back?"

Exasperated by personal questions and the gruesome accusations, George leaned forward and scowled at the lawyer, and in a parched voice said, "Mrs. Moeckel gave the ring back to me."

The audience went quiet.

John Miner walked to his table and savored a long sip of water as he looked at his witness panting on the stand. He returned to continue probing George about the letter that Emma had written. Holding it directly in front of the George's face, Miner asked, "Is this the letter you mailed for Miss Moeckel from Stockbridge?"

George's throat was so dry he could barely speak, but Miner pompously ignored it as he sought George's answer.

"It looks like it, but I cannot say for sure," George hoarsely answered as he coughed.

George Tisch, a prime witness for the prosecution, had been thwacked by the defense. John Miner cracked a wicked smile and said, "I have no further questions of this witness."

The witness was excused. George desperately wanted to walk from the courtroom and never return, but he had been told to be present until the court no longer required him.

Heydlauff's head was hanging low, but his eyes shifted and clearly followed George's every step as he left the stand and walked back to his seat.

Fifth Witness for the Prosecution
George Hannewald

The next witness Charles Blair called was George Hannewald, who walked promptly to the witness stand and was sworn in. Hannewald stood over six feet tall. His rugged face was topped by a full head of auburn hair, his beard closely trimmed. His bushy eyebrows arched above cobalt blue eyes. Hannewald wore a conservative dark suit, white shirt with a high collar, and a dark bow tie.

John Miner's cross-examination of George Tisch had created anxiety in the courtroom. Hoping to calm things down, Blair began his questioning by politely asking, "Mr. Hannewald, please tell us a little about yourself and of your relationship with the Moeckel family."

"I'm forty-nine years old and the eldest child of Waterloo settlers Heinrich and Charlotte Hannewald. I married Louise Frinkle, with whom I've sired twelve children. My farm is two miles north of St. Jacob Church, where my family worships, and where I'm an elder along with Friederich Moeckel, who I've known most of my life."

"Mr. Hannewald, will you please tell the court what you were doing at the Moeckel residence Sunday morning, May 31?"

In a richly toned voice, Hannewald began, "On the way to church with my family I saw Friederich at his door. I had a church matter to talk with him about, so I called for him to come out. As Friederich and I were talking, we heard shots. Friederich ran in and a minute later George Tisch ran out and called me to come in at once. When I got to the parlor, there lay his daughter, Emma, shot dead, and Lewis Heydlauff wounded next to her."

"What did you do when you saw the tragedy?"

"There was no one in the area that could help, so I told my family not to enter the house but to walk the distance to St. Jacob and I would get them later. I rode my carriage to get Lewis's parents. I brought John and Christina back to the Moeckels'."

"When you returned to the Moeckel house, what was happening?"

"Lewis was lying in the yard—we picked him up and carried him to my carriage and took him home."

"Did Lewis talk on the way to the Heydlauff house?"

"Yes. After we got Lewis into my carriage, I held him up and asked why he did the shooting."

"What did the defendant say?"

"Lewis said he wanted to die because Emma had put him out."

George Hannewald was not cross-examined by the defense.

Sixth Witness for the Prosecution
Jacob Heydlauff

The next witness called by Charles Blair was Jacob Heydlauff, who approached the stand wearing dark wool pants and a cream-colored shirt, gray vest, no tie. His hair was cut short and parted down the middle. Before sitting on the stand, he was sworn in by the court.

Blair began by asking, "Jacob, please state your age and relationship to the defendant."

With a slight German accent, he replied, "I'm thirty-four years of age and a first cousin to Lewis. My father's farm is adjacent to Lewis's father's property. I have known Lewis all my life. I'm a member of St. Jacob Lutheran Church."

"Did you help care for Lewis after the shooting?" Blair asked.

"Yes, I did, at his home, the day after the shooting."

"Did you have conversation about the shooting with the defendant?"

"Yes, I did."

Having established that Jacob was with his cousin soon after the murder, Blair said, "Please recall all that was said between you and your cousin Lewis Heydlauff. Remember that you are under oath to tell the truth."

Jacob sat silently for a short time, then resumed, "I asked Lewis why he did it. Lewis told me that he didn't want Emma to get into the Tisch family. He said he felt bad about what he'd done. I told Lewis I felt bad about it, too. Lewis told me he didn't want to see any more womenfolk. I told Lewis he ought not to shoot her. He didn't answer; he felt bad. That's about it, we didn't talk much."

"Thank you. I have no further questions," Charles Blair stated.

On cross-examination John Miner asked the witness, "Jacob, as best you can, please repeat what you just told Mr. Blair, but in exact language."

"Lewis and I spoke only in German. What I told Mr. Blair is about what was said."

There were no further questions from either lawyer, and Jacob Heydlauff was excused.

Seventh Witness for the Prosecution
Justice Orville Gorton

Justice of the Peace Orville Gorton was called by Charles Blair and sworn in by the bailiff. Gorton sat on the stand dressed in a three-piece russet-colored suit, white shirt, and black bow tie.

Blair, having extracted valuable testimony from the defendant's cousin, confidently faced Justice Gorton and began, "Squire Gorton, sir, please tell of yourself, where you reside, and of your relationship with the Heydlauff and Moeckel families."

"Yes, I was born in forty-eight, and I'm forty-eight years of age. I was born in my parents' Waterloo home and have served as Waterloo's Justice of the Peace since April 1891. I have always known both families. My property is east of the Moeckel and Heydlauff farms."

Blair asked, "Sir, how long have you known Lewis Heydlauff?"

"Since he was a boy," Gorton answered.

"And how long had you known Emma Moeckel?" Blair asked.

"Since the time she was a little girl."

"Justice Gorton, when did you interview the defendant, Lewis Heydlauff?"

In an emotionless tone, Gorton recalled, "I met with the defendant on June 2, the Tuesday following the death of Emma Moeckel. I asked Lewis why he killed the girl. Lewis told me he had no intention of shooting Emma when he went to her house. He said he wasn't mad even when he did the shooting, for he kissed her."

"Did you ask the defendant why he carried a loaded revolver when he went to the Moeckel house?"

"Yes, I did. The defendant said that was nothing new, that he had carried his revolver for three or four years and had no intention to shoot Emma, himself, or anyone." Justice Gorton paused and looked assuredly at the jurors, and then continued, "I asked Heydlauff if he might have shot George Tisch if he was in the room. Heydlauff told me he didn't know what he might have done if Tisch was in the room. Heydlauff told me he had never thought to shoot anybody."

"Thank you, Justice Gorton. I have no further questions at this time."

Blair turned his witness over to the defense for cross-examination.

Miner left his table, walked up to the witness, smiled, and began, "Justice Gorton, have you ever heard anything against Lewis Heydlauff previous to this occurrence?"

"No, Lewis was held in high esteem," Gorton answered.

"Did Lewis express any anger toward Miss Moeckel when you met with him?"

"No, I suppose not. He wouldn't have kissed her before he shot her."

When Justice Gorton said "He wouldn't have kissed her . . ." Friederich Moeckel decided he had heard enough about Lewis saying he kissed his daughter before not remembering he shot her. He started to stand ready to shout "*Emma would never have kissed him!*" but was restrained by his wife. As Friederich lowered to his seat he spoke quietly under his breath, "Emma would not have kissed Lewis—he's a liar—it's all a lie." Katharina whispered in his ear that she agreed, but that he had to stay seated and be still. Katharina took her husband's hand, held it tightly, and wept.

The jury noticed what had occurred, surely understanding the father's frustration. Judge Peck had his gavel in hand ready to strike, but put it down when the Moeckels settled.

John Miner had no further questions.

Charles Blair on redirect asked, "Squire Gorton, you were the justice who called the inquest the day Emma Moeckel was killed, is that correct, sir?"

"Yes, that was me."

"Can you recall who you impaneled for the jury?" Blair asked.

"Yes, the jury consisted of John Hubbard, Henry Lehman, Andrew Rumiman, Friederich Artz, Sr., Emanuel Harr, and Charles Crane."

"Where did these individuals reside at the time of the inquest," Blair asked.

"They were all local residents," Justice Gorton answered.

"Do you recall the names of the witnesses who gave testimony at the inquest sir?"

"Yes, I do. They were Friederich Moeckel, Katharina Moeckel, George Hannewald, George Tisch, and Dr. John Conlan."

"And did the jury render a verdict that Emma Moeckel had come to her death by means of gunshot wounds inflicted by Lewis Heydlauff?" Blair asked.

"Yes, that is correct."

Blair continued, "Did you see the body of Emma Moeckel the day she was killed?"

"Yes."

"Justice Gorton, please describe the wounds you observed on Emma Moeckel's body."

"The wounds to the dead girl's body were to her side and directly at her chest. I did not observe the third wound later identified to the back of her neck. I instructed the physician, Dr. Brogan, to make as little examination as was possible and yet satisfy justice because the girl's parents felt so badly about it. There was no doubt to the cause of death."

"Thank you, Squire Gorton. I have no further questions at this time.

On further cross-examination by the defense, John Miner asked the witness, "Had you heard anything against the defendant's reputation prior to the shooting?"

"No, I had not."

Miner continued, "And did you hear anything since the shooting that was against the defendant's reputation before the shooting occurred?"

"Yes, I have," Justice Gorton announced.

Blindsided by Gorton's unexpected reply, John Miner did not press for an explanation, and stated that he had no further questions.

The prosecution elected not to redirect and Justice Gorton was excused.

Eighth Witness for the Prosecution
Sheriff Archibald J. Peek

Sheriff Peek was a giant of a man with a thick brown walrus mustache and brawny physique. He impressively approached the witness stand wearing a dark blue uniform fashioned with a double row of polished brass buttons on the coat, his metal badge placed above the left pocket. When he reached the stand he removed his blue flat-topped hat by its visor and held it over his heart while being sworn in by the court.

Sheriff Peek stated he was forty-two years old and had been the sheriff of Jackson County for two years.

Prosecutor Blair asked Sheriff Peek to describe the physical evidence. The sheriff testified concerning the revolver, bullets, shells, and the dead girl's clothing. He testified that one bullet had remained in the gun and by consent of all parties, ordered it removed and exhibited to the jury. On his own accord, Sheriff Peek inquired as to the defendant's reputation and found that people generally spoke well of him. Before he was excused, Sheriff Peek said, "I didn't hear anyone say an unkind word about the defendant."

Sheriff Peek was not cross-examined and excused from the stand.

Orville Gorton Recalled by the Prosecution

Justice Orville Gorton was recalled by Charles Blair and reminded that he was still under oath.

Blair asked, "Squire, you stated in your earlier testimony that you had heard of something against the defendant's reputation after the shooting. Please tell of what you heard."

"I was told that Lewis Heydlauff had been drinking a great deal prior to the killing. That was all."

The defense declined to cross-examine and Justice Gorton was again excused from the stand.

Ninth Witness for the Prosecution
Katharina Moeckel

Next called by Charles Blair was Katharina Moeckel. She hugged her husband and slowly approached the witness stand dressed in a black crepe mourning gown buttoned at the neck and tightly gathered at the waist. She covered her hands with black cotton gloves. Katharina's golden hair was drawn back into a twist, allowing her freckled face to be fully visible. Delicately arched eyebrows framed her blue eyes. Other than her eye color, Katharina's features shared a close resemblance to Emma's.

Katharina Moeckel was sworn in by the court and took her seat on the witness stand.

Charles Blair thanked Mrs. Moeckel for taking the stand, saying he knew it was difficult, and asked her to tell of the morning that her daughter was murdered in her home.

Her gripping testimony corroborated that of her husband's in all instances.

Katharina's eyes had become swollen from frequently tearing during her emotional statement. After allowing Katharina ample time to drink a glass of water and regain her composure, Blair returned to question her about Lewis before the shooting.

Blair asked, "Mrs. Moeckel, when did Emma start going with the defendant?"

"Oh, that was about four years ago," Katharina answered.

"Did Emma ever go with anyone else?" asked Blair.

"No, she was only with Lewis."

"Did the defendant live in your home last winter?" Blair asked.

"Yes, we allowed Lewis the use of our attic as a bedroom."

Blair then inquired, "Mrs. Moeckel, why did you let the defendant stay in your house?"

"Lewis needed work, so my husband employed him to help build a windmill. Lewis had nowhere else to live, so my husband included the attic as part of his employment; he also allowed Lewis to share breakfast and supper with our family."

"Mrs. Moeckel, what was the duration of that arrangement?"

Katharina swiftly responded, "Five months. Lewis arrived at our home last year on November 4 and departed this year on April 4.

Blair inquired, "During those months did you notice a change in Lewis?"

Katharina looked out to her husband and into his soulful eyes. Friederich's expression was pained. She knew that her husband regretted the day Lewis arrived at their front door. Friederich nodded as if to say *be strong my love.*

Katharina looked at Blair and said, "Yes, I did. At first Emma and Lewis were friendly to each other but, after a while, I noticed a change. Later on, I don't think Emma thought as much of Lewis as before."

"What do you think caused the changes in the defendant's demeanor?" asked Blair.

Katharina again looked at the defendant, whose eyes were closed and appeared to be dozing, and said, "Emma told me it was because Lewis was drinking too much whisky."

John Miner jumped to his feet, "Objection—hearsay Your Honor!"

Judge Peck replied, "Sustained," and instructed that the statement be stricken from the court transcript.

Katharina was startled by Miner's voice when he hollered, "Objection," not understanding what he meant nor by the judge saying, "Sustained." She was simply telling the truth.

Blair gave Katharina a reassuring smile and nod, and then continued, "Mrs. Moeckel, did Lewis talk to you about Emma the morning of the tragedy?"

"Yes. Lewis said he saw Emma with George Tisch at the circus in Jackson. He was very upset. Lewis then told me about a letter Emma sent him saying it was over between them, and asked me how he could get her back. I told Lewis not to worry so much; that matters would come out all right."

Blair very gently asked, "Mrs. Moeckel, when did you last see your daughter?"

"It was Sunday morning when she came home from church. It

was for just a minute, only a minute," answered Emma's mother as heavy tears began falling. Overcome by grief, Katharina put her hands to her face and openly wept.

Others in the courtroom were giving way to tears as the mortifying story progressed. Blair studied the jurors' reactions until Katharina regained her composure.

Judge Peck had sat straight-faced during the emotional scene until it calmed on its own. He then motioned Blair to continue with his witness.

Katharina's face was strained from her heartbreaking testimony. She was dabbing her cheeks when Blair resumed his questioning by saying, "Mrs. Moeckel, how has your son Albert coped with Emma's death?"

"After Emma was killed, Albert developed a nervous trouble. My son has been under the care of a physician," Katharina sadly acknowledged.

"And your son Florenz, how has he been doing after Emma died?"

Katharina sniffled as she told how Florenz had become somewhat withdrawn, and that he goes about his days with little cheer, but for the most part, Florenz was doing better.

Blair paused. He then said, "Mrs. Moeckel, I'm going to ask you some more questions about the defendant."

Katharina agreed with a nod. Blair then asked, "Mrs. Moeckel, had you visited Lewis Heydlauff since the day Emma was murdered?"

"Yes, I visited him once at his home and again when he was in jail."

"Why did you visit the defendant after what he had done?" asked Blair.

Katharina had fully regained her composure and answered, "I visited Lewis at the Heydlauffs' house after the shooting believing he was about to die. I wanted to ask him why he killed Emma; I had to understand why. Lewis was very tired, but he told me that he didn't want to die without Emma. Then he stopped talking and went to sleep. Then after Lewis went to county jail, I visited him again because he asked me."

Blair walked from Katharina toward a table marked, "Evidence." Katharina followed his every step with tears again forming. Blair picked up a cloth bag and looked to the jurymen. He very slowly removed a white, bloodstained dress, and held it up, allowing the gown to drop to its full length. Blair walked end-to-end in front of the jury as he pointed out the bullet holes in the ensanguined fabric. Blair returned to face Katharina and asked, "Is this the dress Emma wore when she was shot?"

Katharina whimpered, "Yes, yes it is."

Blair submitted the clothing as evidence. He then said he had no further questions, and returned to his table.

John Miner approached Katharina for cross-examination and stated, "It has been said that Emma and Lewis had been together exclusively for at least four years. Did you know that they were engaged to be married?"

Taken aback by Miner's assertion, Katharina countered, "No, my daughter would have told me."

Miner asked, "Mrs. Moeckel, knowing that Lewis Heydlauff and your daughter had been together for such a period of time and were engaged, how do now you feel about him?"

Raising her voice, Katharina answered, "My daughter was not engaged to Lewis. I had thought a great deal about Lewis, but I do not feel friendly with him anymore. I don't see how I could after he has taken my dear one like that."

Miner then asked, "Mrs. Moeckel, you stated that you had visited with Lewis at his home and in the county jail. Is there more you can tell the jury about why you visited him?"

"I visited Lewis at his home shortly after the shooting believing he was going to die. I felt badly for his parents because they—"

Miner interrupted, "And why at the county jail?"

Katharina stopped and looked curiously at John Miner, and then answered, "As I said before, Lewis asked for me to come."

Miner asked, "When you were with Lewis at the county jail, did you tell him to pray to God for forgiveness and he would come out all right?"

"I may have," Katharina responded.

"Mrs. Moeckel, during that visit did you tell Lewis that you forgave him for what he did to your daughter?"

Katharina was startled by what the lawyer was asking. She felt betrayed by Lewis that he would share their intimate conversation with his defense attorney. At a loss for words for what to say, Katharina forced her reply, "Yes, I forgave him."

The spectators were bewildered by what they had heard. There was enough chatter in the audience that Judge Peck tapped his gavel and called for silence.

Miner immediately continued, "Did you give Lewis a silver locket that he had given to your daughter for Christmas last year?"

"Yes, when I was with him at the jail."

"Why, may I ask?" Miner inquired.

"I thought he should have it back," Katharina answered.

Miner continued, "Did you kiss Lewis goodbye at the instance of each visit?"

Realizing that her privacy had been violated, she coldly acknowledged, "Yes, on his forehead," sickened by Lewis's breach of trust and Miner's questions.

"When you visited Lewis did you feel sorry for him?" Miner asked.

"No, I did not."

Miner referred to his notes. He looked over to where Albert was sitting with his father, then to the witness and asked, "You stated that your son, Albert, is under the care of a physician. What are the symptoms of his illness?"

"Albert is being treated for a nervous condition. He has had some trouble concentrating since he saw Emma dead."

"Is Albert having any difficulty with his memory?" Miner asked.

"Maybe a bit, you can ask his physician if you wish," Katharina snipped.

John Miner walked to the jury box, put his hand on the railing for several seconds, then turned to face Katharina Moeckel as she was wiping her cheeks with a handkerchief and asked her, "Did you send a letter to the defendant last week?"

Blindsided by the question, she unhappily confirmed, "Yes, I did send a letter to Lewis," as she dabbed more tears.

"Mrs. Moeckel, I have that letter in my possession. Do you recall what you said in it?"

"I do," she replied, alarmed that Lewis had shared such a personal note with his lawyer.

"What did you write in the letter Mrs. Moeckel?"

Tears were bathing Katharina when she said, "I wrote to Lewis that only God will judge him for what he did, and to beg forgiveness from the Almighty. I wrote that, because of my faith in God and acceptance of His teachings, I would not judge him for what he did to my dear Emma, and that someday, if he repents, he would join her in heaven."

The courtroom was silenced by Lewis Heydlauff's extraordinary breach of privacy and by the audacity of John Miner for using it.

Miner had no further questions for Katharina Moeckel and Blair did not redirect.

Before Katharina stepped from the witness stand she looked at Lewis sitting contemptibly with his head lowered. As she made her way to her husband, Lewis ever so slightly raised his eyes and shamefully watched her pass.

When Katharina reached Friederich he could not conceal his disapproval as evidenced by his seething expression. Katharina sat questioning the wisdom of her charity, and now wishing she had never written to her daughter's despicable killer.

The time was late, so Judge Peck instructed the jury to have no talk of the day's proceedings, and then adjourned court until 9:00 a.m. Wednesday.

Blair and Edwards left the courtroom aware they were in for a fight.

Wednesday, December 16
Day Three
Charles Austin Blair

At the opening of court Wednesday morning, Jackson County Prosecuting Attorney, Charles Blair, approached the bench to inform Judge Peck that new information had come to him overnight of a certain conversation which took place between the defendant and another person at the time of the circus in Jackson.

Judge Peck immediately called for John Miner to hear what Blair had to say.

Blair would not offer details other than that it related to the defendant's motive for killing Emma Moeckel. He requested leave of the court to put Friederich Artz, Jr., on the witness list so, if in the expected event the defense put Lewis Heydlauff on the witness stand, the prosecution might thus lay the foundation for cross-examination.

John Miner objected, saying that Artz was not on the prosecution's witness list prior to the trial, therefore the defense was not prepared for whatever his testimony would consist of regarding motive.

Judge Peck noted that the prosecution had not yet rested, and would allow Artz to take the stand, but only after the defense had called its final witness later in the trial. Judge Peck reasoned that that would allow ample time for Miner to prepare for Blair's additional witness.

Miner again objected, saying it did not follow standard court procedure, to which Judge Peck rebuked him, and ruled in favor of the prosecution.

Charles Blair was then sworn in by the court's bailiff, and gave a brief statement as framework for requesting that Artz be added as a witness for the prosecution.

Judge Peck approved the motion and stated, for the record, that the witness could be called only after the defense called its last witness. He then asked Blair if there would be any additional witnesses, to which he responded, "No, Your Honor, that's it."

The Defense of Lewis Herman Heydlauff
Opening Statement for the Defense

Defense attorney Miner approached the jury and slowly walked the length of the jury box. Each of the twelve jurymen followed his footsteps, eager for him to speak.

Miner turned to face them and began his statement.

First, Miner reminded the jurors that only one side of the sad case had been presented and no judgment could be made until all the evidence was before them. The defense, he said, would not deny that the hand of Lewis Heydlauff held the gun which caused the death of Emma Moeckel, but they would show that the defendant was in a condition which rendered him wholly irresponsible and therefore guiltless.

Miner said the defense would show that this unfortunate young man had been so troubled by losing his girl that it unbalanced his mind and turned away his ability to reason. The defense, he said, will show that the defendant had not closed his eyes in sleep for seven days and nights prior to the shooting; that during that entire week he would sit with folded arms and bowed head, speaking to no one; and that he refused to eat or to talk with the children.

Miner described how the defendant had worked in the rain at the Archenbraun house after returning from the Jackson circus, and without any reason or excuse went next door to his sister Paulina Schumacher's house, sat down in the kitchen saying nothing, went away for a while, and then went back to Mrs. Schumacher's kitchen and sat still, saying nothing and giving no reason for his strange actions. Schumacher's little girl, Nora, had seen Lewis outside near the barn, later telling her mother that her Uncle Lewis acted so strangely that the little one said she was afraid of him.

John Miner told that the morning of the shooting Lewis acted so queerly at the Archenbraun residence that his sister Lydia was frightened. He stood in the doorway looking into her bedroom so strangely that Mrs. Archenbraun started to call for help when Lewis went out of the house, and without saying a word he walked away across the fields.

Miner said the defense will show that Lewis Heydlauff contemplated suicide, that he started for home to bid his parent's farewell, and that he had no thought of seeing Emma Moeckel along the way. His mind was in a terrible condition which deprived him of the power to see things clearly; he only remembered that he was going home to say goodbye to his people—that he had lost control of all his reasoning faculties—and did not remember why he was at the Moeckels', which was on his way home.

Miner stressed that the defendant recalled nothing of what he did, vaguely recalled someone saying, "Emma is coming," and was filled with delight when he heard it; that he recalled going into the parlor, putting his arm around his girl and kissing her, but remembered nothing of the shooting or of seeing anyone afterward because the defendant was mentally irresponsible.

John Miner concluded with a touching description of the relations between the two sorrowing families during which time the defendant cried and pitifully sobbed as did his mother and other relatives present in the courtroom. Miner stated that the defense was general insanity, and that expert witnesses would be sworn to testify as to its latent effect on the human brain. Miner promised that everything would be told to the jury and the case would be fully explained.

First Witness for the Defense
Lewis H. Heydlauff

Lewis Heydlauff was dressed in dark slacks, a white-collared shirt, and a loosely knotted brown necktie. He sat glumly next to Richard Price, his eyes red and swollen from crying during Miner's opening statement.

After Miner concluded he returned momentarily to the defense table and conferred with Price. He then told Judge Peck that he was prepared to call his first witness.

"The defense calls Lewis Heydlauff."

Price helped the defendant to his feet. Lewis's face was freshly shaven with a few nicks around his neck; his lips were dry and chapped, the bottom being slightly cracked in the middle. The low light in the courtroom made his pale face appear ghostlike. His short hair appeared to have been hastily combed to the front. Lewis walked with leaded feet to the stand where he stopped and slummed into a hangdog posture.

The court's bailiff held the Holy Bible out to the defendant. Lewis did not respond. Judge Peck then said, "Son, you must place your hand on that book and swear to tell the truth."

He did.

Lewis then took his seat on the stand, placed his hands on his knees, lowered his head, and stared at a space somewhere between his and John Miner's shoes. For many in the court it was painful to watch this once seemingly vibrant person reduced to an empty shell of his former self.

Miner's strategy for Lewis was to use compassionate questioning in an attempt to gradually draw sympathy from the jurors as they observed the woeful defendant eventually—hopefully—weep on the stand.

Miner began his questioning by asking the defendant to state his name and age.

In a weak, raspy voice, Lewis stated, "My name is Lewis Heydlauff. I was born on my father's farm on September 2, 1871. I'm twenty-five years old."

"Lewis, how long have you lived in Waterloo?"

"All of my life."

Miner gently asked, "How long had you known Emma Moeckel?"

Lewis did not answer.

Miner asked again, "Lewis, how long had you known Emma Moeckel?"

Lewis tilted his head down and with his eyes looking up to Miner, whimpered, "I had always known Emma."

Miner asked caringly, "Lewis, how did you spend your time with Emma?"

Lewis's expression lightened as he recalled, "We went to school and church together. We were together when our parents visited. When I was allowed to take the buggy we took small trips together. We did lots of things together—lots of fun things together. I expected to wed Emma someday."

Miner asked, "Lewis, where did you and Emma go on your trips together?"

"We took many little trips. We went to Ann Arbor to see my sister Sarah—sometimes to Chelsea to shop on Main Street. Many times we took the train to Jackson to visit the big city. Once we went together to see Emma's grandparents in Lima."

"Lewis, what do you remember about your trip to Lima?"

Lewis was on the verge of tears as he recalled, "On the way home from Lima we . . ." Lewis sniffled and wiped his nose with his shirt cuff, then continued to say, "Emma . . . Emma promised to marry me."

Miner paused to allow the somber courtroom the opportunity to watch the sad scene develop. After waiting for several moments, he then asked, "How long ago did this take place?"

Lewis's voice broke when he answered, "About two and a half years ago. I even saved over eight hundred dollars thinking the money would get us settled in married life."

"Did you and Emma set a wedding date?"

Lewis looked to the floor and mumbled, "No, we didn't set a date, but I thought it should have occurred last fall."

"Did you or Emma tell other people of your engagement?"

Lewis sniveled, "No, we agreed to keep it a secret."

"Lewis, why was it a secret?"

"I hadn't asked Emma's father."

While Friederich and Katharina Moeckel were listening to Lewis's testimony they, at times, looked at each other in bewilderment. When Lewis said they were engaged, Katharina put her hand over her mouth and gasped. When Lewis said, "I hadn't asked Emma's father," Friederich flinched and grabbed for his chest. His wife asked if he was all right, to which he nodded *yes* and took a deep breath. Emma's parents were certain their daughter would have told them if what Lewis said was true.

Miner gave Lewis an understanding look, and then asked, "Lewis, what can you tell me about your engagement to Emma?"

For several minutes Lewis related little incidents of their engagement and frequently broke down and cried like a child. When he finished talking he dropped his head and went silent. Miner stepped back and looked to the jurors who appeared engrossed by the unfolding drama. Satisfied by their attention to the testimony, Miner turned to Lewis and allowed the defendant to regain a semblance of composure.

Miner started with a new series of questions by asking, "Lewis, did you go to work for Emma's father, Friederich Moeckel, in October, 1895?"

"Yes I did, but the date was actually November 4. Mr. Moeckel asked me if I could help him build a windmill during the winter."

"Did Mr. Moeckel offer to let you live in his house if you worked for him?"

"Yes, he did," said Lewis as he wagged his head.

"Did you accept?"

"Yes," Lewis answered meekly.

Miner continued, "Lewis, were you and Emma cordial to each other during your time at the Moeckels'?"

"Yes, in the beginning we were happy together—not so much later."

Miner paused before asking, "Why do you think that was?"

Lewis squirmed and lowered his head as he faintly said, "Emma changed."

From behind, Miner heard Friederich Moeckel ask his wife what Lewis had just said, and after she whispered the answer to him, Miner heard Mr. Moeckel say, "That liar—he's lying."

Others near the Moeckels heard the same and began making comments to each other. Judge Peck tapped his gavel and demanded silence.

Before continuing Miner looked confidently at the jury and

gestured as if to apologize for Friederich Moeckel for the unfortunate distraction. He then smiled and continued by asking, "Lewis, when did your work finish with Mr. Moeckel?"

"In early April," Lewis answered indifferently.

"Did you then leave the Moeckel residence?"

"Yes, I went to work for my sister's husband, Albert Archenbraun, to help prepare his fields for planting."

"Did you stay in the Archenbraun house?"

"Yes, my sister moved her children around so that I could use a bedroom. It was really nice of her," Lewis described with a slight grin.

Miner smiled in approval, and then asked, "Lewis, do you recall what Emma did after you left the Moeckels?"

"Yes, Emma left her home to work at Henry Tisch's house."

"Lewis, do you know what work Emma was doing there?"

"I heard that Emma was helping with their children and doing housework," Lewis replied, his eyes again welling with tears.

"Lewis, did you ever visit Emma at Henry Tisch's?"

Lewis rubbed his eyes and answered in a faint, breaking voice, "No, I didn't. I didn't think they wanted me there."

Miner left the defendant for his table where he grabbed a paper note binder and returned to Lewis, his body bobbing as he wept.

"Lewis, are you able to continue?" Miner asked compassionately.

"Yes, I think so Mr. Miner," Lewis whined.

Miner waited for the defendant to wipe his tears and blow his nose, and then asked, "Lewis, I'm going to ask you about the circus in Jackson."

Lewis twitched and nodded in agreement.

Miner dropped his empathetic look and asked sternly, "Lewis, did you ask Emma if she would go with you?"

Lewis sat upright, looked angrily at John Miner, and with sudden hostility responded, "Yes, last year. For a long time me and Emma was planning on goin'. Then when it was time to go, Emma said she didn't care to come. Emma told me that if I wanted to go, to go on my own—just go, she said. Emma said she didn't care, she wasn't interested, that she was gonna work that day instead."

"Did you go to the Jackson circus anyway?"

In the same hostile voice Lewis replied, "Yes, I got together with some friends and we took the train from Munith."

Lewis was taking short, rapid breaths when Miner asked, "Was Emma at the circus?"

"Emma wasn't supposed to be there, but yes, she was at the circus," Lewis answered spitefully.

"Was Emma alone?"

Lewis started to stand but stopped in a crouch as he looked angrily out to the courtroom. His face soured as he held his breath, then his pallid face reddened and his eyes bulged, his bottom lip jutted outward, and Lewis exhaled in a strange, growling voice, "No, Emma was with him," pointing his finger directly at George Tisch.

"Lewis, who are you pointing to?"

Lewis shouted, "George Tisch!"

Judge Peck immediately pounded his gravel and demanded that Miner control his witness.

Miner was startled by Lewis's outburst. He had told him to be prepared for the question, but Miner did not expect his startling response.

Miner told Lewis to sit and relax, who then drooped into his seat.

"Lewis, are you able to continue?"

"Yes, Mr. Miner, I'm . . . I'm all right now," Lewis sighed.

"Lewis, when you were at the circus did you talk with Emma?"

Lewis seemed upset by the question, but irritably answered, "I tried to, but all Emma said was 'Hello.' That was all. She walked away with George."

"Lewis, what did you do after the circus?"

"I went back to the Archenbrauns'," he answered quickly.

Miner walked to the jury and turned to the defendant. Lewis's head began lowering as he appeared to be slipping into a stupor. The jurymen followed Miner's lead and curiously watched the defendant's descent into a seemingly mindless state. Miner allowed ample time for them to observe the defendant in his pitiful condition; the courtroom had become so quiet that city sounds from outside closed windows could be easily heard.

Judge Peck decided John Miner's drama had lasted long enough, and firmly said, "May we continue, Mr. Miner?"

Miner answered, "Yes, Your Honor." Miner approached the defendant, and raising his voice said, "Lewis . . . Lewis, I have more questions to ask of you."

Lewis snapped his head up and looked at Miner in a daze.

Miner paused, and then asked, "Lewis, what do you remember about the next morning—the morning after the circus?"

"I . . . I don't re . . . remember much," Lewis stammered.

"Lewis, do you remember walking to Emma's house?"

Lewis rolled his eyes upward and responded, "I have . . . I do have some memory of being outside looking at the Moeckels' house."

"Did you know if Emma was home when you were in the road?"

Shaking his head, Lewis claimed, "I didn't know."

"Lewis, then why did you walk up to Emma's house?"

"To talk with Mrs. Moeckel," Lewis answered quietly.

"Lewis, why did you want to talk with Mrs. Moeckel?"

Lewis closed his eyes, then opened them and groaned, "About Emma—I wanted to tell her about Emma . . ." Lewis broke out in tears, "I wanted to say to Mrs. Moeckel that Emma was with George at the circus. I wanted to ask Mrs. Moeckel how to get my girl back."

Miner then asked, "Lewis, who let you into the Moeckel's house?"

"Fred did."

"Once you were in the house, did you talk with Mrs. Moeckel?"

"Yes, I told Mrs. Moeckel about Emma."

"What did Emma's mother say?"

"She asked me why I didn't ask Emma to the circus."

Miner asked, "What did you tell Mrs. Moeckel?"

Lewis caught his breath, blew his nose into a soiled handkerchief, and then said, "I told Mrs. Moeckel that I did ask Emma but she told me she wouldn't go. I told Mrs. Moeckel that Emma went back on me. I asked her what I could do to get Emma back."

"What did Mrs. Moeckel say to you, Lewis?"

Lewis's lips quivered as he replied, "Mrs. Moeckel told me not to worry, that she would talk to Emma when she got home."

Miner stared at Lewis for a minute without saying a word. He then continued with a series of questions that brought out the whole history of the preceding week: that Lewis wrote a letter to Emma Sunday night and received a reply from her on Friday; that Emma wrote back and in her letter said all was ended between them; that George Tisch's name was in the letter and he ripped it out in anger; and that he felt very bad after reading the letter.

Miner paused to allow the jurors to ponder the defendant's thirty-minute melancholic testimony about his and Emma Moeckel's letters to each other.

Miner then continued by asking Lewis about the Barnum circus in Munith.

"Lewis, were you drinking alcohol during the Barnum show in Munith?"

"No, I was not. I went to the show with Fred Artz and came home with my friends."

"Did you see George Tisch or Emma at the show?" Miner asked.

"No, I did not, but at church on Sunday, George Tisch did say he saw me."

Miner stepped back and paused. He looked at Lewis long enough for the jurymen to wonder—to wonder what questions were coming next. Miner then readdressed Lewis by asking, "Lewis, have you ever been drunk?"

Lewis raised his head, looked directly at John Miner, and said, "I will not deny that once I drank more than I oughta have."

"What can you tell me about it, Lewis?"

"Once I had a bad toothache. Emma told me I should get the tooth pulled. So I asked my Uncle Gottlieb what I should do. He said, 'Let's go to a saloon and have a good drink of whiskey and the pulling won't hurt so much.' So Emma, my uncle, and two of my cousins went to Chelsea. We went to a saloon and I drank one or two glasses of whiskey. We then went to have my tooth pulled out. I admit that I got sick on the way home."

"Lewis, when else did you drink too much?" Miner inquired.

Lewis raised his head, looked attentively at Miner and boasted, "That was the only time I remember ever having too much to drink."

When Lewis gave his answer the courtroom erupted in chatter—the newspapers had reported that Lewis had been drinking considerably and there were some in the audience that could easily contradict his statement. One reporter was overheard suggesting that maybe the defendant didn't remember because he was always drunk. Friederich Moeckel overheard the comment, and nodded in agreement. The spectators went quiet when Judge Peck banged his gavel.

Miner then continued, "Lewis, I'm going to ask you about the night before Emma died. You said that you went back to the Archenbrauns' after the circus. What do you remember about being there?"

"I'd promised to drag an Archenbraun field, so I was doin' it."

Miner asked, "Did you talk with anyone while you were working?"

"Yes, I saw Emma's brother, Albert," said Lewis.

"What time of day was it?"

"It was later in the day. I had been workin' for about an hour. It may've been around six o'clock."

"Where was Emma's brother going?"

"Her brother said he was goin' to Munith to bring Emma home. Albert said his sister was at Henry Tisch's house and that was where he goin' to get her."

"Did you have other conversation with Albert?" Miner asked.

"Yes. I told Albert that I saw Emma in Jackson with George Tisch. I told him that his sister had put me out. I might've been a little mad when I said it."

Miner referenced his notes and asked, "Lewis, Albert Moeckel claimed that you said 'If you saw Emma, you would choke her, and that if she married George Tisch, she would have a damn hard life before she died.' Lewis, did you say that to Albert—or to anyone else?"

Lewis raised his head, looked directly at Miner, and coldly announced, "No, sir, I did not. I only told him 'bout his sister putting me out, that's all."

There was considerable conversation among the spectators after Lewis answered; it was a direct contradiction to Albert Moeckel's earlier testimony. Albert's mother glared at her husband with a look that said it all: *Lewis is lying.*

Judge Peck picked up his gavel and the courtroom settled.

Miner then asked, "Lewis, when and where did you buy the revolver that was used to shoot Emma Moeckel?"

"About three years ago in Chelsea."

"Why did you buy it?" Miner asked.

"No particular reason," Lewis answered nonchalantly.

Miner held back his next question for a minute. He wanted the jury to think about the defendant's answer—that he had bought the revolver years earlier. He had not acquired the gun to shoot Emma Moeckel. Miner then continued, "Lewis, had you ever used it before May 31, 1896?"

Lewis smiled oddly as he responded, "I did shoot at a mark once when I was with Mr. Moeckel, and there was a time I thought to shoot one of my uncle's ugly dogs."

There was some chuckling in the courtroom, to which Judge Peck immediately demanded quiet.

Miner looked at Lewis and asked, "Did Emma know you had the gun?"

"Yes . . . and others. Everyone knew I had it."

"Lewis, how often did you carry it with you?"

Lewis eyes darted as he said, "On Sundays."

"Lewis, I'm going to ask you about the Sunday morning when Emma died; when you got out of bed, what were you thinking?"

With his eyes still downcast, Lewis squirmed and answered matter-of-factly, "I decided to commit suicide. I thought about taking poison but I decided to shoot myself instead. I wanted to say goodbye to my family—especially my parents—before I did it."

"Lewis, were you thinking about Emma?"

"Yes and that I loved her. I didn't wanna live without her," Lewis uttered teary-eyed.

Miner turned and glanced at the jury to make certain all eyes were focused on the tearful defendant, then back to Lewis as he asked, "Did you think of killing Emma?"

Lewis sobbed as he responded, "No, no, no . . . I never thought to do such a thing. I loved my Emma."

At this point, Lewis Heydlauff began crying uncontrollably. The women of his family added their own tears to his; even some seated on the Moeckel side broke down.

Miner turned to face the jury. He caught the eyes of each jury-man, looked back at his blubbering witness, and then glanced out to the many sorrowful spectators in the courtroom knowing the ju-rors would followed his lead and see the copious tears falling to the courtroom's floor. Miner emotionally rubbed his own eyes until they wetted, and then turned to again face the jury; he was pleased to see several moist eyes among the twelve. Satisfied with the jurors' teary reaction, Miner returned to the defendant and sympathetically asked, "Lewis, can you go on?"

"I . . . I . . . think so, Mr. Miner," Lewis mumbled through child-like sobs.

"Lewis, when did you see Emma again?"

Lewis flushed. He half-closed his swollen, bloodshot eyes. His face contorted. He looked down and stammered, "At . . . at . . . her, at Emma's house."

"What were you doing there, Lewis?"

"I . . . I don't remember. I sort of re . . . mem . . . remember walking across , , , across the fields, and then . . . and then I recall talking to Mr. and Mrs. Moeckel and that . . . that Emma was com-ing home."

Perturbed by Lewis's constant stammering, Miner paused until Lewis settled, then asked, "Lewis, what do you remember about Emma after she came home?"

Lewis was sniveling but said clearly, "When I heard someone say 'Emma's home,' I felt happy. Then I remember being in the parlor with Emma and asking her why she put me out. I remember putting my arm around her neck and kissing her. Then everything goes dark. All I remember after that is being out on the yard."

"Lewis, what do you remember about your gun?" Miner asked.

"Nothing—I remember nothing."

Whispering amongst the spectators could be heard. Judge Peck allowed it as Miner continued. "Lewis, do you remember taking a gun out from your pocket?"

Again with a stammer, Lewis answered, "No . . . no . . . si . . . sir.

John Miner announced that he had no further questions and returned to his table.

Jackson County Prosecuting Attorney, Charles Blair, approached the stand and looked at the despicable defendant—the lowly witness testifying on his own behalf—whose head hung low, his hands now clasped between his knees as he swayed from side to side.

Blair began his cross-examination by asking, "Mr. Heydlauff, may I call you Lewis?

"If you want," Lewis sulked.

"Thank you. Lewis, did you write Emma Moeckel a letter the week before you killed her?"

Lewis raised his head and exposed his bloodshot, swollen eyes, and abruptly countered, "I don't remember killing Emma."

"All right Lewis, that's not what I asked. What I did ask was if you wrote Emma Moeckel a letter before she died?"

"I already said I did," Lewis answered rudely.

Blair quickly asked, "Lewis, what did you write in your letter to Emma?"

John Miner jumped to his feet and shouted, "I object, Your Honor."

"On what grounds?" questioned Judge Peck.

"The letter is lost, Your Honor; it is now irrelevant," Miner insisted.

Judge Peck paused, and then declared, "Overruled. I'll allow the question." He looked at the defendant and said, "Mr. Heydlauff, tell whatever you remember of the contents of the letter you wrote to Emma Moeckel."

Lewis began rocking back and forth on the stand as Judge Peck watched in wonderment, as did the stunned spectators in the courtroom. Blair looked to the judge and cleared his throat to get his attention.

Judge Peck broke from his stare and with a loud voice said, "Mr. Heydlauff, answer the question."

Lewis jerked, looked at the judge and asked, "What question?"

Blair got Lewis's attention by saying, "Lewis, you said that you wrote Emma Moeckel a letter. What did you say to her in your letter?"

Speaking in a rapid, monotone voice, Lewis nervously summarized the letter's contents: that he wrote to ask Emma what she meant by going back on him and what had he done wrong to deserve it. Lewis said he asked what he could do to win her back. He claimed that was all he could remember.

Blair continued his cross-examination by having the defendant retell the story of his secret engagement with Emma, who Lewis continued to refer to as "my girl." He had Lewis admit that he had some quarrels with her but nothing serious, and that he once told Emma that if she ever left him he would go crazy and kill himself sooner than be shut up in an asylum. Lewis explained that there had been no work for him at home, so he had gone to Moeckel's house and had spent most of last winter there because Fred Moeckel had asked him to come over and help him with a windmill. He said he had gone home frequently. At that point, Blair caught the defendant off guard by suddenly asking, "Lewis, after the Jackson circus, did you tell anyone, 'that would be the last time Emma Moeckel would go with George Tisch?' "

Lewis pouted at Charles Blair, and then startled him and many in the courtroom by loudly stammering, "No . . . no . . . I ne . . . never said that . . . I never said anything of the sort to nobody."

This denial caused some commotion in the courtroom, especially among those following the minute details of the case, as one article in the *Jackson Citizen* attributed Fred Artz Jr. to having made that statement. The room went silent as Blair walked to the jury box, put his hands on the front rail, and caught the eyes of each juror. Blair's expression seemed to ask, *How can you believe anything this man is saying*? Blair then returned to Lewis and asked him to recall the Sunday morning that Emma Moeckel was shot dead.

Lewis, at times condescendingly, repeated much of what he had said earlier; that he got up early Sunday morning, and made up his mind to die, but before pulling the trigger on himself wanted to say goodbye to his parents. He added that he intended to kill himself near a boulder pile at the edge of his father's main field. He recalled that he had thought of committing suicide frequently all that week. Lewis said that he left his sister's house for his parents', but did not remember why he stopped at the Moeckels', nor if he thought of suicide when he was in their house before Emma arrived. Lewis could not remember talking with any of the different witnesses immediately after the shooting, but thought he may have told Fred Moeckel that he could use the money owed him to help pay for his girl's coffin.

Friederich lowered his head and grunted "liar" as the loathing for his daughter's killer again audibly surfaced. His wife put her arm around his neck and spoke softly into his ear, "Hush, my love. Justice will be served." Friederich raised his head and regained his stoic composure.

There was considerable hushed conversation among the onlookers at this point, some asking each other, "If Heydlauff couldn't recall anything of the shooting, how could he have known that Emma needed a coffin?"

Blair did not challenge Lewis's peculiar recollection. Rather, he began a line of attack by asking all sorts of questions in rapid succession, clearly, so it seemed, to test Lewis's recollection of the various events surrounding the murder in an attempt to have him contradict himself.

Blair asked, "Lewis, did you see Emma come home Sunday morning?"

"Yes, I remember her coming to her father's house."

"Was Emma coming home to stay?"

"I remember her carrying her satchel, that's all," Lewis reckoned.

Blair wanted to establish that Lewis had planned an ambush at the Moeckels'. Again he probed, "Lewis, did you know that Emma was coming home to stay?"

"I thought not," Lewis claimed without expression as he further lowered his head.

Blair grilled the defendant in rapid succession. "Lewis Heydlauff, when Emma came into the house, did you follow her to the parlor?"

"I presume I did," said Lewis arrogantly.

"Why did Emma go to the parlor . . . what was she doing?"

"I don't remember what she was doing in the parlor," Lewis insisted as he defiantly cocked his head.

"Where in the parlor was she?"

Lewis was becoming overcome at the rapid questions. He again started stammering as he answered, "I . . . I think she . . . she . . . she was stan . . . standing in the mi . . . middle . . . ah . . . of the parlor . . . and looking . . . looking at me."

"Was she frightened of you, Lewis?" asked Blair.

Lewis bit down on his split lower lip and answered, "I . . . I wouldn't think so."

Blair looked at the jurors for several seconds and then continued. "Lewis, why did you have a gun with you at the Moeckels'?"

Lewis looked spitefully at Blair and sneered, "I had my best clothes on. My gun is always in my hip pocket when I wear my best clothes on Sundays."

Blair asked, "Did Mr. Moeckel know you owned a gun?"

"Yes, I said that before," Heydlauff indignantly replied.

Blair again looked to the jurors and saw that he had their full attention. He turned to Lewis and asked, "What did Mr. Moeckel say to you about carrying a gun?"

Lewis lowered his head and meekly recalled, "Mr. Moeckel once told me I ought to be ashamed to carry a gun and that I should stay in at night if I was afraid to go out."

Blair asked Lewis what he had done after returning from the circus in Jackson. Lewis recalled in detail how he had worked that afternoon at the Archenbrauns', dragging a field to get it ready for planting by the next morning. He told of working in the rain, not caring about the lightning or getting struck and killed. He told of not being able to sleep that night, of lying awake thinking of Emma and wondering what he should do about her. He further said he had not slept any night after getting her letter. Lewis said he had had no appetite that week and hadn't eaten much.

"Lewis, your memory seems quite good about what you have just told the court. But you have testified to not remembering much about the shooting. When did you start having trouble remembering things?" Blair asked, dubious of the defendant's truthfulness.

Heydlauff answered, "I've been having some trouble remembering things since I was sick with influenza. I was burning up with fever and ached all over. The doctor said it was the grippe."

"How long ago was it that you were ill with the grippe?"

"About a year and a half ago; after I was sick I started having trouble remembering things."

Blair walked to the jury box and gave the twelve men a skeptical look, then returned and faced Lewis and asked, "Lewis, do you not find it strange that you remember putting your arm around Emma's neck and kissing her, but don't remember pulling the trigger on your gun when you shot and killed her?"

Lewis raised his voice and said angrily, "No. Sometimes I don't remember things. I don't remember that at all."

Blair went on to question Lewis, wanting to learn more about the physician visits to the county jail. He began by asking, "Lewis, did any physicians visit you in jail?"

Lewis looked up and said, "Yes, I recall Dr. Colby, Dr. John Main, Dr. Fred Main, and Dr. DeMay. Dr. Conlan, too—he came all the way from Munith."

Surprised by how quickly Lewis recited the litany of doctors' names, Blair cocked his head and raised an eyebrow, but continued, "Lewis, did they come by themselves?"

"No, not always—sometimes Mr. Miner came with them."

"Lewis, what did you talk about when they visited you?"

Heydlauff looked blankly at Blair, dropped his head, and responded, almost inaudibly, "I don't remember much—they didn't ask many questions. I do remember that Dr. Conlan would ask how I was feeling and looked at my bandages. Oh, and the pastor from church called on me—I don't remember his name."

Blair had been confident he would catch the defendant making contradictory statements, but his questions did not produce the results he had hoped for.

Judge Peck looked at the clock and, it being noon, decided it was time for an adjournment. He told Blair he was to resume his cross-examination after lunch, looked at the twelve jurymen, and sternly addressed them. "I want to advise that you are not to talk about this case amongst yourselves. I also caution that enterprising newspapers are publishing abstracts of the testimonies you have heard. You are not to read any of them. Do not talk of this case with anyone. Court is now adjourned until one thirty this afternoon."

Lewis Heydlauff was led from the courtroom by a deputy sheriff to a secure room in the building where he was later joined by his two attorneys.

Afternoon Session

The afternoon session opened with a great crowd that blocked not only the aisles but the corridors outside. Promptly at 1:30 p.m. all persons in the room rose to their feet as Judge Peck was announced and entered the courtroom.

Lewis Heydlauff was led to the witness stand, where he returned to his lethargic posture, his head lowered, his hands clasped between his knees.

Judge Peck reminded the defendant that he was still under oath and was sworn to tell the truth, and Prosecutor Blair resumed his cross-examination. He intended to show the jury that Lewis Heydlauff had not been entirely truthful during his morning testimony. Blair had decided to carefully attack the defendant's credibility without risking the prosecution's strategy to minimize Lewis's reported heavy alcohol consumption. If he could trap Lewis into denying his drinking altogether, he could, by extension, show that Lewis was not to be believed at all.

He started with "Lewis, when you were living at the Moeckel house from November 1895 to April 1896, did Emma Moeckel ask you to stop bringing bottles of liquor to her house?"

Lewis raised his head. "No, she did not."

"Did Mrs. Moeckel ask you to stop drinking in her house?" Blair asked sharply.

"No . . . no, she di . . . en . . . did not," Lewis stammered loudly as bits of spittle flew from his mouth.

"Lewis, after you went to the saloon in Chelsea to get drunk before your tooth was pulled, did Emma say that you were a disgrace to her?"

"No . . . no sir. She . . . di . . . did not."

Blair had become increasingly outraged by Heydlauff's answers. The defendant was denying much of the sworn testimony given by the prosecution's witnesses and was evidently perjuring himself. "Lewis," he cautioned, "May I remind you that you are sworn to tell the truth."

"Yes, sir, I . . . I . . . I know that," Lewis feebly concurred.

"Did Emma ask you to never again go to a saloon after you disgraced her in Chelsea?"

Lewis flushed. He inhaled deeply, held his breath, then stammered, "Ah . . . no . . . Em . . . Emma never told . . . told me that."

"Lewis, is it true that you frequently went to the Hurst Saloon in Munith and that Mr. Hurst told you that you were drinking too much?"

Lewis looked at the floor and answered, "He never said that to me."

"Lewis, is it true that your mother once called you an 'old drunkard' at home?"

Lewis slowly raised his head and stammered, "No . . . no, she . . . she . . . nev . . . she never said it like that."

Charles Blair walked to the jury cynically shaking his head, then slowly turned and looked skeptically at Lewis. After several seconds, Blair announced, "I have no further questions of this witness, Your Honor."

Defense attorney Miner left his table and approached the defendant, whose head was again bowed, hands between his knees. He began his redirect by asking, "Lewis, did Emma tell you that Mrs. Wenk, the pastor's wife at your church, wanted Emma to leave you and go with George Tisch?"

Blair objected, "Hearsay, Your Honor."

Judge Peck overruled and allowed the question.

Miner asked Lewis to answer.

"Yes, sir," said Lewis as tears again welled in his downcast eyes. "She . . . she told me that in her letter."

John Miner revisited the saloon episode in Chelsea by asking, "Lewis, when you were sick in Chelsea, what did your friends say to you?"

Lewis, now sitting stiffly upright, placed his hands on the chair arms and sputtered, "The boys ridiculed me for getting sick. They said I couldn't hold my liquor—that I should drink more and get used to it."

"What did they say to Emma?"

Lewis was clearly unraveled as he griped, "The boys laughed at Emma because she was holding my head on her lap along the way home."

Miner had no further questions of the defendant and he was excused. Lewis sat for a moment with his head down. As he raised it, many of the spectators could be heard commenting on his appearance. His face was haggard and his eyes were swollen and bloodshot. Lewis's nose and upper lip were beet red from a steady stream of mucus that had been running down and over his upper lip during much of his testimony. The split in his lower lip had opened and was oozing a purulent discharge. As Lewis cautiously stepped down from the stand, Miner took his hand and assisted him to his seat, where he dropped into a sitting hangdog. Once seated, Lewis turned his head just enough to his right to see where the Moeckels were sitting on the other side of the aisle. He inadvertently caught both of Emma's parents' daggers. Friederich was livid. His face was flushed, his eyes burning in anger. As he looked at Lewis he moved his lips without making a sound as if to say, *I was there, Lewis— you ruthless murderer, you liar.* When Katharina looked at Lewis, her face twisted in emotional pain. Appalled that this evil man had sworn on the Holy Bible to tell the truth and had lied throughout his testimony, she whispered to herself, "How can I forgive him?"

Lewis Heydlauff had been on the witness stand for almost three hours.

Second Witness for the Defense
Paulina Schumacher

Next called was the defendant's sister Paulina Schumacher. She walked to the stand wearing a conservative rose-colored, full-length gown over a black, high-collared blouse with tight sleeves and scalloped lace ruffles at the wrist. Her chestnut-brown hair was upswept and knotted at the top.

Once sworn in by the court, Paulina took her seat and stated that she was thirty-eight years old, the defendant's sister, and married for fourteen years to Christian Schumacher. She said that she and her husband had two children, John, age thirteen, and Lenora, age six, and owned a farm in Waterloo less than one mile from where her sister Lydia and her husband, Albert Archenbraun, lived, which was where Lewis had been employed and had been living since April, up to the day of the shooting.

Miner approached her with the intention of showing the jury that Lewis had acted abnormally the day before the shooting. He began by asking, "Mrs. Schumacher, please tell the court all that you remember about your brother Lewis's behavior before the tragedy at the Moeckel house."

"Yes, Lewis came over to our house about four thirty in the afternoon that Saturday. All he said was 'How do you do,' not much else. He looked tired and worried and just stood in our kitchen. He stayed about fifteen minutes and went away."

"Did Lewis come back to your house?" Miner asked.

Paulina, erect and alert on the stand, answered, "Yes, a little later. I told my little daughter, Nora, to go and call her father for supper, but when she went to call him, she saw that her Uncle Lewis was there, too. Nora ran back because she was afraid of her uncle. I told my daughter to stay put and I called my husband. When he came up, I asked him where Lewis was. Chris told me Lewis had gone away again."

Miner walked toward the jury, stopped in front of them to look at his notes, then returned to face the witness. He looked at her and asked, "Mrs. Schumacher, did you see Lewis again that afternoon?"

"Yes, Lewis came back after we had supper and stood at the counter in the kitchen. I asked him, 'What's the matter?' He said nothing. I asked Lewis to sit down and have some supper, but he said he wasn't hungry and couldn't eat. I asked Lewis why he had come to our house. He said he didn't know and apologized for acting queerly. Then he left again, I think to the Archenbrauns'. Lewis had never acted like that before."

Miner asked the witness, "When Lewis came to your house the first time, what do you think scared your daughter?"

"I don't know what frightened my little girl."

Paulina was not cross-examined and was excused from the stand. She returned to her seat two rows behind her brother.

Third Witness for the Defense
Lenora Schumacher

Six-year-old Lenora Schumacher, known as Nora, niece to the defendant, was called by John Miner as the next witness.

Many in the audience smiled as little Nora held her mother's hand on the way to the stand. "Everything will be OK," Paulina told her daughter as they reached the chair on which she would sit. Paulina pointed to where they had been sitting and said, "Sweetie,

I'll be right over there."

Miner helped Nora up the stand where, with his assistance, she used her knee to get up on the chair. Nora's moon-shaped face was covered by a full head of curly, wheat-colored hair. Her big, brown eyes looked nervously out to where her mother was sitting. The little girl leaned forward to pull down her blue and white polka-dot skirt. She then sat upright and tugged at the sleeves of her white ruffled blouse and adjusted a small silver brooch on her neck.

Nora was gently asked numerous questions by Judge Peck to determine her competency as a witness. The girl, though badly frightened, exhibited great intelligence as she answered, her little, oval lips carefully pronouncing each syllable with precision. She seemed to know what it meant to tell the truth but could not answer what would be done to her if she did not tell the truth. Then she began shedding tears, and the judge asked John Miner and Charles Blair to approach the bench.

Judge Peck expressed considerable doubt to the two lawyers as to the child's competency and asked prosecutor Blair if he had any objections to offer. He had none but said he feared so young a child would be unable to distinguish between things she had actually seen and what she may have overheard from the family. Little Nora was then told by Judge Peck that she was going to be asked a question or two by Mr. Miner and that she had to tell the truth.

Miner faced Nora, who sat quietly looking back. Before Miner could say a word, Nora began pouting and her bottom lip quivered. Tears then came bursting from the child's eyes as she commenced crying hysterically, barely able to catch her breath between squeals.

Judge Peck glanced at Nora, closed his eyes, and put his fingertips to his temples. He then looked at the little girl with a slight smile and dismissed her saying, "You are temporally excused, Miss Nora."

Nora was helped down from the stand by Miner, who began to walk the bawling girl back to her mother. Nora broke away from his grip and ran the last few steps and threw herself into her mother's open arms. Little Nora promptly began to settle down as her mother tenderly hugged and soothed her daughter. She gently wiped away Nora's tears with a linen handkerchief as she said, "Hush, sweetie, hush. It's all OK now."

Little Nora Schumacher was held in favor by the court and spectators.

Fourth Witness for the Defense

Lydia Archenbraun

The defendant's sister Lydia Archenbraun was next called by John Miner. She walked to the stand wearing a long, dark-green dress buttoned from top to bottom. Along the buttons were patterns of pink embroidery. Lydia was about two inches taller than Paulina but had a similar hair color, also gathered in a bun. Immediately after Lydia was sworn in by the court, Miner asked her to describe her relationship to the defendant, location of her farm, her house, and the bedroom where Lewis slept while he was employed by her husband.

Lydia Archenbraun stated that she was thirty-one years old and had been married fourteen years to Albert Andreas Archenbraun. They had seven children at home, the youngest being six months of age, and the defendant was her brother, Lewis. She said that their farm was about one mile from her parents'. Their brick and frame house had five bedrooms: three on the second floor and two on the main level. She said that Lewis slept in one of the upstairs rooms. That room had one bed, a dresser, a washstand, two chairs, and a small closet.

After she finished, Miner wanted to get back to having the jury hear of the defendant becoming increasingly unstable. Miner began by asking, "Mrs. Archenbraun, please tell the court how Lewis was acting at your house the week leading to the morning of May 31."

Lydia looked attentively at him and began, "I heard Lewis awake at night all that week because he was making a great deal of noise upstairs. It was so noisy at times that it frequently awakened me as I slept."

"How was Lewis's behavior that week before the tragedy?" Miner asked.

Lydia's frowned as she replied, "The last week Lewis was at our house he acted very strangely—and he wouldn't eat. Lewis would just sit at the table with folded arms looking down. I don't believe Lewis ate or slept that entire week. I saw him in tears several times for no reason that I knew of. Sometimes I heard Lewis make a big sigh and tell the children not to make noises. They bothered him, but they never did before. Lewis always liked my children and would play with them. He was always cheerful before and had something to say to everyone. He became so different."

"What did Lewis do Sunday morning before he left your house?" Miner asked.

Lydia tugged at both her sleeves and then, with a steady voice, replied, "I heard Lewis moving around upstairs before daylight, about five o'clock. He worked at his morning chores, wandered in and out of the house, would sit down but wouldn't stay for a minute, not saying a word, get up and walk around, then sit again. A little later he went upstairs."

"What did you do after Lewis went upstairs?" Miner asked.

"I went to make my bed. Then Lewis came down, came to the bedroom door, and stared at me in a way that frightened me. Lewis didn't say a word and I was too scared to ask him what was wrong."

"Then what did Lewis do?" asked Miner.

Lydia lowered her head, as she now knew what had been on Lewis's mind at the time, looked up with tears, and answered, "Lewis put on his coat and scarf and then went away across the fields."

Miner said he had no further questions.

The prosecution did not cross-examine, and Lydia Archenbraun was excused from the stand.

Fifth Witness for the Defense
Charles Hurst

Charles Hurst was called and sworn in. Hurst was a stout man with mutton-chop sideburns. He kept a saloon on Main Street in Munith and was acquainted with the defendant.

John Miner asked the witness, "Did you see Lewis Heydlauff in your saloon the day of the Barnum Circus at Munith on Saturday, May 16, of this year?"

The saloon keeper cleared his throat, and then replied in a gruff voice, "Yes. Lewis was in my saloon three or four times that day with some of the Realy, Lutz, and Gottlieb Heydlauff's boys."

"Did you notice anything different from what you knew of Lewis Heydlauff that day?" Miner asked.

"Yes, I noticed that Lewis did not feel well. He acted gloomy and seemed to be studying what was around him. He said nothing. I had no conversation with him."

"Did you serve the defendant alcohol while in your saloon?" Miner asked.

"I don't recall," Hurst replied.

"Did the defendant appear drunk while in your saloon?"

Hurst hesitated before replying. He looked down to the floor for a few seconds, then raised his head and replied, "No, I don't recall the defendant being drunk. If he had been, I would've told him to leave my saloon."

Miner said he had no further questions.

Charles Blair approached the saloon keeper and began his cross-examination by asking, "Mr. Hurst, would you say that your saloon was busy the day of the Barnum circus on May 16?"

"Yes, at times my saloon was full that day, especially following the show," replied Hurst.

Blair then asked, "Did you have someone working with you that day to help serve your patrons?"

"Yes, on busy days I have a barmaid come in to help me," Hurst replied.

"Mr. Hurst, is it possible that your barmaid could have served the defendant some alcohol?" queried Blair.

"Yes, I suppose so. It was very busy that day."

"Mr. Hurst, you just testified that the defendant was in and out of your saloon three or four times that day. How, may I ask, could you possibly forget if you or your barmaid served alcohol to the defendant?"

Hurst became agitated and replied harshly, "I don't remember. As I've already said, I was busy."

Blair crossed his arms and challenged the saloon keeper by asking, "Under those conditions, Mr. Hurst, please tell the court how you determined that the defendant had taken ill because he was acting gloomy?"

Hurst, the saloon keeper, was dumbstruck.

Blair did not press for an answer, for it was obvious.

Charles Blair surprised everyone when he then asked, "Mr. Hurst, are you acquainted with the defendant's father, John Heydlauff?"

Mr. Heydlauff flinched when Blair asked the question.

Miner rose to his feet and shouted, "Objection Your Honor, irrelevant to the case."

"Sustained," Judge Peck immediately ruled.

Blair announced that he had no further questions.

Hurst was then excused and returned straight-faced to his seat.

Charles Blair frowned suspiciously at John Heydlauff as he returned to his table.

Sixth Witness for the Defense
Deputy Sheriff William Wheat

Deputy Sheriff William Wheat approached the witness stand wearing a heavy, dark-blue wool uniform, with his polished brass badge pinned above his left coat pocket. He stood at the stand, was sworn in, and took his seat. Wheat said he was employed as the turnkey at the Jackson County Jail and had been for nearly four years. He had charge of Lewis Heydlauff while he was confined to the jail. The turnkey room was just outside Lewis's cell.

Defense attorney Miner began by asking, "What was the condition of the defendant when he came to jail?"

The deputy sat upright, used the back of his hand to brush down his thick walrus mustache, cleared his throat, and answered, "The defendant was very sick when he first came. He would just lie docile in his cell. He seemed despondent and wouldn't talk much."

"Did you have conversation with the defendant while he was in jail?" Miner asked.

"Not much at first," Wheat replied.

"After you became more familiar with the defendant, did he talk of why he was in jail?" Miner asked.

"Yes, Lewis and I had several conversations. He often wanted to talk about his girl and how much he thought of her. I told him to stop; that he'd better not talk about her. He once wanted to talk of what happened and I told him to stop."

"Did you ask the defendant if he remembered how she died?"

Charles Blair stood and objected. Miner withdrew the question, and Judge Peck instructed the court stenographer to strike the question.

Miner asked, "What else do you remember about the defendant while in your charge?"

"Lewis showed me a photo that he kept in his pocket—said it was his girl. He asked me if it would do any harm if he kept the photo. I told him to keep it. Another time Lewis showed me a locket—said his girl used to wear it."

"How would you describe Lewis Heydlauff's demeanor while in your charge?"

"Lewis was very orderly, quiet, a peaceful prisoner. He never expressed a desire to get well or to get out of jail."

Miner had no further questions and the prosecution did not cross-examine.

Seventh Witness for the Defense
John H. Heydlauff

The father of the accused, John Heydlauff, was called by John Miner. He approached the witness stand in a steadfast manner, showing no emotion—even though he had looked tortured at times during Lewis's gut-wrenching testimony.

John Heydlauff was about five feet, ten inches tall, and had a solid physique for his age. He wore a finely tailored dark wool suit with matching vest, a white shirt with a winged collar, and a perfectly tied red silk tie. His face was partially shaven, leaving a trimmed ear-to-ear beard hanging from his weathered face. His beard, bushy eyebrows, and thinning head of hair had turned mostly white.

Heydlauff was sworn in by the court in the usual way. He stated that he was sixty-three years of age and had lived on the same farm for thirty-five years. He said Lewis had been born there; that he and his wife had six children in total, all married except for Lewis, who had lived at home and worked for him until November of 1895.

Miner asked a range of personal questions to establish the witness's good relationship with Lewis. He then asked Mr. Heydlauff why Lewis had gone to work for Friederich Moeckel. Heydlauff answered by saying he had had insufficient work for his son and advised him to find work elsewhere. A few days later Mr. Moeckel offered Lewis employment, so his son went to work for him.

Miner then asked, "Were you and Lewis on good terms when he left home to work for Mr. Moeckel?"

John Heydlauff looked out to Lewis, who was sitting attentively for the first time since the trial had begun, and saw that his son's eyes were tearing. Grimacing, he answered, "Yes, when we settled I gave Lewis all the money we agreed to and more. I gave my son an extra five hundred dollars. I wanted everything to be all right with him. Lewis said he was satisfied."

Hearing this, Lewis lowered his head.

Miner then asked, "Has Lewis ever been seriously ill while living at home?"

"Yes. Lewis had the grippe about a year and a half ago. He was very sick. He had a high fever for a couple of days. The doctor told me it was a bad strain of influenza. I was worried we might lose him, but he recovered."

"After your son recovered, did he have trouble remembering things?" Miner asked.

"Yes. Lewis seemed to have trouble remembering things after

he got well. About a month after he was sick, Lewis jumped out of bed in a fright during the middle of the night, ran down to my room, roused me, and told me he was dying. His brother, August, came in and convinced Lewis there was nothing the matter and made him lie on the couch till morning. He didn't remember anything about it the next day."

Miner had no further questions and walked back to his table as every juryman's eyes followed him to his seat.

The prosecution declined to cross-examine.

John Heydlauff left the stand. As he walked near Lewis he looked at his son, briefly paused, and took a deep breath, slowly releasing it as he continued to his seat.

Eighth Witness for the Defense
Doctor Charles DeWitt Colby

The defense team of John Miner and Richard Price was now ready to launch their plan to educate the jury about brain disease by strategically calling medical experts to scientifically explain the cause for the defendant's sudden mental change that led to death of Emma Moeckel. Richard Price was to handle this part of the defense. Price first called Dr. Charles D. W. Colby, the Jackson County Jail physician.

The tall, robust-looking man strolled very slowly to the stand, holding his head high, his arms swinging by his side. Colby was wearing a gray suit and black vest. His stiff, high-collared white shirt was accented by a broadly knotted red necktie. His hair was precisely combed to the right; his thin mustache was waxed upward, handlebar style. He wore round rimmed eyeglasses. Colby was sworn in by the court and took his seat on the stand. He stated his name, that he was born in Albion, Michigan, and was thirty-one years old. He proudly said that he received his medical training at the University of Michigan and that he was the physician at the Jackson County Jail.

Price began his questions with, "Dr. Colby, did you care for the defendant whilst in jail?"

"Yes, since he arrived on June 8," the doctor replied.

"Please tell the jury of your analysis of the defendant."

Colby slowly removed his spectacles and stated, "It is my judgment that Lewis Heydlauff, while in jail, has been in a continuous state of melancholia—a form of insanity due to extreme depression—the antithesis of mania caused by great excitement."

"What led you to this conclusion, Dr. Colby?" Price inquired.

Colby replied, "I asked the defendant how he held the gun when he shot himself, assuming that the desired information thus elicited might enable me to probe more intelligently for the bullet still in his abdomen. He wouldn't say. When I asked again, the defendant told me he didn't remember about the shooting, didn't care to have the bullet extracted, and was adverse to me treating him at all. When I tried to persuade him, the defendant said he didn't care to live."

Price stepped back, as he had no further questions.

On cross-examination, Charles Blair cynically asked, "How is it that you determined the defendant was in a state of melancholia from not wanting treatment for a bullet wound?"

Colby sat up stiffly and replied, "I did not use only that occurrence to determine his melancholia. I had other conversations with the defendant while in jail. Although the defendant spoke mostly in monosyllables and his answers seemed reasonably intelligent, it was my initial diagnosis that the patient was and is still laboring under a mild form of melancholia. There are cases cited by medical authorities where insanity has been feigned with great success and baffled eminent physicians, but it can usually be detected if watched long enough. I observed Lewis Heydlauff long enough to determine that, in my opinion, he was insane with melancholia."

Blair asked, "If a person had melancholia for only one week, would that person be dangerous afterward?"

"No, a person would not usually become dangerous from one week of suffering from melancholia."

Having no further questions, Blair returned to his table.

Price, on redirect for the defense, put a hypothetical question to the witness asking, "Dr. Colby, considering what you know of the facts and circumstances leading up to and occurring after the shooting in this case, would you consider the defendant insane or otherwise at the time of the shooting?"

"I would consider the defendant in frenzy at the time from undue excitement superinduced by the appearance of the girl. This would not be an unnatural sequence to the onset of melancholia."

There were no further questions, and Dr. Colby was excused. He quickly stepped off the stand, nodded to Judge Peck, and proudly walked to his seat, looking at the spectators along the way.

Ninth Witness for the Defense
Elmer Kirkby

Before Richard Price called Elmer Kirkby as his next witness, he asked Judge Peck for a short break so he could visit the lavatory. The judge frowned but allowed it, telling Price to make haste or he would have John Miner call the witness in his absence.

While Price was out of the courtroom there was considerable talk amongst the news reporters awaiting Kirkby's testimony. Kirkby was well known in the county. Four years earlier, in the November, 1892, general election, Kirkby, a Democrat, was running for reelection as the incumbent Jackson County Prosecuting Attorney against the Republican, George Blair—Charles Blair's brother. It had been a mudslinging campaign in which Kirkby's supporters spread contemptible rumors that George Blair was addicted to the use of liquor, essentially accusing him of being a hopeless drunk. George Blair countered that he had not had a drop of liquor for several months leading to the 1892 election, and produced multiple notarized statements swearing to the fact. Kirkby also claimed that George Blair was running on the coattails of his father, the honorable Austin A. Blair, who had served as governor of Michigan during the Civil War, and that his opponent lacked any valid credentials to hold office. But Kirkby lost the election, and George Blair took office. But, during George's third year as Jackson County Prosecuting Attorney, he inexplicably resigned, and Charles agreed to serve out his brother's term.

By 1896, the political winds in Jackson County had changed. Kirkby, in the recent November election for the same office, had narrowly defeated the Republican candidate, Henry E. Edwards, who was now sitting next to Charles Blair at the prosecution's table. Bad blood boiled between Blair, Edwards, and County Prosecuting Attorney-Elect Kirkby—who was scheduled to retake the office in sixteen days, on January 1, 1897. Miner and Price believed that having Kirkby testify on behalf of the defendant's reputation was, at a minimum, questionable, and could have an unfair influence on the jury.

Kirkby, a tall, well-built man, wore a smug smile on his sharply featured face as he strolled grandiosely to the witness stand dressed in a perfectly tailored, dark wool suit with matching vest, a white cotton shirt with linen collar and cuffs, a plaid bow tie made of silk, and fancy black leather half-boot oxfords.

Kirkby was sworn in by the court and took his seat. He stated that he was thirty years of age, was raised in nearby Grass Lake, and currently resided in Jackson, where he served as a public defender attorney.

Richard Price approached and asked, "Mr. Kirkby, how long have you known Lewis Heydlauff?"

"About fifteen years."

"How would you describe the defendant as you know him?" Price asked.

"Lewis has always been a peaceful, orderly, and quiet man," Kirkby assured.

Price then asked, "Mr. Kirkby, have you ever witnessed the defendant under the influence of alcohol?"

"No, Mr. Price. I've never seen the defendant in that state, nor have I ever seen him drink any form of alcohol," Kirkby insisted.

Price thanked Elmer Kirkby for taking time from his busy schedule to vouch for the defendant's impeccable reputation.

Blair was taken aback to see Kirkby called as a witness. Blair knew Kirkby was well-acquainted with John Heydlauff and saw nothing to glean by cross-examining his replacement-elect. As Kirkby was excused from the stand, he offered both Charles Blair and Henry Edwards a slight nod and smirk as he returned to his seat.

The news reporters looked disappointed that there was no cross-examination, hoping for suppressed hostilities between the lawyers to boil over during Kirkby's time on the stand. One reporter was overheard as saying, "That's it?"

Kirkby was the last witness to be called for the day. Before Judge Peck adjourned, Charles Blair approached the judge and formally admitted evidence to the court based on the testimonies of Dr. John Conlan, Justice Orville Gorton, Friederich Moeckel, Katharina Moeckel, Albert Moeckel, George Hannewald, and George Tisch, all of which were taken at the defendant's preliminary examination.

Judge Peck then adjourned court until Thursday at 9:00 a.m.

Lewis was led back to jail where he picked at his supper. Afterward, he sat in the corner of his cell with his knees pulled up to his chest, holding the photo of Emma in one hand and the silver locket in his other. At 8:00 p.m., a guard barked at Lewis to get into bed, where he would lie in his clothes for most of the night without sleeping.

In the morning he was required to dump his chamber pot, provided a breakfast of granola and warm milk, then waited to be cuffed and led again to the county courthouse.

Thursday, December 17
Day Four

It was a cool, blustery morning in Jackson, Michigan, when court opened promptly at 9:00 a.m. with the usual large attendance. Lewis was led into the courtroom by two deputies, where he was joined by Miner and Price. It appeared as if the defendant had slept in his clothes—the same clothes he had worn since the trial began. Rough stubble covered his pale face. Lewis's eyes were sunken as if he had not slept in days—his bottom lip still split and crusted. When he reached his chair at the defendant's table, a deputy removed his handcuffs. At once, Lewis sat and took the same dejected, hopeless demeanor—his head drooped low, hands between his knees. Behind Lewis were a large number of relatives who wanted to somehow sustain him in any possible way, as they had done throughout the trial.

Recalled by the Prosecution
Deputy Sheriff William Wheat

Deputy Sheriff William Wheat was recalled to the witness stand by prosecuting attorney Charles Blair. Judge Peck reminded the witness that he was still under oath.

Blair asked a series of questions relating to the food provided to prisoners in jail and whether Lewis Heydlauff ate any of it.

Wheat told the court that the defendant had two meals a day brought to his cell from a restaurant. The deputy could not say whether Lewis ate all of the food or not, but he was sure he ate some.

There were no further questions of the witness, and he was excused.

Tenth Witness for the Defense
Officer John G. Holzapfel

Next called by Richard Price was John Holzapfel, police patrolman for the city of Jackson, thirty-two years old. He approached the stand wearing his blue, formal uniform, his coat secured by a single row of polished brass buttons. He stood tall as if at attention, removed his stiff constable's hat, held it to his chest below his badge, and was sworn in by the court.

Price faced the witness and asked in his usual strong voice, "Officer Holzapfel, how do you know Lewis Heydlauff?"

"I once lived in Waterloo. I'm a few years older than Lewis, but I have known the defendant since I was a very young man," Holzapfel replied sharply.

"How would you describe the defendant?" Price asked.

"Lewis Heydlauff has always been quiet—didn't talk too much. I have always heard him well spoken of. He has a good reputation."

The defense attorneys believed it important to have a lawman vouch for the defendant's reputation. Holzapfel seemed to have oddly impressed the jury, as all twelve paid unusually close attention to Holzapfel's rather unimpressive, routine witness testimony. Price thanked the officer for his testimony.

The prosecution did not cross-examine, and the witness was excused.

Eleventh Witness for the Defense
Doctor John Trafton Main

On Wednesday, county jail physician Dr. Charles Colby was the first physician to testify that he believed Lewis Heydlauff to be insane with melancholia. Richard Price was now to reinforce Dr. Colby's conclusion with his foremost expert witness, the venerated Dr. John Trafton Main, who was held in high esteem throughout the entire State of Michigan's medical community.

Price called his witness.

Dr. Main rose from his seat and leisurely walked to the witness stand. The astute-looking doctor was dressed in a blue, double-breasted wool suit and a high-collared white shirt, its cuffs linked by ornate, golden studs. He sported a perfectly knotted, large bow tie. His long platinum hair was combed back and flowed over the back of his suit collar. He wore a flawlessly trimmed mustache that flared to his cheeks and a pointed goatee. Dr. Main's eyes were a crystal-clear blue that sparkled when he looked out to the people packed into the courtroom.

Dr. Main reached the witness stand and was sworn in by the court bailiff. After he sat, Dr. Main looked at the jury—some of whom looked back at him as if they were in the presence of royalty. The jurors, sensing that Dr. John Main was about to provide crucial information regarding the defendant, leaned forward in unison as they intently awaited his testimony.

Price smiled politely to the audience, nodded to Dr. Main, and then presented the celebrated physician to the jury by asking, "Dr. John Main, for the record, please tell the jury about yourself and of your credentials."

In an upper-New England accent, Dr. Main began to speak, pronouncing each syllable distinctly as he said, "I was born in Albion, Maine, on May 25, 1831. I attended the China Academy in Maine, the Medical College at Castleton, Vermont, and finally the Harvard Medical School in Boston, Massachusetts, where I received my medical degree in 1857. Whilst at Harvard, I was for some years a private pupil of Oliver Wendell Holmes. I also served as a private tutor in the study of microscopy. During the Civil War, I served as assistant surgeon in the Second Maine Regiment. In 1872, I came here, to Jackson, to practice medicine. I also teach anatomy at the University of Michigan in Ann Arbor. I have been practicing medicine and surgery for thirty-nine years. I've been married to my charming wife, Ferrie, for thirty-seven years, and we have one son, Dr. Frederick W. Main, with whom I practice medicine here in Jackson."

The jury was mesmerized as they listened to Dr. Main tell of himself with such a refined voice. Not one of the twelve had ever seen nor heard such a distinguished person up close. Sensing the jurors' fascination with the man, Price slowly walked to the jury box and looked deliberately at each of the jurymen—and each looked back, as if to say, *I'll listen carefully; I know he speaks with knowledge and truth*. Price nodded to them collectively, then returned to the doctor and asked, "Dr. Main, you are recognized as one of the most capable physicians in the American Northwest. Thank you for testifying. You stated that you've been a physician for almost forty years. During this time, have you treated people afflicted with diseases of the brain?"

"Yes, during my many years of practice I have treated many people suffering from diseases of the brain, which are not infrequent. I have also examined patients prior to them being sent to asylums."

"Dr. Main, did you examine the defendant, Lewis Heydlauff, in jail?"

"Yes, I did," Main replied as he stroked his chin while looking directly toward the jury.

Price looked to the jury as well and proceeded, "Dr. Main, please tell the court of your conversation with the defendant."

Dr. Main straightened himself on the stand and continued his testimony, saying, "Yes, I have seen Lewis Heydlauff in his jail cell. I asked the defendant a number of questions to bring out his cerebration, the working of his brain, his memory of past events, perception, and reasoning faculties."

Price asked, "Dr. Main, after you met with the patient—"

"Objection, Your Honor!" Charles Blair called out.

"On what grounds?" demanded Judge Peck.

"Your Honor, Lewis Heydlauff is not the patient—he's the defendant in this case," Blair specified.

"Sustained. Counsel, please refer to Lewis Heydlauff as the defendant. You may continue."

Richard Price smiled as he rephrased his question by asking, "Dr. Main, after you met with the defendant, did you form an opinion of his state of mind?"

"Yes, it is my opinion that the defendant was, at the time I interviewed him—and is currently—suffering from a mild form of melancholia."

Richard Price then said, "Dr. Main, I would like to ask your expert opinion of a hypothetical case."

Price began to describe his hypothetical case by giving a brief history of the lives of Lewis Heydlauff and Emma Moeckel together with a review of the various persons connected to the tragedy, showing a remarkable command of the evidence. While addressing his witness, he frequently looked over to the jurymen, who were listening intently with great interest. When Price reached the point where the defendant was alone in the parlor with Emma, he looked at the jurors until he was certain he had their undivided attention, then returned to face the doctor and asked, "Dr. Main, in your expert opinion, may I ask how you would describe the mental condition of the boy at that very moment?"

Before Dr. Main could answer, Blair rose to his feet and strongly called out, "Objection, Your Honor! The witness cannot offer an opinion to a hypothetical case that involves the defendant considering he has not disclosed any information relating to his examination of the defendant upon which such expert opinion could be based."

Judge Peck had both attorneys approach the bench and engaged in a sidebar discussion for several minutes. He shuffled through some papers as the attorneys watched, located the document he was looking for, and called the jury to his attention. "There is a U.S. Supreme Court ruling, decided last December, Davis v. United States, which I will reference. I want you to clearly understand what was stated; I'll read it to you now: 'The question to an expert must be answered on the facts stated and not on the witness's exclusive knowledge of the case. The law presumes every man is sane, and the burden of showing it is not true is upon the party who asserts it. The responsibility of overturning that presumption, which the law recognizes as one that is universal, is with the party who sets it up as a defense. The government is not required to show it. The law presumes that we are all sane; therefore, the government does not have to furnish any evidence to show that this defendant is sane.'

Judge Peck looked at the jurors and stated, "In other words, the expert's opinion must be based on evidence previously submitted."

At the bench Richard Price contended to the judge that he sought an answer from Dr. Main based only on his examination of the defendant as already recited in evidence. After more discussion, Judge Peck instructed Price to have Dr. Main provide more detailed information of his examination of the defendant and to rephrase his hypothetical question before again asking for the doctor's medical opinion.

Judge Peck overruled Blair's objection and allowed Price to continue as instructed.

Blair returned to his table, and Price resumed questioning the doctor.

"Dr. Main, please tell the court exactly on what evidence you base your opinion that Lewis Heydlauff is suffering from melancholia."

The doctor replied, "I asked several questions of the defendant to determine what memory he had of shooting the girl and himself. During the conversation I found him to be sluggish, apathetic, and indifferent. He seemed to have only one central thought, and that was, *he couldn't live without his girl.* There was lack of coordination in his thought; his brain's processes were uncertain. His power of reason was apparently suspended. It was impossible to arouse him."

Price was now ready to revisit his original question. He asked, "Dr. Main, I would like to return to my hypothetical question. Based on your examination of the defendant and from the evidence so far testified to in this case, what may have been the defendant's state of mind leading to the shooting of the girl and himself in her family's parlor?"

Without objection by the prosecution, Dr. Main began, "In the parlor the presence and touch of the object of his affection and the girl's statement that all was over between them produced acute mania. The defendant was unable to distinguish right or wrong. He was incapable of governing himself or exercising will power. His mind was in a chaotic condition and passed from control. He could not distinguish this or any other matter. The defendant reached a form of insanity known as melancholia. Whilst in this state of insanity, the suicidal tendency or homicidal impulse is very likely to crop up—it occurs very commonly." Dr. Main adjusted his spectacles and stroked his goatee several times. He then continued, "Melancholia is a form of insanity—a diseased condition of the brown substance of the brain. It produces a set of symptoms that interfere with thought and reason. On certain subjects the patient won't talk, while on others he is likely to become excited and violent. In melancholia the tendency is to depression rather than elation. Often the patient will drop his employment without any cause, wander away, or return without purpose. The patient will exercise the utmost caution on matters of no importance, refuse to talk, and exhibit the utmost depression. The depression is produced in many ways, but all governing power will be destroyed by the transition to frenzy or acute mania. In long-term dementia, destruction of the brain follows."

Following the doctor's riveting description of melancholia, Price asked, "Dr. Main, in your opinion, is Lewis Heydlauff insane by melancholia?"

"As I stated earlier, yes, the defendant is currently suffering from a mild form of melancholia."

Having no further questions, Price walked to his table. Along the way he looked intently at each juror, all of whom looked intently back.

Charles Blair began his cross-examination by asking, "Dr. Main, if the defendant was suffering from melancholia, would it not be obvious to the jury from his testimony on the stand?"

Dr. Main seemed annoyed by Blair's question and responded, "I don't believe the jury would be quite as capable of judging a person's sanity as would a physician such as myself."

Blair turned to face the jury and cynically stated, "Gentlemen, may I remind you that the Supreme Court has practically decided that ordinary people, whether they be jurors like you or not, are about as able as an expert to decide whether a fellow is crazy or not."

Light laughter surfaced in the courtroom. Without hesitation, Judge Peck reprehended the people, telling them, "This is a court of law and not a circus. There will be no further outbursts."

Blair continued, "Dr. Main, who requested you to examine the defendant in jail?"

The doctor replied, "Richard Price requested that I examine this defendant in jail."

"Did Mr. Price explain why the defendant was in jail?"

"Yes. He informed me that the defendant was charged with murder and had attempted suicide. Mr. Price did not make an extended statement of the case prior to my examination."

"What did you report to Richard Price following your examination of the defendant?" asked Blair.

"I told Mr. Price that it was my diagnosis that the defendant was suffering from melancholia at the time," Dr. Main contended.

"Dr. Main, what will typically cause a person to develop melancholia?" Blair queried.

"The melancholia form of insanity is frequently brought on by sudden shock or great grief. It may approach slowly or acutely, according to the circumstances."

"Are you saying that grief will bring on melancholia?" asked Blair.

Main replied, "No, grief does not necessarily bring on melancholia. But if a sudden shock triggered an acute attack, the patient may remain in a dazed condition for a few hours or a day or more. Depression, sluggishness, and torpor are usual in such cases."

Blair then asked, "Would it be unusual for a man suffering from such an acute attack to obey when told to sit down in a house and a minute later to run out and pound his head with a brick?"

Dr. Main tugged at his goatee and replied, "That would be an ordinary manifestation of the disease. The fact that a man acts reasonably and as usual under these circumstances is not certain evidence of his sanity; he may appear rational, but not necessarily."

Blair folded his arms, took one step, and looked inquisitively at Dr. Main as if assessing the doctor's credibility. Blair then presented a hypothetical question: "Dr. Main, if the defendant came cordially to the Moeckel residence, spoke rationally with Friederich Moeckel about farming, with Katharina Moeckel about Emma, spoke sensibly and calmly with Emma when she arrived, then followed her into the parlor, asked why she had gone back on him, quoted portions of the letter she wrote him, asked her to take back what she said in the letter, and when she refused to come back to him, he shot her—and the only thing he could not remember about it was the number of shots fired—then using this as a basis, would it be evidence that the man had acute mania?"

Richard Price rose to his feet and shouted, "Objection!"

Judge Peck asked, "On what grounds, Mr. Price?"

"Its conjecture, Your Honor. Only the defendant would have known and he doesn't remember," Price explained.

Judge Peck considered Price's objection for a few seconds then announced, "Overruled," and allowed the question.

Dr. Main speculated on the hypothetical question by saying there are symptoms only a trained expert would recognize, then dithered somewhat by saying, "Taking the question alone, outside all associated circumstances, there would be no evidence of insanity or mania."

Blair continued, "Dr. Main, have eminent physicians and experts of brain diseases ever been deceived by symptoms of insanity?"

Before the doctor could answer, Richard Price loudly objected, "Question by the prosecution is irrelevant, Your Honor."

Judge Peck asked Blair on what basis he was asking this question of Dr. Main.

Blair cited a case in which the distinguished New York physician, Doctor Mary Putman Jacobi, author of several essays relating to diseases of the brain, committed a man to the asylum because when swatted in the face by a cold moonbeam he would immediately explode with insanity, but later stated that the man was simulating insanity and declared she had made a mistake.

The defense argued at length that this was immaterial and irrelevant to the case. The judge agreed and the question was rejected.

Blair, by not having his hypothetical question fully answered, had captured the jury's attention by simply asking it. He continued with the doctor by asking, "Is it true that melancholia patients have wild delusions, such as believing the devil is after them or some horrible catastrophe is imminent?"

Dr. Main replied, "There are such instances, but no, this sweeping statement is not necessarily factual."

Blair continued, "Dr. Main, do melancholia patients stop eating?"

The doctor cocked his head and tugged again at his goatee, then answered, "With the majority of melancholia patients, loss of appetite is usual, especially with anemic subjects. In most cases, it's more likely that female patients have this symptom."

Blair walked to his table as every set of eyes in the overcrowded courtroom followed his every step. At the attorneys' table Henry Edwards had a stack of six leather-bound books in front of him. He handed one over to Blair.

Blair proceeded to bring one book at a time from the table to the witness stand, opened each to a premarked page and read definitions of insanity to Dr. Main. As he did so he looked to the members of the jury following each description, who listened intently to each. The descriptions from the medical books, some ancient, some recent, were very much mixed. One author stated that "Brain disease occurs at a mature age but rarely in the young." Others stated the opposite. Blair cited a study by Dr. R. V. Pierce in his book, *The Peoples Medical Advisor* that "Men are frequently made temporarily insane by drinking liquor; when habitually using alcoholic beverages they are often led to excesses, debauchery, and crime by moral and physical derangement."

After Blair finished reading excerpts from the six books, he asked the doctor, "Dr. Main, which of these is correct?"

Price rose to his feet and shouted, "Objection, Your Honor! What relevance do these paragraphs have without knowing the context in which they are written?"

"Sustained," Judge Peck returned.

Blair then restructured his question by asking, "Dr. Main, do Dr. Pierce's observations of conditions that lead to insanity conflict with yours?"

Dr. Main weighed Blair's question for several seconds, then carefully responded, "All these descriptions could be considered. I will state that one of the certain accompaniments of the form of insanity known as melancholia is expressed by the term 'hangdog.' "

" 'Hangdog'? Will you please be specific about this manifestation of melancholia you call 'hangdog'," Blair requested.

"'Hangdog' is a slang description for an individual suffering from melancholia. The disease exhibits itself by the physical stature of lowered head, bent shoulders, and sluggish gate, accompanied by morose behavior."

"So if an individual has poor posture and is having a bad day, would that person be suffering from a brain disease?" Blair asked sarcastically.

"Objection, Your Honor," Price called out.

"Sustained," Judge Peck ruled without comment.

Blair then asked, "Dr. Main, considering the opinion you gave in your testimony earlier that you believe the defendant is suffering from a mild form of melancholia, what is your prognosis for the defendant?"

Dr. Main straightened his back and sat perfectly upright, twirled the tip of his mustache, and replied, "My prognosis of the defendant must be guarded. I have not examined the defendant physically but only mentally on one occasion. My assessment is that it's probable he will recover. Although, I must caution, nothing is certain. There is a possibility the defendant could experience further deterioration and, ultimately, the destruction of his brain."

Blair momentarily scrutinized the doctor's self-assured analysis, then walked to the jury, carefully read each of the twelve faces for their reactions to the testimony, returned to the witness, and asked, "Dr. Main, if a person decided that life was not worth living without the object of his affection and rather than permit a rival to have her he should kill her, then reflecting over the horrible crime, is it not possible that a man would go stark mad?"

Dr. Main pondered the question as he smoothed his goatee. He then stated, "It is probable—if the man had a conscience. Otherwise, it is not."

The courtroom was left silent as the spectators and the jury contemplated Dr. John Main's answer. Blair broke it by saying, "I have no further questions, Your Honor."

Noting the time, Judge Peck adjourned court for the noon recess.

Afternoon Session

The courtroom and corridors were densely packed when court was reopened at 1:30 p.m.

Dr. John Trafton Main returned to the witness stand and was reminded by Judge Peck that he was still under oath.

The spectators, reporters, and jury had been waiting in suspense for more testimony from Dr. Main, and were grateful that he was again on the stand.

Price began his redirect by calling Dr. Main's attention to a certain passage in the medical work by Dr. R. V. Pierce, which attorney Blair had cited earlier, by reading, "'Insanity symptoms that indicate aberration of mind may at first be very slight and trifling.'"

Blair stood and called, "Objection, Your Honor. Dr. Main has already given his opinion to this medical book."

Judge Peck without hesitation announced, "Sustained," and reference to the book was withdrawn.

As before, Price had the courtroom hanging on his every word. He asked another hypothetical question. "Dr. Main, what effect would a sudden, serious gunshot wound have on a person suffering from melancholia?"

Dr. Main made a fist and placed it under his chin. He then said, "A sudden, serious wound as you describe would likely restore the patient from an acute attack of insanity or frenzy."

Having the full attention of the jury, Price continued, "Dr. Main, considering all that has been testified heretofore, what would be the mental condition of a patient suffering from melancholia?"

The doctor was becoming noticeably exhausted from his prolonged time on the stand. With his tired voice trailing off, he looked in the direction of the jury and stated, "A person suffering from melancholia lives in a state plagued by delusions. The patient is indulged in a life that is not worth living, believing that everyone is an enemy, that danger is present, and that the thought of suicide is almost constant. I must mention that melancholia is often, but not always, accompanied by uncontrollable homicidal mania . . .," Dr Main's voice was weakening, so he paused for a drink of water, cleared his throat, and then continued, "Melancholia results from a diseased organ, the brain. I tell you: all insanity is a manifestation of a diseased brain." Dr. Main took a deep breath and slowly exhaled, then yawned.

Price stepped back from his expert witness to observe the demeanor of the jury; they were glued to the edge of their seats wanting to hear more from the distinguished physician. Satisfied that the jurors had been collectively enticed by Dr. Main to continue learning about the mortifying effect of brain disease inflicting an unfortunate victim—Lewis Heydlauff—and of the resulting symptoms of a poor soul stricken with melancholia—Lewis Heydlauff—and that Dr. Main had concluded that the defendant was suffering from melancholia, Richard Price announced that he had no further questions.

Charles Blair declined to recross for the prosecution, and Dr. John Trafton Main was excused.

Judge Peck then called for a fifteen-minute recess.

Court Resumes

John Miner's next three witnesses all vouched for the defendant.

Friederich D. Artz, Sr., the thirteenth witness, testified that he had never heard of Lewis Heydlauff being in any sort of trouble, and that his son, Fred, Jr., was a trusted friend of the defendant.

Witness fourteen, Hiram N. Barber, testified that Lewis Heydlauff had always been an upright citizen, just like the boy's father, John.

Jacob Waltz, the fifteenth witness called, said he had always known the Heydlauffs, and that Lewis was well bred, and equally as respectful and peaceful as his entire family.

Most in the courtroom had yawned throughout their testimonies. Friederich Moeckel had not. He became increasingly agitated as his neighbors, persons he had been friendly with for most of his life, painted Lewis as an outstanding man. Friederich knew differently, and had become suspicious of their bubbling testimonies praising his daughter's killer. Regardless of when it began, Lewis had become a callous coward—a monstrous drunkard—and the unrepentant liar who ruthlessly murdered Emma. Others in the community were surely aware of it; how could they not know?

Blair had declined to cross-examine any of the three. He did not believe their testimonies were relevant.

John Miner was aware that the jurors had become inattentive during the prior three testimonies, some fighting heavy eye lids while Jacob Waltz was on the stand. The key to Miner's strategy was to use physicians as expert witnesses to convince the jurors into believing they too were capable of observing symptoms of brain disease. But he also had to show the jury that the defendant was a respectable man who had no control over falling victim to melancholia. More medical testimony was to come, but there was another character witness to call.

Sixteenth Witness for the Defense
Jacob Realy

Miner had the good fortune to see his next witness, Jacob Realy, dressed interestingly for court, and decided to announce him in such a way to awaken the jurors. Miner stood beside the bench and thunderously proclaimed, "The court now calls Mr. Jacob Realy!"

Realy sprung to his feet. He marched to the witness stand wearing slightly tattered blue trousers and a wool, dark-blue Union Army coat with freshly polished brass buttons—from the Civil War. Realy stopped at the foot of the witness stand and turned to the bailiff. Realy put his hand on the Bible, swore to tell the truth, and took his seat.

Miner smiled and complimented Realy on how well he graced his Union uniform. He then asked his witness to tell the court about himself.

Realy gave the judge an earnest glance and nod, his deep-set eyes barely visible through thick, bushy brows, then looked out to the spectators and began, "My name is Jacob Realy. I recently turned fifty-seven years of age and have been married to my devoted wife, Catherine, for twenty-eight faithful years. Our farm is about two miles north of John Heydlauff's."

Miner interrupted to ask, "Mr. Realy, where did you serve during the War?"

Realy began to smile, but then abruptly turned solemn when he replied, "I volunteered for the Michigan Twentieth Infantry, Company K. We engaged the rebels mostly in Tennessee and Virginia. There were about a thousand of us in my group, lost over a hundred. It was hard to see my fellows shot and killed; I was lucky, only took a slug at Spottsylvania," said Realy as he tapped his upper chest. He then continued, "At Spottsylvania we battled the rebs for two weeks. There were so many dead." Realy wiped his eyes with the back of his hand and sighed, "God help us if we ever have another war like that."

Miner paused to allow the jury time to appreciate the Civil War survivor's story, and then continued by saying, "Mr. Realy, our country thanks you for your sacrifice, and may we all thank God for the peace in our great Union."

Miner then asked, "Mr. Realy, how do you know the defendant?"

Realy responded by saying he had known the defendant since the time Lewis was a little boy, and was friends with his father, John. Realy vouched that Lewis had never caused any trouble. He then said, "I would've been proud to have a young man like Lewis fighting next to me during the War." Realy then looked sadly at the defendant and concluded his testimony by saying, "I don't understand why Lewis did it."

Miner flinched. Shockingly tongue-tied, he simply said, "I have no further questions."

Charles Blair was content with the witness's last words and elected not to cross-examine.

Seventeenth Witness for the Defense
Doctor John H. DeMay

The jurors had been revived by Jacob Realy's testimony and were now inching forward on their seats, hungry for more expert medical testimony.

Dr. DeMay was called by Richard Price. He approached the stand dressed in a gray suit and knotted silk tie. The barrel-chested man's head was nearly bald, but from the ears down he had a salt-and-pepper beard. He wore round, golden-framed spectacles.

After being sworn in, Dr. DeMay stated his age as forty-five years old, that he had practiced medicine for eighteen years, six in

Jackson, and had considerable experience with insanity cases, having made frequent examinations of persons alleged to be insane for the purpose of testing their sanity.

Price began, "Dr. DeMay, have you examined the defendant, Lewis Heydlauff?"

"Yes, I saw Lewis Heydlauff in the county jail."

"Doctor, considering the circumstances of Lewis Heydlauff's case, and from your examination of him in jail, please tell the court your diagnosis of the defendant."

Dr. DeMay looked out to the courtroom, and with a booming voice stated, "I am confident that the defendant, at the time of the shooting, was suffering from acute mania—he was not able to distinguish right from wrong or to control his emotions."

Price asked, "Dr. DeMay, what would cause a man to fall into such a state of mind?"

"Acute mania is frequently triggered by an unbearable emotional shock that is preceded by a rapid series of depressing episodes. The human brain has a limit to how much pain it can tolerate. The final shock leads to a momentary state of chaos. The brain can no longer operate as it did before, resulting in insanity."

The packed courtroom went quiet. Only the sounds from reporters busily taking notes and flipping pages could be heard.

Price stepped back, studied the jury, and continued, "Dr. DeMay, is acute mania permanent?"

"Not necessarily. Insanity caused by acute mania is frequently temporary. With proper treatment, the brain will again function as before.

Price had no further questions.

On cross-examination, Blair asked Dr. DeMay to name any recent cases of acute mania that he had diagnosed. The doctor named Mrs. Debbie Deyo as one who he had examined who was afflicted with the disease.

Blair asked, "Dr. DeMay, please tell the court what determined your diagnose of acute mania of Mrs. Deyo?"

The witness paused, and then began, "Mrs. Deyo was unable to function as a normal being. She had lost all ability to communicate with others; her sentences were incoherent. Her body movement was spastic, and at times threatening.

Blair asked, "What was your recommendation for the care of Mrs. Deyo?"

He answered, "I recommended that she be treated in an asylum. My colleague, Dr. G. J. White, concurred, and she was then committed."

"How long ago did this occur?" asked Blair.

Dr. DeMay paused, pondered the question, and then answered, "Late March, 1895."

Blair put his hands to his hips and queried, "Dr. DeMay, has she recovered from her acute mania?"

Dr. DeMay's voice lowered when he answered, "I haven't heard of Mrs. Deyo's treatment since she was committed, but I can assure you, she is receiving competent care."

Blair walked to his table, guzzled a drink of water, and returned to the witness and asked, "Dr. DeMay, earlier you testified that the defendant was suffering from acute mania at the time of the murder. How do you now regard his mental condition?"

The doctor replied, "I regard the defendant as being mildly insane; he is not of sound mind."

Blair gathered his notes from prior testimony and referenced them as he reviewed how the defendant had reasoned prior to the shooting. At the Moeckel residence, he appeared the same as usual, talking about farming with Mr. Moeckel, speaking to Emma when she arrived, and then following her into the parlor; he argued with her about a letter, put his arm around her neck, and kissed her.

"Dr. DeMay, does that conduct indicate insanity?"

The doctor cleared his throat, tugged at both his coat lapels, and then declared, "Such conduct does indicate a certain amount of calculation and sanity."

Blair opened his arms to the doctor and asked, "Would that have indicated acute mania?"

Dr. DeMay shuffled in his seat. He nervously rubbed his hands together and answered, "No, not necessarily."

The courtroom gasped when Dr. DeMay answered Blair's question by saying, "No, not necessarily." Someone in the back of courtroom was heard saying, "Heydlauff's not crazy!"

Judge Peck demanded silence as he tapped his gavel to its sounding block.

Charles Blair had no further questions.

On redirect, Richard Price asked, "Dr. DeMay, could the defendant's acute mania have resurfaced when he was alone with the girl in the parlor?"

Blair shouted, "Objection Your Honor, it has not been established that the defendant was suffering from acute mania."

"Sustained," Judge Peck agreed.

Price stepped back and announced he had no further questions, and Dr. DeMay was excused from the stand.

Katharina Moeckel Recalled by the Defense

Katharina Moeckel, mother of the murdered girl, was recalled to the stand and reminded by Judge Peck that she was still under oath.

Defense attorney Miner asked, "Mrs. Moeckel, do you know the defendant's sister, Sarah Vogel?"

"Yes, I do," Katharina replied coldly.

"Did she come to your house after your daughter was killed?"

"Yes, Mrs. Vogel came to my house once or twice."

"What did you talk about during her visit?" asked Miner.

"We talked about Lewis," Katharina matter-of-factly replied.

Miner asked, "Did you tell Sarah Vogel to give your best regards to Lewis when she would see him next?"

"Yes, I did."

The prosecution did not cross-examine, and she was excused.

Eighteenth Witness for the Defense
Sarah A. Vogel

Sarah Vogel, sister of the defendant, was next called by John Miner. In contrast to her brother, who was dressed in wrinkled clothes and hunched lazily in his chair, she strolled gracefully in a fashionable burgundy gown to the witness stand, glancing at Lewis with her large brown eyes as she passed. After being sworn in, she smiled warmly at Judge Peck as she took her seat.

Miner began by asking, "Mrs. Vogel, please tell the court where you live and of your relationship to the defendant."

Sarah replied, "I'm thirty-two years of age and married to Charles Vogel. We are residents of Ann Arbor. The defendant is my brother."

"Mrs. Vogel, are you close to your brother?" Miner asked.

"Yes, I've always been close Lewis. We frequently confide in each other," her eyes glassing as she responded.

"Mrs. Vogel, do you know the parents of Emma Moeckel?"

"Yes, I have known Mr. and Mrs. Moeckel for quite some time."

"Have you visited Mrs. Moeckel at her residence since the day her daughter died?" Miner thoughtfully asked.

"Yes, twice. I wanted to pay my respects."

"Did Mrs. Moeckel seem glad to see you?"

"I believe so. We have known each other for many years and have always been friendly."

"Did you talk of Lewis during your two visits?" Miner asked.

"Yes, we did. When I called on her last, Mrs. Moeckel said she was sorry to see Lewis cooped up in jail and to give her regards next time I would visit him."

Miner probed Sarah as to why Mrs. Moeckel would say she was sorry that Lewis was cooped up in jail, to which Sarah tearfully replied, "I don't know, but maybe Mrs. Moeckel thought that my brother didn't know what he was doing. Perhaps she felt badly for him."

Miner had no further questions and the prosecution declined

cross-examination, so Sarah Vogel was excused.

As she walked back to her seat, Sarah burst out in tears after passing her sickly looking brother sprawled lethargically on his chair.

Nineteenth Witness for the Defense
Doctor Frederick W. Main

Dr. Frederick W. Main, son of Dr. John Trafton Main, was called by Richard Price.

The younger Dr. Main, who preferred being called Fred, was taller and leaner than his father, similarly dressed but with spectacles. His face was shaven, and his head was covered by thick, curly, cinnamon-colored hair cut short. He approached the stand confidently and was sworn in by the court. Dr. Fred Main had a commanding presence on the witness stand. He stated that he was age thirty-five and practiced medicine in partnership with his father; he had been active in Jackson for twelve years and had treated several cases of insanity.

Price asked Dr. Main if he had examined the defendant in jail, to which he replied, "Yes, I found him to be suffering from melancholia." Price then called upon the court stenographer, Thomas Daniel, to read the statement made by the doctor's father during the morning session regarding his diagnosis of the defendant.

Daniel paged to the morning's record and located Dr. John Trafton Main's testimony. From the transcript, the court stenographer read verbatim the hypothetical question that the senior Dr. Main had answered earlier describing the events in the Moeckel house the morning the girl was killed. When the stenographer reached the point where Richard Price had asked, "Doctor, in your opinion, was Lewis Heydlauff insane by melancholia?" he paused. Then the stenographer continued with the doctor's testimony, reading from the transcript, "As I stated earlier, yes, the defendant is currently suffering from a mild form of melancholia."

"That's sufficient," Price informed Daniel.

The silent courtroom breathlessly awaited Price's next question.

He then asked Dr. Main, "As a medical expert and based on what was just read, along with the conclusion from your personal examination of the defendant, what is your opinion of the mental condition of Lewis Heydlauff at the time he fired his revolver?"

Dr. Main immediately responded by saying, "I should consider the defendant not responsible for his condition or acts. His mental faculties were blank, his sense of memory blunted, and his mind was all confusion. The defendant was not capable of controlling his reasoning powers, or his will."

The doctor had the full and complete attention of the jury and spectators as the defendant went unnoticed, sitting lethargically during the duration of the riveting testimony. The defense was succeeding in dehumanizing the dead girl as only a secondary object in a scholarly hypothetical medical debate. The pathos for Emma and her family was being lost. Lewis Heydlauff was being cast as the victim, tortured by events out of his control—events so destructive that they drove him insane. All those big words used by the experts had some of the jurors believing that they had indeed become educated in the medical science of brain disease.

Price felt good as he sensed the jury members being properly swayed, and believed it an excellent point to stop with his witness. Stating that he had no further questions, Price turned Dr. Fred Main over for cross-examination.

Charles Blair approached the doctor in a slow, but deliberate stride as he looked sternly at the jurymen along the way. He sensed that some of the jurors were being significantly influenced by the physicians' testimonies. Blair realized he was underprepared to effectively challenge the experts—he had neglected to have the defendant interviewed by a physician who could have supported the prosecution's case by declaring Lewis Heydlauff as sane—before, during, and after—he murdered Emma Moeckel. Blair was in a bind by not being able to offer an expert medical challenge. He was alarmed that the defense had twisted the case in a way that was drawing sympathy from the jury for the defendant, and that it was imperative to focus the jurors on the hard fact of the case: *Lewis Heydlauff had killed Emma Moeckel in a jealous rage.*

He asked Dr. Main, "Earlier, Dr. DeMay testified that the defendant, while at the Moeckel house the morning of the shooting, acted in a calculating way that indicated a degree of sanity. From what you have learned of the events, do you agree with Dr. DeMay?"

Dr. Main weighed the question for a time before responding. He then looked directly to the jury and said, "I will not agree or disagree with Dr. DeMay. What I will say is that the defendant is said to have gone without sleep for seven days and had worked every day of those seven. A man should be weakened physically and mentally under these conditions. It would likely reduce his mind to a dazed condition. Much would depend upon the exciting cause that had produced the trouble. Insanity at the time is likely."

Blair felt trapped by the reply and decided it best to not proceed further. There were no further questions, and Dr. Fred Main was excused from the stand, who then returned to his seat in a very quiet courtroom.

Ninth Witness for the Prosecution
Fred D. Artz Jr.

Fred Artz Jr. was the person Blair had added to the prosecution's witness list as court opened on Wednesday morning. Judge Peck had allowed it when Blair claimed that Artz had information that would show the defendant had revealed a motive for killing Miss Emma Moeckel.

Blair asked to approach the bench. He informed the judge that his witness was absent. Judge Peck inquired why, to which Blair replied that he didn't know, but perhaps it was due to the weather, or maybe he took ill. The judge reminded Blair that if he intended to call a witness, he must appear in court as scheduled.

Making note of the time, Judge Peck decided to adjourn court until 9:00 a.m. Friday. He sternly warned the jury to not talk with anyone regarding the case, nor read any of the newspaper stories about the trial, saying, "Go home, eat supper, and go to bed." Before leaving, the judge advised Blair that his witness was expected to be in when court opened in the morning.

Blair returned and sat at his table. He flipped through his notes relating to Fred Artz Jr., which included a newspaper article published in the June 1, 1896 edition of the *Jackson Patriot* about the shooting. The story was written using early information gained by interviews with persons in and around the vicinity of the Waterloo shooting. The article told of Lewis having been at the Jackson circus with friends, and attributed Fred Artz Jr. as having heard Lewis say *George Tisch would never take Emma to any more shows*. Blair concluded that Heydlauff must have said something along those lines to Artz while in Jackson. Considering Lewis had killed Emma Moeckel the very next morning after seeing her with George Tisch, the Heydlauff statement attributed to Artz was strong circumstantial evidence for supporting motive.

Charles Blair was unnerved by Artz not showing up. He questioned if issuing a subpoena to a friend of the defendant's, potentially a hostile witness, had been in the prosecution's best interest. He decided to sleep on it and make the decision in the morning whether or not to call Artz to testify.

Friday, December 18
Day Five

The cold, dry weather during the week had been mostly cooperative for travel on the dirt roads in Jackson County. Friday, December 18, was different. A warm front had blown in from the south, and with it gloomy gray clouds that produced a sloppy mixture of rain and sleet.

The court's doors opened at 8:50 a.m. Within minutes an overflowing crowd filled the humid, musty-smelling courtroom. The wooden benches and seats felt tacky from the dampness in the air. The room's electric lighting gave off a ghostly yellow hue. Little of the morning's dreary daylight entered through the windows.

Lewis Heydlauff, flanked by the same two officers, entered the room looking worse than the day before. One of the officers removed his cuffs and Lewis wilted into his chair and lowered his head, showing no apparent interest in his surroundings.

Because of the poor weather, extra time was allowed for all the jurymen and witnesses to arrive and take their seats. By 9:10 a.m. all those required, except for Fred Artz Jr., were present.

The attorneys for both sides were fully aware they would soon be delivering their closing arguments. Their speeches had been meticulously prepared and practiced throughout the better part of their nights; the lawyers had even decided how to dress for greater impact. But first, there was more testimony.

Blair and Edwards had their heads together discussing whether to call Artz when, or if, he arrived. Blair concluded that he could modify his line of questioning if his witness became antagonistic.

At 9:15 a.m., Artz abruptly rushed through the door wearing a heavy wool overcoat and looking disheveled from the windy, wet weather outside. He brushed the wetness from his shoulders, removed his overcoat, ran a comb through his longish auburn hair, and waited to be called to the witness stand.

Everyone stood as Judge Peck entered the court dressed in his black robe.

Fred D. Artz Jr. takes the Witness Stand

Fred Artz Jr. was called by prosecuting attorney Charles Blair.

Artz stood and began walking to the stand. When he reached to where Lewis was sitting, Lewis turned and looked at his friend. Their eyes met and Artz nodded. Lewis responded with a slight smirk that only Artz would understand. Artz reached the stand, was sworn in by the bailiff, and took his seat.

Blair faced his witness and cynically greeted him by saying, "Good to see you here, Mr. Artz. The court is relieved that you made it safely into court this morning."

Without uttering a word, Artz cocked his head and smiled.

Blair then asked, "Mr. Artz, please tell of your relationship with the defendant, Lewis Heydlauff."

Artz leaned forward, looked in the direction of Lewis, and said, "Lew and I are about the same age—I'm twenty-six years old. He and I have been best friends since childhood. I live at my parents' house, which is not far from where Lew had lived until about a year ago. We attended school together and we go to the same church."

Blair had noticed Artz nod to the defendant when he approached the stand but did not think much of it—perhaps he should have. Blair continued, "Mr. Artz, during the month of November, 1895, did you see Lewis Heydlauff drinking alcohol with Jud Armstrong at the Hurst Saloon in Munith?"

"Objection!" shouted Richard Price.

"On what grounds?" asked Judge Peck.

Price explained, "This question is asking for new evidence only meant to attack the credibility of the defendant, Your Honor."

Blair responded by saying, "Your Honor, I have already laid the foundation for the question when I cross-examined Charles Hurst on Wednesday."

Both attorneys were instructed by the judge to approach the bench. After considerable sidebar discussion, Judge Peck ruled out the question.

Price returned to his table and perused his notes.

Blair, perturbed that his last question had been disallowed, asked Artz, "Did you go to the Forepaugh Circus in Jackson with Lewis Heydlauff on May 30 of this year?"

"No, sir, I did not go to that show with Lew."

Artz's answer conflicted with what Blair had been told.

Blair asked again, "Mr. Artz, were you at the Forepaugh Circus with the defendant on May 30?"

"I did not attend the circus with Lew," Artz insisted.

The courtroom began erupting in noisy chatter as the conflict was unfolding. Judge Peck pounded his gavel twice and reminded the spectators, "This is a court of law and I will empty this court-room if there are further outbursts."

Blair had believed that an article relating to the Emma Moeckel murder published in the *Jackson Patriot* the Monday following the shooting was accurate. But now, the witness's testimony did not correspond with what was printed: Artz was at the circus with the defendant. Blair found himself in a quandary—was he to challenge the witness's credibility or continue with questions that might draw out the truth? Artz was the witness who he expected to testify that while at the circus, he heard Lewis say George Tisch would never take Emma to any more shows. How could Artz have heard that from Lewis if they weren't together at the circus? Blair knew that the reporters had to have interviewed someone who said that—maybe it wasn't Artz. Maybe Artz told someone else—but whom? Blair had not verified the newspaper's source, and if he attempted to draw it out from Artz, he knew the defense would repeatedly and successfully object to his questions as hearsay. Blair had to move forward.

Blair learned from his interviews with residents in Waterloo that Lewis Heydlauff and Fred Artz Jr. had been close friends for years and assumed that Artz should know every detail of Lewis's relationship with Emma Moeckel. In an attempt to salvage any evidence for the prosecution from his witness, Blair asked, "Mr. Artz, did you at any time have conversation with the defendant about Emma Moeckel and George Tisch?"

"Objection, Your Honor!" Price shouted.

Judge Peck, without hesitation, overruled and ordered the question to be answered. The judge looked down to the witness and reminded Artz, "Son, you are under oath. Answer the question."

Artz looked out to Lewis, who was sitting upright and listening, and answered, "I've heard Lew speak of Emma and George, but I don't recall what was said. I don't think it was anything much, otherwise I would've remembered it."

Blair was befuddled. He assumed his witness had perjured himself, but he had no way of proving it. Only Artz and Lewis knew the truth; maybe one or both of the defense attorneys knew the truth, but Blair had lost his witness. Feeling foolish and certainly displeased, he stated that he had no further questions. After Blair returned to his table he sat and looked blankly at his witness; it then flashed through his mind: *I didn't ask Artz if he was even at the circus.* As quick as the thought came it vanished, as Blair had had enough of being made a mockery by his failed effort.

Richard Price was grinning as he approached Blair's witness. He began his cross-examination by motioning to Lewis with his hand, who was strangely sitting upright. Price asked, "Mr. Artz, how long have you known the defendant?"

Artz smiled and answered, "Like I said to the other lawyer, I've known Lew for most of my life."

"Do you consider the defendant a close friend?" asked Price.

"Yes, I do," Artz replied.

Price continued, "The prosecution wanted to ask if you saw the defendant drinking alcohol at the Hurst Saloon last November in Munith. I'm not going to ask that question again. But I will ask you, have you ever seen the defendant drunk from alcohol?"

"No, sir, I have not."

With that answer, some in the courtroom began talking: the reporters near the back, and in the front, those supporting the Moeckel family.

Judge Peck tapped his gavel and reminded the audience that his court was in session and to remain silent.

Price said, "Thank you, Mr. Artz, I have no further questions.

Blair was unnerved what had transpired on the stand. He informed the court that the prosecution had no further questions for the witness, and Fred Artz Jr. was dismissed.

As Artz left the stand, he again nodded to Lewis, whose eyes followed his friend as he passed. Lewis then sagged into his chair.

Blair wondered if he had asked his questions incorrectly, allowing the witness to give misleading answers, or had he encountered a moral failure that should warrant condemnation—or was the statement attributed to Artz in the newspaper inaccurate. But he knew one thing for certain—he regretted having called Fred Artz Jr.

Charles Blair needed time to recover from his disappointment before calling his next witness. He approached the bench and asked

Judge Peck for a short break.

Judge Peck allowed the request and called for a fifteen-minute recess.

Recalled by the Prosecution
Lydia Archenbraun

Charles Blair recalled Mrs. Albert Archenbraun, sister of the defendant. After she took the stand, Judge Peck reminded her that she was still under oath to tell the truth, which she acknowledged.

Blair started by asking, "Mrs. Archenbraun, did you visit the Moeckels the Monday after Emma was killed?"

"Yes, I wanted to offer my deepest sympathy for what had occurred."

"While you were talking with Mr. and Mrs. Moeckel in their kitchen, did you tell them that you didn't notice anything peculiar about Lewis before the shooting, otherwise you would have spoken to them about it?"

"Objection!" shouted Richard Price.

"Overruled. Answer the question," Judge Peck instructed the witness.

Lydia Archenbraun sat with her head, neck, and shoulders stiff as a board. She answered unflinchingly, "I don't recall saying anything of the kind."

The defense declined to cross-examine, and the witness was excused.

Recalled by the Prosecution
Friederich Moeckel

Charles Blair recalled Friederich Moeckel to the stand. Judge Peck reminded the witness that he was still under oath. Moeckel nodded and took his seat on the stand.

"Mr. Moeckel, did Lydia Archenbraun visit your house the day after your daughter was killed?"

"Yes, she did."

"Did you and your wife talk of Lewis with Mrs. Archenbraun while in your kitchen?" Blair asked.

"Yes, we did."

"What did Lydia Archenbraun say about Lewis?"

Friederich looked first at Lydia Archenbraun where she sat in the courtroom with her eyes cast down, looked at the judge and then to Charles Blair, and answered, "Lydia Archenbraun said she didn't notice anything peculiar about Lewis before the shooting. If she had, she would've spoken to him and tried to find out what was the matter."

The courtroom was stunned by the contradiction between the two testimonies. There was considerable conversation among the newspaper reporters—the spectators were speechless.

The defense did not cross-examine.

Friederich Moeckel was excused. As he returned to his seat, he looked in the direction where Lydia and most of the defendant's family and friends were sitting and shook his head in disgust.

The prosecution had no further witnesses to call, so Charles Blair returned to his table, unnerved that Mrs. Archenbraun's testimony was inconsistent with what she testified to Wednesday afternoon.

Recalled by the Defense
Doctor John Trafton Main

Richard Price approached the stand and recalled Dr. John Main.

The elder Dr. Main walked confidently to the stand, where Judge Peck reminded him that he remained under oath.

Price began by asking, "Dr. Main, it has been testified that the dead girl was shot in the sternum, had another bullet wound in the side of the abdomen, and one to the back of the neck. Is it possible that the wound to the back of the neck was caused by the same bullet that entered the sternum, glancing upward and passing out the neck?"

"I believe it possible," Dr. Main replied. "Had a thorough examination of the girl's body been made, it would have settled the matter. But at the request of the parents and with agreement by Justice Orville Gorton, the examination was brief. It is impossible to say for certain what direction the bullet might have taken."

There was no cross-examination by the prosecution, and the witness was excused.

The defense had no additional witnesses to call, so Richard Price announced, "The defense rests, Your Honor." He returned to his table, where he joined John Miner and the seemingly uninterested defendant, Lewis Heydlauff.

Judge Peck looked to Charles Blair and asked, "Mr. Blair, do you have any additional witnesses to call?"

Blair stood and replied, "No, Your Honor, the prosecution rests."

Final Motions

Jurymen Leave the Courtroom

Judge Peck ordered the jury to be sent out to a separate room, as both sides had rested.

The judge was to hear final motions from the attorneys and then decide on how the case would be explained to the jury before their closing arguments.

Richard Price began by asking the court to strike out all references to the clothing the deceased had worn at the time of the shooting. No evidence had been presented to indicate from the clothing where the bullets had entered the deceased; consequently, the clothing had no place in evidence. Charles Blair objected. Judge Peck thought the clothing proper evidence, but attorney Price argued that it served only to excite sympathy from the jury. The judge disagreed with the defense and sustained for the prosecution. The clothing remained in evidence.

Blair asked to have all the evidence stricken that related to the Lutheran minister's wife having been requested to interpose her influence to get Emma Moeckel away from Lewis Heydlauff and induce her to go with George Tisch, as it was too remote to have had any influence on the defendant's mind at the time of the shooting.

Price objected, and Judge Peck agreed. The evidence would remain.

Judge Peck then sought to get from the defendant's attorneys a concise statement of their theory relating to the mania that they claimed possessed the defendant at the time of the shooting, the purpose being to get the exact definition of melancholia as used in the case. The judge informed the attorneys that the terms "melancholia," "frenzy," and "acute mania" were not legal phrases. Judge Peck told the attorneys that the only terms that could be used were *compos mentis*—being responsible—or *non compos mentis*—therefore, irresponsible. The defendant was either sane or insane.

Judge Peck asked each side how long they required for their closing arguments. After a brief discussion, it was agreed that each side should occupy no more than three hours of arguments. Afterward, the court would at once submit the case to the jury.

There were no further motions, and Judge Peck called for a twenty-minute recess.

The Jury Returns for Closing Arguments

Final motions had occupied about forty minutes. During that time the courtroom swelled in attendance to where some spectators could no longer jostle forward to a spot where they could easily see or hear much of the proceedings. Many were denied entrance and spilled back into the hallways, where they relied upon news of the trial being verbally relayed. By the time some of that information reached the end of the line, it could have been from an entirely different trial.

Lewis Heydlauff occupied his time during the final motions sitting at the defense table showing no interest in the proceedings, sitting listlessly, as usual.

There was a steady din in the courtroom as the spectators milled about waiting for the judge's return. The attorneys for the prosecution, Charles Blair and Henry Edwards, and for the defense, John Miner and Richard Price, sat reviewing their notes as they readied their closing arguments. It was apparent by the attorneys' swollen eyes that neither side had slept much during the week.

The twelve jurymen returned and took their seats.

"All rise," the bailiff commanded as Judge Peck entered the courtroom. When the judge appeared the four attorneys stood, with Miner and Price helping Lewis stand to his hangdog stance and Blair and Edwards skeptically observing.

Judge Peck took his seat at the bench.

"You may be seated," announced the bailiff.

The courtroom settled, but an annoying din resonated from outside its doors. Judge Peck threatened to have the doors closed if it was to continue. Word got to the corridors, which quickly went silent.

Judge Peck began by addressing the jury. He informed them that all of the evidence had been provided, and now they were to hear the closing arguments from both the prosecution and defense. He told the jury that after each side had concluded its arguments he would give them final instructions before they left to deliberate the case and reach a verdict.

Closing Argument for the Prosecution

Blair and Edwards acknowledged that the defense was rather effective in using the testimony of their medical experts to cast the defendant as an ordinary person with a latent brain disease that surfaced, by no fault of his own, which led to his unconscious act of shooting the girl he loved. They now had to convince the jury that Lewis Heydlauff's alleged insanity was nothing but an insidious ruse for what he did, and that the prosecution is bound by the facts—the truth—and that truth is that intense jealousy led to the defendant's motive for killing Emma Moeckel. Blair and Edwards agreed that they had to walk the jury through the fog of deceit that the defense had created through their cunning reasoning that Lewis Heydlauff was victimized by another man's interference in his life; that Heydlauff refused to lose his girl to another man, and so he ruthlessly planned his every step before shooting three bullets into Emma Moeckel, making sure she was dead by sending the third into her neck. They intended to prove, without a doubt, that motive with malice was absolute, and therefore Heydlauff was fully responsible for his heinous act—and must be found guilty of murder.

Henry Edwards led for the prosecution. He rose from his seat wearing a dark blue three-piece, wool suit, white shirt with a high, round collar and a tightly knotted, gold and blue striped necktie. His reddish hair was neatly combed away from his clean-shaven face. The assistant prosecuting attorney looked dashing as he stood tall and confident before the court.

Edwards approached the jury holding a leather-bound notepad. Before speaking he smiled to the jurymen, stepped back one pace, and for an instant caught the eyes of each juror.

Edwards started his closing argument by saying, "Members of the jury, you have heard the evidence from both sides. The intent of the prosecution is to present the case fairly, laying aside prejudice and feeling, guided only by our sworn duty to enact the laws of the State of Michigan."

The courtroom and corridors stayed silent as Edwards began by passionately stating, "Much that was spoken by Lewis Heydlauff's attorneys was an attempt to invoke sympathy for their client. Sympathy is but a golden fabric woven in heaven itself to cover the sins of a frail humanity. They want you to feel sorry for this unhappy man. Even though you may have some feeling for him in this regard, you must not forget the poor mother who sits here like the Bible's Rachel weeping for her firstborn. Emma was the pride of her mother's life, the daughter whose life was so violently torn from her with so little reason."

Edwards shook his head in disgust as he looked at Lewis, and then boldly addressed the jury stating, "A law of the State of Michigan has been violated. A commandment of God has been desecrated; it was written on the tablet of stone atop Mt. Sinai, '*Thou Shalt Not Kill.*' "

The courtroom remained quiet except for an occasional sniffle, a quiet sob.

Edwards continued, "The law makes it an offense to even touch another person without consent. In this case, a human life has been taken—a fair young soul was sent to meet its creator without a moment's preparation, without an opportunity to say a word of farewell to the mother and father to whom she was so dear. If you believe that was wrong, then you have a duty to perform as jurors."

Edwards looked over to Lewis, who sat expressionless as if none of what was being said applied to him, then turned to face the jury and forcefully said, "If the defendant knew at that time he killed Emma Moeckel that he was doing wrong, and that is the only test to be applied in this case, then he must be punished. I have no doubt Lewis Heydlauff has traveled through the burning depths of the hell of remorse since that foul crime was committed. The punishment of the law is feeble beside it. The only question is: *was the defendant conscious of what he was doing?* It is necessary for the prosecution to show that Lewis Heydlauff did the shooting intentionally, knowing and desiring that his act would end the life of Emma Moeckel. I want you, you twelve men of the jury, to accept that all the witnesses on the stand believe they told the truth. In regard to the German witnesses from Waterloo, they are honest, frugal, truthful people. Their evidence is not conflicting in any essential particulars." Edwards continued by saying he would comment somewhat upon the testimony given by the defendant, but would have very little to oppose from the evidence of other witnesses.

Edwards paced the length of the jury box while referring to his notepad as the jurors impatiently anticipated his continued discourse. Edwards then stopped midway and said, "Much has been said about the defendant's melancholia. There is not one shred of evidence that the defendant was inflicted with it prior to the murder. How, may I ask, could melancholia have inflicted the defendant in the space of less than just one week? Did it start the instant Lewis Heydlauff saw Emma Moeckel in Jackson with George Tisch when he supposed she was at work? Up to that time, was Lewis perfectly sane? No witness has successfully stated that he was insane prior to that day or at any time prior to killing Miss Moeckel. Murder is no evidence of insanity. Suicide is no evidence of insanity. If this had been a case of simple assault and battery, do any of you in the jury suppose a plea of insanity would be entered here? Not a bit of it! Lewis Heydlauff may have been desperately in love with Emma Moeckel, even insanely so, but if Emma thought best to no longer be with Lewis Heydlauff and not marry him, does she not have the right to do as she wished? Emma Moeckel had the inalienable right to come to the circus with any man, whether it was George Tisch or anyone else.

"Dr. John Main stated his opinion of the defendant's insanity wholly upon the loss of his memory, saying Lewis Heydlauff could not recall things. Was that so? Lewis Heydlauff was perfectly rational when he saw Emma at the circus here in Jackson; also when he received the letter from Emma casting him off. Think of what the defendant did. Lewis Heydlauff tells of it on the witness stand; he took Emma's letter and went to a field where he could read it alone—a natural proceeding for a man in love. All his acts show method, memory, sanity." Edwards paused and pointed to Lewis, whose eyes had closed, and continued, "The defendant says he cannot remember the shooting or much of anything that occurred in the parlor when he killed Emma Moeckel. But sworn witness testimony tells that when he awakened at his father's house, Lewis told of the shooting and why he did it—yet he claims no memory! If he didn't remember the shooting, then how did he know Emma was dead?"

Edwards went on to attack the theory that Lewis Heydlauff was insane the entire week before the shooting—and that the defendant's actions did not sustain the theory. Edwards referred to his notes, and then continued his speech saying, "No one testified to any strange action except for his sister, Lydia Archenbraun, who later was said to have told Mr. Moeckel that she did not notice anything peculiar about Lewis before the shooting, and if she had, she would have spoken to her brother and tried to find out what was the matter. The supposition is that for one entire week, the defendant worked all day without eating and went wholly without sleep. Seven days and seven nights—yet attracted so little attention? This is impossible to believe."

The courtroom and corridors remained dead silent, save for the occasional cough, sniffle, and paper shuffle, but each juryman, each spectator awaited Edwards's next word. Lewis Heydlauff remained leaning listlessly forward, elbows on table, head on hands, eyes nearly closed. Whether Lewis was destined for a prison cell or to be set free did not seem to concern him.

Edwards continued, "The week before the defendant shot and killed Miss Moeckel, the seven days and seven nights before seeing Emma with George Tisch at the circus, he contemplated suicide; his thoughts all tended to that end. It was a terrible purpose that he had made up his mind to destroy himself, but he was not insane."

Edwards raised his voice and proclaimed, "The defendant, in his own words, remembers what happened. He knew that Emma was coming home to stay. He knew that she'd be home after church, so he hastened there. He knew she was coming because Emma's young brother told him so the night before. Lewis Heydlauff remembered it!"

All eyes were focused on the dynamic prosecutor as he spoke—except for Lewis, who had yet to budge. Edwards went on to say, "The terrible thought of suicide was uppermost in the defendant's head. He left his sister Lydia Archenbraun's home that morning without saying goodbye; he tried to say it when he went to the door of her room where she was doing her work. She said he acted strangely, tried to speak; he wanted to say goodbye. He longed for a word of a woman's tender consolation."

Edwards looked over to Lewis Heydlauff's family who were seated behind the defendant, the jurors' eyes following his lead, and observed their collective grief as they wiped their eyes and noses with handkerchiefs. Edwards then opened his arms wide, as if to embrace the entire family, and announced, "Oh, this whole case from first to last is pitiful. The defendant went twice to see his sister Paulina Schumacher but couldn't speak. He was contemplating death, wanted to say farewell but dare not, as that would expose his intention. The defendant began to walk across the field to bid farewell to his parents, but on the way he stopped at the home of Emma

Moeckel. What his real purpose was may never be told, no one now knows, but the prosecution must present a theory." Edwards paused, and then lifted his voice saying, "That theory is simple: the defendant acted upon a deliberate plan to wait for the girl and kill her."

The sorrowful sounds from the Heydlauff family suddenly stopped.

Edwards repeated, "Lewis Heydlauff acted upon a deliberate plan. He was in possession of all his faculties as he conversed intelligently with Mr. and Mrs. Moeckel as he waited for Emma to come home. He was in possession of all his faculties when Emma's brother announced her arrival. He was in possession of all his faculties when he said '*Good morning*' to Emma as she entered the house and followed her into the parlor. He was in possession of all his faculties when he asked her to take back what she said in the letter, which she refused. He was in possession of all his faculties when he forced his arm around Emma's neck and kissed her. He was in possession of all his faculties when he drew the revolver from his hip pocket and shot the girl in the side first, then in the chest. He was in possession of all his faculties when he fired again, striking the girl's neck and causing instant death. He was in possession of all his faculties when he fired two shots into himself and fell in a swoon. It all occurred in a moment, but his next words, just minutes later when he regained consciousness, were to Mr. Moeckel when he said, '*Fred, for God's sake help me up, I am dying.*' That was a natural thing to say, it was a rational thought. The defendant's next statement was to Dr. Conlan, *that he could not die and leave her behind.* The defendant later told his cousin Jacob that the reason he killed the girl was because he couldn't bear to have Emma get into the Tisch family. Jacob Heydlauff is an honest man; he tells the truth on the witness stand. All these statements prove thought, memory, and sanity."

The courtroom remained still while the jury focused intently on Edwards's every word.

Edwards walked to the evidence table and solemnly held up the bloodstained clothing Emma Moeckel wore when she was shot for all the jury to see. Many in the audience gasped at the sight; many began sniveling. Edwards then caringly folded the dress and gently placed it back on the table. He walked to the attorney's table, looked at Lewis Heydlauff slumped reprehensibly as if he had no feelings for the suffering surrounding him, turned and looked at Emma's mother as she wiped away her tears, and at Friederich, his eyes reddened from the agony of again being forced to imagine his daughter's last seconds of life. Edwards stood silently near them for a time to make certain each of the jurors understood the enduring anguish Emma's parents were suffering. Edwards walked to the jury box and offered each of the twelve jurors a candid look, and then concluded his argument by saying, "You have been presented evidence that will help you decide the fate of Lewis Heydlauff. This case has been about his love for Emma Moeckel and what led him to kill her. But you must not forget the mound of earth over in the cemetery of the Lutheran church at Waterloo where all summer and winter the heart of the bereaved mother will turn in sorrow for which there is no cure. Take that thought to the jury room and render a verdict not for sympathy, but for justice." Henry Edwards continued looking intensely at the twelve jurymen for over a minute before returning to his table.

It was noon. Judge Peck called for a thirty-minute recess.

Closing Argument for the Defense

Fearful of losing their seats, very few spectators broke for the lavatories or anywhere else during the half-hour recess.

The defense's closing argument had been evolving daily since the beginning of the trial. Both John Miner and Richard Price had been taking copious notes during the prosecution's witness testimonies, underscoring statements that Miner could potentially use later to invoke sympathy for the defendant and, for Price, to use in discrediting their statements; all part of their Trident strategy to defend, deny, attack.

Court reconvened. John Miner stoutly approached the jury dressed meticulously in a stylish gray suit, crisp white shirt with its cuffs joined by gold links, and wide, black silk tie. The courtroom, with the apparent exception of the defendant, eagerly awaited his oration.

Miner put both his hands on the jury box rail and began by saying, "Men of the jury, the human mind is mysterious and complex. We all posses this greatest gift from God, but as we know, we are all a little unlike. We can experience events sometimes differently from each other. One of us may welcome the beauty in a late-spring snowfall; another may consider that same snowfall as an unwanted nuisance. One may feel peace, the other anger—we're all different. Some events are far more than a simple snowfall. Some events grip our innermost emotions. It might be from the loss of one's finest horse. It can be from having a severely sick child. Or it can be from the loss of a loved one, whether it be by death or from being rejected. One intellect might stand such an event, another could become unbalanced. The unbalanced mind can lead to despondency, fitfulness, rash impulsiveness, mania, insanity, and suicide. It was the loss of Emma Moeckel to another man that dethroned the mind of Lewis Heydlauff. It was the loss of the girl with whom he was insanely in love that caused his mind to become unbalanced.

From where he stood in front of the jury, Miner pointed to the defendant, and then with thoughtful voice continued, "Lewis Heydlauff has lived a productive and honorable life. All who have come to the stand in his defense have told of his good reputation from all the time they have known him. It was the loss of his sweetheart that caused Lewis Heydlauff's mind to become unbalanced. It has happened to others; the great mind of Abraham Lincoln was nearly lost as a young man when his sweetheart, Ann Rutledge, died at twenty-two years of age from typhoid. It is told that Mr. Lincoln became severely depressed from the sad event, so grievously that he experienced the deepest gloom, and melancholy settled into his mind. At her grave, it is told that Mr. Lincoln said, *'I can't bear to think of her out there alone.'*

"Abraham Lincoln was honestly and truly in love with Ann Rutledge, it having been said that he never stopped loving her, even as he married Mary Ann Todd and later as president of our United

States of America."

Miner had many in attendance spellbound by his comparing Lewis Heydlauff with President Lincoln. Lincoln was held in greatest esteem in Jackson County, as it was only a short distance from the courthouse that the Party of Lincoln had been established. Miner intended for the jury to know of President Lincoln's depression—his melancholia—while deliberating a verdict for Lewis Heydlauff, *he too* being a *victim* of melancholia.

John Miner had the courtroom—most importantly the jury—fully captivated. He paced the length of the jury box, turned, and looked back to the feeble defendant, who had taken a position of having his head bowed and arms folded across his chest.

Miner shook his head slowly, and continued, "Lewis Heydlauff loved his girl so much he wanted to die if he couldn't be with her. Earlier this century, in Dublin, Ireland, Robert Emmet, an Irish patriot, loved his sweetheart, Sarah Curran, so completely that he surrendered his life for her. The two lovers were driven apart by rebellion, but aspired a way to escape here, to America, so they could be together for life. But Robert Emmet was arrested at the instruction of the girl's father for treason and thrown into prison. All he could do was dream of Sarah's loving touch as he was savagely held in a dark, dank cell. The two found a way to pass passionate love letters to each other, but Sarah and Robert were betrayed. In fear that his letters to Sarah, if found, would cause her great hardship, perhaps her life, he arranged an escape to warn her, knowing if he were captured, he would be executed. And yes, as he frantically tried to reach her he was quickly captured—with Sarah's precious letters in his pocket. At the young age of twenty-five, the same age as Lewis Heydlauff, Robert was cruelly hanged to death in the public square of Dublin. Robert could have chosen to live, but he was so in love with Sarah—insanely in love with his girl that, in a frenzy to protect her, gave up his life.

John Miner removed a folded page of parchment from his coat pocket, slowly opened it, and then continued, "The Irish poet, Thomas Moore, writes of Sarah Curran's anguish. She had voyaged from Ireland for Sicily in hopes of recovery from the torment of losing the great love of her life, the man she would never again embrace, the man to whom she could never again say '*I love you*,' the man who gave his life to rescue hers." Miner took a deep breath, looked sadly at the defendant, then warmly to the jurors and theatrically read:

> She is far from the land, where her young hero sleeps,
> And lovers are round her, sighing;
> But coldly she turns from their gaze, and weeps,
> For her heart in his grave is lying!
> She sings the wild song of her dear native plains,
> Every note which he lov'd awaking
> Ah! little they think, who delight in her strains,
> How the heart of the Minstrel is breaking!
> He had lov'd for his love, for his country he died,
> They were all that to life had entwin'd him,
> Nor soon shall the tears of his country be dried,
> Nor long will his love stay behind him.
> Oh! make her a grave, where the sun-beams rest,
> When they promise a glorious morrow;
> They'll shine o'er her sleep, like a smile from the West,
> From her own lov'd Island of sorrow!

There was whimpering in parts of the courtroom, particularly behind the defendant, who had resurrected from his near catatonic state during Miner's impassioned performance and began to stare perplexingly at the jurors, some of who looked at Lewis with moist eyes. Miner waited several seconds for their sentiment to infect the other jurors, and then continued as he raised his voice to emphatically proclaim, "It is the same frenzy of disappointed love, unfulfilled love—lost love—that has filled our asylums with bright minds and countless graves with broken hearts. Lewis Heydlauff doesn't deserve any of this. He loved his girl and, I boldly say, Emma's equal love for Lewis was conflicted only because of another man's selfishness."

Miner walked to his table for a drink of water as the sounds of sniffling and nose blowing filled the courtroom. Judge Peck was expressionless as he allowed Miner to catch his breath.

The tragic event of May 31, 1896, involved Germans from their enclave in Waterloo, but it was the jury in Jackson that was to decide the fate of Lewis Heydlauff, and those twelve men were mostly of Irish and English heritage—they knew the story of Sarah and Robert. They were the ones sniffling the most—an insight to the defense's rigid jury selection. John Miner, in his systematic approach to create sympathy for his client, took the opportunity to catch the eyes of the jurors, focusing on those with teary eyes to offer a look of compassion. Miner knew he was creating pity for the defendant; he was confident that he had been successful in transforming Lewis from defendant to victim in the minds of some of the jurors, and for them, a victim needs a villain—and Miner was about to give them one.

Miner changed his expression from compassionate to smoldering anger. He then explosively addressed the jurors as he bellowed, "The killing of Emma Moeckel was an insane act—Lewis Heydlauff had nothing to gain by it. He had no malice toward Emma. If Lewis had any ill feeling it would have been against George Tisch. He knew George Tisch dictated the letter that Emma wrote, for Tisch alone knew what went on at the circus in Munith. But Lewis seemed to have no feelings against Tisch. He knew that the pastor's wife had been requested to break up the engagement and get Emma to go with Tisch. Was it George Tisch who persuaded the pastor's wife to sway Emma away from Lewis?"

As Miner was addressing the jury Lewis's sympathizers could be heard grieving in the background. He stopped talking and waited long enough to allow the depressing whines to impact the jurors. Miner then threw his arms up and in a fiery voice boomed, "George Tisch is the cause of all this trouble. If Lewis had any malice in his heart it would have been directed against Tisch, who put up the job on him. When Lewis came on the Moeckel porch after the shooting with a gun in his hand, he saw George Tisch standing by his horse just a few feet away."

Raising his voice higher, Miner thundered, "If Lewis Heydlauff had malice in his heart he might have blown George Tisch's miserable head off. He could have had reason to feel hatred for this fellow; he had been the cause of all his trouble. But this poor boy had no malice against anyone—his mind was diseased, he was in a state of frenzy, he was insane. The physicians all testified on the stand that Lewis Heydlauff was insane when he committed the act."

At this point, the elegance of John Miner's rhetoric in pleading sympathy for Lewis because of his insanity caused a tempest of more tears and uncontrollable emotion amongst the many relatives and friends of the defendant. Lewis had also been affected. He had not changed his sitting position much, but was exhibiting strong grief while Miner was speaking. Lewis may have appeared comatose earlier, but he was now surely listening to what was being said. Miner continued as he emotionally cried out, "Lewis has traveled through the burning depths of the hell of remorse since that horrid act was committed."

Throughout the courtroom and corridors and down the halls there was a crescendo of mixed emotions being heard in the form of tearful cries and heated rumbling. For the second time during the trial, contrast between the Heydlauff and Moeckel emotions were obvious.

Miner powerfully stated, "What occurred in that parlor was an insane act, the most insane act I have ever heard of a gentleman. This defendant loved the girl he killed, loved her more dearly than the blood that flows in his veins. He cannot tell how it happened—whether this defendant fired the first shot at himself or at the girl he loved, God only knows. His admission is that he didn't remember anything. Asked if he would have shot Tisch if he had seen him, the defendant replied perhaps he may have, but that he didn't know. Lewis Heydlauff had no malice against George Tisch or he would have shot him!"

Lewis was bawling. His mother, sitting directly behind him, was noisily sniffling. Christina leaned forward and passed a clean handkerchief to her grieving son while his father wiped his eyes and cleared his throat. Miner waited before continuing—to allow the jurors ample time to observe the blubbering family—and then said, "Lewis's father knew there was something the matter with Lewis; he gave instances where he acted queerly during his testimony. Emma's father came upon the stand and corroborated Lewis's father. Mr. Moeckel said Lewis had changed; Lewis had become sullen and morose whilst working and living at his house.

"The prosecution says crime must be punished. There was no crime committed, for this poor boy had no will or purpose to commit what he has been charged with. There was no motive. Wrong cannot be righted by the commission of another crime. The crime to punish for what—for being innocent? What Lewis did could not be prevented."

Miner took pause as some of the crowd was showing emotional sympathy for Lewis Heydlauff, with an equal number expressing distain for the killer. Miner calculated that the groans were possibly greater than the grunts. Both sides were causing a great deal of disturbance in the courtroom. News reporters were rapidly taking notes of the occurrence. The jury sat mesmerized by John Miner's oratory and by the commotion surrounding them. None of the jurymen had ever been in a situation like this—had never imagined it when they were sworn to hear the case and render a verdict.

Judge Peck demanded silence in his court as he forcefully pounded his gavel not once, not twice, but three times and shouted, "This is a court of law, not a saloon!"

The jurymen snapped out of their trances as John Miner, having taken pause to allow the scene to unfold and satisfied by the occurrence, raised his voice above the settling uproar to say, "Lewis Heydlauff comes from an outstanding family. They are prominent residents of Jackson County. They have built a reputation of honesty, industry, and obedience to the law. They have helped build this land of ours into a great land. I ask you twelve jurymen to not disgrace his family by unjustly sending this poor broken boy to prison to spend years, perhaps until death claims him, for an act for which he is not responsible. Think of Emma Moeckel. She is now in heaven. She knows what Lewis was going through. She knows what drove him to his insane act. She wouldn't ask for a conviction. The people of Jackson do not seek the kind of vengeance the prosecution is demanding, for it isn't needed. Lewis Heydlauff was insane and not responsible for the death of the girl he so dearly loved."

Miner looked at the jurors for a long period of time, and then told them, "You will next hear Richard Price continue with our case for the acquittal of Lewis Heydlauff."

John Miner concluded his captivating portion of the defense's closing argument at 1:15 p.m.

Judge Peck recessed the court until 2:00 p.m.

Afternoon Session

Closing Argument for the Defense Continues

Court reopened at 2:10 p.m. with the largest crowd yet in attendance. Outside the courthouse, news had spread that the trial was reaching its climax, drawing locals who loitered in a carnival-like atmosphere as they waited word of a verdict.

Richard Price, who was dressed as if he had coordinated his wardrobe with John Miner, stood at the entrance to the jury box as court was about to reconvene. As each juror filed past him, Price made it a point to catch their eyes and offer a distinguished nod of recognition as they took their seats. Some of the twelve settled comfortably into their seats, others leaned forward to relieve pressure from tired backs.

Charles Blair and Henry Edwards had returned to their table and were busily shuffling papers and comparing notes.

Richard Price joined John Miner at their table, where the defendant was sitting lethargically as before, seemingly not at all interested in the proceedings.

Court attendees stood as Judge Peck entered the room, took his seat at the bench and reminded everyone that they were in a court of law and to respect the rules of his court. He was resolute in saying that he would have any spectator removed as he saw fit—the entire assembly if necessary—if a ruckus occurred as earlier.

After the judge made his threat, an uncanny quiet overcame the room, except for muffled exchanges between newspaper reporters, and muted sounds from corridors outside the courtroom, which were packed. The corridors quickly calmed as Judge Peck's stern warning was relayed. It seemed as if the entire Jackson County Courthouse went mute, except for an occasional clink or clank that didn't seem to originate from anywhere.

Judge Peck, satisfied that he had made his point, quietly told the defense to continue their closing argument.

John Miner had focused his speech on the emotional aspects that led to Lewis Heydlauff's insanity. He had prepared the way for Richard Price to make a systematic argument for Heydlauff's clinical innocence.

Price left his table and approached the jury. Those in the courtroom that could see him keenly focused on his every move. Price stopped and faced the jury, offered a warm smile, and nod to the group—just as he had when they reentered the court. He then stepped back, and with a clear and prominent voice began, "Jurymen, I feel it unnecessary to remind you of the importance of this case. There is no question that a girl is tragically dead. Was there an intent that led to her death? The answer is no, there was not. There is nothing more important than this fact."

Price looked intensely at the jurymen and continued, "The defense will not attempt to work on sympathies for the defendant, but will solely address the evidence presented in this case. Some parts of this case are undisputed. For example, it is concluded that a homicide occurred.

"It was said during reliable testimony from esteemed medical experts in the field of insanity who took the stand and testified under oath that certain persons will go insane under certain circumstances. Asylums are filled with the sad evidence of this fact, and among those unfortunates are a great many, perhaps a majority, who go there through disappointment in love. We have thousands shut up in asylums who would, if liberated, commit homicide the same as this defendant did, for the same reason: they couldn't help it. The prosecution has essentially acquitted this defendant of willful murder; the testimony of their witnesses proves it. They now ridicule expert testimony and illogically tell you that any man is as good a judge of insanity as the most experienced physician, like Dr. John Trafton Main. The good doctor stated as the result of long experience and from examination of numerous insane persons that the defendant was suffering from insanity at the time of the homicide. The prosecution had the resources of the whole county available to them. They might have called medical experts to examine the defendant, but they dared not do it, for they knew any reputable physician who had experience in such matters would at once tell them the accused was insane. Their case is so weak they couldn't risk expert testimony, knowing it would be against them."

The courtroom remained hushed, save for the occasional sniffle and sounds of handkerchiefs being used to wipe noses and dab tears. Price walked to his table and collected some notes, returned to face the jury, and said, "I am going to read from the sworn testimony of George Hannewald, the witness who brought the defendant to the Heydlauff house after the shooting. I'll begin with Hannewald's testimony when he first encountered the defendant:

Witness Hannewald: "Lewis was lying in the lane; we picked him up and carried him to my carriage and took him home."
Blair to witness Hannewald: "Did Lewis talk on the way home?"
Witness Hannewald: "Yes. After we got Lewis into my carriage, I held him up and asked him why he did the shooting."
Blair to witness Hannewald: "What did the defendant say?"
Witness Hannewald: "Lewis said he was beside himself because Emma had put him out and wanted to die."

Price lowered the notes and, with a sad inflection in his voice, told the jury, "Lewis didn't say he knew Emma had been shot and was dead in the parlor. He only knew he had shot himself and wanted to die."

Price then read Dr. John C. Conlan's entire evidence, emphasizing his conversation with the defendant when he reached the point when Dr. Conlan testified:

Witness Conlan: "Lewis told me he wanted to die and could not leave her behind him. Lewis told me he expected to die, and thought he made a mess out of it. Lewis asked me to give him poison, or leave it behind so he could take it and die. I refused of course. Lewis was greatly excited and wanted to die. He asked again for poison, saying he couldn't live without Emma and wanted to die."

After Price concluded reading Dr. Conlan's testimony, he looked passionately at the defendant who was sobbing as a child, then back to the twelve jurymen and stated, "Lewis Heydlauff never intended to shoot and kill his sweetheart. He loved the girl and could not bear to live without her—only he wished to die."

Lewis's mother, seated directly behind her son, was conspicuously weeping, as were many throughout the courtroom. Lewis began growling in an uncanny guttural voice. Judge Peck lightly sounded his gavel and, without saying a word, the room settled.

Price continued by referring to Justice Orville Gorton's testimony concerning the defendant's stated reason for bringing his revolver to the Moeckels' house, reading from the court transcript:

Blair to witness Gorton: "Did you ask the defendant why he carried a revolver when he went to the Moeckels' house?"
Witness Gorton: "Yes, I did. The defendant said that was nothing new; that he carried his revolver for three or four years and had no intention to shoot Emma, himself, or anyone. I asked Heydlauff if he might have shot George Tisch if he was in the room. Heydlauff told me he didn't know what he might have done if Tisch was in the room. Heydlauff told me he had never thought to shoot anybody."

Price went on to say that the evidence was clearly consistent and not one bit of it indicated malice, motive, or intention. He attacked the only testimony that inferred such—Albert Moeckel's. Price referred to his notes and read from Albert's testimony:

> Witness A. Moeckel: "Emma was going back on him and he said that if she didn't come back to him he would kill himself. Lewis told me that if he had hold of Emma he would choke her, and if she married George Tisch she would have a hard life before she died."

Price bellowed, "These statements are untrue. Albert Moeckel testified at the Justice Court and never mentioned a word of this conversation. He was asked over and over to tell everything he knew, but said none of this, because it never occurred."

Albert was sitting with his family directly behind the prosecution table where Charles Blair and Henry Edwards listened intently to Price's heated diatribe. Albert looked sadly to his parents wanting to say something, but his father hushed him.

Price continued to blast Albert's testimony saying, "Lewis didn't say anything like that to Albert Moeckel. His mother tries to explain that he suffers from a nervous condition and his memory is impaired. She wishes to excuse him, but in doing so, shows no mercy for this poor defendant who has been and is now insane."

Katharina pulled Albert close when he wanted to protest; Friederich was breathing rapidly, his face flushed scarlet as ready to burst.

Price loudly stated, "Witness after witness tells of the defendant's peculiar behavior. Expert witnesses tell of his insanity. Mr. Moeckel noticed it early in the spring. Mrs. Moeckel noticed it, and others observed it. Lewis Heydlauff's brain was diseased. He had become insane!

"The prosecution's case is weak; it shows no cause for murder in the heart of the defendant. Their witnesses all prove that Lewis Heydlauff was insane—he didn't know what he was doing. Lewis was religiously reared—Henry Edwards said this morning, "*Those Germans are honest—they tell the truth.*" The truth is that Lewis Heydlauff has no knowledge of shooting Emma Moeckel. He didn't plan it or intend it; it is all a blank to him. Allow me to repeat—it is all a blank to him."

Price stood motionless, looking at the jurymen for several seconds. Satisfied that the twelve were hanging in suspense, Price went on to attack George Tisch as the origin of all Lewis's troubles as he mockingly said, "If this defendant had been a George Tisch, he would not have gone insane over the loss of the girl. If he were a George Tisch, he would probably have gone to the girl and demanded his miserable, fifty cent ring back and told himself, 'Just let her go.' But Lewis Heydlauff was cast from a different mold. Lewis loved that girl with his whole soul."

During Price's closing most of Lewis's family and close friends had watery eyes and were sniffling. Even John Heydlauff had a tear trickling down his weathered, stoic face as he lamented Lewis's unsettling behavior at home—and telling his son to find work elsewhere—when he knew Lewis was fearful of leaving home. After learning of brain disease from the physicians, John Heydlauff now thought his son to be sick, and wondered if he had triggered Lewis's path to insanity by his action. John Heydlauff was feeling a father's culpability for his child's demise, and a haunting guilt that Emma would still be alive if he had not started the whole mess by what he had done.

There was no sympathy for the defendant amongst the Moeckel family. Each time the defense made reference to Lewis's epic love for his girl, Friederich clenched his teeth so hard it triggered painful pressure throughout his entire head. During the winter, Friederich had learned who Lewis really was: a resentful coward hiding behind the veneer of a respected family name. Lewis Heydlauff was rude and disrespectful to his daughter—who was now dead and buried—because he could not be a man and walk away.

Others on the Moeckel side also knew precisely what happened the morning of May 31, 1896. Dr. John Conlan heard Lewis confess to shooting Emma, as did George Hannewald. Albert Moeckel re-membered exactly what Lewis told him: that Lewis said he would choke her and to be sure to *bring her home* the night before he killed her, only to see her dead at home. Jacob Heydlauff was deeply troubled as he recalled what Lewis said when he visited his cousin shortly after the shooting. They all had asked themselves how Lewis could claim no memory of what he had told them—and wondered why he was being shielded by a group of people that testified Lewis had no memory of what he had said.

Katharina Moeckel had once been fond of Lewis; she thought that he and Emma made a nice couple. She now felt betrayed by the entire Heydlauff family for trying to protect their deceitful killer from the truth. The entire Moeckel side was enraged when the devi-ous lawyers implicated George Tisch for Emma's death by portray-ing Lewis as the hapless victim who lost the girl he loved because of another's interference. They all knew the truth: *Emma was murdered trying to escape Lewis because she found true love in someone else.* The Moeckel side collectively questioned how Lewis's unscrupu-lous lawyers could morally twist the truth—had they any decency? They all were in agreement that Lewis Heydlauff was guilty of cold-blooded murder.

Richard Price assessed the spectators' emotions, and they were what he had planned for. There was more than enough pathos for the defendant to bleed into the jury box—as it contained only those who mattered—and it had. Price read the faces of the jurors and was confident he had swayed some to his side. Price continued to work the juror's emotions as he cried out, "Lewis's heart was bro-ken. Emma's mother loved her daughter, but no mother could love a dying child with a stronger affection than what Lewis had for Emma in his tortured heart."

Katharina cried out, "Oh my God, Friederich, how can that man say that?" as she broke down and wept against his shoulder.

Judge Peck glared at Price in condemnation; the silence in the courtroom was deafening.

Price was unaffected. He turned to the Moeckels, shrugged, and then pivoted sharply to the jurors and forcefully said, "I have seen a mother go stark raving crazy at the bedside of her dying child and yet, the prosecution claims that the defendant couldn't become insane in so short a time as seven days—the seven days when Lewis brooded over his misfortunes, the seven nights when he wept for the loss of his girl and couldn't sleep as he contemplated suicide. Are we going to progress backward and refuse to believe that insanity is a brain disease?

"Look about this courtroom. You can see the overflowing sympathy for the defendant all around you. This poor boy has been dragged into this court and has had to endure the pain of being told by the prosecution that he is an evil man who willingly killed the girl he loved—when he has no memory of it whatsoever! Lewis Heydlauff loved his girl so much he didn't care to live without her. He only wanted to see her one last time before he was to die and have one last kiss to take with him to the grave. This is not the action of a hateful, evil man. This is the action of a man who loved as no other can imagine. The prosecution is determined that you, the jury, shall believe the defendant is simulating insanity—is a hypocrite as well as murderer. Dr. Colby showed how impossible it was for this boy to deceive the physician who attended him in jail. The physicians all testified alike that the defendant was not responsible for the death of Emma Moeckel."

Price returned to implicating George Tisch as he said, "Emma and Lewis were together—they were engaged and planning to wed. Everything between them was good. Maybe they had a small argument or two—who doesn't in a romance? It was George Tisch who ruined it. He didn't love Emma—he only coveted her. If Tisch had stayed out of Emma's and Lewis's affairs, this trial would not have been necessary because Emma would be alive."

Richard Price's provocative statement caused a commotion in the court—angry grumbling reverberated from the Moeckel family and friends, and loud chatter amongst stunned reporters. Some on the Heydlauff side turned to find George where he sat and frowned at him with spiteful eyes—they had someone to blame.

George grimaced and shook his head in despair. As an innocent man, he felt like he was being condemned to the gallows by a lynch mob in an arena of hate. George wanted to escape, but felt captive by the horde surrounding him, so he sat and waited forlornly for the noose to tighten.

Judge Peck pounded his gavel and bellowed, "Order, order, I'll have order in my court!"

Price had hit a nerve with the jury. He observed that some of the jurors, perhaps most of them, looked provoked. Before the court-room noise fully subsided, Price began loudly pleading with the jury, saying, "Lewis was led to insanity because of his complete and total love for his girl—from the total devastation of losing Emma because of the actions of another man. I implore you to accept the truth. The truth is that Lewis Heydlauff's brain is diseased; he was driven to insanity because his girl was leaving him for another man. He was insane the day of the shooting, is insane now, and is not re-sponsible in any way for the death of Emma Moeckel. Do not send an innocent, unfortunate, afflicted boy to prison for the rest of his life and cast a stigma on him and the name of a worthy family."

Richard Price concluded his appeal by saying, "Men of the jury, I regret that there is nothing further I can present. The truth has been told and the defendant is innocent. I fully believe in Lewis Heydlauff's innocence and ask you to do the same. Thank you."

Richard Price ended his argument at 4:20 p.m. He had spoken for over two hours.

Judge Peck called for a fifteen-minute recess.

Court Reconvenes

Rebuttal by the Prosecution

George Tisch direly wanted to flee the courtroom during the blistering attacks that both John Miner and Richard Price had lev-eled at him throughout their closing speeches, but was paralyzed by their horrid accusations. George now sat alone, his stomach violent-ly churning and fearful of vomiting. His prolonged suffering from losing Emma was worsened by each lie the lawyers told—lies that repeatedly slashed at his very soul. Katharina Moeckel had given George a sympathetic look during Richard Price's vicious condemnation, but now he felt abandoned. George's spirit was broken. As many of the spectators stood and stretched, George Tisch got up—unnoticed—and left the courtroom, not to return.

While court was in recess, word was sent down the corridors and to those lingering on the street that the trial was nearing conclusion. The county courthouse swelled in attendance as even more people forced themselves through the entrance and into every crammed space.

The sun was low on the horizon, so the building's electric arc lighting system was all that illuminated the room. Some of the windows in the courtroom were opened to allow fresh, cool, December air to flow through the stuffy confines.

Jackson County Prosecuting Attorney Charles Blair accepted that he was in a ferocious fight against a formidable defense team. At the beginning of the case Blair had never expected the extent of chicanery Miner and Price would turn to, much of it made possible through the deep pockets of the defendant's father.

Blair was aware that some of the jurors had been notably influenced by John Miner portraying Lewis Heydlauff as the unfortunate victim in the case. Blair also knew that Richard Price had been effective in making the case that Heydlauff was driven insane because his sweetheart—the girl he loved—put him out after being pursued by another man: George Tisch. To win the jury, Blair had to completely refute the insanity defense and negate the portrayal of Heydlauff as the hapless victim. Blair had to bring the jury back to the only hard fact in the case: Emma Moeckel was murdered in cold blood by Lewis Heydlauff—Emma Moeckel *was* the victim.

Blair had to reestablish the truth regarding Lewis Heydlauff's reason for committing his heinous act of murder. He had to convince the jury that it was not insanity—*but jealousy*—that led to the defendant's motive for murdering the girl. Blair needed to use his rebuttal to convince the twelve jurymen to consider *only the facts*, and not let their emotions become a diversion as to why Lewis Heydlauff deliberately pushed the barrel of his revolver against Emma Moeckel's body and pulled the trigger three times—murdering an innocent girl.

Judge Peck entered the room at 4:45 p.m. and reminded the spectators that he demanded quiet; if there was to be any disruptive outburst he would empty the room without hesitation.

Charles Blair's normally clean-shaven face was shadowed with late afternoon stubble, but he looked refined in his well-tailored, black, long-length three-piece suit with wide lapels. Before leaving his table to deliver the prosecution's rebuttal, he tightened the knot on his gray tie, brushed his lapels, and then approached the jury.

Blair studied the expressions of the twelve exhausted jurors. He looked at each face in an effort to measure their reactions to Richard Price's emotionally charged onslaught to determine who looked sympathetic or not, and who appeared indifferent. Uncertain of it all, Blair knew he had to make a powerful, convincing speech—the speech of his career—to dispel the defense's outrageous myth that Lewis was the victim and not the villain.

Charles Blair began by saying, "Members of the jury, this has been a remarkable trial. You have heard conflicting statements, confusing statements, and emotional statements that have been made during the past four days regarding the defendant's reason for his murderous act. I come to you with no feeling for or against Lewis Heydlauff. I come to you asking that you only consider the facts leading to the murder of an innocent girl. This case is the most singular case I have ever witnessed: a man was jealous because a girl he wanted chose not to be with him, but to be with another. So he killed her. It's that simple."

Blair stopped to read the juror's faces. To his dismay, there were only four, maybe five nods of agreement. The others, nothing—just blank looks.

He continued, "The defense wants you to see it another way. They want you to believe that the defendant was led to insanity. How do they present it?"

Blair scoffed and raised his voice saying, "They even put their crazy man on the stand for hours to testify regarding his own sanity!

"You heard the defendant's testimony: he talked rationally; he told what he did and why; he told what he thought and why; he talked just as any other man would do. Is he insane now? The experts say he is. Was he insane when he fired his revolver at Emma Moeckel, not once, but again, and again?" Blair again raised his voice and methodically stated, "Lewis Heydlauff decided to kill Emma Moeckel, went to her house, waited for her, and bang, bang, bang—Emma Moeckel was dead. That's the whole case."

Blair walked the length of the jury box without taking his eyes off the twelve, pivoted, walked back, and stopped halfway. He then looked over to the defendant, sitting slothfully as usual, looked back to the jury and said, "If Lewis Heydlauff was sane *he must be punished*! The law is not vindictive. It doesn't seek alone to punish only this defendant; it aims to deter others from crime—to restrain future discarded lovers from killing the girl who rejected them for any reason—then setting up a plea of emotional insanity. You, the jury, must only consider the facts and lay aside any sympathy as well as prejudice and hold only the highest regard for the fair balance of justice. The defense has done what they could to make this an emotional case in an attempt to obscure the facts.

"Decisions are made only on facts. During the defense's closing argument you were told to consider the supposed sympathy within this courtroom for the defendant. I have never, in all my years, seen such an exhibition of disrespect to a jury in a court of record. If I had done such a thing as a prosecutor for the people, the Supreme Court would reverse the verdict and send the case back for another trial. You twelve men are the jury—not the spectators—in this courtroom. You alone will decide the fate of Lewis Heydlauff, not the persons sitting in the back row, not the crowd pushed against the walls, not the news reporters, not anyone but you.

"The defense brought several expert witnesses to testify before you. I won't pooh-pooh the use of an expert, but I will assure you that their opinions are no better than the opinion of any other person. I ask each of you: do not consider their opinions superior to yours. Dr. John Main expressed two different opinions in his testimony. He determined the first from visiting the defendant once, I repeat—*once*—while in jail, that Lewis Heydlauff was insane when he put three bullets into Emma Moeckel. But when asked if the defendant would have been insane as he talked rationally with Emma Moeckel's family, and later with Emma when she came home before shooting her dead in the parlor, Dr. Main said there would be *no* evidence of insanity. What is it, the first opinion or the second?

"The defense wants you to believe that four so-called medical experts who met with the defendant for only short periods of time have somehow determined he was going insane the week leading to the murder of Emma Moeckel. You have to wonder why the defense hadn't put on the witness stand the men who had worked with this defendant during the week leading to the murder, men who could raise the picture of the past with his present. Yet the defense dared not ask any of them if they thought the defendant insane. They dared not ask Dr. John Conlan if the defendant was crazy. He attended to the defendant and had rational conversations with him; the defendant told the doctor what he did and why he did it. Why didn't the defense call his brother-in-law, Albert Archenbraun, the man who employed him and with whom he worked every day that week, to tell of his mental condition? Why didn't they put Christian Schumacher, another brother-in-law, on the stand? Mr. Schumacher knew the defendant well. Why didn't they put him on the stand to tell of the defendant's insanity? How is it that the defense wants you to take only the opinion of four supposed experts who had never known the defendant until *after* he shot and killed Emma Moeckel—an innocent girl who the others all knew, loved, and respected?"

Blair began observing nods of agreement from some of the jurors, but knew that he had to negate any sympathy the defense had created for the defendant.

Blair continued by saying, "I don't disagree that Lewis Heydlauff was a devoted lover of Emma Moeckel. But Emma decided to end her romantic bond with him. That was her choice, not the defendant's. The defendant rationally thought of what to do about it. The defendant decided he had two choices: one was to choose death if he could not have Emma; the second was to live to see Emma the wife of another. Lewis Heydlauff chose death. The morning of Sunday, May 31, 1896, he made his choice. He resolved to make one last attempt seeking to get Emma to make up with him and if he failed, he intended to take his life. That was a decision of a desperate man, but not an insane man. When Emma rejected him in the parlor for the last time, Lewis's love for Emma was monopolistic—he would not allow another to love her. This defendant finally resolved to end everything and take Emma with him to the valley of death. All of the defendant's actions bear out this theory."

Blair looked at Lewis who was now leaning forward on bent elbows with open eyes. After a long moment he pointed to the defendant and, raising his voice, proclaimed, "If this defendant is crazy, then we are all crazy. A man who can correct a lawyer on the stand is crazy? A man who can clearly recall the names of each doctor that visited him in jail is crazy? Nonsense! Allow me to remind you that the esteemed doctor, Mary Putman Jacobi, had declared a man insane because a cold moonbeam swatted him in the face—it was nonsense. At least Dr. Jacobi admitted the error of her initial diagnosis. The four self-proclaimed medical experts who testified say they are better than you at deciding someone is insane or not—it's all nonsense!"

Blair put his hands on the front rail of the jury box and looked at each of the jurors for a full minute. The absolute silence in the courtroom was deafening. Charles Blair was generating the reactions he was striving for—a slight nod, a hint of smile, brief eye-to-eye contact—all signs that the jury was listening and forming opinions based on what he was saying.

Blair continued, "When the defendant's lawyer, Mr. Miner, spoke to you this morning, he certainly swept the strings of the harp of human passion and yes, he made the strings resound. His oratory was an elegant pathos aimed to confuse you, while the defendant's other lawyer, Mr. Price, later gave you the so-called evidence that proves, so he says, that the defendant was insane when he killed

Emma Moeckel and therefore innocent of his crime. As an attorney, I wish to compliment them both for their cleverness."

The jury was listening intently. Blair sensed that he was bringing them back to considering only the truth in the case, but also knew that he had to continue attacking the allegations of the defense's closing arguments.

Blair further stated, "The defense has attempted to draw on your emotions to distract you from the fact that an innocent girl was gunned down in cold blood. It's absurd to think of Lewis Heydlauff as the victim here. *Emma Moeckel was the victim—she's dead. Lewis Heydlauff murdered the poor girl!*" Raising his voice, Blair proclaimed cynically, "Lewis Heydlauff cannot be compared with Abraham Lincoln! The defendant cannot be compared to Robert Emmet! Is the defense implying that both these revered men were driven insane over the women they loved? Nonsense! Neither Abraham Lincoln nor Robert Emmet pulled the trigger of a revolver, not once, not twice, but three times—the third to be sure an innocent girl was dead. Abraham Lincoln and Robert Emmet did not kill their sweethearts! Don't let yourselves be misled by these ridiculous comparisons. You, the jury, must simply follow the facts in this case and be guided by the truth."

Blair had been caught off guard during defense witness testimonies when their medical experts testified that Lewis was not only insane when he killed Emma Moeckel—but was currently insane, and that convincing the jury of that diagnosis was their only possible hope for acquittal. Blair realized he had to fully discredit their physicians to convict Heydlauff of murder as charged. Blair continued, "The defense has called upon their self-proclaimed experts who used words to confuse you, one in particular: *melancholia*. Beware of that word. They have used it over and over the past four days. Melancholia is but a cloak used to hide the same old stalking horse until it fell into disrepute—the same old cloak under which guilty men have sought to hide and escape from justice for years. This defense is nothing new. It's all they have. Consider only the evidence. All the evidence states that this defendant's symptoms are not those of a melancholiac."

Blair walked to his table, gathered his notes, and returned, saying, "Allow me to read the sworn testimony from Dr. John Conlan when I asked him what the defendant said after the shooting:

Witness Conlan: "I had several conversations with the defendant as I was treating him. He was greatly excited and thought he was about to die."

Blair to Witness Conlan: "Did you ask the defendant why he shot Emma?"

Witness Conlan: "Yes, Lewis told me he shot Emma because he asked her to take back what she wrote to him in the letter and to be his girl again, and when she said no he put his arm around her and shot her."

Blair looked at the jury and asked quizzically, "How was it that the defendant remembered what he did and why he did it after committing the murder—but during this trial, he doesn't remember? The fact is that Lewis Heydlauff told Dr. Conlan exactly what happened."

Blair raised his voice and boldly stated, "That is the whole tragedy as it occurred: Lewis Heydlauff knew precisely what he did and why he did it."

Blair was making his final case for conviction and believed the jurors were accepting the truth of what he was restating. He continued, "This is a strange case at every step if you try to believe this defendant was insane. But all is plain when you see that Lewis Heydlauff was determined to commit suicide and take the girl with whom he was obsessed along with him—he admits it! This repugnant thought was in his mind all the week before that dreadful Sunday morning. This hideous thought made him moody, morose, and peculiar—his heart was filled with an ugly passion. Yes, he was consumed with suicidal thoughts, but he was not insane. Allow me to repeat: he was not insane. Lewis Heydlauff knew precisely what he was doing when he murdered Emma Moeckel."

Once again Blair attacked the medical experts by saying,

"Months after the defendant killed Emma Moeckel, physicians were called upon by the defense to meet with Lewis Heydlauff in jail for five minutes, or fifteen minutes, maybe an hour, to talk with the accused, while never taking his pulse or examining his physical condition or inquiring about his eccentricities. They then come away to glibly swear on the witness stand that this man was insane when he killed the girl, and that he was still insane this week during the trial when he gave rational testimony for almost three hours. The defendant's every action disproves their opinions. Gentlemen, you have a sworn duty to consider only the facts as you understand them. I ask that you do not believe any testimony that cannot be proven. As the prosecutor in this case, I assure you that the witnesses against the defendant told the complete truth. Do not let yourself fall into the snare the defense has set for you. Expert testimony is not always based on facts. During my career I have encountered juries that have been swayed by emotions. I admit that some verdicts have greatly angered me, not because I may have lost the case, but because justice for the people was not served by their misguided decisions. Again, only consider the facts—only the truth."

The crammed courtroom remained captivated by Blair's speech. He stood boldly looking at the twelve, his head held high. Charles Blair was confident. His inflection and tone were convincing as he spoke, "Men of the jury, you have heard all the evidence. Some of it was presented in an attempt to confuse the case. Consider only the facts in the case, not the emotions. The truth is that Lewis Heydlauff willfully shot and killed Emma Moeckel. There is no mistake about that. She lies buried in a dark grave at the German church. Her parents sit here in the courtroom brokenhearted. They didn't have the opportunity to say goodbye. The defendant pulled the trigger three times, the third to assure she was dead. Lewis Heydlauff took Emma Moeckel's life because she rejected him. Does this atrocity deserve mercy? Of course not—it deserves justice. It is your sworn duty to vindicate the law and discharge your duty honestly upon the evidence, regardless of what people may think. This case has an important lesson to teach: you can't hide from the law by a cloak of insanity. Do your duty without fear or favor. Lewis Heydlauff must pay the price for his crime."

Blair stood before the jury, confident from their expressions that he had successfully made his case for a conviction—a verdict of guilty. When he returned to his table Edwards nodded in approval of his impassioned speech. Both were convinced that a conviction for anything less than murder would be a travesty of justice.

Charles Blair had spoken to the jury for one and a half hours, concluding his elegant, impassioned rebuttal at 6:00 p.m.

Judge Peck, noting the late-afternoon hour, informed the court that there were to be no further breaks, and that he was now to address the jury.

Instructions to the Jury

Not a single person left the courtroom. Every seat and any possible standing space were occupied. The corridors were swarming. Police officers monitored the hallways to maintain silence and order, and to keep open narrow passageways by forcing people tightly against the walls.

Judge Peck began his charge to the jury by saying, "Men of the jury, you have heard the sworn testimonies from both the prosecution and the defense in this case. You have seen the physical evidence. I will now give you final instructions before you leave this courtroom to deliberate a verdict.

"It is your sworn duty to determine the facts. You alone are the judges of the facts. You have heard testimonies from multiple witnesses. You are not to make decisions based on the number of witnesses called for either side. What is important is how believable the witnesses were and how much weight you think their testimonies deserve. You must apply these facts to the law, which I will explain to you.

"The defendant, Lewis Heydlauff has been charged by the people of Jackson County, Michigan, with murder for the killing of Miss Emma Moeckel on May 31, 1896 in Waterloo. The defendant entered a plea to this charge of 'Not Guilty due to General Insanity.'

It is the obligation of the government to prove he is guilty. This means that the defendant is not guilty unless the government convinces you beyond a reasonable doubt that he is guilty."

The jury box, the courtroom, the hallways—they were silent as everyone strained to hear the Honorable Erastus Peck. The distinguished judge continued, "I will now explain to you the legal definitions, to which you must listen carefully." Judge Peck referred to a journal he was holding, and then addressed the jury by reading, "'Murder is an act of a person of sound mind, who, with malice, prepensely takes the life of another person.' I'll explain prepensely: it means the defendant planned the murder in advance."

The judge waited to be certain the jurors understood what he had read. He then continued by reading the legal definition of malice: "Malice is the intention to inflict injury, harm, or suffering on another, either because of a hostile impulse or out of deep-seated spitefulness." Without taking his eyes off the jury, Judge Peck said, "I will repeat: murder is an act of a person of sound mind, who with malice prepensely takes the life of another. Murder is deliberate, willful, and premeditated. In this case, it will be necessary to prove willfulness, as it is not necessarily implied."

Judge Peck paused. The courtroom remained hushed. The twelve jurors sat upright and alert, concentrating on Judge Peck. The defendant appeared to be in another world—head resting on the palm of his left hand, his elbow low on the table. Judge Peck leaned toward the jurors and said, "Besides murder, you have an option of convicting the defendant for the lesser crime of voluntary manslaughter." Judge Peck again read from his journal, " 'Voluntary manslaughter is the unlawful act of a sane person who takes the life of another person without malice or premeditation while in a sudden fray, a state of high emotion and passion, and not in self-defense." Judge Peck looked to the jury and said, "You will decide from the evidence whether the crime is murder, voluntary manslaughter or, that no crime was committed and the defendant is therefore innocent."

Judge Peck went on to explain presumption of innocence by saying, "You must accept that the defendant is presumed to be innocent of all charges against him as you enter your deliberation. He then read from his journal, " 'Presumption of innocence is a fundamental protection for a person accused of a crime which requires the prosecution to prove its case against the defendant beyond a reasonable doubt. Beyond a reasonable doubt means that if there is no other rational explanation as to the cause of the alleged crime, then the prosecution has proven the defendant's guilt and he must be found guilty."

He looked at the jury and said, "What is reasonable doubt? Reasonable doubt is a fair doubt. If the prosecution's evidence leaves your mind in such an uncertain condition that you cannot decide, the defendant must be presumed innocent and therefore be found not guilty." Judge Peck set his journal down and said, "The main questions in this case are: was the defendant of sound mind when the homicide was committed—and was he legally responsible? The law has no theories on insanity, but holds everyone sane unless clearly shown to be *non compos mentis*, which in English means 'not of sound mind.' A sound mind is rational and adequate to reason when it comes to making ordinary judgments. An unsound mind is the opposite—if unsound, it must have resulted from disease. If you find that the defendant did not have sufficient power of mind or willpower to know the act was wrong and to control his conduct, then he would be not guilty of the charge. The burden of proof rests on the prosecution. They must prove that the defendant had such power of intellect and willpower as would enable him to control his conduct and prevent the homicide.

"The question you must answer amongst yourselves is: what was the defendant's mental condition at the time of the act? It would make no difference whether he was sane or not before or after the homicide. I repeat, you must agree upon what the defendant's mental condition was at the time of the homicide. If the act resulted from mere passion and the homicide was the result of it, then he cannot be excused—the law holds him liable. If the defendant allowed violent passion to gain possession of his mind until he was no longer able to control his acts, then he is also responsible. If disease caused the act, then he was *non compos mentis*, and therefore not guilty." All eyes remained on Judge Peck, with the exception of the defendant's, as he sat leisurely in his chair. As the judge gulped from a glass of water, the arc lighting in the courthouse flickered, causing a strobe of sporadic brightness. Lewis sat up, looked to the ceiling, squinted, and hissed. Miner nudged Lewis, who then sagged back into seat.

Judge Peck waited for the lights to settle and referred to his notes. He then continued to address the jurymen, "During this trial physicians offered their expert testimonies to show that the defendant was not of sound mind when he did the shooting. Their testimony is not conclusive. You, the jury, should give it such weight as you believe entitled. If you believe the expert testimony to be contrary to facts in the case or clearly the result of wrong motives, it should be rejected. You must reach your verdict from all the evidence. Do not let rumors, suspicions, speculation, or anything other than the facts, as determined by you, influence you in any way. You will decide that if the defendant was of sound mind, he is guilty. If not, he must be acquitted."

Judge Peck paused and looked resolutely to the twelve men sitting in the jury box, then asked, "Do any of you have questions?"

There were none.

Judge Peck then said to the jurors, "You will now be led to a jury room to deliberate on your verdict. If you require anything from the court, you are to speak only to a bailiff, who will be stationed outside the room."

After addressing the jurors for more than an hour, Judge Peck sat back as two bailiffs were assigned to secure the jury. One bailiff led the twelve to the jury room as the second followed. When the entire jury was in the room, the door was closed and both bailiffs stood guard at the entrance. Judge Peck retired to his chambers. Lewis Heydlauff was cuffed, shackled, and then escorted by two deputies to the courthouse's basement cell. Lawyers for both sides gathered their notes. Charles Blair then spoke for a short time with the Moeckels while John Miner talked with the Heydlauffs. The lawyers then exited the courtroom for their respective offices, leaving behind assistants to wait; they were instructed to immediately contact them when word arrived that a verdict had been reached.

Newspaper reporters gathered in clusters, some predicting how long the jury would deliberate, others wondering if they had time to grab a quick supper, some flipping through their handwritten notes to be sure their stories included all the pertinent information of the day's proceedings. They were all destined to kill time awaiting the verdict. The family and friends of both victim and defendant stayed in their seats, not knowing what to do or where to go. It was announced that the courthouse was to stay open and that some of the lights would remain lit until word arrived of a verdict—until morning if necessary.

John and Christina Heydlauff sat together with only an occasional word whispered between them. On the opposite side of the aisle sat the parents of Emma Moeckel. Friederich looked straight ahead not saying a word. Katharina read from her Bible.

For many years the Heydlauffs and Moeckels were the best of neighbors. Now, far more than the location of St. Jacob Church separated them. Before May 31, 1896, the two couples would have been sitting together, John and Friederich discussing their work, their community, their church, their sons and daughters. Christina and Katharina would have been talking proudly of their children and what their futures might entail. Everything had changed. Where once conversation flowed freely, now there was none. For the Moeckels, resentment had replaced friendship. For the Heydlauffs, disgrace had replaced dignity. In the courtroom, neither acknowledged the other.

Most of the courtroom's lights were dimmed an hour after the jury left for their deliberation. As the filaments inside the large, glass bulbs faded from white to orange before going dark; the two bulbs that remained lit produced a muted yellow glow that erased the expressions on the faces of those still seated.

SATURDAY, DECEMBER 19, 1896   MORNING EDITION

JACKSON DAILY CITIZEN

Oratory in Court

JURY HAS YET TO RENDER A VERDICT

In the Heydlauff trial, Friday, the attorneys' final arguments before the jury, which occupied the entire day, were unusually brilliant and at times intensely dramatic. The necessarily condensed reports of their speeches, published in The Citizen, fail to do justice to the commendable eloquence of the talented quartette.

Henry E. Edwards occupied two hours with a complete review of the testimony, showing not only perfect grasp of every salient point in the case, but a command of language that held the attention of the audience to the close.

John W. Miner surprised and delighted his friends at the bar with the brilliancy and dramatic force of his plea. He left the systematic force of the evidence to his associate, Mr. Richard Price, and devoted his limited time to the emotional features of the case, carrying the audience with him in paroxysms of sobs and tears as proof of his eloquence.

Richard Price closed the defendant's case with a powerful argument of two hours, in which he analyzed the evidence with great care, incidentally ridiculing the people's case with a power on invective that was quite discouraging to the attorneys for the prosecution. Mr. Price's memory of the evidence was quite remarkable.

Charles A. Blair, in closing for the people, exhibited some irritation over the previous argument and it aroused him to make one of the finest pleas in the recent history of the circuit court. For an hour and a half Mr. Blair discussed the evidence, ridiculed the defense, and denounced expert testimony as a snare and humbug. His close was noteworthy and brilliant.

Judge Peck's charge was comprehensive, exhaustive, and very fair towards the defendant before the jury was sent out for deliberations at 7:15 o'clock this evening, who had yet to render a verdict as of this writing.

The key to this whole sad tragedy that plunged into the depths of grief and underserved shame for several worthy county families is found in the miserable little revolver which Lewis Heydlauff bought some years ago and carried in his Sunday clothes. If Lewis had never bought or carried a pistol this terrible tragedy would not have occurred and Emma Moeckel would doubtless be alive and well today.

The moral and warning for all young men is to beware of carrying revolvers, which are invariably more dangerous to friends than foes.

Saturday, December 19

Day Six

Verdict

Many people loitered about the county courthouse throughout the night, waiting for word of a verdict. Dawn was eventually observed as a soft, violet glow through the courthouse's tall, frosty windows. At daybreak the sky brightened and a strong wind started howling, its powerful gusts pounding against the window glass and through tiny fissures around their frames producing high-pitched whistling sounds.

Many who spent the entire night had slept in their seats, including court officers who remained stationed within the courtroom and outside the jury room. The lawyers' sleepy clerks remained sprawled on the court's benches.

As overnight spectators rose to their feet, stretched, and found their way to one of the building's lavatories, noisy chatter began filling the courtroom as edgy family members, friends, and the curious started making conversation regarding the overnight jury deliberation. The early morning rumor was that the jury was split—hopelessly deadlocked and unable to reach a verdict.

Shortly after 7:00 a.m., the jury requested the journal Judge Peck used to define the legal guidelines for determining a verdict. Word quickly spread that the jury had made contact with the court. A few minutes later the full array of courtroom lights was activated, and with morning sunlight bursting through the rattling windows, the room became brightly illuminated.

Seats vacated during the overnight hours quickly filled. The victim's and defendant's families had never left; news reporters had stayed as well. By 8:00 a.m. the courtroom was nearly full as a line of spectators in the hallway continued elbowing their way into the courtroom.

Just before 9:00 a.m., word circulated that the jurors had reached a verdict and would announce it when the judge and defendant arrived. Everyone waited at the edge of their seats. Those in the hallway pushed their way to the courtroom doors, hoping to hear the jury's foreman make the announcement. Everyone waited, and waited. The hour hand on the large regulator clock behind the judge's bench reached X, then XI. The clock's hour and minute hands met at XII—still no judge, defendant, or jury. The clock hands seemed stuck in time. Then slowly it became 1:00 p.m.—then 2:00 p.m. Many who had been waiting in the corridors had left the courthouse in frustration, but not one from within the courtroom exited. Most who remained looked exhausted, some faint from hunger and lack of sleep. Newspaper reporters took turns running out for food, but they too were fatigued.

The pendulum on the clock swung rhythmically back and forth, back and forth. Still, there was no word, no rumors—nothing at all. Then it was 3:00 p.m. It had been over twenty hours of waiting as the clock's minute hand clicked to 3:36 p.m. At that precise moment, a clerk hurriedly entered the courtroom and announced, "The jury has reached a verdict. Those of you waiting on behalf of the attorneys must contact them immediately."

Notification was sent to the judge, to the basement cell where the defendant was being held, to the court clerk, to the stenographer, and to all who were required for the reading of the verdict.

The entire courthouse broke into frenzy. As word spread, many who had left earlier found their way back to the corridors. Others in Jackson following the case in the newspapers rushed to the courthouse only to be turned back because the building quickly filled to capacity.

Assistant Prosecuting Attorney Henry Edwards entered the courtroom first and was led through the noisy gathering to his table with the help of a sheriff's deputy. Defense attorney John Miner followed just behind and made his way to the defense table. Minutes later, Richard Price pushed his way through the crowd and took his seat next to Miner. Henry Edwards nervously awaited Prosecution Attorney Charles Blair, who then came into the courtroom aided by a deputy sheriff who led him to Edwards. Blair turned to face Friederich and Katharina Moeckel, both drained from the long ordeal they had been enduring since their daughter's death, and nodded confidently to indicate that justice was about to be served. Across the aisle, Miner and Price were talking to John and Christina Heydlauff, whose weary faces looked to have aged a decade during the seven traumatic months leading to this point in time.

The two sheriff's deputies took positions on either side of the judge's bench. One called for the crowd to settle and to take their seats if possible. The other left his position to clear the front of the room, moving spectators and news reporters toward the sides and back.

The room went silent as Lewis Heydlauff, flanked by two uniformed guards, shuffled into the courtroom with his hands cuffed and feet shackled. It appeared Lewis had not slept. Perhaps visions of living and dying within the confines of a wretched prison cell prevented his eyes from closing—his mind flooded with ideas of how to finish the job that he started on May 31 and join his girl in death.

Lewis's pale face was covered by six days of spotty stubble; his hair was matted and oily. Lewis's lips were severely chapped, the split in the middle of his lower lip heavily crusted. His sunken eyes were glassy and lifeless. The defendant was unbound and released to his lawyers.

Lewis sat between his attorneys and rested his head on his left hand, grasping a soiled handkerchief in the other. Lewis's mother, sitting behind him, placed her hand on his shoulder, causing him to flinch and turn to her. Christine looked affectionately to her son and was then told by an officer that she was not to touch the defendant. Lewis slid back into his chair.

At 4:00 p.m. Judge Erastus Peck entered from his chambers wearing his long black robe. All in attendance were commanded to rise as the judge stepped up to his bench and sat. Immediately afterward, the steady cadence of footsteps from the jurors being led by a bailiff was heard as they marched into courtroom. The twelve jurors then filed one by one to their seats in the jury box. While this was occurring, Lewis had not changed position, apparently indifferent to the activity around him.

A bailiff then told the assembly in the courtroom to be seated.

Friederich sat and leaned forward with his hands tensely clasped in front of him; Katharina rested her head against her husband's shoulder as she firmly clutched her Bible.

With tension building and everyone at their positions in the courtroom, the spectators waited in silence. All that could be heard was an occasional cough and the shuffling and tapping sound of nervous feet. Then the county clerk, Arthur M. Baker, walked to face the jury. With little hesitation, he asked, "Has the jury agreed on a verdict?"

Foreman John Rockwell arose and replied in a strong, articulate voice, "We have."

The two defense lawyers rose to their feet. John Miner then grabbed Lewis's arm and pulled him up from his chair. Miner and Price flanked the defendant, who now stood in his usual drooped posture—his hangdog.

Arthur Baker looked at Foreman Rockwell and asked, "In the case against Lewis Heydlauff, who has been charged with murder for the killing of Miss Emma Moeckel on May 31, 1896, in Waterloo, what is your verdict?"

"Not guilty," Foreman Rockwell proclaimed boldly, his strong voice echoing off the courtroom's back wall.

Baker then asked, "In the case against Lewis Heydlauff for the crime of voluntary manslaughter in the death of Miss Emma Moeckel, what is your verdict?"

"Not guilty," John Rockwell announced loudly.

There was a peculiar silence for a few seconds. Then the full force of the not guilty verdict was fully comprehended by John Heydlauff, who was sitting with his wife behind their son, who could not repress his feelings of joy. He rose to his feet and began to clap his hands. Then others sitting on the Heydlauff side stood and cheered as they applauded the jury's verdict.

On the Moeckel side, wide-eyed disbelief was quickly followed by gasps, tears, and angry shouts. Charles Blair hit his fist on the table in anger; Henry Edwards buried his face in his hands. Katharina dropped her Bible and closed her eyes; Friederich shook his head back and forth as he looked despairingly at the exonerated boy—who did not appear to realize the consequence of the verdict.

Lewis had not changed his position nor had he raised his eyes from the floor.

Judge Peck, markedly displeased by the verdict, slammed his gavel to its wooden sound block with such force that it flipped the square onto the floor in front of Charles Blair. The angry judge had beads of sweat dampening his face, which had turned an unhealthy shade of red as he stood and sternly rebuked the audience, shouting, "This is a court of justice, not a beer hall. The jury has performed its duty and they are not to be applauded." Judge Peck looked at Lewis Heydlauff and said, "The defendant has been found not guilty of all charges by a panel of his peers and is free to go."

When Judge Peck said this, Lewis continued standing, seemingly unaware of what had occurred. Judge Peck repeated that the jury had rendered a verdict of not guilty and told Lewis he was free to leave. John Miner smiled at Lewis as he slowly explained that he was a free man. Lewis then lifted his head high, put his hands together as in prayer, looked up, and stared soullessly at the ceiling. Judge Peck glared briefly at Lewis Heydlauff, bit down on his lower lip, and then scowled at Lewis's cheering supporters. After several minutes of divided emotions being expressed amongst the spectators, no one had noticed that Judge Peck had sat down and rested his head on the back of his chair. Trapped by the doldrums of his judgeship's sworn duty, he stared listlessly at the commotion in his courtroom, trying to accept what had just occurred.

After the room settled, the county clerk polled the jury. Judge Peck then thanked them for their service and discharged the twelve men. It was then learned that the jury had been deadlocked for twenty hours following the first ballot, which tallied eight for acquittal and four for conviction of murder, and that this position had been maintained all night. It wasn't until just before 3:30 p.m. that the four for conviction had joined the others and the verdict of not guilty was agreed to. Further deliberation quickly dismissed the voluntary manslaughter option. In the end, they had agreed that the defendant had been insane with melancholia when he killed Emma Moeckel and therefore not responsible. Guided by Judge Peck's instructions, they had found the defendant innocent due to *non compos mentis*.

The Honorable Erastus Peck then left the bench and retired to his quarters, and the notable criminal trial closed and passed into history with the acquittal of Lewis Heydlauff.

While Lewis was looking at the ceiling, his mother had left her seat and embraced her son, as did his sister Sarah. John Heydlauff then herded them through the crowd as a reporter from the *Patriot* shouted out, "Lewis, how does it feel to be free?"

Another asked, "Lewis, did you expect that verdict?"

A young reporter from the *Jackson Citizen* called out, "Hey, Lewis! Are you thankful for the verdict?"

Lewis stopped at that reporter's question. He looked at him and replied apathetically, "Yes, I suppose so—it was better than I expected. I had hoped for this but never believed it would come."

John Heydlauff told his son, "Don't talk to anyone else and keep your head down."

The Heydlauffs rushed from the courthouse and hurriedly hailed a streetcar for Central Station where they boarded the Grand Trunk for Munith. Lewis sat alone facing his parents.

Steam began hissing and the engine's giant iron wheels squealed as it began inching away from the station, its four passenger cars lurching forward with it. As the train gained speed, little was said. Along the way, Lewis's expression grew complacent as he gazed out the window at the spectacle of spacious fields and stately houses wrapped in snow—he had almost forgotten what it looked like. While watching he had dismal thoughts of being deprived of freedom, recalling that when he arrived at the county jail he only wished to die. Last night, as Lewis spent his final hours of imprisonment, he once again contemplated suicide rather than enduring one more day of confinement. He now realized that he had escaped being condemned to rot in prison.

As the train rumbled along he conceded that living in freedom was better than dying behind bars. Lewis thought of his friends in Waterloo, smiled, stretched his arms, and yawned. He then reached into his pocket and grabbed hold of Emma's silver locket, chose to leave death behind, and closed his eyes.

Lewis may have been liberated by law, but he would never be free in Waterloo—or elsewhere in Jackson County. Before the trial, John Heydlauff, hopeful for a favorable outcome, had made arrangements for Lewis to live with his sister, Sarah Vogel, and her husband, Charles, thirty miles from Waterloo in Ann Arbor, a populous city in Washtenaw County where an unknown acquitted killer could feasibly live and work undetected. It was decided that Lewis was to spend Christmas at home, then pack his belongings and move to his new residence on Monday, December 28, 1896.

Lewis Heydlauff was about to enter a labyrinth in search of freedom.

CHAPTER TWENTY-NINE

Next Step

The disheartened Moeckels had stayed seated after the trial until most of the room had emptied. For the crestfallen family, the verdict was a travesty. Justice had not been served—the trial had ended as a mockery of justice.

After watching Emma's exonerated murderer walk from the courtroom, Friederich questioned both prosecuting attorneys regarding what had occurred, asking Blair if there was anything more in the law that could serve some sort of justice to Lewis for what he did.

Blair replied, "I believe there is. There's a provision in the law that can be invoked to send Heydlauff to the asylum for the criminal insane to test his mental condition and, if insane, cause his incarceration for treatment."

Friederich asked, "How long would he be confined?"

"That's difficult to predict. During the trial, Heydlauff's physicians testified that he was still insane with melancholia. Assuming the asylum's physicians concur, perhaps one or two years. But because Lewis Heydlauff is known to be a killer, he could potentially be held for several years. But first, he has to be charged with another crime. It's obvious that he lied during his staged testimony on the witness stand—that's perjury. Mr. Moeckel, you will have to swear out a perjury charge against Lewis Heydlauff."

Friederich asked, "What if it's determined he's not insane?"

"Lewis will then face trial in circuit court for perjury. When found guilty, he'll spend a year or two in prison."

"That's what I want. Lewis is a murderer and a liar. He must be punished."

Blair replied, "Leave it to me."

CHAPTER THIRTY

HEADLINES

Newspapers throughout Michigan reported on the unexpected verdict. Some stated only the jury's decision; others offered details, especially relating to the reaction of the Heydlauffs as they applauded the verdict and of Judge Peck's stern rebuke. There were more headlines to come.

SATURDAY, DECEMBER 19, 1896

The Saginaw Evening News

VERDICT, NOT GUILTY

Lewis Heydlauff, Who Murdered His Sweetheart, IS ONCE MORE A FREE MAN

TEMPORARY INSANITY WAS THE PLEA OF THE DEFENDANT'S ATTORNEY —VERDICT DOES NOT MEET WITH APPROVAL

Jackson—After being out for 20 hours the jury in the case against Lewis Heydlauff, charged with the murder of his sweetheart, Emma Moeckel, brought in a verdict of not guilty Saturday afternoon. The plea of the defense was temporary insanity. The verdict does not meet with approval, the general opinion being that the verdict should have been manslaughter.

CHAPTER THIRTY-ONE

PERJURY

Monday, December 21, 1896

With Friederich Moeckel, Charles Blair had prepared the application to swear out a warrant against Lewis Heydlauff for perjury and brought it to Justice Rudolph Worch in the county courthouse.

"Good afternoon, Rudy," Blair called out as he entered Justice Worch's office.

"Hello Charles, rough trial last week. I was surprised at the verdict; it appeared the jury was leaning toward a manslaughter conviction."

"Yes, but Henry Edwards and I were confident for the murder conviction, not manslaughter—certainly not an acquittal. The defense team, Richard Price in particular, was effective in confusing the jury with his so-called brain experts. They convinced the jurors that Heydlauff had no control over his actions. They had them believing that the defendant was victimized by melancholia because his girl left him for another man, and that it drove him crazy enough to kill her. I admit that John Miner also did a notable job by working the sympathy angle for Heydlauff. It was all nonsense, but the jury bought into it," Blair explained.

"What can I do for you, Charles?" asked Worch.

"Lewis Heydlauff killed an innocent girl. If he was acquitted because the jury decided he was crazy, then the question has to be asked: *why is he not in an insane asylum?* Rudy, Heydlauff lied on the stand. Three prosecution witnesses swore that Heydlauff told them that he not only shot the girl, but more importantly, why he shot her. When asked on the stand, Heydlauff testified that he didn't remember anything. Rudy, that's just hogwash. The murdered girl's father wants to charge Heydlauff with perjury. Rudy, I'm requesting that you issue a warrant, at the request of Friederich Moeckel, against Lewis Heydlauff for perjuring himself during his testimony at the trial."

"Charles, what do you hope to achieve?" asked Worch.

"Justice," Blair replied.

"Charles, perjury is a capital charge that requires a trial similar to the one you concluded. Perjury is difficult to prosecute; witnesses are subject to challenging questioning and, in the end, it's up to the jury to believe who and why. You would be retrying the case you just lost. But, I will admit, convictions can result in significant jail time if that's your goal.

Blair replied, "The object in arresting Heydlauff is to take the proceedings into court to determine if he is insane as the medical experts claimed during the murder trial. If it's determined that he's crazy, he'd be committed to an asylum for the criminal insane. I'll use the provisions of section 19, act 119 in the 1895 Michigan penal code—"

Justice Worch interrupted to say, "Charles, slow down . . . please tell me exactly what that provision states."

Blair removed a large, hardbound book from his leather briefcase. The book was titled: *1895 Compiled Laws of the State of Michigan, Volume One.* Blair opened it to page 676 and moved his finger down the page until he stopped at section 19, and read,

When a person accused of any crime shall have escaped indictment, or shall have been acquitted upon trial upon the grounds of insanity, the court, being certified by the jury or otherwise, shall carefully inquire and ascertain whether his or her sanity in any way continues and if it does, shall order such person into safe custody and to be sent to the Michigan asylum for the dangerous and criminal insane, or to any one of the state asylums for the insane. If any person in confinement under indictment for any crime shall appear insane, the judge in the circuit court of the county where he or she is confined shall institute a careful investigation. He shall call two or more respectable physicians and other credible witnesses and the prosecuting attorney to aid in the examination; if it is deemed necessary to call a jury for that purpose, he is fully empowered to compel the attendance of witnesses and jurors. If it is satisfactorily proved that such person is insane, said judge may discharge such person from imprisonment and order his or her safe custody and removal to the Michigan asylum for the criminal insane, or to any one of the state asylums, at the discretion of such judge, where such person shall be retained until restored to his or her right mind.

Blair paused, looking up at Justice Worch.

"Rudy, shall I continue?"

"No, I understand the premise. If Heydlauff is committed, how long would he be in the asylum?" asked Worch.

"That would be determined by the superintendent of the asylum. Within sixty days their physician will determine the degree of mental illness. Afterward, probably two years, perhaps longer if he's actually insane," Blair replied.

Justice Worch looked inquisitively at the frustrated prosecuting attorney and asked, "Charles, did you consider using this provision during the murder trial?"

"Yes, but it wasn't much of a consideration. It was, and still is my belief, that Heydlauff is sane. Why would I have asked for him to be certified sane with the evidence I had for conviction? It was the defense's hired physicians who convinced the jury that a sane man was insane. Rudy, if that's what the jurors believed, I need to use this provision."

"And if he is declared sane, will you pursue the perjury charge?" Worch asked rhetorically.

"Yes. In two weeks my term as county prosecutor expires, and it will be up to my successor, Elmer Kirkby, to prosecute the charge. I can't trust him to continue with the case. That's the reason for citing section 19."

"Charles, why wouldn't Kirkby continue with either section 19 or the perjury charge?"

Blair crossed his legs, took a deep breath, and began telling the story about the contentious campaign two years earlier between his brother, George, and Elmer Kirkby for county prosecuting attorney. He told of Kirkby's mudslinging, during which he attempted to destroy his brother's character by accusing him of being a drunk. He explained the relationship Kirkby has with the Heydlauff family, and that he was even called as a character witness for Lewis Heydlauff during the murder trial.

"All right, Charles, I understand; you make a compelling case. But Charles, I must caution that you will meet legal resistance from Heydlauff's attorneys if you take this route. Are you certain this is what you want'?"

"Yes, Rudy, some sort of justice must be served," Blair responded.

"All right, I'll grant your request, but I will not deviate from the law."

Justice Rudolph Worch signed the warrant and sent it to Constable George J. Rosencrantz, who was instructed to at once enforce the warrant for the arrest of Lewis Heydlauff.

Tuesday, December 22

Back to Jail

On Tuesday at about 2:00 p.m. loud knocking on the front door of the Heydlauff's Waterloo residence startled the owner. When John Heydlauff opened the door, he was surprised to see two burly, uniformed police officers standing in front of him. A third officer was tending two large horses hitched to a black police coach parked in the lane to his house.

"How may I help you?" John Heydlauff asked without inviting them in from the cold.

"One of the two officers announced, "My name is Constable Rosencrantz. I'm here by order of the Jackson County Justice Court to serve a warrant to Lewis Heydlauff."

John Heydlauff's facial expression went blank. "A warrant for what?" he asked in angst.

"Perjury. The warrant is signed by Justice Rudolph Worch. If Lewis Heydlauff is in this house please call for him to appear at once," Rosencrantz demanded.

"On whose behalf?" John Heydlauff questioned.

The constable showed the warrant to John Heydlauff, and when he saw that it was issued at the request of Friederich Moeckel, he shook his head and under his breath snapped, "Leave it alone, Fred; it's over. Leave my son alone."

Lewis had been standing around the corner leading to the front door listening to the exchange between his father and the constable. He decided to enter the foyer and faintly announce, "I'm Lewis."

Holding the warrant, Rosencranz declared, "Lewis Heydlauff, you are under arrest on a charge of perjury."

John Heydlauff demanded, "Under whose authority?"

"Justice Rudolph Worch. He has issued this warrant against Lewis Heydlauff for perjury during last week's trial. Mr. Friederich Moeckel swore out the complaint. Lewis, I need for you to come with me now."

"What!" John Heydlauff exclaimed. "What does that mean? Lewis, you stay put."

"It means that your son is now under arrest and is to come with me at once to Jackson," Rosencrantz replied.

Lewis looked at his father and said, "It's all right. I don't believe I have a choice in the matter. I'll gather my coat, hat, and gloves and go with them straight away."

John Heydlauff demanded he should accompany his son, to

which the constable replied, "Sir, that will not be possible. You must arrange for your own travel."

The two officers walked Lewis to the carriage. Lewis and Constable Rosencrantz stepped into the coach and closed the door. The other officer joined the driver, who took the horses' reins in hand and began the eighteen-mile, four-hour ride to Jackson. John Heydlauff, deeply alarmed and angered at the occurrence, began making his plans to take the train from Munith.

Early Tuesday evening the black police coach transporting Lewis Heydlauff arrived in Jackson. The accused was ushered into the Cortland Street police station and confined to a holding cell. John Heydlauff arrived two hours later at 8:00 p.m. with his attorney, John W. Miner. They were told bail would not be set until the next day and that the accused was to remain overnight. John Heydlauff was allowed to see Lewis for a limited amount of time. He then left with John Miner for Richard Price's house. At the Price residence the three spoke of the perjury charge and how to defend it. After an hour, John Miner invited Mr. Heydlauff to spend the night at his home.

Wednesday Morning, December 23
Justice Sought

John Heydlauff arrived at the Cortland Street police station with John Miner and Richard Price at 8:00 a.m. Miner asked the officer stationed at the front desk if there was any word from Justice Worch. Nobody in the station had any information. Thirty minutes later, Jackson County Prosecuting Attorney Charles Blair arrived. Price walked to Blair and asked condescendingly, "Not happy with the verdict, Charles? Whatever your scheme, it's not going to work."

Before Blair was able to reply, a physician came into the station asking for Prosecuting Attorney Charles Blair. "Here I am," Blair announced as he left Price. Within minutes, three additional physicians arrived and joined Blair. As he and the four doctors talked, Justice Worch arrived, nodded to the lawyers in the room, and walked over to the front desk officer, where the two began conversing. Fifteen minutes later, a young man arrived carrying a stenotype machine and asking for Justice Worch.

"Hello, son, you must be the court stenographer. I'm Justice Rudolph Worch."

As the assembly of lawyers and physicians bumbled about, the station's door swung open and Elmer Kirkby rushed in followed by a blast of cold air.

Blair saw that it was Kirkby and gave him an icy glance.

Worch called out to the crowd, "Please, follow me," and led the group to a small, makeshift courtroom inside the police station. Already inside the room were two police officers standing either side of Lewis Heydlauff, who was dressed in the clothes he left home in, looking bewildered.

Worch asked the court stenographer to use a small table and chair next to a raised desk. He instructed the police guards to sit with Lewis Heydlauff in the first row of chairs facing him.

There were about twenty other chairs scattered in the room. Worch offered them to the lawyers and physicians if they cared to sit, which some did.

Worch then asked, "Is everyone comfortable?" There were no replies, so he stepped up to the raised desk and announced, "All right then, Justice Court is now in session."

Blair, who was still standing, asked to approach. He informed Justice Worch of his intention, to which Justice Worch told Blair that he needed to formally make his request. Blair stepped back and allowed Worch to say, "Before the charges against the accused are read, may I ask for what purpose have you called these physicians to court, Mr. Blair?"

Blair announced, "Lewis Heydlauff has been charged with perjury. Under section 19, act 119 of the laws of 1895, I request that the court allow these four qualified physicians present before you to interview the accused to establish his mental capacity before proceeding with the charge against him."

Miner and Price both jumped to their feet, Miner calling out, "I object! This is only a preliminary examination of the charge. The accused has not been arraigned!"

"Sustained," Justice Worch stated as he looked tentatively at Blair. Worch then asked Blair to present the complaint sworn against Lewis Heydlauff.

Charles Blair read the charge, which accused Lewis Heydlauff of having committed perjury during his trial for the murder of Emma Moeckel. He stated that the charge was sworn out by Friederich Moeckel, and signed by Justice Worch.

Worch looked at the accused and asked, "Lewis Heydlauff, do you have a lawyer present?"

Lewis turned around and looked at his father, who was sitting with John Miner and Richard Price.

"May I approach the bench, Your Honor?" Miner called out.

"You may approach the bench," Worch replied.

John Miner informed Justice Worch that he was representing the accused and asked if he could sit next to his client, to which Justice Worch agreed.

"OK now, will the accused, Lewis Heydlauff, stand and face the bench?" Justice Worch ordered.

Miner instructed Lewis to stand next to him and face Justice Worch.

Lewis looked confused by what was occurring, but stood alert, showing no hangdog as he did just days earlier.

Justice Worch then said, "Lewis Heydlauff, you have heard the charge of perjury read against you. To this charge, how do you plead?"

Without answering, Lewis promptly drooped into his signature hangdog and said nothing. Miner looked indignantly at Justice Worch and also remained silent.

Justice Worch asked again, "What is your plea?"

Receiving no answer, Worch stated, "It is noted that the court enters a plea of not guilty."

Miner at once demanded an examination of the charge for his client, which was granted, and set for Monday, December 28 at 9:00

a.m., at the county courthouse.

"Bail is fixed at five hundred dollars," Justice Worch announced and then declared his court adjourned.

John Heydlauff furnished bail money and signed the necessary bond. Lewis was released and left with his father, both walking vigorously to Central Station, where they caught the train back to Munith and to their Waterloo home.

Charles Blair met hurriedly with the four physicians he had asked to attend the proceeding and told them he would arrange for them to perform their medical interviews at a later date.

As the doctors walked away Kirkby came to Blair and said, "Charles, I give you credit for your persistence. You lost a big one— why don't you let it go and get on with your new practice?"

Blair countered, "Elmer, you've been in my shoes before—how can we, as prosecution attorneys, be satisfied by a guilty man walking free?"

Kirkby smugly responded, "Last I heard, Lewis Heydlauff was deemed innocent."

Blair scoffed.

Kirkby grinned.

Before leaving Courtland station Kirkby commented, "Charles, I did notice that Lewis looked quite well until the perjury charge was leveled against him. It's impressive how quickly his hangdog returns when he senses trouble. Maybe he's actually a trained dog!" Kirkby laughed. "Charles, first you insisted that Heydlauff is sane, now you demand he be certified insane . . . do you actually believe he's crazy?

Blair stood, speechless.

"Have a good day, Charles," Kirkby quipped as he turned and strolled out of Courtland Station. A strong gust of frigid air hit Blair as the door shut.

While Kirkby was bantering Blair, John Miner had spoken with Justice Worch, saying he did not object to an evaluation of Lewis Heydlauff's mental condition, but not until after preliminary hearings. He also asked that the interviews be made by physicians selected by both sides of the case and by order from the court.

Blair then met privately with Justice Worch and asked him why he didn't allow the physicians to interview Heydlauff. Worch told him, "Charles, I don't have the legal authority to commit Heydlauff to an asylum prior to an arraignment. To have that boy committed beforehand requires the consent of a family member, and if that was the case, it wouldn't be in this court—that proceeding would be held in probate court."

Blair replied, "If this carries on past December 31, the charge could be dismissed by the incoming Prosecuting Attorney Kirkby. I was hopeful that Heydlauff would be arraigned today—that you would not have granted an examination."

Justice Worch said, "I understand, Charles. I'm sworn to follow the law. December 28 is only five days from now. I'll do what I can."

CHAPTER THIRTY-TWO

FRUSTRATION

Wednesday Afternoon, December 23

Charles Blair returned to his office furious. He had been humiliated by losing the most sensational case in years during his tenure as the Jackson County Prosecuting Attorney, and now his scheme to have Lewis Heydlauff committed to an asylum had stalled in Justice Worch's court. Blair had few remaining days before his term as prosecutor expired, and had to have Lewis Heydlauff arraigned immediately following the Monday, December 28 hearing. If not, the case would undoubtedly roll into the New Year and out of his control.

Some of the newspapers had been critical of Blair's prosecution of the Heydlauff murder case. The *Jackson Patriot,* in particular, implied carelessness by the prosecution's failure to use medical experts to evaluate Lewis Heydlauff's mental condition before the trial. The *Patriot* was critical by inferring neither Charles Blair nor Henry Edwards was properly prepared for trial. The *Patriot* got under Blair's skin when it reported that the community expected a conviction and questioned how the prosecution could have bungled the case so badly that it resulted in acquittal.

Blair refused to let go of the Heydlauff saga, believing he had a moral, personal, and political reputation to uphold. He and Edwards had seventeen convictions during 1896 and only two acquittals. Blair did not want to begin private practice with his new law firm of Blair, Smith, and Townsend, to be located in an elite suite of offices in the heart of Jackson, on a sour note. He wanted some form of punishment served to Lewis Heydlauff as justice for the grieving Moeckel family.

Charles Blair also sought exoneration from the *Patriot's* sharp criticism over his handling of the case. Blair decided to bring his case to the people of Jackson by telling his account of the trial, in writing, to James O'Donnell, editor of the *Jackson Citizen,* the *Patriot's* chief competitor. He carefully crafted an outline until exhaustion caused him to put down his pen and retire for the night.

Charles Blair awakened at dawn Thursday, December 24. He bathed, dressed, and left home for his office in the county building with his outline and notes, stopping for breakfast along the way. After finishing his second cup of black coffee, he paid his tab and soon afterward was sitting at his desk with a stack of blank paper and started to write. After several hours, he read and reread what he had written, then left for the *Jackson Citizen,* where he delivered his letter addressed to the paper's editor. He returned home as his wife Effie and their children were readying for supper.

CHAPTER THIRTY-THREE

CHRISTMAS

Christmas was solemnly observed at the Moeckel household. The family had suffered mightily throughout the trial as they had to relive the awful details of Emma's murder. Lewis Heydlauff's acquittal profoundly intensified the Moeckels' anguish. As a family, they were shocked at the cheers Lewis received when the jury rendered their verdict of not guilty. They were devastated that the trial had shifted from Lewis being a calculating killer to Lewis being the guiltless victim.

Friederich and Katharina were immeasurably offended by John Heydlauff, their once-caring neighbor, when he applauded his son's verdict. They were sickened by the devious lawyers implying that Emma was somehow responsible for her own death—*because she wanted to be with a different man!*

After hearing Lewis lie during the trial, Katharina was tormented by why she faithfully forgave him for the most ungodly of all acts. She was now equally tortured by wanting to take it back. The conundrum was testing her faith.

Friederich knew the details leading to the shooting on May 31: Lewis was not crazy when he approached him while working his field; Lewis was not crazy when he came to his home to see Emma the morning he killed her; Lewis was not crazy when he shot her and certainly was not crazy when he admitted to doing it. Friederich was becoming increasingly infuriated by the jury's verdict. He could not understand why twelve seemingly sensible men refused to accept the truths of George Hannewald, Dr. John Conlan, Jacob Heydlauff—and his own—that Lewis admitted that he willfully killed Emma to not leave her behind when he shot himself. Friederich was unable to understand how the jury could have believed all the lies professed so readily during the trial, and why they had accepted the pompous opinions given by the so-called experts.

Friederich was furious that Lewis was out on bail for the perjury charge and celebrating Christmas with his family—while his daughter lie dead in her grave.

Emma's two brothers were changed by having witnessed the events of May 31—Albert especially, as he frequently thought of what Lewis told him on the road the day before his sister was murdered. He was also confused by being accused of having made up the story—it was true. Albert carried a guilt that maybe his sister would still be alive if he had told his parents what Lewis said about Emma.

Florenz became withdrawn after Emma died. He went about his days not saying much, but at night he was often heard sniffling as he said his nightly prayers, finishing with, "God, please bless my sister Emma."

The Moeckel family did not attend the Christmas Eve service at St. Jacob. The trial had left them hollow. They could not sing a glorious hymn; they simply wanted to be at home. They also let it be known that their annual Christmas Day open house was not to be. They wished to spend the day in isolation.

Down the road at the Heydlauff house, John and Christina, who also stayed away from St. Jacob, were hosting an early dinner, a celebration of sorts, which included their son Emanuel and his family; the Archenbraun and Schumacher families; August, his wife Carrie, and young daughter Hannah; and from Ann Arbor, the Vogel family—in total, about thirty relatives and close friends.

Lewis looked remarkably well. He was clean-shaven. His hair was trimmed and he was dressed in clean clothes. Lewis appeared happy to be surrounded by so much family after spending almost seven months in jail. There was no conversation about his time in custody, the trial, or the pending perjury charge. Lewis mostly played with his nieces and nephews before dinner—their parents carefully watching. Shortly after eating, Lewis's three sisters and his brother Emanuel gathered their loved ones and left for their homes, where they could fully relax and enjoy the remainder of the day. Soon after, the last of their friends departed. Lewis and August helped their parents put the house back together and, at about 6:00 p.m., they retired to the parlor. Lewis sat and lowered his back onto an elegant, black-velvet chaise lounge and stretched out his legs, relishing the comfort of being home. August, sitting across the parlor in a plush, upholstered chair, caringly asked, "Lewie, how are you feeling?"

Lewis smiled and replied, "Quite well, actually."

From the kitchen, Christina commented, "I'm glad you're feeling well, Lewis. It's been quite an ordeal."

Lewis took a deep breath, and as he lazily exhaled replied, "Yes, it has. It's been a time I care not to remember."

Lewis said he was tired and went to his bedroom. He opened a dresser drawer and retrieved the photograph Emma had given him the prior Christmas. He stared at it. He then held Emma's locket, opened it, and revealed the empty space meant to hold a photograph. He then took out the scarf Emma had knitted, wrapped it around his neck and curled up on top his bed. He closed his eyes and tried to reminisce the way he once felt about his girl, but the memory was elusive. Lewis returned the photograph, locket, and scarf to the dresser drawer and closed it shut.

John Heydlauff had been sitting at his desk in the library shuffling through various papers. He leaned back in his chair and thought about the upcoming perjury hearing, and wondered if Lewis's problems with the law would ever end. He once again refused to accept the possibility of Lewis being locked up in jail or sent to an asylum, and would continue doing whatever possible to prevent it—regardless the cost.

John Heydlauff also knew that Lewis could never again live in Waterloo.

George Tisch rode to Christmas Eve service at St. Jacob with his parents. Before entering the church, George stood by himself at the warming fire, still reeling from the merciless attack he had endured seven days earlier at the trial. The outlandish accusations made by the defense attorneys further weakened his fractured heart. Feeling almost as an outcast, George's spirits were lifted when a small group of young revelers came to him singing Christmas greetings. George forced a smile and awkwardly replied, "Merry Christmas," as he was thinking, What's merry in my life? For just a little time the group engaged in small talk with George and then moved on, leaving him feeling lonely as before.

As George watched the jovial troupe dance away, his heart leaped when, from behind, he heard a voice like Emma's say, "*Fröhe Weihnachten, mein Freund.*" He turned around to see his friend Charlotte Hannewald smiling, her warm, blue eyes looking kindly up to his.

"Hello Charlotte—oh, I meant to say, Merry Christmas!" George was delighted to reply.

"I'm relieved to see that you still understand German!" Charlotte joked.

The ice surrounding George's heart suddenly broke. For the first time in many months a smile emerged on its own. He thought of Emma when he heard Charlotte's voice, but now he was hearing a new song in hers.

"I've been thinking about you, George. You've been through so much; I could never imagine how you must feel."

"Thank you, Charlotte, it's been difficult," George lamented.

Charlotte took George's hand in hers and said, "I know you must have loved Emma dearly; I'm so sorry for you. George, you don't need to be alone all the time. We don't live far apart—please, let me help you heal."

George's eyes moistened as he replied, "Charlotte, you are a good friend. Yes, I would welcome your company. I do need someone to confide in."

As the bonfire's embers glowed and crackled, Charlotte moved close to George and gave him an affectionate hug, then left to join her family. George walked to find his, who were talking with Charlotte's parents.

Then the church bell started ringing to call remaining congregants into St. Jacob.

The Tisch and Hannewald families entered and sat together.

Christmas day dinner was hosted by George's brother Charles and wife Caroline. Their two young sons, Ezra and Emra, helped set the table where their parents sat with Henry and wife Reicka. George sat next to Reicka, who had been especially consoling to George as he suffered from the events of May 31. Ezra and Emra sat next to their Oma and Opa Tisch. Reicka held little Martha while her other children sat at a small table next to the dining room table. Conversation was light, the children occupying most of the attention.

After dinner was finished, the women left to work in the kitchen. George and his brothers gathered the restless children and led them to the parlor. George asked his nephews and his niece Sarah to squeeze together on the couch and save a place for him in the middle. Henry held his daughter Martha while sitting in a rocker across from the couch.

From the top shelf of a tall bookcase George removed a hardbound book titled *A Treasury of Pleasure Books for Young Children*, by Joseph Cundall, then sat between his nephews.

"Let's start at the beginning with Little Bo-Peep," said George as he held the book up and displayed an illustration of a cheerless young girl. He began to read:

Little Bo-Peep has lost her sheep,
And can't tell where to find them;
Leave them alone, and they'll come home,
And bring their tails behind them.

George continued reading story after story, showing the color illustrations for each. The entire family had found their way to the room and took seats. They knew George was lonely and heartbroken, and prayed that he would regain his spirit and love again.

The little ones listened to every word and studied each illustration until falling into a sound sleep.

———— ⟨∞⟩ ————

At noon on Christmas Eve, John Miner and Richard Price met at the Park Hotel, across the street from the Jackson County Courthouse, and ordered a cold bottle of Krug Champaign. Two crystal glasses were then filled with the bubbly libation and the blithesome lawyers toasted to their improbable victory, agreeing that their Trident defense strategy had worked—although neither had actually expected an acquittal. They concurred that Dr. John Main was so credible with his testimony that it nearly convinced them of Lewis's melancholia, and that using unfortunate George Tisch as the catalyst to causing Lewis's illness to surface created genuine sympathy from the jury.

Both lawyers were astonished by the prosecution's apparent lack of preparation. Miner commented to Price that Charles Blair presumably thought the evidence was more than sufficient to gain a quick and easy victory. Both Miner and Price agreed that jury selection was crucial—that the prosecution did not seem to recognize the subtle questions being asked that allowed the jury box to be filled with men who seemed open-minded to the theory that a latent brain disease could contribute to an insane act, and that the medical experts did a splendid job in convincing them.

Miner and Price then refilled their glasses and toasted each other's closing arguments, Miner saying lightheartedly to Price, "You should send Tisch a sympathy note—I almost felt badly for him sitting out in that courtroom trying to take it like a man."

Price laughed as he replied, "John, the city of Jackson is about to have a new opera house—I think you should consider theater after the way you read Thomas Moore's poem. You had me in tears!"

They finished their lunch after quickly discussing Heydlauff's upcoming perjury hearing, agreeing that there was more fortune to be gained after having their contract with John Heydlauff extended.

Early Christmas morning, John Miner and his wife Louise, along with Richard Price, his wife Ida, and their seven-year-old daughter, Hazel, met for an early breakfast at the Yellow Front Restaurant on Francis Street in Jackson. After finishing their meals, they attended 10:30 a.m. mass at St. John the Evangelist Catholic Church, where they sat across the middle aisle from each other. Father Casper Schenkelberg preached that the coming of the Christ child made all things in life possible. After Father Schenkelberg said, "Made all things in life possible," Miner and Price both leaned forward and looked over to each other from across the aisle, smiled, and nodded their heads in agreement that yes, all things in life are possible. Both acknowledged that the acquittal they had won for Lewis Heydlauff adhered to that very premise.

Charles Blair, his wife Effie, and their young son George attended the Christmas morning service at the Unitarian Church in Jackson. Service was conducted by Reverend Walter Taylor, who preached on the marvels of the Nativity. Blair did not hear a word of it as he was preoccupied with how to cage Lewis Heydlauff.

The remainder of Blair's day was spent at home with his family. He tried to relax but was exhausted from the trial, infuriated by the verdict, frustrated by Heydlauff being out on bail, and obsessed with wanting to convince the people of Jackson County that he had taken every rational step in his unsuccessful attempt to have Lewis

Heydlauff convicted for murdering Emma Moeckel. The letter to the editor of the *Jackson Citizen* he wrote and personally delivered would be published the following day, and his thoughts of how it would be received concerned him.

Charles Blair had just one week remaining as Jackson County Prosecuting Attorney. What should have been a celebratory week was destined to be fraught with controversy.

Henry Edwards had nearly come to terms with his defeat in the November election to Elmer Kirkby, and was let down by the shocking verdict in the Heydlauff trial—but refused to dwell on either.

Henry walked into Christmas morning service at the First Congregational Church of Jackson holding hands with his wife, Mabel, and their five-year-old daughter, Harriet. Reverend W. E. Strong presided, his homily focusing on the charity freely offered by the Bethlehem innkeeper that provided Joseph and his pregnant wife, Mary, a stable in which to take shelter. He emphasized that everyone has an obligation to do charitable work whenever possible. At the end of his preaching, Mable squeezed her husband's hand and whispered into his ear, "Henry, I'm with child. Our glorious blessing will arrive sometime July next."

Henry Edwards spent the remainder of Christmas joyfully at home with his family and close friends. Throughout the day Henry peacefully cuddled his pregnant wife.

CHAPTER THIRTY-FOUR

CHARLES BLAIR'S LETTER TO THE EDITOR

SATURDAY, DECEMBER 26, 1896

THE HEYDLAUFF CASE

STATEMENT FROM PROSECUTING ATTORNEY CHARLES BLAIR

To the Editor of the Citizen.

In view of the attacks upon me for failing to call experts to meet the so-called expert testimony on the part of the defense in the Heydlauff case, and prosecuting him anew in bad faith, I desire to say a few words to the people of Jackson County. I fully admit that the testimony of the experts took me entirely by surprise so far as it related to Heydlauff's insanity since the murder. I expected that the defense would call experts to testify upon the basis of hypothetical questions that Heydlauff was insane at the very time he fired the fatal shots. I certainly did not have the slightest reason to suspect that they would produce experts who would testify the defendant was insane at the time of the trial. I had no reason to anticipate such testimony, but quite the contrary. The testimony of Dr. Conlan, his family physician, of Justice Gorton, of Jacob Heydlauff, of Mr. and Mrs. Moeckel was clear to the effect that before, at the time of and after the shooting, the defendant was rational and sane. After he was brought to this city and confined in jail, the sheriff frequently reported to me how he was improving in health, but never at any time intimated the faintest suspicion of his sanity. He told me since the trial, that he does not now believe and never has believed Heydlauff to have been insane, while in his custody. Heydlauff's attorney, Mr. Miner, several times requested me to allow Heydlauff to plead guilty to manslaughter, which plea could only have been offered upon the theory of his sanity and legal accountability. In short, everything which came to my knowledge indicated Heydlauff's unquestioned sanity since the shooting. The sheriff and myself both proceeded upon this assumption and could not have acted upon any other theory, without doing violence to our senses. I never supposed for a moment that anyone would question his sanity since the shooting till four physicians testified in the case that he was insane as he sat before the jury.

I never knew, till they testified to it, that these four physicians had made an examination of Heydlauff at the jail. The sheriff informs me that he did not know of the examination himself, and therefore he, of course, could not inform me of it. The jail physician, who is a county officer and would seem to be under some obligation to advise the prosecuting attorney, as well as the defendant's attorney, of the condition of prisoners charged with crimes, said not a word to me. The first intimation he gave to me of possessing any knowledge affecting the case was when he took the witness stand and swore that he had treated Heydlauff at the jail, that he had been insane during all that time, and was insane then.

When it is remembered that Heydlauff was charged with murder, and that the jail physician knew this fact, he must have known that it was of the highest importance to the prosecuting attorney to know if Heydlauff was insane. It seems to me that the conduct of this officer, in withholding from me the information which he swore he had, is at least worthy of consideration by the board of supervisors. If the prosecuting attorney cannot rely upon being informed about what takes place at the jail, with reference to a murder case, his situation is somewhat forlorn. Certainly, if the jail physician had notified me what he and his fellow experts claimed to have discovered, I should have taken steps to at once ascertain the truth, and this is probably why I was not notified. In the absence of such notification, I think no candid, intelligent man will hold me blameworthy for relying on what all my information showed to be the fact, viz: that Heydlauff was perfectly sane. I do not wish to be understood that I think the testimony of these so-called experts raised a reasonable doubt as to Heydlauff's sanity in the case, did not of necessity, require scientific testimony, and that they were not bound by the testimony of the experts, but could exercise their own common sense, upon all the facts in the case. The most prominent fact in the case was that the defendant testified before the jury, for about three hours, and never made an irrelevant answer. He detailed the events of his past life for years back and corrected the memories of others. He manifested a proper understanding of the relations between different facts and only failed in memory, when to have remembered would have condemned himself to state prison for life. He talked rationally, with everyone who ever talked with him, even the experts, and no one ever suspected his sanity except these four experts. He had no delusions, illusions or hallucinations whatever, and was as openly and notoriously a sane man, in the meaning of the law, as any man upon the jury. Although in the opinion of these illustrious experts, the mere sight of his sweetheart threw him into a state of maniacal frenzy, he was able to sit for five days and listen to the dreadful details of the murder without the faintest indication of frenzy. The fact is he proved his own sanity in the very face of the jury.

The people's case was established by the evidence within every rule of law, or common sense, and every fair-minded man who heard the evidence, or read it, knows it was. This verdict is the result of that maudlin sympathy, which loses sight of the inoffensive victim and the outraged law, to lavish its sickly sentimentality upon the murderer.

The defendant's attorney never hoped for such a result. He told me at the conclusion of the trial that he thought the jury would find the respondent guilty on the first ballot, but hoped they would convict of manslaughter. His client evidently held the same opinion, since he said, as reported in the Patriot, "I am thankful, you bet; it was better than I expected. I had hoped for this, but never believed it would come."

The maniac had better sense than the jury.

The Patriot has done all it could to mold public opinion in the favor of this murderer. Only the Sunday before the trial began it published, in a conspicuous place, an item to the effect that, "It is believed that Heydlauff was insane when he killed Emma Moeckel." The plain purpose of this was to convey to the jury the impression that the public generally believed he was insane. I called the attention of the circuit judge to this item and he wrote a letter to the editor, calling his attention to the impropriety of such comments. This morning it comes out of ambush and charges that the prosecution for perjury is in bad faith, for the reason that insanity of Heydlauff might have been certified by the jury, or otherwise to the judge under the first part of section 19, of act 119, of the laws of 1895. These are several reasons why the proceedings, under the first part of the section, were not open to me. In the first place, it was my firm belief, at the trial, as it always has been and is now, that Heydlauff was sane and responsible for his acts, and I could not satisfy myself by asking the jury to certify his sanity.

In the second place, it is apparent that several of the jury did not believe that the defendant was insane and only came over to the majority, if my information is correct, upon the theory that there was a reasonable doubt of his sanity.

Third. As I am now proceeding, if a jury to be charged by the circuit judge with the duty of determining the question of Heydlauff's insanity find that he is sane, as I believe he is, the prosecution for perjury may be proceeded with and, if found guilty, he may be partially punished for his crime. In my opinion it is monstrous reproach to the administration of justice that this man should go free; and it is the duty of every right-minded citizen to insist that no step be omitted by the officers of the law to bring him to justice.

Mr. Wasson, of the Patriot, stated to me that he had hardly found a man who approved of this verdict. If this be true, as I believe it is, it can only be upon the ground that the people believe he was proven guilty. I do not believe that the people of Jackson County will consider the question of expense in a proceeding of this importance, neither do I believe that they are willing that if this man is insane and liable to an attack of homicidal frenzy if a moonbeam strikes his face, that he should be allowed to go at large until he kills someone else. In its anxiety to assist the defense, the Patriot misrepresents the facts. I did not ask that any Star Chamber examination be made of Heydlauff. I notified Mr. Miner to be present and he and Mr. Price were present and refused to consent to my examination. I then stated to Mr. Miner that I was entirely willing that any physician they chose should be present, and asked him if he would fix a time after the arraignment for an examination by physicians, which he refused to do. It is quite generous on the part of Mr. Miner to be willing that a petition be filed in the probate court for his admission to an asylum, since such a petition can only be filed by the relatives or friends of Heydlauff. Any man with the brains of a peacock will have no difficulty in understanding the point of the objection.

When Heydlauff came into the justice's office and took his seat, incoming county prosecutor, Mr. Kirkby, called my attention to the fact that Heydlauff's "hangdog" look had disappeared, but when the justice began reading the perjury complaint, he remembered his lesson, and cast his eyes down as of yore.

I do not deprecate criticism. I believe there is too little criticism of public officers, but I do ask that the facts be not warped to my prejudice, and that an attack upon me be not made the means of distracting attention from this heinous crime. If, during the entire course of my office, I have failed in my duty, the Patriot need have no hesitation in declaring such failure to the public and I will bear the burden. I have doubtless made many mistakes and I may be a bungler in law, as you suggest, but I deny, with all the vehemence of my nature, that I have consciously done a wrong act as prosecuting attorney. I am entirely content to submit my entire conduct of that office to the candid judgment of the people of Jackson County, but I protest against being judged by the defendant's attorneys.

CHAS A. BLAIR,

Dec. 24, 1896.

CHAPTER THIRTY-FIVE

REACTION

At 4:00 p.m. Saturday, December 26, Richard Price was at home on Biddle Street and received his copy of the *Jackson Citizen*. After glancing at front page stories, including reports of a huge fire in New York City that destroyed four large buildings, causing over one million dollars in damages, and of Cuban insurgents dynamiting a Spanish train outside of Havana, killing over forty Spaniards, he turned the page and was fascinated to see the headline "THE HEYDLAUFF CASE."

When Price saw that it was a letter to the editor from Charles Blair his eyes popped. He started to read: "In view of the attacks upon me by the Patriot for failing . . ."

Price got mad as he continued reading Blair's rant, his outrage increasing with each paragraph. Price was apoplectic at the end when he read: "I protest against being judged by the defendant's attorneys."

Price sat for a few minutes, and then reread Blair's letter. He stood and began to laugh thunderously as he called out to an empty room, "Now I know for certain at least one person involved in the case has gone stark-crazy mad." He thought more about that concept and, as he did, his reaction changed from irate to a peculiar, giddy feeling. Price smiled as he imagined Charles Blair challenging him and John Miner to a duel.

About two hours after reading Blair's letter, Price folded the paper in half and stuffed it into his briefcase with his Heydlauff trial notes and walked to John Miner's house, about one mile away on Washington Street.

Richard Price walked up the lane to Miner's house and rapped twice on the door's brass knocker. After waiting in anticipation for less than a minute, an upbeat John Miner opened the door and, seeing it was Price, said with a laugh, "Oh, yes, I've read it! Come in. Let's decide how to respond."

Miner asked Price if he cared for a spot of brandy, to which he replied, "John, that's a superb idea."

As Miner poured, Price commented on why Blair would have sent his letter to the *Citizen*, saying, "I reckon Charles went with his friends at the *Citizen* knowing they would print his letter without comment. If he had chosen the *Patriot*, the paper would have torched him with a harsh rebuttal. Blair is careful not to damage his thin skin!"

"Cheers!" Miner chimed as he clicked his snifter to Price's. "Now, let's get to work."

They discussed whether or not to counter the claims Blair had made. Miner, sensing that Price was reacting more ardently then himself, asked if he would like to pen the reply, to which he replied, "You bet I do."

The two lawyers then spent the next two hours outlining a response. Once they were satisfied, Price said he would write the letter at home and bring it by Sunday afternoon for Miner to read. He would then deliver it, in person, first thing Monday morning to the *Jackson Citizen*.

Price got home as his family was getting ready for bed. Effie asked her husband to please join her but was disappointed when Richard told her he had work that would keep him busy for a couple of hours. The house went quiet after his family retired. In Price's study a single mantle light burned brightly at his desk. Richard sat, placed his outline to the left, and started writing. After almost three hours, he was pleased by what he had written and joined his wife in bed.

Price was at Miner's house Sunday afternoon at 3:00 p.m., where the two lawyers critiqued the written response. After about an hour of making minor edits, Price left for home and enjoyed a satisfying supper with his family.

———————

At dawn, Monday morning, Richard Price entered through the front door of the *Jackson Citizen* and found his way to the editor's office, where he waited to hand deliver his letter.

CHAPTER THIRTY-SIX

EXAMINATION OF THE PERJURY CHARGE

Early Monday morning, December 28, 1896, before the day's edition of the *Jackson Citizen* containing Richard Price's counter to Charles Blair's letter to the editor was for sale on the streets, the four lawyers who battled it out in the Heydlauff murder case were at the Jackson County Courthouse. The examination of the perjury charge against Lewis Heydlauff was scheduled for 9:00 a.m. in Justice Worch's court.

Before the courtroom was scheduled to open at 8:30 a.m., John and Christina Heydlauff and their son Lewis were in the lobby talking with John Miner and Richard Price. In a conference room nearby, Friederich and Katharina Moeckel were meeting with Charles Blair and Henry Edwards. Up one flight of stairs, near the locked doors to Justice Worch's courtroom, family members and friends of the Heydlauffs were waiting.

The Moeckels were mingling in a hall near the courtroom with a few newspaper reporters and a growing number of unfamiliar faces.

The doors opened on time and people began flowing in. The room was not as large as that used for the murder trial, but the layout was similar. Lewis and his parents took the front seats to the left of the judge's bench. Blair and Edwards entered from a private door to the side of the bench with the Moeckels, who sat in the front row to the right

Just before 9:00 a.m., the court stenographer took his station. Two uniformed officers then positioned themselves on either side of the bench. Five minutes later it was announced by a bailiff that Justice Worch was entering the courtroom. All stood until he took his seat.

Before the proceedings began, John Miner approached Justice Worch and requested a postponement so he could file objections to the case.

Justice Worch, fully understanding that the defense strategy was to delay the case until Charles Blair's term in office expired in three days, granted the request—until after lunch. He ordered court adjourned until 1:30 that afternoon.

During the adjournment more spectators arrived, filling the courtroom to standing room only along the walls and in the back.

Before 1:00 p.m. the Heydlauffs, with Miner and Price, had already taken their customary places. Lewis, well dressed and nicely groomed, sat between his two attorneys at their table, his parents directly behind.

Blair and Edwards walked in together a few minutes later and took seats at their table across the aisle. The Moeckels sat in the first row behind the two attorneys.

Promptly at 1:30 p.m. Justice Worch entered the room, took his seat on the bench, and announced that court was in session. He then shuffled through a few papers on his desk and said, "I see that no objections to the Heydlauff perjury charge have been filed. Is this correct, Mr. Miner?"

"Yes, Your Honor," Miner replied.

"Then court shall proceed. Mr. Blair, call your first witness."

"The people call Thomas I. Daniel," announced Blair.

Mr. Daniel was sworn in and took his seat on the stand. He told the court he was the circuit court stenographer at both the Lewis Heydlauff preliminary examination in July and at the recent murder trial.

Blair walked to his desk where Edwards handed him a dull-green hardbound journal about four inches thick. He walked to the stand and handed it to Mr. Daniel and asked, "Is this the record you made as the circuit court stenographer for the Lewis Heydlauff preliminary examination?"

Mr. Daniel opened the journal, flipped through a few pages, and replied, "Yes, it is."

Blair then returned to Edwards and exchanged the journal for five others like it, each about six inches thick, and brought them to the stand and placed them next to Mr. Daniel and asked, "Are these the court records you made during the Heydlauff murder trial?"

One by one, Mr. Daniel examined the five journals, and when he had finished, declared, "Yes, these are the records for the Heydlauff trial."

Blair submitted all six journals as evidence, stating that they proved that Lewis Heydlauff had made contradictory statements under oath at both the July examination and the December murder trial.

Blair had no further questions and the defense declined to cross-examine. Thomas I. Daniel was excused from the stand.

Next called was Dr. Charles Brogan from Stockbridge. Dr. Brogan was sworn in. He was then asked if he had examined the body of Emma Moeckel who had been killed by Lewis Heydlauff the morning of May 31, 1896. He said he had and described the wounds to her body.

Blair asked, "In your opinion, Dr. Brogan, do you consider the bullet wounds to have been inflicted at random or deliberately?"

Dr. Brogan replied, "In my opinion they were deliberately inflicted. The shot to the neck assured the girl was dead."

Blair turned to Justice Worch and stated, "I suggest to the court that the accused knew what he was doing at the time of the shooting, as he made sure the girl was dead. The accused claimed no memory of the shooting during the murder trial. I assure you that witness testimonies recorded in the journals will prove otherwise."

Blair had no further questions and the defense declined to cross-examine.

Dr. Brogan was dismissed and returned to his seat.

Next called was Dr. John Conlan of Munith. He was sworn in and took his seat on the stand.

Blair stood before the doctor and asked, "Dr. Conlan, you swore at both the preliminary examination and the murder trial that Lewis Heydlauff told you, while attending to him as his physician, that he killed Emma Moeckel and then shot himself after seeing that she was dead. Is this correct, doctor?"

"In essence, yes, that is what Lewis Heydlauff told me."

Blair faced Justice Worch and said, "Lewis Heydlauff swore during his murder trial that he did not remember what he told Dr. Conlan. I ascertain that Lewis Heydlauff perjured himself during that trial when asked if he remembered shooting Emma Moeckel."

Blair had no further questions and the defense declined to cross-examine. Dr. Conlan was excused.

Blair then announced to Justice Worch that he had no further witnesses to call.

Justice Worch asked John Miner if he had anything he wanted to say, to which Miner simply replied, "No, Your Honor."

Worch announced, "The evidence submitted is accepted by the court."

Worch then noted that it was nearly 5:00 p.m. He looked at his calendar, gripped a pen, and made a note.

Justice Worch stared emotionless at Lewis Heydlauff for a long moment, turned to face Charles Blair and took a deep breath. "Court will resume," he said, looking again to his calendar and tracing his finger to a spot only he could see. He took a second deep breath, slowly exhaled, and then announced, "Saturday, January 23, 1897, at 10:00 a.m. Court is now adjourned."

John Miner and Richard Price smiled.

Charles Blair dropped his head in defeat. He turned to Friederich Moeckel, who wore a confused expression, and simply shook his head in disgust. Without saying a word, Blair collected his papers and went in search of Justice Worch, leaving Edwards to try and explain to the Moeckels what was occurring.

John Heydlauff spoke briefly with Miner, gathered his wife and Lewis, and left the courthouse. Outside, they flagged a streetcar heading to Central Station, where they boarded the Grand Trunk train for the return trip to Munith.

A greatly displeased Charles Blair quickly tracked down Justice Worch.

"Justice Worch, why did you adjourn until January? I explained to you that this case could be jeopardized when Elmer Kirkby takes office."

Worch looked pensively at Blair and replied, "Charles, my schedule is full for the remainder of this week. I am obliged to not show any partiality in the case by attempting to grant favor by accelerating it without merit and, regretfully, am compelled to adhere to standard procedures. Elmer Kirkby will have the obligation to examine the evidence you submitted today, and it will be his sworn duty to pursue justice."

Blair's options were exhausted. He fought back his displeasure to thank Justice Worch for what he was able to do and that he understood his ruling.

Blair left the courthouse dejected and angry. As he stepped from the door to the street, the first sound he heard was from a newsboy carrying a stack of freshly printed *Jackson Citizen* newspapers: "Get ya news here, get ya news here." Blair flipped the young hawker a nickel for a copy, glanced at the headlines, and then turned the page only to spot his name in print. He immediately saw that it was a return volley from his letter to the editor two days earlier and it was not friendly. Blair walked to his office in a very, very foul mood.

CHAPTER THIRTY-SEVEN

RICHARD PRICE'S LETTER TO THE EDITOR

MONDAY, DECEMBER 28, 1896

JACKSON DAILY CITIZEN

THE HEYDLAUFF CASE

STATEMENT FROM RICHARD PRICE, ONE OF THE ATTORNEYS FOR THE DEFENSE

JACKSON, Mich., Dec 28, 1896

To the Editor of the Citizen

I see by Saturday's issue that Mr. Blair is still trying the Heydlauff case. It is a trite saying among the members of the bar that it is a privilege of every attorney who is beaten in a case to d--n the court or jury as the case may be, but it is a bold innovation on the part of the prosecuting attorney to undertake to do this through the medium of the press. Indeed it would almost seem from a perusal of his communication that Mr. Blair had lapsed into a condition of melancholia since the trial of the Heydlauff case.

It appears from an article published in yesterday's Patriot that Mr. Miner has taken Mr. Blair to task for misstatements as to a conversation which occurred between them and which was referred to in Saturday's article. I have no personal knowledge of what that conversation was, but if Mr. Blair's statement of it is as far from being correct as most of his other statements contained in his article, then there is but little doubt that he misrepresented Mr. Miner.

The prosecuting attorney seeks to convey the impression to the public that the experts who were sworn in behalf of Heydlauff testified that he was insane at the time of the trial in the sense that he was irresponsible for his acts. Not one of the experts testified, and there can be no excuses for such a statement on the part of the prosecutor. What the experts did say on this point was that Heydlauff in their opinion was at the time of the trial in a condition of melancholia, but that he knew what he was doing—was rational and talked rational. Dr. Colby testified in substance that the medical profession applied the term insane to every person whose mind was not in its normal condition, but he distinctly said that this did not necessarily mean that the law recognized such persons as insane, or that they were irresponsible for their acts. Neither the law nor the medical profession regards a man as irresponsible for his acts, unless his insanity reaches such a degree as to render him non compos mentis, or no longer a free agent. No one claimed that Heydlauff was irresponsible for his acts during the trial or at any other time, except the time of the shooting and some portion of the week prior thereto, and it is inconceivable how the prosecutor should get such a notion in his head unless he obstinately prefers to take that view of it.

Mr. Blair complains bitterly about his "forlorn situation" of not being constantly informed of what was taking place in reference to a "murder case." I have no recollection of the defendant's attorney being invited to attend the conference which the prosecuting attorney and his witnesses had with reference to the same "murder case" as he is pleased to call it. What was there which took place at the jail which rendered his condition as "forlorn"? Simply a 15-minute talk between some of the physicians and the defendant. The people's physician, Dr. Conlan, and other witnesses for the people, had repeated interviews with Heydlauff when he was lying in bed expecting to die at any minute. They examined and cross-examined him with reference to the shooting to their hearts content. He answered them willingly and they admitted to it, and yet with death staring him in the face not a single statement did he make to them inconsistent with his testimony upon the stand.

One would think to read the plaint of the prosecuting attorney that once a man is arrested it becomes the duty of the jail physicians and all the other jail officers to enter into a league with the prosecuting attorney to bring about his conviction by hook or by crook. Dr. Colby testified to what he saw of the defendant's condition—he noticed at one time that the pupil of one of his eyes was dilated and also that he was in a depressed state of mind. He also testified to what the defendant said to him when he was trying to extract the ball. Had he no right to tell these things? Must he go and ask Mr. Blair's permission? Could not Mr. Blair find these things out by interviewing Dr. Colby the same as the defendant's attorney did? And if Dr. Colby went to the prosecutor and told him these things, does anybody believe that the prosecutor would put the doctor on the stand and have him swear to them? I agree with Mr. Blair that the doctor is "worthy of some consideration by the board of supervisors." He ought to be allowed an extra $50 for having manhood and courage enough to tell the truth at the risk of incurring the displeasure of the prosecuting attorney.

Mr. Blair says that the people proved their case within every rule of the law, and that the testimony of Dr. Conlan and others showed that at the time of and after the shooting the defendant was rational and sane. If there was a solitary witness for the people who swore that he thought Heydlauff was sane at any time, I have entirely forgotten it. I have in my office every word of the testimony of Dr. Conlan, Orville Gorton and Mr. Hannewald, the three principal witnesses for the people, and any citizen who desires is welcome to come and read it over and satisfy himself as to the correctness of the prosecutor's statements. The only witness who swore to anything of consequence which would tend to show malice or intent on the part of Heydlauff was Albert Moeckel, and his statement was so thoroughly refuted by his former statement on the examination that Mr. Blair did not dare to refer to it in his argument. As for Mrs. Moeckel, her admission that she went to see the defendant, both at his home and in jail, that she kissed him on at least two of those occasions and she told him to trust in God and all would come out right, and even a week before the trial had sent her regards to him, showed conclusively that she did not regard him as the murderer of her daughter, and Mr. Blair has admitted to me that this was a strong point against him in the case. The fact is the people's case was weak and tottering as made by their own evidence, and even if no defense had been made, there was enough in the people's case to raise a reasonable doubt in the minds of the jury as to Heydlauff's sanity.

Mr. Blair sneeringly refers to the "illustrious, so-called experts," who took the stand in behalf of the defense. He forgets that the most illustrious of the so-called experts, and the one whom he particularly denounced in his argument, was Dr. J.T. Main, who had testified as an expert for Mr. Blair in the Pelky case which was tried before the Heydlauff case. In the Pelky case, Mr. Blair stood before the jury, several of whom also sat in the Heydlauff case, and exhausted his vocabulary in lavishing praise upon Dr. Main and referred to him as a physician of the profoundest learning and highest integrity—and I agreed with him. In one short week, Mr. Blair would have us believe Dr. Main descended from the high plane of wisdom and honesty to the low level of a dishonest pretender to knowledge which he did not possess, willing under the sanctity of an oath to exploit false notions as to the mental condition of Lewis Heydlauff. I wonder if the prosecutor imagines that the public are so shallow as not to see and understand the animus which prompted his childish attack upon the jury and expert witnesses, or whether he thinks that any of those gentlemen are obliged to accept a character from his hands?

The field of expert testimony was as open to the people as to the defendant. The prosecuting attorney brought into court a book which treated of insanity and culled out some sentences which he read and questioned Dr. Main about. When I proposed to read the remainder of the same paragraphs from which he had been reading, he objected and the objection was sustained. I then proposed to him that he might put all of his books in evidence and read them to the jury, if he would permit us to do the same; but he very adroitly refused by saying that if we did that we would all be crazy before the trial ended. Here was a chance for the prosecutor to dispense with the experts and take the books for it, and if defendant's experts had said anything which was not sustained by writers on the subject, it could be easily discovered. But Mr. Blair knows if he has given the subject any study, that all the books fully sustain every statement made by the defendant's experts.

I do not wish to be understood as intimating that the prosecutor ought to have introduced expert testimony, or that he would have helped his case by so doing. On the other, I think that no expert, were he to be honest, could help his case; because he would be obliged to stand by the learning of his profession, and could not avoid testifying to much that would favor the defendant. I believe that Mr. Blair was aware of this, and that is why he did not introduce expert testimony. Lewis Heydlauff was acquitted simply because at the time of the shooting he was unaccountable for his action, and the only criticism which can be made is upon the course which the prosecutor has taken since the trial. It is true that some people think the verdict a wrong one, but the majority of those whom I have heard express themselves, think the verdict was right, and I am credibly informed that some of the oldest and most experienced members of the bar who are not interested in the case have said that under the evidence the verdict could not be otherwise.

I look upon Mr. Blair's article as meriting a reply, not only because of the unseemly and unjustifiable assault which he made upon the experts and the jury, but also because of the mischief which it is to do by deceiving people into the notion that justice has been cheated, and that a murderer has escaped punishment. It has come to a fine pass when a jury cannot honestly and conscientiously perform their functions under oath, without being libeled and maligned by the prosecuting attorney; when physicians of undoubted ability and unblemished character cannot take the witness stand and declare their honest opinions, without being similarly reviled and slandered; and when a man who has been honorably and fairly acquitted by a jury of his peers, is criticized because he does not carry a "hangdog" look to suit the caprice of the prosecutor of Jackson County.

Mr. Blair told the jury during his argument that he had often got out of his patience with juries, often lost his temper and criticized them, because they had beaten him; but that after he cooled off and had time to reflect calmly, he always came to the conclusion that the jury was right and that he was wrong. Others of us have had the same experience, and this is but another case to add to Mr. Blair's list. It is too bad that he did not cool off before he wrote the article. If he had waited another week, he would never have written it, and I venture the assertion that when he has had time to reflect, he will be heartily ashamed of his performance.

The developments since the Heydlauff trial have demonstrated the perniciousness of our present system which lodges with the prosecuting attorney the whole duty and power of saying whether a man shall be arrested on the charge of crime. No one can read Mr. Blair's article without observing at a glance how utterly impossible it is for him in his present frame of mind to be anything like impartial in anything which concerns Lewis Heydlauff. It is a blot on our civilization that a prosecuting attorney, or any other individual should have the power, by the scroll of his pen, to order a man thrown into prison whenever the whim seizes him, without investigation or inquiry. The grand jury ought to be revived, or some other means ought to be provided to guard the rights of the people. If the law were such that the prosecuting attorney were not charged with the responsibility of launching criminal proceedings, he could then approach the trial of criminal cases with much more fairness and impartially. Whichever way the case resulted, he could not then be blamed for starting it, whereas under our present system the prosecutor too often believes that in order to save himself from criticism, he must convict every man whose arrest he orders, whether he be guilty or not.

Respectfully yours,

RICHARD PRICE

CHAPTER THIRTY-EIGHT

THE NEW YEAR

January 1, 1897

When the first day of 1897 arrived, the horrifying events of 1896 haunted three families.

Friederich and Katharina Moeckel had lost their beloved Emma in the most senseless and gruesome way any loving father and mother could imagine. Their son Albert had developed a serious nervous condition after seeing his sister dead in a pool of blood. Katharina's faith had been challenged as she struggled with the concept of forgiveness. Friederich carried unrelenting remorse for inviting Lewis into his house that dreadful Sunday morning. And now, Friederich was outraged by lack of justice. He was infuriated by the untruthful story Heydlauff's lawyers created to characterize Lewis as an innocent victim, and by all the lies told during the trial. Friederich was disheartened with the stalled perjury charge, and by what the new prosecuting attorney, Elmer Kirkby, may or may not do with Lewis.

Friederich and Katharina had lost their friendship with John and Christina Heydlauff. They had come to the belief that they knew all along that Lewis had a dark side and did not care to do anything about it. They came to think of Lewis as a rabid dog that escaped its chain—a killer dog. In looking back, Friederich regretted hiring Lewis for his windmill project; Katharina was anguished by having

Lewis disrupt the harmony in her home; Albert and Florenz hated the tension Lewis had created by his treatment of Emma. On May 31, the pinnacle of misery erupted with Emma's slaughter in the parlor of their home. From that morning on, each day brought punishing memories for each of them—and it was not over. Friederich Moeckel would pursue every avenue possible to see justice served. The days leading to January 23 were to be agonizing for Friederich in particular, as he feared the worst—that the killer would somehow evade punishment for the carnage he left in his path.

———— ⟨⟩ ————

John and Christina Heydlauff had, in essence, lost their son Lewis. Yes, he was alive and at home after the acquittal, but there was the pending perjury case that could either send him to prison or confine him to an insane asylum. If free, there was no possibility of Lewis living in Waterloo or anywhere else in Jackson County. Lewis had a few sympathizers among his family and friends, but outside of that, he was shunned by those who believed he had gotten away with murder.

One of Lewis's sympathizers was his sister Sarah. She was four years older than Lewis and, as they grew up together, became confidants. When Lewis reached adolescence, he asked Sarah intimate questions about girls, who enlightened him with details only a woman could provide. Later, when he became enamored with Emma, he repeatedly asked for advice—Sarah urging him to always be respectful and never boorish.

When Lewis told Sarah that Emma had pledged herself to him on her sixteenth birthday, she was surprised. Sarah had known Emma for the same number of years as her brother, and knew of their close friendship. However, Sarah did not believe that Emma Moeckel shared the same amorous feelings for Lewis as he did for her. Sarah was concerned when Lewis announced that Emma was now his girl and that he was determined to marry her someday. When Sarah asked if Emma had ever told Lewis that she loved him, he became irritated, and told his sister that Emma did not have to say it, because he knew she did.

In May of 1895, Sarah married Charles W. Vogel from Ann Arbor, a widower with three children. John Heydlauff had known Vogel for a number of years as a local meat supplier. Lewis's future, if there was any, was to be exiled to Ann Arbor to live with them. Sarah agreed, along with her reluctant husband, to house Lewis for a time if he were to be acquitted of the murder charge. Now that plan was on hold.

For the next twenty-three days, Lewis's life would be in limbo. Lewis stayed out of sight, imprisoned in the coziness of his parents' house.

Lewis frequently paced the house, questioning himself why he chose to kill Emma. The doctors told him he was insane when he did it. But Lewis knew differently.

The feelings Lewis once had for Emma had faded away, and he no longer cared to be with her in death.

On the train home following his acquittal, Lewis concluded that living at home was better than dying in prison. He was content with his choice.

Lewis had the occasional visitor. His sisters came, but not their husbands or any of the children.

Some of the Waterloo boys visited—his friends who had earned a reputation for their drunken rowdiness.

Pastor Wenk, a frequent visitor before the trial, had other souls to save and figured Lewis could visit him at St. Jacob if he so wished.

John Miner and Richard Price came by weekly to explain to Lewis what to expect and how to act in Justice Worch's courtroom on January 23. They assured him he would not be taking the stand and that they would answer any questions for him. On those occasions, the two lawyers spent the majority of their time meeting privately with his father in his library.

John Heydlauff continued to interpose his influence wherever he could to free Lewis, and in the process, banish him from Waterloo to a place where he would be virtually unknown—the city of Ann Arbor, thirty miles away.

The days leading to January 23 were to be filled with gut-wrenching anxiety for John Heydlauff as he would exhaust his options to sway the court by means he would never divulge.

John Heydlauff was determined to keep his son from being committed to an insane asylum—or to prison for perjury—and to save his family name, which Lewis had tarnished.

George Tisch was devastated by the lingering avalanche of emotions from Emma being ripped away at the beginning of their loving relationship. George had fought to hide the brokenhearted pain he was enduring when he was called to the witness stand during the trial. George's stomach sickened while being roasted by John Miner—and when Richard Price declared to the courtroom that had George stayed out of Emma's affairs she would be alive. George was flattened by an enormous weight of unwarranted guilt. He had thought of every scenario as to how he may have saved Emma from her dreadful fate—but she was still dead.

Besides the pain from Emma's murder and from the grilling at the trial, George was worried by Lewis's acquittal. He knew that Lewis had come to the Moeckel house the morning of May 31 with a fully loaded revolver and carton of cartridges. George often wondered why Lewis did not shoot himself in the head with one bullet if he had actually wanted to commit suicide. He feared Lewis would someday ambush him like he had Emma. George hoped that January 23, 1897, would somehow result in Lewis being put away for life. That day could not come soon enough

CHAPTER THIRTY-NINE

•··•————⟨◦⟩⟍⟨◦⟩————•··•

ALBERT FRANK'S TAVERN

January 23, 1897
Perjury Examination, Continued

The morning of January 23, 1897, was frosty, sunny, and bright. A fresh dusting of fluffy white snow nearly blinded those making their way to the Jackson County Courthouse for the continued examination hearing of Lewis Heydlauff's perjury charge.

It had been almost a month since the preliminary examination was held in Justice Worch's court. By 9:00 a.m., a group of persons consisting of relatives and friends of the Heydlauffs, several spectators obsessed with the Lewis Heydlauff saga, some newspaper reporters, and a small number of Moeckel supporters were waiting outside the closed doors to Justice Worch's courtroom.

Already inside were John Miner and Richard Price, who were meeting with John Heydlauff and his healthy-looking and nicely dressed son, Lewis. Also inside was *former* county prosecuting attorney, Charles Blair, along with his two partners from the new law firm of Blair, Smith, and Townsend, who were talking with Friederich and Katharina Moeckel.

At 9:30 a.m., the *new* Jackson County Prosecuting Attorney, Elmer Kirkby, surprisingly entered the room from the judge's chambers behind the bench. He saw Blair and approached him. Just as the two began speaking they were interrupted when a bailiff opened the courtroom's doors and a small group of boisterous young men burst noisily into the room. The first person through was Fred Artz Jr., followed by three others—all Lewis Heydlauff's friends—his Waterloo boys—who rushed to the front of the spectator seats. When Lewis saw his friends he smiled sheepishly—until John Miner reminded him that he was in court.

Lewis promptly lowered his head.

During the ruckus, Kirkby left Blair without saying much and sat at the prosecutors' table behind a stack of binders. Blair returned to the Moeckels, where his law partners sat with them in the audience in anticipation of a favorable resolution.

About ninety additional spectators had filled the courtroom almost to capacity.

Exactly at 10:00 a.m. Justice Rudolph Worch was announced. Everyone in the courtroom stood as he appeared from his chambers and took his seat at the bench.

Before Justice Worch opened court, Elmer Kirkby rose to his feet from the prosecutors' table and called out, "Your Honor, I'd like to make a motion for dismissal of the perjury charge filed against Lewis Heydlauff, and that he be discharged immediately."

Pandemonium erupted, causing Worch to fumble for his gavel and pound it soundly against a square wooden block on his desk. With a stern voice he called out, "Calm down people—this is a court of law!"

The crowd settled somewhat but there was an obvious excitement as to what may be expected next.

Justice Worch asked Kirkby and Heydlauff's two lawyers, who were sensing what was to come, to approach the bench. Worch asked Kirkby, "On what grounds do you make your request for dismissal of the charge, Mr. Kirkby?"

Kirkby pointed to six dull-green hardbound journals stacked on his table and replied self-assuredly, "Your Honor, the day after I took office I read the entire transcript from the Lewis Heydlauff murder case and carefully compared the witness testimonies that allegedly conflicted with Lewis Heydlauff's sworn testimony. After critical review of these testimonies I do not believe there is enough evidence to support the perjury charge. I have also interviewed the two witnesses who gave testimony at the preliminary examination for this charge, doctors Conlan and Brogan, along with other witnesses subpoenaed by the people, and have arrived at the conclusion that there is insufficient evidence to secure a conviction in circuit court. Therefore I ask that the charge of perjury be dismissed and the accused discharged accordingly."

Most of those in the courtroom heard what Kirkby was saying and exploded with chatty commotion. Worch, for the second time, pounded his gavel and the room settled. Worch could be heard quietly asking Kirkby if he was absolutely certain that the perjury evidence was insufficient to take the case to trial, to which the new prosecuting attorney could be heard saying, "I have spent the past three weeks evaluating the evidence submitted for this charge, and from what there is, it conflicts in such a way that I have no confidence in prosecuting this charge."

Justice Worch looked at Heydlauff's attorneys and asked, "I don't suppose either of you has any objection to the perjury charge being dismissed?"

Miner suppressed a grin as he replied, "No, Your Honor."

Price looked at Miner, trying his best to look emotionless, and concurred by saying, "No, Your Honor, I have no objection whatsoever."

Justice Worch instructed Miner and Price to return to their seats, but allowed Kirkby to remain standing to the right of the bench. Before Worch was to announce what almost everyone in the courtroom anticipated, Kirkby caught Blair's repugnant glare, and in an instance only the two would share, he taunted Blair with a wink.

Worch scanned the spectators in the courtroom, most of who were sitting at the edge of their seats. He then looked toward Charles Blair, and when their eyes met, Blair grimaced and put a hand to his mouth to keep his tumultuous emotions from causing him to shout

out *"No, don't do it!"* Worch then looked at the face of Friederich Moeckel, who could not conceal his dread of what was about to occur, and at Katharina who had burst into tears, and finally at the accused, Lewis Heydlauff, who was sitting with his head hanging low—hangdog low—with his eyes clearly looking up to the bench. Justice Worch tapped his gavel, and then loudly announced, "The prosecution has declared *nolle prosequi*—that is, the prosecution declines to prosecute. Based on lack of evidence and at the request of the county's prosecuting attorney, the court dismisses the charge of perjury against Lewis Heydlauff. Mr. Heydlauff, you are free to go."

John Heydlauff stayed seated and clapped once as the Heydlauff supporters jumped to their feet and cheered at the announcement.

Blair's law partners patted Blair on his back, then left their seats and pushed their way toward the exit. Friederich and Katharina remained seated, stunned by the ruling.

Lewis sat sneering with his head hanging slightly. Miner bent down and spoke into his ear, "Lewis, you are free to go. It's finally over—you are free, free to go."

Lewis's head popped up as he jumped to his feet. He rolled his eyes to the ceiling and smiled; then released a series of shrill cackles. Lewis turned to his friends, who were wildly clapping and cheering, and proclaimed with a giddy laugh, "I'm free, boys, I'm free!"

Friederich, shocked by the decision, looked at Blair, who was shaking his closed fists in a gesture of abject failure. Friederich then looked at Lewis in utter disgust, sickened to see the man who had viciously killed his daughter smiling.

Moeckel turned to Blair and asked, "What does this mean?"

"It means we lost. Heydlauff is free to go," Blair replied resentfully.

"This can't be!" Friederich replied frantically, his eyes bulging with furious animosity, his entire body shaking.

Katharina grabbed her husband's hand and said, "My dear, let's go home."

"Charles, is there anything else we can do to hold that killer responsible?" Friederich asked desperately.

Blair put his hand on Friederich's shoulder and replied dismally, "Mr. Moeckel, there is nothing more we can do. The law has been twisted to allow Lewis Heydlauff to be unaccountable for his crimes. He was acquitted for murdering your daughter by a jury, and the perjury charge has been legally dismissed by the court. Unless he commits another crime, our options are gone."

Hearing this, Friederich and Katharina looked back at the chaotic celebration. Friederich seethed at the sight of Lewis cheerful and laughing with his family and friends while Katharina meekly watched. Friederich then thanked Charles Blair as best he could; Katharina offered a weak smile of gratitude. Both gathered their belongings, took one last look at Lewis, and left the courtroom. Outside, Friederich hailed a horse-drawn taxi, helped his wife into the carriage, and then were driven to Central Station to board the Grand Trunk for the serene journey back to Munith and Waterloo. They then sat closely together, tightly holding each other's hands in an olive-green passenger car. Along the way, both stared vacantly through frosty windows. Neither could see the beauty in the snow-covered landscape, nor could they hear the pleasant sounds of three energized children sitting nearby with their attentive parents.

John Heydlauff met briefly with the defense team of Miner and Price and thanked them for successfully defending Lewis. He then worked his way to his daughter Sarah, who was near the back of the room. When he reached her, they could be seen talking in a serious manner.

Elmer Kirkby was nowhere to be seen. He had discreetly left the courtroom during the mayhem.

Lewis was joined by Fred Artz Jr. and the other Waterloo boys who had come in his support. They patted Lewis on the shoulders and on his back, and congratulated him on his freedom. Lewis left them to talk to his father, during which he thanked him for all he had done and asked if he could return home later, to which his father hesitantly agreed.

Sarah caught Lewis's attention by calling out, "Lewie, I'm

looking forward to you spending time with us in Ann Arbor."

Lewis's smile vanished as he replied, "Yes, me too, Sarah."

———— ⚬⚬ ————

It was almost noon when Lewis and his friends left the courtroom and hurriedly navigated their way through the building's corridors to the Main Street exit. Once outside, Lewis stopped at the edge to the red brick road. He was quickly surrounded by his Waterloo boys. Lewis stood pompously with his hands on his hips and sneered as he looked up to the blinding, noon sky. He outstretched his arms, sucked in a deep breath of cold, fresh air, and as he exhaled, produced a cloud of frozen haze as he proclaimed, "You know boys . . . it's been a long, long time since I've had a good drink of whiskey—do y'all think this calls for one?"

One of the Waterloo boys shouted out, "You betcha, Lewie—let's get goin'!"

Lewis smiled and said, "Boys, there are over forty taverns in Jackson—follow me, let's start at Albert Frank's—I'll buy!"

With that proclamation, Fred Artz Jr. let out a huge belly laugh. He turned to face Lewis, looked deeply into his dark eyes, placed his hands firmly on his friend's shoulders, and said, "Lewis Heydlauff, you must be crazy."

EPILOGUE

Lewis *Heydlauff* did not have many days to celebrate his freedom in Waterloo. The murder trial and subsequent perjury charge had tarnished the John Heydlauff family name. The acquittal of the murder charge came as a great surprise to the surrounding community, and rumors were that Lewis got a break with the perjury charge. Insane or not, he had killed a popular young girl. Rather than being shunned in Waterloo, his sister Sarah and her husband, Charles Vogel, had agreed during the trial to allow Lewis to live in their Ann Arbor home, in Washtenaw County, adjacent to the east of Jackson County, far enough away that he would be essentially unknown.

Within days of the perjury charge being dismissed, Lewis was unpacking his bags at the Vogel residence. He would spend the next few years at the Vogel's as he stayed out of the public eye.

———

George Tisch survived the shock of hearing the gunshots that killed Emma Moeckel and seeing her lying dead as blood pooled around her lifeless body.

George stoically held himself together during the funeral as he silently wept. As fate would dictate, Emma and George's kindred spirits' were not to be united.

George endured multiple morbid legal proceedings following the murder. George suffered through the unfair roasting during the trial. Within days he was vindicated as the community realized the accusations made at the trial were unjustified and untrue, and acknowledged that Lewis Heydlauff was a drunkard, and insane or not, was driven by jealousy to wantonly kill Emma Moeckel. Folks quickly concluded that George Tisch had nothing to do with the killing and that he had lost the girl with whom he had fallen deeply in love.

Emma Moeckel was in a place she feared. It was the dark place she experienced in a dream, the nightmare that tortured her after the Christmas afternoon with Lewis. The dream Emma had longed to live, the glorious dream of being with the man she loved, was that of the sunny and fateful Sunday morning of May 31, 1896. But that dream was not to be, as time forever stopped just hours later in the parlor of her parents' Waterloo home when the flame burning in her heart was extinguished by the rapid discharge of three bullets. Emma Moeckel's future was to be placed in a plain wooden coffin, at age twenty, and buried in a dirt grave alongside the little wooden church just down the road.

Emma Maria Moeckel
March 11, 1876 – May 31, 1896

Emma's Granite Gravestone at St. Jacob Church Cemetery

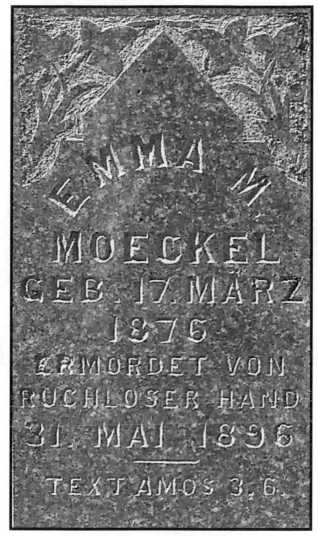

Inscribed in German:
Ermordet Von Ruchluser Hand

In English:
Murdered by a Ruthless Hand

TEXT: Amos 3:6
Shall the trumpet sound in a city, and the people not be afraid?
Shall there be evil in a city, which the Lord hath not done?

This was Emma's Waterloo.

AFTERMATH

Further Reading

Lewis *Heydlauff* went free, but if Judge Erastus Peck could have given the jury the option of "guilty but mentally ill" at the murder trial, Lewis would have, in all likelihood, been committed to a Michigan Asylum for the insane facility before serving actal prison time. But that legal option (GBMI) would not be available in Michigan until 1975. GBMI determined that a defendant's need for mental treatment does not excuse him from legal responsibility and a specific prison sentence for the crime.

In the 1900 Federal Census Lewis was listed as a servant serving his sister Sarah Vogel's household in Ann Arbor.

Sarah (Heydlauff) Vogel had married Charles Vogel on May 28, 1895. Charles had been a widower with three daughters. He lost his first wife, Mary Elizabeth, four years earlier when she burned to death trying to save the life of the Vogel's sixteen-year-old servant girl, who also perished in the flames. Charles Vogel owned a market in Ann Arbor that John Heydlauff supplied meat products to and was also involved with the Britton Pressed Brick Company in nearby Ridgeway Township, its management office being in Ann Arbor. Charles Vogel was a director and John Heydlauff a shareholder in the business. With those connections, John Heydlauff was able to find a place for Lewis to work and live. It's uncertain how long Lewis lived with the Vogels, but the 1910 census listed Lewis Heydlauff as one of eight boarders in a property owned by Rasho

Underwood in nearby Ridgeway. In a 1980 account of oral history by James Verling Moeckel, the other boarders found out about Lewis's past. Afterward, he became very disturbed about it, and walked the floors nightly.

It can be assumed that Lewis was employed at the Britton Company, it being a company his father was involved with.

Within one year it appears that Lewis changed jobs and moved back to Ann Arbor as a teamster for Luick Brothers, a supplier of lumber. On June 26, 1911 the Ann Arbor *Daily Times News* published the following:

The Daily Times News

ANN ARBOR, MICHIGAN, MONDAY, JUNE 26, 1911

Teamster Badly Hurt

Lewis Heydlauff, a teamster at Luick Bros., suffered a painful accident while attempting to board a train at Milan last night. He slipped on the step and fell and cut a hole in the side of his head. He was unconscious until late last night. Dieterlo's ambulance met the train and took him into the Central Hotel, where he lives. He was removed to the hospital this morning. Dr. Heyderman, the Ann Arbor railroad's physician, attended him.

The Central Hotel was located at Fourth and Ann Street in Ann Arbor. The Charles Vogel residence was on East Ann Street, just a short distance away. Considering Lewis's history with alcohol and reading between the lines of the *Daily Times News* article, it could be assumed that Sarah, who must have had a heart of gold for her brother, may have wanted Lewis nearby so she could try to protect him from himself; she knew that Lewis struggled greatly with his demons.

Lewis later lived nearby at the Ann Arbor YMCA on Fourth Street. He was employed by the Ann Arbor Artificial Ice Company as a driver and delivery man. He would have been required to load his horse-drawn wagon with blocks of heavy ice for delivery to customers throughout the city. It's uncertain how long he held the job, although it was implied he had lost it for arriving intoxicated.

During January of 1916, Lewis was hospitalized at St. Joseph's Sanatorium, a small private hospital with seventeen beds located in a residential house at the corner of State and Kingsley streets in Ann Arbor, not far from the Vogel house. Nine months later, on Wednesday, September 20, 1916, the Ann Arbor *Daily Times News* published the following:

The Daily Times News

ANN ARBOR, MICHIGAN, WEDNESDAY, SEPTEMBER 30, 1916

L. Heydlauff Dead

Lewis Heydlauff, age 46, for the past few years a driver for the Artificial Ice Company, died this morning at one of the local hospitals where he had been taken for treatment.

He is survived by two sisters and two brothers, of Munith, Mich., and one sister, Mrs. Charles Vogel, of this city.

Funeral services will be held at Dieterlo's undertaking parlor Friday afternoon at 1 o'clock. Rev. G. A. Newmann officiating. Burial will take place at Forest Hill Cemetery.

The opening paragraph of the article states that Lewis Heydlauff *"died this morning at one of the local hospitals where he had been taken for treatment.*" It is a fair question to ask: *what treatment?* James Verling Moeckel's 1980 oral history says he died after jumping from the second floor of a building. Another local oral history, provided by Lillian Schmidt, states: *he jumped from a hospital window in Ann Arbor, and died.* Lewis Heydlauff's signed death certificate does not indicate suicide, but rather:

CAUSE OF DEATH:
Chronic alcoholism followed by acute mania with acute dilatation of heart.

Duration: Six Months

Chronic Alcoholism: A pathologic condition resulting from the habitual use of alcohol in excessive amounts. The syndrome involves complex cultural, psychologic, social, and physiologic factors and usually impairs an individual's health and ability to function normally in society. Symptoms of the disease include anorexia, weight loss, neurologic, and psychiatric disturbances (most notably depression).

Acute Mania: The sudden onset of a manic episode. Manic episode is a manifestation of bipolar disorder characterized by elevated, expansive, or irritable mood, lasting for at least one week, which is severe enough to cause difficulty or impairment in occupational, social, educational or other important functioning.

Acute dilatation of the heart: Compensatory enlargement of the cavities of the heart, with thinning of its walls. This condition leads to an enlarged heart, which loses its ability to pump blood effectively, often resulting in congestive heart failure.

Lewis may not have succeeded in committing suicide on May 31, 1896, after killing Emma Moeckel, but after twenty years of struggling with intense guilt, he finally achieved his goal, not necessarily by plunging from a building, but by drinking himself to death.

Did Lewis Heydlauff actually attempt suicide that day in May, or was it a ruse—did he aim low only to injure himself, or was he simply too vain to put a bullet into his head? Was he truly insane at the time or was his judgment impaired from alcohol abuse?

The physician who attended to Lewis during his last two days of life determined he was insane. Did he make his diagnosis from the way Lewis appeared at the time, or was it influenced by what Sarah Vogel may have told the doctor of her brother's past? Was he slowly driven insane by what he had done twenty years earlier? Whatever the reasons, at 6:00 a.m., September 20, 1916, Lewis Herman Heydlauff finally escaped his demons as a single and lonely man.

His grave at Forest Hill Cemetery in Ann Arbor is marked by a small stone of gray granite.

August Heydlauff and his family stayed on the family farm with the parents, John and Christina. In the 1900 census, August is listed as head of household. Tragedy occurred on June 30, 1908, when his wife, Carrie, pregnant with her second child, developed placenta previa, and she and her baby both died during the ill-fated delivery.

George Tisch began courting George Hannewald's daughter, (Emma) Charlotte, one year after Emma Moeckel's death. The courtship led to marriage at St. Jacob Church on February 16, 1898. George, twenty-eight years old, and Emma, age nineteen, lived in an apartment in Stockbridge for two years, where they had the first of their nine children, Louis, who was born on February 9, 1899, during the coldest night of the century. They moved to George's mother's house following the death of his father, Wilhelm, who died on November 13, 1900.

Wilhelm Tisch's *Last Will and Testament* left varying amounts of assets to his children—most notably, the farm to George. Wilhelm's will was immediately contested by George's two eldest siblings, Anna and William, who hired Richard Price to represent them, making the claim that Wilhelm was incompetent when he wrote and signed it. George's mother, Katherine, hired Charles Blair to represent enforcement of her husband's final wishes. The arguments between the two sides became so contentious that the case ended up before a jury in circuit court. In the end, there were minor changes with one exception: Katherine was given ownership of the farm, which would immediately transfer to George upon her death, which occurred on December 30, 1914.

George faithfully continued to operate the farm, which consisted of 125 acres, ten cows, and four horses. He significantly grew the threshing business and was one of the first in the county to modernize by adding steam-driven tractors. George Jacob Tisch died at home on November 17, 1943, at age seventy-four. His wife, Emma Charlotte (Hannewald), followed thirteen years later at age seventy-eight. They left seven adult children: Louis, George, Lenora, Carl, Clare, Emma, and Rayner. They had lost their ten-month old son, Albert, in 1909 to a fever, and years later, their twenty-seven-year-old daughter, Luella, to an infection in 1939.

------~------

Charles Blair lost the most controversial case of his term as Jackson County Prosecuting Attorney. Following his stint with the county, he entered the firm of Blair, Smith and Townsend, (*Charles* A. Blair, *Charles* H. Smith, *and Charles* E. Townsend. But he did not leave his aspiration for seeking justice.

Blair was influenced by being raised in a political household. His father, Austin Blair, rose from humble beginnings in Tompkins County, New York, to being admitted to the bar in Tioga County, New York, in 1841. He left that year for Michigan, where he settled in Eaton County, adjacent to the northwest of Jackson County, where he was elected County Clerk in 1842.

After serving his term he moved his family to Jackson, where he was politically active as a founder of the Republican Party and rallied successfully to end the death penalty in Michigan. Austin Blair was an outspoken opponent of slavery in the United States. He held several elected offices before serving as the governor of Michigan during the Civil War years of 1861 to 1865.

Charles was taught law by his esteemed father while earning his bachelor's degree from the University of Michigan. He passed the bar in 1878, sharing the same philosophy as his father when it came to justice. The same year he passed the bar, he married Ellie North. They had their first child, Ella, in 1882. Two years later Walter was born. Charles Blair began to build his practice and life was good. Then December of 1886 arrived. The community was ravaged by a sickness that manifested itself with high fever and severe dehydration. Charles and Effie lost their two-year-old son, Walter, on December 7 of that year; Ella became inflicted by the same illness and died one week later, on December 14. Somehow, the distraught parents had the courage to dig out from the anguish of losing both their beloved children.

Charles Blair practiced law at Blair, Smith, and Townsend, and for five years before successfully running on the 1902 Republican ticket for Michigan's attorney general. Two years later he became a Michigan Supreme Court justice. While in office, he was struck with Bright's disease, which led to kidney failure. He died on August 30, 1912, at age fifty-four. He left behind his wife, Effie, and two children, George and Helen.

———————— ❦ ————————

John W. Miner continued to practice law in Jackson, where he built a reputation as one of the area's most prominent defense attorneys. He and former county prosecutor Elmer Kirkby were both active in the Jackson Democratic Party. They worked behind the candidates who ran for office while maintaining their lucrative law practices. Miner served in several capacities for the Democratic Party, including chairman, while Elmer Kirkby served as secretary.

Miner invested successfully in business and heavily into Jackson real estate. Within twenty years he was Jackson's largest real estate owner; his specialty was acquiring prime business blocks and updating the property to fill the space with high-end retail, business, and offices. In the process he networked with Jackson's most influential people and by 1918 was a director for the Jackson City Bank, Union Bank, and the Jackson State Savings Bank. He also was the principal owner of the Orpheum Theater. In 1918, he became president of the Patriot Company, publisher of the *Jackson Patriot* newspaper.

On Sunday, May 27, 1918, virtually twenty-two years after the Emma Moeckel tragedy, the *Jackson Patriot* ran a poem written by Arthur Brooks Baker, a roving news reporter and poet. It included a handsome photograph of John W. Miner. Was this a tribute or a thinly veiled critique?

The Velvet Hammer

By Arthur Brooks Baker
NO. 70

Some people grind their fortunes out with hard and patient toil, while others puncture nature's store of rich and pungent oil, and as it flows it lathers from the bosom of the rock, they sell their stimulated friends a thousand barrels of stock. John Miner found the field of oil a good place to invest, and filled with rapid revenue his large and stately chest.

He stakes his fat and handsome seads [sic] in Jackson property, whose small and gentle risk could never frighten such as he. A late one is the Orpheum, whose fine and fancy bills have filled all our folks with keen, delightful thrills; for entertainment is a thing for which we all aspire, a thing of daily diet which we rightfully require.

John Miner stands before the court and turns the jury's mind from plans of speedy vengeance to emotions soft and kind. He shows them that the man accused is human as are they: that it would be a crime to take his liberty away. So touchingly he braces up a crippled alibi that many of the jurymen are not ashamed to cry.

In democratic politics he likes to play his part, and much delights in firing off his oratoric art. For it's the right of every man who's done some things of size, to holler "Mr. Chairman!" and to stand up and advise; while small potatoes which have grown but sparsely in the hill should cultivate the art of looking wise and keeping still.

John W. Miner left an indelible mark on Jackson as a remarkable attorney, politician, and businessman. He died April 26, 1943, at the age of seventy-eight. His wife, Louise, died in 1957. They left behind an adult daughter, Kathleen.

———— ⟨∽⟩ ————

Elmer Kirkby, the Democrat who defeated Henry E. Edwards in the 1896 election as Jackson County Prosecuting Attorney, took office on January 1, 1897. His first action was dismissing the Lewis Heydlauff perjury charge. Before his term expired, he resigned his office in May of 1898, and moved his family to Colorado Springs, Colorado. His friend and fellow Democrat, Richard Price, served out Kirkby's term. Kirkby returned to Jackson one year later, where he remained for the rest of his life, working as an attorney and staying politically active within the Democratic Party.

Elmer Kirkby played a significant role in combating the growing temperance movement in Michigan. By 1914 several counties had voted to prohibit the sale of alcohol, but not Jackson County, which had upwards of sixty saloons—forty in the city of Jackson itself. Because of an ever growing antisaloon movement within the county, several laws were passed in an attempt to satisfy the calls for a *dry* county, but they were rarely implemented by Jackson County Prosecuting Attorney Reuben H. Rossman, who was known to be soft on violators. The champion of the saloon keepers was Elmer Kirkby. He worked with fellow attorney Wellington E. Van Camp, who acted as a settlement fixer between plaintiffs claiming injury due to illegal liquor sales and the saloonkeepers Kirkby represented. Kirkby was active with the Liquor Dealers Bonding and Indemnity Company of Grand Rapids, served as Toastmaster for the Michigan State Retail Liquor Dealers Association Meeting in July 1914, and represented the Jackson Liquor Dealers Association. In August of 1916, Kirkby led the *wet* debate against prohibition in Michigan. His efforts failed. Later that same year Michigan voters passed an amendment to the state's constitution prohibiting the manufacture and sale of alcoholic beverages. Adding enforcement strength to the constitutional amendment, the Michigan legislature passed the Damon Law in May 1917. The Damon Law prohibited the *bringing in* of liquor to Michigan. The *dry* laws took effect on May 1, 1918. None of this legislation prohibited individuals from possessing or consuming alcoholic beverages in the privacy of their homes. Some residents had accumulated generous stocks of beer and liquor prior to May 1. Once their private stocks were depleted, many of Michigan's drinkers resorted to liquor smuggling. By the time nationwide prohibition was implemented by the United States Eighteenth Amendment on January 16, 1920, Michigan smugglers had mastered their trade of *bootlegging* booze from Canada.

Kirkby died in Jackson on March 18, 1941, at age seventy-five. He left behind his wife, Minnie, who would follow him in death nine years later at age eighty-one. They left behind three sons, Ray, Eugene, and Walter.

———⸺———

Henry E. Edwards was not successful in following Charles Blair as the next prosecuting attorney for Jackson County, but that did not stop him from being active within the Republican Party in the fast-growing city of Jackson. In 1898, Edwards was nominated by President William McKinley (the second Republican president to be assassinated, Abraham Lincoln being the first), to be postmaster of Jackson, Michigan, which he served until 1902. He also continued with his law practice. Edwards was active with the Knights of Pythias, a secret society consisting of lawyers, politicians, and businessmen committed to world peace. He was soon elected as chancellor of the Jackson lodge.

Henry Edwards became enamored with automobiles. According to the *Jackson Patriot* on July 24, 1912:

Henry E. Edwards returned from Milwaukee with a beautiful new six cylinder "Kissel Kar" with horsepower galore. It rides like a boat and moves as quietly as a dove. On Thursday Mr. and Mrs. Edwards, with Dr. and Mrs. Fred Main, leave for a motor trip through the Berkshires and the coast of Maine.

Henry Edwards ventured into the Jackson automobile industry in 1915 and was issued a U.S. patent for his invention of a new type of carriage top. In 1922 he started another business in the growing automobile industry, Rodney Weeks Inc. in Detroit, with his daughter Harriet and her husband, J. Rodney Weeks. Henry E. Edwards died in Birmingham, Michigan, on July 13, 1943, at age seventy-nine. His wife, Mabel, preceded him in death. They left behind two children, Harriet and Joseph.

———◦∞◦———

Richard Price continued to practice law in Jackson, primarily as a defense and personal injury lawyer. He also served as the attorney for the Central State Bank in Jackson, becoming one of its three directors in 1922. Price stayed active in the Jackson Democratic Party throughout his life.

A devout Catholic, Price was active with the local Ancient Order of the Hibernians and the Knights of Columbus lodges.

He was recognized in Jackson as an expert in using impaired mental reasoning as part of his legal approach. He was successful with his defense for Lewis Heydlauff and in contesting Wilhelm Tisch's *Last Will and Testament.*

In December of 1915 he defended a double murderer, John H. Carson, for killing his mother-in-law and her male companion following a heated exchange during which Carson pumped several bullets into both victims. He used a similar strategy as in the Heydlauff case, this time arguing that John H. Carson *was under a spell from epilepsy* triggered by mental and physical disease during the killing. Carson swore he had no memory of the shooting and that he was innocent, for he loved his mother-in-law, Mary Madden, and thought the highest of her companion, Ed Madden. Unlike the Heydlauff case, the prosecution put two expert medical experts on the stand before the defense had the opportunity to do the same. The jury did not believe a word of what the defense had to say. Carson was convicted of both murders and sent to prison for life. It was discovered later that Carson was a convicted swindler, had deserted two wives only to illegally marry a third, and had a checkered past ranging from Arkansas to Chicago and finally to Jackson.

Price died on July 20, 1935, at age seventy-six, leaving behind his wife, Ida, and daughter, Hazel.

Reverend Emil B. Wenk served as pastor at St. Jacob Lutheran Church in Waterloo from 1896 to 1902. Oral history tells of bonds between certain parishioners being greatly strained or broken by the events leading to Lewis Heydlauff's acquittal for the murder of Emma Moeckel. Rumors persisted that certain witnesses, including some parishioners, were paid to lie at the Heydlauff trial. Not knowing the historical dynamics between his long-term parishioners, Pastor Wenk would have been greatly challenged in his attempts to reconcile conflict within his congregation.

It was also noted by some in the congregation that John Miner, Lewis Heydlauff's lead defense attorney, built a new, palatial house in Jackson following the legal proceedings—allegedly from money he earned from John Heydlauff.

Talk of how alcohol may have fueled Lewis Heydlauff's killing of Emma Moeckel reawakened the dormant temperance society in the area. It was agreed that the Waterloo boys and others like them were not just a public nuisance but a growing danger to the community. Within months the movement gained momentum, and on Friday, December 31, 1897, the *Jackson Citizen* reported:

A dispatch from Munith says: The young people of Munith organized an antisaloon league Monday night with 21 charter members consisting of many of the most popular young people in town. At one time, Munith had the largest temperance organization in the state. For the past few years, however, Munith has been noted for the drunkenness which prevails in the village. A crusade against the saloons was begun last week, and as a consequence Christmas day and Sunday were exceedingly "dry" days in the village.

------⟨∞⟩------

Honorable Surnames

The three Waterloo Township family surnames that were dramatically affected by the tragedy of May 31, 1896, were Moeckel, Heydlauff, and Tisch.

The *Moeckel* name came to Waterloo in the 1840s from Bavaria, Germany. Johann and his wife, Elizabeth, acquired 180 acres and built a cabin. Old-growth trees and underbrush were cleared with the help of other early settlers. Their son, Friederich C. Moeckel, was born in 1844. As Friederich grew he worked the farm along with two older brothers, who each saved money to acquire their own property. In 1875, Friederich married Katharina Joos from Lima, Michigan, and within one year, their daughter, Emma M. Moeckel, was born. After Friederich's father passed, inheritance allowed him to acquire property in Waterloo. In 1896 the Moeckels were highly respected and known to operate a successful farming business.

The *Heydlauff* name came to the Michigan Territory during the mid-1830s. Martin and Elizabeth Heydlauff had been living among other German immigrants in New York along the Mohawk River near Utica. When the nearby Erie Canal was expanded in 1836, news traveled quickly that public land in the lower part of the Michigan Territory was open for sale. Seeking new opportunities, they moved westward with their children, including their young son John. After spending a few years farming near the hamlet of Ann Arbor, Martin purchased 180 virgin acres in Waterloo and moved his family there in the 1840s. After constructing a cabin, he continuously improved the land for cultivation. In 1860 John Heydlauff married Christina Riethmiller, daughter of John Riethmiller, an early settler from Germany, and purchased a tract of land nearby. After Martin died in 1868, his sons received inheritances and John acquired additional land. John and Christina had six living children, Lewis H. Heydlauff being number five. In 1896 the John Heydlauff property exceeded 300 acres and the family was considered one of the wealthiest in the area.

The *Tisch* name came to the area by way of Marietta, Pennsylvania, which is near the east bank of the Susquehanna River. During the year of 1852, Wilhelm and his wife, Katherine, along with an infant daughter had departed the hamlet of Herxheim am Berg, in southwestern Germany, for America. After working at a cousin's Pennsylvania farm for about three years and having two additional children, Wilhelm and Katherine were encouraged by Katherine's brother, Heinrich Hannewald, who resided in Waterloo Township, Michigan, to come to Michigan as there was still fertile land available for a good price. Wilhelm, Katherine, and their three young children made the journey. Upon arrival, Wilhelm purchased 125 acres of land, some of it marsh, in the northern section of Waterloo Township near the village of Munith. Wilhelm built a cabin using lumber harvested from the land along with milled wood from a local sawmill. Wilhelm then began the task of readying the land for cultivation. Within a short time the farm was productive, and Wilhelm expanded to raising livestock. A few years later he established a successful threshing business. Wilhelm and Katherine raised seven children, George Jacob Tisch being the youngest. In 1896 the Tisch family was well thought of and operated a profitable threshing business.

These three families were part of the established German enclave in Waterloo Township, Michigan. They worked together and worshiped together. One young individual from each family was destined to an unimaginable event of horrific magnitude on Sunday morning, May 31, 1896, at a comfortable farmhouse near the little wooden church—just down the road.

Das Ende

HISTORICAL PHOTOGRAPHS AND ILLUSTRATIONS

**St. Jacob Lutheran Church, Waterloo
(Grass Lake), Michigan, circa 1880
Photograph shows school, parsonage, church, and stable.**

Organ and Altar at St. Jacob, circa 1900
Emma Moeckel played this instrument.

Martin Luther's Seal

**St. Jacob's steeple with round stained
glass window, circa 1880**

Jackson, Mich. County Court House, view from Central Park.

**Jackson County Courthouse
on Main Street**

City of Jackson, Michigan, showing interurban streetcars on Main Street

Steam locomotive with coal car

Jackson Central Railroad Station

Albert Frank's tavern, 228 Main Street, Jackson

Common nineteenth-century horse-drawn carriages

Coffin being placed in glass-windowed funeral hearse

Michigan State Prison, Jackson, Michigan, circa 1890

Michigan Asylum for Insane Criminals, Ionia, Michigan, circa 1890

PROPERTY OF STEPHEN SIEGFRIED,
SEC 25 WATERLOO TP MICH

Waterloo's Trist Mill Pond, a popular swimming spot

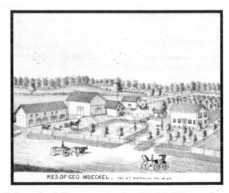

RES. OF GEO. MOECKEL, SEC 27 WATERLOO TP MICH

Moeckel Property in 1874 Waterloo

Perkins Windmill

The Great Forepaugh & Sells Brothers Circus publicity posters

Nineteenth Century Farm House and Perkins Windmill in Waterloo Township. Property once belonged to Jacob Realy, neighbor to the Heydlauffs and Moeckels. Now maintained by the Waterloo Farm Museum.

Waterloo Township Plat map, Jackson County, Michigan, 1894

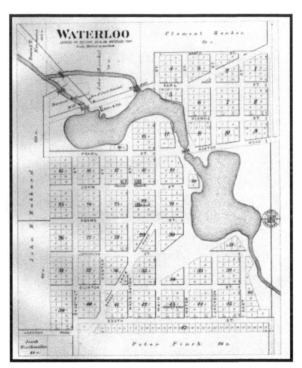

Village of Waterloo, 1894

ACKNOWLEDGEMENTS

In memory of my brother and family genealogist:
Dr. Robert J. Tisch
(March 29, 1941 – October 2, 2006)

To my wife, Susan, for her patience and encouragement

To my brother, David, and his wife, Judith,
for their advice and guidance

To Reverend Kurt and Karen Uhlenbrauck, for access to the archives at St. Jacob Evangelical Lutheran Church, Grass Lake
(Waterloo), Michigan

For reading and commenting on my manuscript, I sincerely thank:
Charles T. Tisch, Telluride, Colorado
Jason R. Tisch, St. Charles, Illinois
Paul L. Tisch, Boulder, Colorado
Susan M. Tisch, Glenview, Illinois
Herbert C. Driver, Muskegon, Michigan
Robert J. Driver, Summerlin, Nevada
Amy Frankel, Northbrook, Illinois
Richard Gruendel, Arlington Heights, Illinois
Graham Jackson, Glenview, Illinois
Debra Lowe, Glenview, Illinois
Barry Mandell, Glenview, Illinois

Susan Pelzek, Wilmette, Illinois
Lawrence Rose, Glenview, Illinois
Reverend Susan L. Sommer, Glenview, Illinois
Kristine Wyatt, Pacific Palisades, California

NOTES

In chapter one, the newspaper article, "Killed His Sweetheart," is attributed to The *Stockbridge Sun*. The author was unable to locate the source of this article, which is from an actual clipping. It is reproduced verbatim from the clipping, which was supplied by Mrs. Emma (Tisch) Roland, Stockbridge, Michigan, and therefore attributed *to The Stockbridge Sun*, which was published from 1884 until it merged with the *Stockbridge Brief* in 1907. The *Stockbridge Brief-Sun* was published until 1965. It was this article that inspired *Emma's Waterloo*.

Stockbridge Newspapers
(http://michigannewspaperhistory.pbworks.com/w/page/20854467/Ingham%20County)

Waterloo Farm Museum and Dewey School:
　　The owner of the Waterloo farm was Jacob Realy, whose property was in the same township as the residents mentioned in *Emma's Waterloo*. It contains the original farmhouse, an authentic log cabin, and a Perkins windmill. The museum complex contains several outbuildings, making it a genuine example of rural life in the mid-to-late 1800s. There is little doubt that members of the Moeckel, Heydlauff, Tisch, and other families mentioned in *Emma's Waterloo* would have set foot in this historic house. The one-room Dewey School is located a short distance away. Its location on Territorial Road is directly across from the property that Wilhelm Tisch, and later his son George, once owned. http://www.waterloofarmmuseum.org/

Families/Germany:
Family relationships and German origin were determined by finda-grave.com, and FamilySearch.org. There were marriages between Moeckel and Hannewald (Freiermuth), Tisch and Hannewald (Freiermuth), Heydlauff and Moeckel, plus several secondary rela-tionships, and Hannewald and Heydlauff.

Freiermuth + Hanewald/Hannewald:
https://familysearch.org/ark:/61903/1:1:J4Z3-8QG

Hanewald/Hannewald + Moeckel (Freiermuth):
http://www.findagrave.com/cgi-bin/fg.cgi?page=gr&GSln=freierm uth&GSiman=1&GScid=2212458&GRid=18780327&

Heydlauff (Gottlieb) + Moeckel:
http://www.findagrave.com/cgi-bin/fg.cgi?page=gr&GSln=heydlau ff&GSiman=1&GScid=2212458&GRid=18780026&

Tisch + Hannewald:
https://familysearch.org/ark:/61903/1:1:J4R3-TVN

Hannewald + Freiemuth:
http://www.findagrave.com/cgi-bin/fg.cgi?page=gr&GSln=freierm uth&GSiman=1&GScid=2212458&GRid=18779989&
https://familysearch.org/ark:/61903/1:1:J4R3-T6L

General Points of Origin in Germany (Surnames in story):
Moeckel: District- Bad Durkheim
http://www.findagrave.com/cgi-bin/fg.cgi?page=gr&GSln=heydlau ff&GSiman=1&GScid=2212458&GRid=18780026&

Tisch: Herxheim am Berg /District- Bad Durkheim
https://familysearch.org/ark:/61903/1:1:J4R3-TVN

Heydlauff: Knittlingen/District- Enz; Baden-Wurttemberg
https://familysearch.org/ark:/61903/1:1:NCW4-Z8J

Hanewald/Hannewald: Herxheim am Berg /District- Bad Durkheim
https://familysearch.org/ark:/61903/1:1:J4R3-TVN

Holy Bible, Amos 3:6: DOUAY-RHEIMS 1899 AMERICAN
EDITION (DRA) Publisher: Public Domain

Erie Canal:
http://eriecanal.org/index.html

Early Michigan:
http://geo.msu.edu/extra/geogmich/michigan_fever2.htm

Price of Land:
Michigan State University, http://geo.msu.edu/extra/geogmich/
michigan_fever.html
Detroit Historical Society, https://detroithistorical.org/learn/
encyclopedia-of-detroit/detroit-land-office

Log Cabins:
http://www.nps.gov/tps/how-to-preserve/briefs/26-log-buildings.
htm

Early Jackson County/Waterloo Township:
https://archive.org/details/historyofjackson00chic
http://genealogytrails.com/mich/jackson/waterlootwp.html

History of Michigan:
https://books.google.com/books?id=IXpzq-XS6KcC&printsec=fro
ntcover&dq=inauthor:%22COLONEL+CHARLES+V.DELAND%
22&hl=en&sa=X&ei=8OI2VYDJO7LgsAT564Ew&ved=0CB4Q6
AEwAA#v=onepage&q&f=false
Internet Archive

History of Michigan 1881
Interstate Publishing Chicago May 1881
https://archive.org/stream/historyofjackson00chic#page/n1161/
mode/2up

Potawatomi Treaty:
http://www.kansasheritage.org/PBP/books/treaties/t_1832_c.html

Passenger Ships:
http://americanhistory.si.edu/onthewater/exhibition/2_3.html

St. Jacob Lutheran Church:
Thanks to Pastor Rev. Kurt Uhlenbrauck
http://stjacobgrasslake.org/site/dbpage.asp?page_id=140002150&
sec_id=140002012

Republican Party/Under the Oaks:
http://www.jacksonmich.com/markers/mark1.htm
http://www.mlive.com/living/jackson/index.ssf/2011/07/peek_
through_time_the_republic.html

Jackson County Court:
Thanks to Kim Willkie
http://www.genealogyinc.com/michigan/jackson-county/

Schools:
http://en.wikipedia.org/wiki/Prussian_education_system

Windmills:
T. Lindsay Baker. University of Oklahoma Press, Jan 1, 1985 -
Technology & Engineering
Perkins Brand: https://books.google.com/books?id=7M9C1Adp0y
QC&pg=PA284&lpg=PA284&dq=perkins+windmill&source=bl&
ots=MGdQQ1a9Ze&sig=lpygJAqJdMX_KYOIsb-VfqbA22I&hl=

en&sa=X&ei=HgELVabHM4ekgwTtxIGIAw&ved=0CDoQ6AEw
Bg#v=onepage&q=perkins%20windmill&f=false

Holidays:
"Christmas in the 19th Century" by Penne Rested
History Today Volume 45 Issue 12 December 1995
http://www.historytoday.com/penne-restad/christmas-19th-century-
america
http://christmas.lovetoknow.com/German_Christmas_Traditions

Music:
"Tell Me I'm Not Dreaming" by J.P. Skelly: 1893
New York Public Library Digital Collections
https://digitalcollections.nypl.org

Austin Blair:
Austin Blair Family Papers
University of Michigan
Bentley Historical Library

Trist Millpond:
Paper: *Chelsea Update*
A History of Trist: A Little Town That Is No More
August 10, 2014

Circus:
Circuses and Sideshows Dot Com
http://circusesandsideshows.com/circuses/adamforepaughcircus.
html
http://circusesandsideshows.com/circuses/barnumandbaileycircus.
html

Holy Cow:
Paper: *Jackson Citizen Patriot* (Jackson, MI)
Thursday, May 14, 1896 Volume: XXXII

Issue: 44, Page: 3
GenealogyBank.com

Waterloo Township Detailed Maps:
Maps used for reference only.
http://www.historicmapworks.com/Map/US/21740/
Waterloo+Township++Norvell/Jackson+County+1911/Michigan/
http://www.historicmapworks.com/Map/US/21343/Waterloo+Tow
nship++Hanover+++Village/Jackson+County+1874/Michigan/

Newspaper History:
http://michigannewspaperhistory.pbworks.com/w/page/20854472/
Jackson%20County

Newspaper Articles:
Story contents are based on articles published in the following
newspapers. The articles contained within the *Jackson Patriot* and
Jackson Citizen was located with the help of Jeannette McDonald
at the Jackson Public Library (Jackson, Michigan), Reference
Department, and to GenealogyBank.com

"Killed his Sweetheart. Horrible Tragedy near Munith, Jackson
County. Emma Moeckel Shot by Lewis Heydlauff":
Date: Monday, June 1, 1896
Paper: *Jackson Citizen Patriot* (Jackson, MI)
Volume: XXXII
Issue: 60
Page: 6
Jackson Public Library
GenealogyBank.com

"Murdered his Sweetheart":
The *Yale Expositor.* (Yale, St. Clair County, MI), 05 June 1896.
Chronicling America: Historic American Newspapers. Lib. of
Congress.

<http://chroniclingamerica.loc.gov/lccn/sn98066406/1896-06-05/ed-1/seq-3/>

Hitchcock:
Central City Brevities
Date: Wednesday, June 3, 1896
Paper: *Jackson Citizen Patriot* (Jackson, MI)
Page: 7
Jackson Public Library
GenealogyBank.com

"Killed his Lover":
Date: Friday, June 5, 1896
Paper: *Michigan Argus* (Ann Arbor, MI)
Page: 1
 Jackson Public Library
GenealogyBank.com

"Heydlauff Still Lives, But Is Failing Fast—He Wishes to Die":
Date: Friday, June 5, 1896
Paper: *Jackson Citizen* (Jackson, MI)
Page: 5
Jackson Public Library
GenealogyBank.com

Emma Moeckel Funeral Cortege:
http://www.findagrave.com/cgi-bin/fg.cgi?page=gr&GSln=moeckel&GSfn=emma&GSbyrel=all&GSdyrel=all&GSob=n&GRid=18780348&df=all&

Funeral:
Central City Brevities
Date: Friday, June 5, 1896
Paper: *Jackson Citizen* (Jackson, MI)
Page: 4

Jackson Public Library, GenealogyBank.com

"Lewis Heydlauff Arraigned. He Demands an Examination, Which Was Set for July 6":
Date: Monday, June 22, 1896
Paper: *Jackson Citizen Patriot* (Jackson, MI)
Volume: XXXII
Issue: 78
Page: 7
Jackson Public Library
GenealogyBank.com

"Charged with Murder. A Warrant Issued for the Arrest of Lewis Heydlauff ":
Date: Friday, June 5, 1896
Paper: *Jackson Citizen* (Jackson, MI)
Page: 4
Jackson Public Library
GenealogyBank.com

"Lewis Heydlauff not so well":
Saturday, June 6, 1896
Paper: *Jackson Citizen Patriot* (Jackson, MI)
Volume: XXXII
Issue: 65
Page: 11
Jackson Public Library
GenealogyBank.com

"Lewis Heydlauff taken to jail":
Thursday, June 11, 1896
Paper: The *Stockbridge Sun*
Vol. XIII No. 3

"Louis Heydlauff. Charged With Killing Emma Moeckel, on Examination before Justice Palmer":
Date: Monday, July 6, 1896
Paper: *Jackson Citizen Patriot* (Jackson, MI)
Volume: XXXII
Issue: 90
Page: 7
Jackson Public Library
GenealogyBank.com

"Adjourned for Two Weeks was the Examination of Lewis Heydlauff- Charged with Murder":
Date: Friday, July 10, 1896
Paper: *Jackson Citizen* (Jackson, MI)
Page: 4
Jackson Public Library
GenealogyBank.com

"Lewis Heydlauff Arraigned,
Circuit Court, Saturday":
Date: Tuesday, September 15, 1896
Paper: *Jackson Citizen* (Jackson, MI)
Page: 5
Jackson Public Library
GenealogyBank.com

TRIAL
"The Heydlauff Case. Louis Heydlauff Charged with the Murder of Emma Moeckel in Court--Selection of jury in progress":
Date: Monday, December 14, 1896
Paper: *Jackson Citizen Patriot* (Jackson, MI)
Volume: 229
Issue: XXXII
Page: 7
Jackson Public Library

GenealogyBank.com

"Heydlauff's Trial for the Murder of Emma Moeckel. The Tragedy Occurred in Waterloo Last June":
Date: Tuesday, December 15, 1896
Paper: *Jackson Citizen Patriot* (Jackson, MI)
Volume: XXXII
Issue: 230
Page: 6, 3
Jackson Public Library
GenealogyBank.com

"Trial of Heydlauff the Evidence so Far--Testimony of the Dead Girl's Mother—The Pathetic Story":
Date: Wednesday, December 16, 1896
Paper: *Jackson Citizen Patriot* (Jackson, MI)
Volume: XXXII
Issue: 231
Page: 6, 3
Jackson Public Library
GenealogyBank.com

"Heydlauff's Trial for the Murder of Emma Moeckel Tuesday":
Date: Friday, December 18, 1896
Paper: *Jackson Citizen* (Jackson, MI)
Page: 8, 1
 Jackson Public Library
GenealogyBank.com

"Drawing to a Close. The Trial of Louis Heydlauff Charged with Murder of Emma Moeckel":
Date: Friday, December 18, 1896
Paper: *Jackson Citizen Patriot* (Jackson, MI)
Volume: XXXII
Issue: 233

Page: 6, 3
Jackson Public Library
GenealogyBank.com

Davis v. United States, 160 U.S. 469 (1895)
U.S. Supreme Court
No. 593
Submitted October 30, 1895
Decided December 16, 1895

"Not Guilty. The Heydlauff Trial for Murder. Seven Hours Speeches
to the Jury":
Date: Tuesday, December 22, 1896
Paper: *Jackson Citizen* (Jackson, MI)
Page: 5, 8
Jackson Public Library
GenealogyBank.com

The *True Northerner.* (Paw Paw, MI), 23 Dec. 1896. "Chronicling
America: Historic American Newspapers." Library of Congress.
‹http://chroniclingamerica.loc.gov/lccn/sn85033781/1896-12-23/
ed-1/seq-3/›

"Oratory in Court":
Date: Tuesday, December 22, 1896
Paper: *Jackson Citizen* (Jackson, MI)
Page: 4
Jackson Public Library
GenealogyBank.com

PERJURY CHARGE
"Warrant for Louis Heydlauff, He Is Charged with Perjury":
Date: Tuesday, December 22, 1896
Paper: *Jackson Citizen Patriot* (Jackson, MI)
Volume: XXXII

Issue: 236
Page: 7
Jackson Public Library
GenealogyBank.com

"On a New Complaint. Officers Are After Louis Heydlauff, Who Was Acquitted of Murder":
Date: Wednesday, December 23, 1896
Paper: *Kalamazoo Gazette* (Kalamazoo, MI)
Page: 1
GenealogyBank.com

"Released on $500 Bail. Louis Heydlauff Arraigned on a Charge of Perjury—A Plea of Not Guilty":
Date: Wednesday, December 23, 1896
Paper: *Jackson Citizen Patriot* (Jackson, MI)
Volume: XXXII
Issue: 237
Page: 6
Jackson Public Library
GenealogyBank.com

"Louis Heydlauff Discharged. The Evidence against Him Deemed Insufficient to Convict on the Perjury Charge":
Date: Saturday, January 23, 1897
Paper: *Jackson Citizen Patriot* (Jackson, MI)
Page: 7
Jackson Public Library
GenealogyBank.com

"Heydlauff a Free Man":
Date: Friday, January 29, 1897
Paper: *Michigan Argus* (Ann Arbor, MI)
Page: 1
GenealogyBank.com

LETTERS TO THE EDITOR
"The Heydlauff Case. Statement from Prosecuting Attorney Blair":
Date: Saturday, December 26, 1896
Paper: *Jackson Citizen Patriot* (Jackson, MI)
Volume: XXXIII
Issue: 239
Page: 6, 3
Jackson Public Library
GenealogyBank.com

"The Heydlauff Case. Statement from Richard Price, One of the Attorneys for the Defense":
Date: Monday, December 28, 1896
Paper: *Jackson Citizen Patriot* (Jackson, MI)
Volume: XXXII
Issue: 240
Page: 6, 3
Jackson Public Library
GenealogyBank.com

Pelky v Palmer:
Pelky v Palmer, 109 Mich 561, 564; 67 NW 561 (1896), where it held it was incorrect to limit the standard to a particular locality or neighborhood. [11] Thus, the basic Michigan standard is the practice in the same or similar communities.
The *Northwestern Reporter*, Volume 67, page 561

"Lewis Heydlauff/ Teamster hurt in fall":
Date. Monday, June 26, 1911
Paper*: Ann Arbor News* (Ann Arbor, MI)
Page: 8
GenealogyBank.com

"Lewis Heydlauff Dead":
Wednesday, September 20, 1916

Paper: *Ann Arbor News* (Ann Arbor, MI)
Page: 3
GenealogyBank.com

Lewis Heydlauff Grave
Find A Grave
https://www.findagrave.com/memorial/36111259/lewis-herman-heydlauff
Findagrave.com

CARSON CASE
"Carson's Troubles Drove Him Insane Attorney Says Temporary Insanity is to be Plea of Defense":
Date: Tuesday, December 7, 1915
Paper: *Jackson Citizen Patriot* (Jackson, MI)
Page: 10
GenealogyBank.com

"John H. Carson Convicted; Life Sentence Penalty Jury Finds Slayer of Mrs. Mary Palmer Guilty":
Date: Saturday, December 18, 1915
Paper: *Jackson Citizen Patriot* (Jackson, MI)
Page: 10
GenealogyBank.com

"Dry days in Munith"
Central City Brevities, *Jackson Citizen*, December 31, 1897, page 5
GenealogyBank.com

Prohibition
"The Booze Protectors"
Date: Monday, August 3, 1914
Paper: *Jackson Citizen Patriot* (Jackson, Michigan)
Page: 4
GenealogyBank.com

"Prohibition Debate to Be Held Oct. 27 Neither 'Wets' Nor 'Drys'
Ready to Announce Who":
Date: Thursday, October 19, 1916
Paper: *Jackson Citizen Patriot* (Jackson, Michigan)
Page: 3
GenealogyBank.com

"Repeals by Implication: Prohibition in Michigan":
Michigan Law Review
Vol. 17, No. 6 (April, 1919), pp. 495-497
Jstor.org

"Guilty but mentally ill" (GBMI):
Michigan Legislature: THE CODE OF CRIMINAL PROCEDURE
(EXCERPT)
Act 175 of 1927.
http://www.legislature.mi.gov/(S(cv5ccpzedk2revjn4byueyix))/mi-
leg.aspx?page=GetObject&objectname=mcl-768-36

Photos, Images, and Illustrations:
St. Jacob photos courtesy of Pastor Rev. Kurt Uhlenbrauck. St.
Jacob Lutheran Church Archives. http://stjacobgrasslake.org

Author's photo courtesy of Susan M. Tisch.

Photo of Emma Moeckel courtesy of Mr. Ken Briggs (From Judith
Moeckel, granddaughter of Florenz Moeckel, Emma's brother).

Photo of Emma Moeckel's cemetery marker at St. Jacob courtesy of
Rev. Kurt Uhlenbrauck.

Photo of Nineteenth Century Farm House. Waterloo Farm Museum
and Dewey School. http://www.waterloofarmmuseum.org/

Photo of Perkins Windmill at the Waterloo Area Farm Museum near Grass Lake, Michigan. Shirley Krause, Waymarking.com

Ionia State Hospital, postcard view. Michigan Historical Psychiatric Project. http://projects.leadr.msu.edu/mhpp/items/show/5

Steam Engine. Public domain. University of Michigan Bentley Historical Library.

Albert Frank's tavern at 228 Main Street, Jackson, MI (1981 Copy Negative).
University of Michigan Bentley Historical Library. Copyright Regents of the University of Michigan. http://quod.lib.umich.edu/b/bhl/x-hs18404/hs18404. Creative Commons license (CC BY 4.0) https://creativecommons.org/licenses/by/4.0/

Forepaugh & Sells Brothers: Strobridge Lithographic Co. poster images from the United States Library of Congress's Prints and Photographs division. No known restrictions on publication. The works are in the public domain in the United States because they were published (or registered with the U.S. Copyright Office) before January 1, 1925.

Standard atlas of Jackson County, Michigan, including a plat book of the villages, cities, and townships of the county . . . patrons directory, reference business directory, and departments devoted to general information . . . compiled and published by Geo. A. Ogle & Co. Author: Geo. A. Ogle & Co. Collection. Michigan County Histories and Atlases.

Combination atlas map of Jackson County, Michigan/compiled, drawn, and published from personal examinations and surveys by Everts & Stewart. Everts & Stewart. Michigan County Histories and Atlases.

Plat book of Jackson County, Michigan/compiled and published by the American Atlas Co. American Atlas Company (1894-1901). Michigan County Histories and Atlases.

History of Jackson County, Michigan. History of Michigan. Michigan County Histories and Atlases.

Interurban Station Jackson, postcard view. Michigan Railroad History/RRHX.

Postcard: Bird's Eye View, Michigan State Penitentiary, Jackson, Mich., ca. 1912. University of Michigan Bentley Historical Library. Copyright Regents of the University of Michigan. http://quod.lib. umich.edu/b/bhl/x-hs18405/hs18405. Creative Commons license (CC BY 4.0) https://creativecommons.org/licenses/by/4.0/

Jackson Central Railroad Depot, postcard view. Courtesy of Tom Tisch.

County Court House, view from Central Park, Jackson, MI (1981 Copy Negative made from a postcard). University of Michigan Bentley Historical Library. Copyright Regents of the University of Michigan. http://quod.lib.umich.edu/b/bhl/x-hs18398/hs18398. Creative Commons license (CCBY4.0) https://creativecommons. org/licenses/by/4.0/

Martin Luther's Seal. Lutheran council of Great Britain.